John Harvey

# WASTED YEARS

# LIVING PROOF

This edition published by Arrow in 2003
an imprint of The Random House Group
20 Vauxhall Bridge Road, London SW1V 2SA

Copyright © John Harvey 2003

The right of John Harvey to be identified
as the author of this work has been asserted by
him in accordance with the Copyright, Designs
and Patents Act, 1988

*Wasted Years* copyright © John Harvey 1993
*Living Proof* copyright © John Harvey 1995

Papers used by Random House UK Ltd are
natural recyclable products made from wood grown
in sustainable forests. The manufacturing processes
conform to the environmental regulations of the
country of origin.

A catalogue record for this book is available from
the British Library

Printed and bound in Great Britain by
Bookmarque Ltd., Croydon, Surrey

ISBN 0 09 189149 3

# Wasted Years

John Harvey

The lines on page 309 are from
'Ghost of a Chance' and
those on page 312 are from
'Temps Greatest Vol II'
both by John Harvey and published
in *Ghosts of a Chance*
(Smith/Doorstop,
Huddersfield, England, 1992).

Although this novel is set in a real city, it is a work of fiction and its events and characters exist only on its pages and in the author's imagination.

# 1969

# One

'Don't forget the Boat, Charlie. Half-eight, nine. Okay?'

Resnick turned at the sound of Ben Riley's voice, picking out his face without difficulty, the only one among the crush of supporters hard against the fence not jeering, calling abuse. Two minutes from the end of an apparent nil-nil draw, a war of attrition played out in the no man's land of late-season mud, the ball had skidded out towards the wing and the few blades of grass remaining on the pitch. The winger, shaking off one challenge, sprinted thirty yards before cutting in. At the edge of the area, uncertain whether to pass or shoot, a defender felled him from behind, sliding in, feet up, to leave his stud marks high inside the winger's thigh. The free kick, mishit, spun off an outstretched boot and crossed the line into the net. One-nil. Fifty or so visiting fans charged their opponents' end, sharpened coins bright in tight fists.

Resnick had lost his helmet in the first scuffle, something wet sticking to his hair that he hoped was spittle, nothing more. They were trying to pull the troublemakers out of the crowd, the worst of them; diving in among the flailing feet and words, punched and kicked, not caring, get your hands on one and drag him clear, show you mean business.

He had one now in a headlock, blue and white scarf, bomber jacket, jeans. Doc Martens with steel toe caps that had caught Resnick's ankle more than once.

3

'Better be there, Charlie.'

The last of the players had left the pitch, those in the crowd who'd come with their kids were pushing them towards the exits. 'Get down here and give a hand,' Resnick called above the noise. 'I'll be away sooner.'

'No chance,' laughed Ben Riley. 'Off duty. 'Sides, you're doing okay. Overtime, i'n't it? Come in handy later, buy me a pint.'

The youth wriggled his head out from under Resnick's arm and ran on to the pitch. His feet had already started to slither when Resnick's tackle sent him sprawling, the pair of them headlong and thick with mud.

'Right state you've got yourself in there, lad,' Resnick's sergeant said to him outside the ground, vans filling up with those arrested, shuttling them to the station to be booked. 'Have your work cut out getting that clean. Early shift tomorrow, aren't you?'

Resnick walked along the river bank towards the bridge, the football ground at his back. The last straggle of fans moved grudgingly aside to let him pass, muttering, avoiding his eyes. Oarsmen were lifting their boat from the water and carrying it towards the nearest of the two rowing clubs that stood back from the path, side by side. Later that evening the buildings would be transformed by flashing lights and speakers pushed almost to distortion. 'The Boat, Charlie. Half-eight, nine.' Resnick thought he might be lucky to get there at all.

Resnick's landlady had his uniform jacket off his back almost before he was through the front door. 'Let me have them trousers, duck, and jump into bath. Water's hot. I'll have this lot like new by morning, not to fret. Trouble at match, again. I s'pose. Ship lot of 'em off into t'army, best thing for 'em. Nice bit of fish tonight, keeping warm in oven.'

Resnick handed her his trousers round the bathroom door. Fifty-eight years old and with three lads of her own escaped out into the world – two down the pit, one in Australia – she lavished mushy peas, strong tea and what passed for common sense on her lodger with steely determination. Each night for the past six months, Resnick's planned announcement of his intention to move had foundered upon the direction of her stare. Her need of him. Him and next door's cat she tempted in with scraps, the budgie moulting in its parlour cage.

He finished running the cold and lowered himself into the water. There was a bruise the size and shade of a large orange on his calf, another on his upper arm; he winced as he rubbed soap across his ribs. Careful, the tips of his fingers traced a ridge of dried blood through his hair. Once his transfer to CID came through, that would see an end to all this, alternate Saturdays as punch bag and kicking pole. Object of derision and hate. Once his transfer came through he could go to Mrs Chambers, clear conscience, and explain. Find a flat on his own, somewhere he could relax, ask people back, liberate his record collection from the tea chest where it languished. How long now since he had heard Paul Gonsalves taking chorus after chorus in front of Duke's band at Newport, the slow fall of Ella's voice in 'Every Time We Say Goodbye'?

Resnick walked along Arkwright Street, away from the city, the muffled bass patterns audible before he stepped on to the bridge. In shadows close by the river, young men made one-handed assaults upon girls' clothing, metal clasps and elastic, glow of cigarettes cupped between their fingers. A Hammond organ surged as Resnick handed over his money, stepped inside. Thick with bodies, the room swam with the scent of sweat and tobacco and the possibilities of sex. The sweet odour of dope which he willed himself not to recognize. On the stage, a seven-piece band was playing 'Green Onions'. In those days, they were always playing 'Green Onions'.

'Charlie! Here. Over here.'

Ben Riley was over by the wall, one hand resting against it, arm extended past the head of a girl with mascara eyes and a plum mouth. Not a minute over seventeen.

'Charlie, this is Lesley. Reckons as how she's here every week, on the bus from Ilkeston, but I told her, got to be having us on. Here that often, we'd've seen her for sure. Eh, Charlie?'

Ben Riley winked and Lesley glanced at Resnick's face and then away, a glass of rum and black held close against her waist.

'Lesley's got a mate, haven't you, Lesley? Carole. Off dancing with some bloke right now, but she'll be back any minute.' Ben winked again. 'What d'you reckon, Lesley? Think she'll go for Charlie, here? Your mate, Carole?'

Lesley giggled.

The band took a break.

Carole turned out to be stooped, self-consciously tall, a narrow-faced girl with fair hair and a soft voice that was lost almost as soon as it left her body.

'Can't win 'em all,' Ben Riley said, squashed up against Resnick in the crush for the bar. 'Maybe she's got hidden talents.'

Resnick shook his head. 'It doesn't matter,' he said. 'I'm not interested.'

'Come on. Don't be such a ... Two pints, love, rum and black and a lager top.'

'You carry on,' Resnick said. 'I'll catch up with you tomorrow.'

Ben handed him one of the pints and the rum and blackcurrant. 'All right, you have Lesley. We'll do a swop. Another couple of these and they won't notice anyhow.'

Resnick sighed and pushed his way back to where the two girls were waiting. 'Here you go,' Ben said cheerily, 'reinforcements.'

'We'll have to be going soon,' Lesley said. 'Our last bus.'

'No, s'all right,' Ben grinned. 'You don't have to worry about that. We'll see you right.'

Resnick handed over the drink and stepped away. 'Tomorrow then, Ben. Okay?' He nodded at the girls and moved off into the crowd.

'What's up with him?' he heard Lesley ask.

He was moving too fast to hear Ben Riley's reply and besides, by then the band was back on the stage.

Nursing his pint, Resnick found a space up close but out of range of the dancers – he'd ducked flailing arms enough for one day as it was. The tenor player squirted out a quick spiralling phrase and set to readjusting his reed. A jazzman by nature, Resnick reckoned: given a mid-tempo blues and the chance to stretch out, he was worth careful listening. Now, though, it was a quick run through 'Time is Tight', a change of riff, a spotlight – 'Put your hands together for the fabulous . . .' – the horns hit three notes hard and the singer launched into 'Tell Mama' as if her life, or the next thirty minutes, depended upon it.

Ruth Strange.

Ruthie.

Resnick had seen her before, this band and that, one club or another. A small woman with a rash of auburn hair, cheekbones that threatened to pierce the skin where they touched. She wore a black sweater, sleeves pushed back to the elbow, black skirt, black tights, red high-heeled shoes. One hand gripped the mike stand when she sang, the other punched or tore or windmilled through the air. A voice that seemed to come from some other – larger, older – body altogether.

Before the applause for her first song had begun to fade, she had signalled to the keyboard player, closed her eyes, thrown back her head, beaten in the tempo with an open hand against her thigh.

Slow blues in three flats.

Wedged into the middle of the floor, Ben Riley and the stoop-shouldered girl stood with their arms around each other, scarcely moving.

*Wasted years . . .* Ruth sang, raw-edged.

'Sure you don't want to dance?' Lesley's voice close by Resnick's shoulder.

'No, thanks. Really.'

A suit-yourself shrug and she was turning away.

> *Every night I spend waiting,*
> *All those dreams and wasted tears,*
> *Every minute, every second, babe,*
> *The worst of all my fears,*
> *When you walk back through my door again,*
> *All you'll have for me are empty arms,*
> *And empty promises,*
> *And ten more, ten more, oh baby,*
> *Ten more wasted years.*

The band driving hard behind her, the final note torn and ugly, a wrench of pain. Arms loose now by her sides, she stood, head bowed. Applause. Resnick finished his pint and checked his watch. Early shift. Ben Riley no longer in sight. He left his plastic glass on the corner of the bar, rather than have it splintered underfoot. A final glance over his shoulder as he moved towards the door.

'Hey!' A woman's voice, sharp and aggrieved.

'I'm sorry.'

'I should think so, too.'

'I was just . . .'

'Leaving. Yes, I can see. And I was coming in.'

'I didn't mean . . .'

'Difference was, I was looking where I was going.'

'Look, I said, I'm sorry. I don't know what else . . .'

'To say. No, I don't suppose you do. Walking all over my feet like that. It's a wonder I didn't go flying back down the stairs. And don't stand there grinning.'

Resnick bit his lip and looked at her seriously: not tall, around the same age as himself, mid-twenties, not pretty, anger bringing brightness to her eyes, a glow to her skin. Her shoe, where he had trodden on it, was scuffed; her tights were torn.

He reached towards his pocket. 'Maybe I could buy you . . .?'

'A new pair of tights? Don't bother.'

'I was thinking more of a drink.'

'What?' Eyes widening. 'And pour it down my front.'

'Elaine,' a voice said off to the side and Resnick realized for the first time that she was not alone.

'All right,' she said, withering Resnick with one more look as she squeezed past. 'Coming.'

Outside on the bank, the water looked dark. Buses moved in slow convoy across the bridge, heading towards the lights of the city. Gravel crunched lightly underfoot. 'Elaine,' Resnick said quietly, testing the name on his tongue. It would be more than four years before he would say it to her face.

# 1992

# Two

'Espresso, inspector?'

'Please.'

'Full, yes?'

Resnick nodded and unfolded the early edition of the local paper, thumbing through the pages in search of hard news, knowing he wouldn't like what he found. Fifteen-year-old youth wounded by four girls in knife attack; old woman of eighty-three robbed and raped; Asian shopkeeper driven from estate by racist taunts and threats of violence. In the magistrates' court, a man explaining why he pushed a petrol bomb through his neighbour's letter box – 'Night and day they had this music playing, night and day. I asked them to turn it down but they never took no notice. Something inside me just snapped.'

Setting the newspaper aside, Resnick sipped the strong coffee and, for a moment, closed his eyes.

The Italian coffee stall was located among the market stalls on the upper level of one of the city's two shopping centres. Vegetables, fruit and flowers, fish and meat and bread, Afro-Caribbean and Asian specialities; the two Polish delicatessen stalls where Resnick did much of his shopping, replying to greetings offered in his family's language with the flattened vowels of the English Midlands. His stubborn use of English was not a slight; merely a way of saying *I was born here, this city, this is where I was brought up*. These streets. Eyes open,

Resnick scanned the other customers sitting round the U-shaped stall: middle-aged shoppers whose varicose veins were giving them gyp; mums with kids who couldn't make up their minds which flavour milk shake and would never sit still; old men with rheumy eyes who sat for hours over the same strong tea; the photography student from the Poly who drank two cappuccinos back to back and whose fingers smelt of chemicals; the solicitor who could eat a doughnut without getting as much as a granule of sugar on the skirt of her power suit; the tramp who waited till someone bought him a drink, then skulked off by the photo machine to finish it, legs visible through the rags of his trousers. These people.

Angled across from where Resnick was sitting, Suzanne Olds licked her finger ends clean with the fastidious delicacy of one of his cats. Lifting her leather brief-case from the floor, she slid from her stool and approached. The last time they had spoken, one of the solicitor's clients had been up on five charges under sections 18 and 47 of the Offences Against the Person Act, shuffling alibis like a dog-eared pack of cards.

'Inspector.'

'Ms Olds.'

'I was at dinner with a new colleague of yours a few nights ago. Helen Siddons. Very bright. Sharp.' Suzanne Olds smiled. 'Aware of the issues.'

'I thought crime was the issue: solving it, preventing it.'

Suzanne Olds laughed. 'Come off it, inspector, you're not as naive as that.'

Resnick watched her walk away, incongruously elegant and somewhat intimidating as she passed between local-grown spinach and pink and white shell suits, the latter greatly reduced, council clothing vouchers welcomed. He had met Helen Siddons a number of times since she joined the local force; transferred from Sussex, detective inspector at twenty-nine, eighteen months and she would have moved on. A graduate with a degree in law, she was being propelled by the Home Office along a fast track towards the highest ranks. She should be looking at Assistant Chief Constable by the time she was forty. Resnick could see how well she and Suzanne Olds would have got along; serious conversations between courses about the sexism endemic in the force, racism, the errors – careless or malicious – in police evidence which had led to conviction after conviction being so publicly overturned.

Why was it, when he agreed, at heart, with most of the beliefs women like Helen Siddons and Suzanne Olds held, he found it so hard to give them his support? Was it simply that he found them a threat? Or the almost certain feeling that the support of men like himself, career coppers for more than twenty years, would not be welcomed?

'Another?' asked the stall owner, whisking his cup into the air.

Tempted, Resnick checked his watch and shook his head. 'Got to be off. Important meeting. Maybe see you later. Cheers.'

And he ambled away, shoulders hunched, a wave at the man from the fish stall forever on at him about giving a bit of a talk to the Church Fellowship, a bulky man in a shiny suit that had been beautifully tailored by his uncle more than fifteen years before – for somebody else and not for him.

Reg Cossall was standing on the steps of the central police station, swopping tales of arson with the senior officer from the fire station alongside.

'Hey up, Charlie,' Cossall said, falling into step with

Resnick as he pushed through the front door. 'Heard the latest?'

Resnick was sure he was going to, any minute.

'They only reckon Grafton's going to get Tom Parker's spot. Can you believe that? Malcolm bloody Grafton a chief inspector. Over the likes of you and me.'

Resnick grunted non-committally and started on the stairs.

'Tell you what, Charlie. That bastard's done so much sucking up, must have a gullet like anyone else's large intestine. Not to mention wearing through three sets of kneecaps.'

Resnick opened the door and waved Cossall through ahead of him. Most of the other officers were already present, a round dozen, inspector and above. Maps marked with coloured pins and tape hung from the walls; memos and computer printouts lay in plastic wallets on tables of walnut veneer. The overhead projector was in place, screen pulled down. Jack Skelton, Resnick's superintendent and heading up this particular task force, stubbed out one of his rare cigarettes, poured a glass of water from the jug, cleared his throat and called the meeting to order.

'Operation Kingfisher, let's see what we've got.'

Eighteen months previously, five men, masked and wearing track suits, had forced their way into a bank in Old Basford right on closing time. The two remaining customers had been told to lie on the floor, the cashiers bound and gagged; one of the weapons the gang had been carrying, a shotgun with sawn-off barrels, had been placed against the assistant manager's head. They had got away with close to forty thousand pounds, changing cars three times in making their escape.

Driving in to open a newly refurbished supermarket

at Top Valley five months later, the manageress had her Orion forced off the road and a pistol flourished in her face. Only after she had facilitated the opening of the safe was the gun withdrawn from sight. All the manageress could tell the police about the person threatening her was that he was average height and wearing a Mickey Mouse mask.

. Mickey was on hand when the Mansfield branch of the Abbey National was held up one busy Saturday. It was Goofy, though, who placed a suitcase beside the protective screens on the counter and informed the nearest cashier that it contained a bomb. None of the staff felt like testing the possibility that it was just a bluff. Nor did they appreciate suggestions that the whole thing was a publicity stunt on behalf of EuroDisney.

The most recent robbery, three weeks ago now, took place in the inner city, Lenton Boulevard, just as the sub-post office was opening for the day. The door was locked from the inside and, while a line of grumbling customers grew along the pavement, the staff were tied to one another, shut inside a cupboard and warned that if they tried to get out or raise the alarm, shots would be fired through the door.

Four robberies: close on half a million pounds.

Five men: all wearing gloves, instantly disposable clothing, masks. All armed.

Between three and five cars, stolen days in advance, used on each occasion.

Threats of violence, so far not carried out.

Some of the stolen money had surfaced in places as far apart as Penzance and Berwick-on-Tweed; most of it, it was assumed, had already been laundered abroad for a fat commission.

Operation Kingfisher had been set up after the second incident; between thirty-five and fifty officers had been involved. All of the information gathered had been entered by civilian operatives on to disk and checked against the Home Office's central computer. Possible links were being followed up in Leeds, Glasgow, Wolverhampton. Known criminals implicated in similar raids were being tracked down and interviewed. Comparisons with similar robberies in Paris and Marseilles were being made. Flight manifests at East Midlands and Birmingham airports had been checked.

Sooner or later, somebody would make a mistake; so far, no one had. Resnick hoped it wouldn't be some building society clerk or bank teller acting out of bravery or panic, a misplaced sense of loyalty to his employers.

'You know what, don't you, Charlie?' Cossall said as they were leaving, best part of two hours later.

'What's that, then, Reg?'

'What this lot reminds us of. That bloody business – when was it? – ten year ago.'

But Resnick didn't want to be reminded. Not then or ever. Refusing Cossall's offer of a quick pint in the Peacock, he slipped into a pub on High Pavement he rarely used and where he was unlikely to be known. *That bloody business ten years ago.* Never one to drink in the middle of the day, Resnick surprised himself with two large vodkas, one sharp after the other, with the tonic he had bought to dilute them still open and unused when he pushed his way back on to the street.

# Three

Peter Hewitt farmed several hundred acres in what had once been known as Rutland – the smallest county in England. To those families whose roots had taken long before local government rationalizations, it still was. To them, Hewitt was an outsider, welcomed guardedly. He represented new blood, new stock, new ideas.

Hewitt had not always been a farmer. Brought up, as farm children always were, to take his share of the work from an early age, he had turned his back on the land at seventeen and gone to sea. As an officer in the Royal Navy, he had served in the Falklands campaign, a lieutenant commander on HMS *Argonaut*. Along with other vessels, his ship had come under heavy hostile fire in Falkland Sound: her fellow frigate, the *Ardent*, had been sunk with the loss of over twenty lives; the *Argonaut* had been more fortunate – she had remained afloat and only two of her crew had died.

Only.

The word teased Hewitt cruelly still.

He thought of the parents of these men when they heard the news; thought of chance and misfortune, stability and flow, the sea and the land. As soon as he was able, he left the navy.

Hewitt's father had retired: rather, the recession and rheumatoid arthritis had retired him. Now he lived quietly in a cottage in Northamptonshire, grew vegetables, kept goats, grew lonely. Peter had bought a farm near him but not too near; his intention had always been to go his own way. He had given this a great deal of thought and it seemed right that his methods and means should be as organic as good business sense and the land would allow.

In addition to the acreage given over to crops, Hewitt kept a herd of Friesian cows and had several contracts to provide organic milk. His wife, Pip, ran a profitable farm shop. Together, they encouraged local groups and schools to visit the farm so that they could explain their methods. Spread the word. Hewitt found himself increasingly in demand as a speaker in various parts of the country, occasionally in Holland or even France.

This work, as an ambassador for organic farming, he took seriously, just as he did his time as a school governor, his stint as a JP. If you take something from the community, he told friends less convinced, you have a duty to put something back. It was the way he felt about the land. It was why he had accepted the invitation to be on the Board of Visitors at the local prison without hesitation. Part of his duties there was to serve on the Local Review Committee, whose recommendations were forwarded to the Parole Board.

This was why he was driving in today, beneath low skies, to interview a long-stay prisoner whose application for parole was due for review. *Showing a callous disregard for the safety of others, you were prepared to threaten and use violence in the pursuit of personal gain.* Hewitt had read the judge's summing-up before leaving the house. The man he was going to see had been found guilty on five separate counts and sentenced to fifteen years. The nature of the offences, the use of violence, meant there would be no automatic release once two-thirds of that sentence had been served. After ten years, however, there was the question of discretionary parole.

Hewitt slowed as the side road leading to the prison came in sight, checked his rear-view mirror, changed lanes, signalled his intention clearly.

The moment he walked through the twin doors and heard them close behind him, Peter Hewitt felt something leave his body. He would not regain it until some hours later, pacing the fields of his farm, marvelling over visible horizons.

'Good one for you today, sir,' the warder remarked. 'Very nice fellow, I'm sure.'

Prior was sitting in a room without view or natural light: plain wooden table, metal chairs with cloth seat and back. He scarcely glanced up as the door opened.

'One thing we didn't succeed in teaching him,' the warder said, 'manners.'

'Thank you,' Hewitt said. 'We shall be fine.'

As the door was being closed, Hewitt introduced himself and offered his hand. Sitting, he took out the packet of cigarettes he had bought that morning at the village shop and slid them across the table. Box of matches, too.

Prior said thanks and helped himself, lit up and looked at his visitor squarely for the first time.

'You understand, of course, the importance of this interview?' Hewitt asked.

Something of a smile floated at the back of Prior's eyes. 'Oh, yes,' he said.

Prison had stripped weight away from him, made him strong. It was that way for some, a few; those it didn't institutionalize or weaken, break down. The ten years had greyed Prior's skin to putty, but it was tight; the muscles of his legs and arms, chest and back were strong; the eyes were still alive. Sit-ups, push-ups, stretches, curls. Concentration. Save for one occasion, whenever he had been tempted to lash out, respond, overreact, he had thought about this moment, this meeting. He had kept himself largely to himself, waiting for this: the possibility of release.

'Before I can make a positive recommendation,' Hewitt was saying, 'I have to be convinced in my own mind that you have no intention of offending again.'

Prior held his gaze. 'No problem, then, is there?'

Hewitt blinked, shifted the position of his chair. 'The offences you committed...'

'Long time ago. Different life.' Prior released smoke through his nose. 'Wouldn't happen again.'

'It did then.'

'What I think,' Prior said, 'people change.'

Hewitt leaned forward, leaned back.

'You believe that, don't you?' Prior said.

'Yes. Yes, as a matter of fact, I do.'

'Well, then...' This time the smile was unbridled. 'There you go.'

'Have you thought,' Hewitt asked after some moments, 'about work, finding a job?'

'Used to be a chippie...'

'Carpenter?'

'Joiner, yes. That's my trade.'

'Good, good. I'm sure your probation officer will try to find something for you. After all, having a skill, a real skill, it's what so many men in your position sadly lack.'

Way this is going, Prior thought, better than I could have hoped.

'You've friends on the outside?'

'A few.'

'That might be willing to help you find work?'

'They might.'

'And you've a wife.'

'No.'

'Surely you're married?'

'Legally, maybe, but no. Not any more. Not really.'

'Ten years, it's a lot to withstand. It takes a very special woman . . .'

'Oh, she was that, all right.'

'Was? She isn't . . .?'

'I haven't seen her. Don't know where she is.'

'I'm sorry.'

Prior shook his head. 'One of those things. Can't put in the sort of time I have, expect everything to stay the same.'

Hewitt was thinking what he would do if for any reason Pip left him. A partnership, that was how he referred to it when he was making his after-dinner speeches, a partnership in which my wife is the strongest part.

'What I want to do,' Prior was saying, 'start my life over again, do things right, before it's too late.'

'Of course, I understand.' Second chances, second lives, they were very much what Peter Hewitt was about. One of the two men killed on board the *Argonaut* had been celebrating his eighteenth birthday that day. No second chances in his life. Hewitt hated the waste, the brave waste.

'Exactly,' he said again. 'I do understand.'

Prior looked into his face directly, held his gaze. 'Good,' he said several seconds later. 'Good. Because too much of my life has been wasted. There are things I want to do while I still have the time.'

# Four

Darren knew about prisons. YOIs anyway. Young Offender Institutions. Places like Glen Parva, where, if you didn't find a way of topping yourself in the first few months, chances were you learned enough to graduate into the big time.

Glen Parva: that's where he'd met Keith. Walked into his cell, free time, thinking to scrounge a snout and there was Keith, all five-five of him, struggling to loop his towel around one end of the upturned bed.

'What the fuck d'you think you're up to?' Darren had yelled. One thing for certain, what Keith hadn't been doing, devoting himself to spring cleaning.

Keith's only answer had been to hide the towel behind his back and blub: tears like some six-year-old caught offing sweets from the corner shop.

'You don't want to do that,' Darren had said, sitting on Keith's bunk. 'Give these bastards the satisfaction of cutting you down. How much longer you got to do, anyway?'

'Couple of months.'

'You'll get through that.'

Keith hung his head. 'I won't.'

Darren looked at him, pathetic little bugger, sticky-out ears and soft skin and hands like a child's. No wonder they'd been at him again in the showers, gang-banging him most likely, smearing smuggled-in-lipstick round his mouth before making him suck them off.

'S'okay,' Darren had said. 'I'll look out for you. Anyone tries anything, let them know they got to deal with me.'

Keith was looking at him in wonder. 'Why d'you want to do that?' he asked.

Darren had seen this film once, staying at his sister's, Sutton-in-Ashfield, western it'd been. This soldier, cavalry, spurs and sabre and yellow stripes, big deal, he saves the life of some Indian chief and after that the Indian follows him everywhere, waiting for the chance to do the same for him. Some kind of crazy blood brothers. Shit! That wasn't what it was like with Keith and him. Reason Darren hung around with Keith after they were released, nothing to do with that old bollocks. What he put up with Keith for, there wasn't nothing Keith didn't know about cars. No car he couldn't nick.

Crossing towards the parade of shops, lunchtime, Darren looked at his watch: one fifty-four. If Keith was late, he'd take his legs off at the knees. Laughing aloud: poor sod was any shorter he'd be underground.

Keith had cased the multi-storey from top to bottom: nice Orion worth making off with, owner obligingly leaving the parking ticket sticking out of the ashtray. All Keith had to do at the exit was hand over a quid – as cars came, this was cheap at the price.

What he hadn't reckoned on was road works on the ring road, single-lane traffic and there he was, trapped behind some geriatric in a Morris Minor – nice motor, though, well looked after, likely worth more now than when it was new.

Keith knew full well Darren would be less than happy. No way he was going to make it on time now. Working the horn wasn't going to make a scrap of difference. Boring, aside from anything else, not even a radio to listen to. Almost the first thing he'd noticed, sizing up the car, some bastard'd already had the radio away, torn wires all over the place, owner too tight to get it replaced.

The road suddenly widened and Keith stood on the accelerator. Too close to two for comfort: Darren wasn't going to be worth speaking to.

It had been a pizza place last time Darren had been there. Deep dish or thin 'n' crispy. Hawaiian a speciality. Darren had made the mistake of having one once. Pineapple chunks that stuck in your throat like gobbets of vomit: ground beef and gristle a dog wouldn't cock its leg to piss on.

Before that, what? A Chinese chippy. Paki sweet shop. When he was a kid, one of them bakers where they sold stale cobs in bags of three, half price, the morning after – cheese and onion or turkey breast or haslet with a touch of Branston pickle.

Across the street the Co-op offices had been bulldozed flat to make way for a spanking new DIY superstore – three floors of wallpaper, fake Formica and self-assembly kitchen units that fell apart faster than you could screw them together. Darren had got a job there once, sixteen, humping great boxes about the back, ten quid and callouses at the end of the day, no tax, no questions asked. That had been before he had the good fortune to get himself nicked and sent away: before he had learned there were easier ways to make a living.

Now there were signs plastered across the superstore windows – *Everything at Half-Price – Must Go – Closing Down*. The pizza place was boarded up: fly posters for Soul II Soul and Springsteen and The Fabulous Supremes LIVE at Ritzy's torn and graffitied over. In the doorway, cardboard boxes and a nest of rags: somebody's home.

Out of the remaining six shops set back from the street, only three were still in business. A newsagent's with metal grilles at its windows, a sign – *No More Than Two Schoolchildren At Any One Time* – taped to its door. A factory textile shop, direct from the makers to you, cut out the middle man, sold tea towels and shirts with little to tell the difference between them. Between those two, a sub-office of the Amber Valley Building Society, closed for lunch between twelve forty-five and two.

It was now almost a quarter past.

Darren looked across at the door, open sign hanging down; half a mind to go in on his own, get the business done. But then what? Legging it down the main road, sack on his back?

He was flexing the fingers of his right hand when the blue Orion slipped into sight and eased towards the kerb, Keith's face just visible in the lower half of the windscreen.

'What happened to you? Go by McDonald's for a Big Mac and a chocolate shake?'

'Chicken McNuggets.'

Darren had hold of the front of Keith's T-shirt, like to choke him, before he realized it was a joke.

'Anyone go in yet?' Keith asked, once Darren had let him go.

Darren shook his head. They had watched the office carefully the past three days; not once had they had a customer between reopening after lunch and twenty minutes past the hour. It was now two seventeen.

'Why don't I dump the car?' Keith suggested. 'Try again tomorrow.'

'Like fuck we will!'

Keith shrugged, not about to argue. He knew that tone in Darren's voice all too well; had seen him break a glass in a youth's face once, just for asking him was he sure he didn't have a light?

'The talking,' Darren said. They were crossing the patch of bricked-off earth in front of the shops, stepping between the dog turds.

'What about it?'

'Leave it to me.'

Keith nodded: as if he needed telling.

Lorna willed herself not to turn her head towards the clock, up there on the wall between the aerial photograph of the High Peak and a poster advertising High-Yield Tessa returns. This was the part of the day that always dragged, right from when she got back after having her packet of Slimma Chicken and Vegetable soup for lunch, two pieces of Swedish crispbread with just a scraping of extra low-fat margarine, from there through to tea, four or four fifteen, Marjorie fretting over the kettle, leaving the tea bag in too long, shaking a tin of custard creams under her nose no matter how many times Lorna pursed her lips and waved them away.

Marjorie back there now with Becca, practically fawning over her, turned Lorna's stomach, that's what it did. Becca in her smart little grey suit with its high collar and tapered skirt she wasn't above sliding up her skinny legs whenever the area manager happened to pop in. Three years of elocution lessons and a polytechnic degree in Modern Languages and they'd made her acting branch manager about as soon as she'd finished her training. Two years older than Lorna, nothing more.

'It's still confidential, of course, but Mr Spindler says I'll be moving on to one of the main branches within the year.'

She'd heard her one day, telling Marjorie as if she was

doing her a big favour, letting her in on a secret, and Marjorie, all soggy-eyed, 'Oh, Becca! How lovely!'

'Never mind the way Spindler treated Marjorie herself, patronizing bastard, 'Well, Marjorie, keeping these two youngsters in order, are we?' Seventeen years she'd worked there, Marjorie, passed over every chance of promotion there was, all the while pretending that it hadn't happened.

Not me, Lorna thought, that's not what's going to happen to me. Eighteen months tops and I'm putting in for a transfer and if I don't get it I'm straight off to the Halifax, the Abbey National, the Leeds. And I don't care who knows it.

Twenty-three minutes past two. There – I looked.

Oh, well.

Lorna eased her back against the padded chair and turned the pages of last week's *Bella*, which was resting on her knees. In the raised area behind her, she could hear Becca and Marjorie at their desks: Becca going on about her holiday in Orlando; Marjorie retelling the story of her sister's ovarian cyst, the size of a small baby – Sunday mornings going round car-boot sales for a shawl and a second-hand cot before she realized the truth.

The door opened slowly and Lorna's eyes flicked back towards the clock. Twenty-five past. Old Mr Foreman in his carpet slippers and his zip not properly fastened, paying in fifteen pounds and withdrawing five – 'Did you see such-and-such last night? Bloody tripe! Don't know why those people get paid.'

She closed her magazine and slid it beneath the ledger.

Darren stood just inside the door, Keith behind him. Already he could feel his heart pumping. Three women, one at the front, behind the only cashier's window in use, the others further back, neither of them looking round, paying any attention. The girl at the window, though, round glasses, staring at him through big round glasses, surprised. Well, he'd give her something to be surprised about.

'The door,' he said to Keith, moving forward.

'Uh?'

'Watch the door.'

Lorna sat readying her smile, a new customer, probably nothing more than an inquiry, how d'you go about opening an account?

'Lorna Solomon?' smiled Darren, reading her name off the engraved plate at the side of the window.

He wasn't bad-looking when he smiled.

'Yes,' she said. 'How may I help you?'

Darren laughed, more of a chuckle than a laugh. He opened the front of the loose leather jacket he was wearing and pulled out a bin bag, black. 'Here,' he said, passing it through to her. 'Fill that.'

Behind the blue-framed glasses, Lorna blinked. It had to be a joke, a wind-up, someone kidding her for a bet, a dare.

'Do it,' Darren said. 'Don't make no fuss. Do it now, eh?'

It wasn't a dare.

Lorna's gaze shifted towards the second youth, far shorter, over by the door. Neither of them older than she was herself.

'Don't keep me waiting,' Darren said, his voice a little louder.

'Miss Solomon,' came Becca's toffee-nosed voice from behind. 'Is something the matter?'

'This gentleman has a query, Miss Astley,' Lorna said, turning her head. 'Perhaps you should deal with it yourself.'

30

'What the fuck're you playing at?' said Darren, face thrust close against the screen.

'What's going on?' said Keith, stepping away from the door.

Trim legs on the short flight of steps, Becca saw the plastic bag in Lorna's hand, read, uncertainly, the expression on her face, saw the movement of the young man behind.

Becca threw poise and elocution to the winds and screamed.

Darren pulled the hammer clear of his coat and smashed it against the centre of the screen.

Fumbling with his pass book, trying to free it from its plastic cover, Harry Foreman came through the door, whistling through his half-dozen remaining teeth the theme from 'Limelight'. Always one of his favourites. That Mantovani, couldn't be beat.

'Keith, where the hell did he come from?'

Keith wasn't certain: about anything.

'Here . . .' said Harry.

The third time Darren hit the screen, it splintered, top to bottom.

Lorna crouched beneath the counter, shielding her eyes. Becca ran back up the steps, turned and ran back down.

'Here . . .' said Harry Foreman, as Keith grabbed hold of his bony arms and pushed him back against the wall.

Marjorie eased her way across the rear of the office towards the telephone.

'Stuff the money in that bag,' yelled Darren, 'and quick.'

But Lorna didn't seem to be listening. Inch by inch, she was sliding her hand towards the alarm.

'Take your hands off of me,' Harry said, ducking his

31

balding head towards Keith's face. 'Don't think I'm going to be pushed around by the likes of you.'

Darren knocked away a section of screen and vaulted on to the counter. Becca stopped screaming and cried instead. 'Hello,' said Marjorie quietly into the receiver she was shielding behind her size-sixteen dress, 'I want to talk to the police.'

Lorna squinted up at Darren's black jeans, the worn soles of his Nike trainers, fear and fury on his face, and pressed her thumb against the button hard.

'Darren!' called Keith. 'The alarm!'

'Fucking genius!' Darren said. 'That's you.' He aimed a kick at Lorna's head and missed, swung wildly with the hammer and liberated several inches of varnished chipboard from the counter top.

Harry Foreman stuck out a leg and Keith half-tripped, staggered wildly before breaking open the skin above his left eye on the corner of the wall beside the door.

'What's this?' Darren said, jumping down. 'Home fucking Guard?'

'Don't think I'm frightened of you,' Harry said.

Darren swung the hammer two-handed and cracked it against the side of his head, just in front of the ear. Before the old man had finished falling, Darren was out of the door.

In front of him, Keith was skating across several yards of mud like they were glass. An Asian face peered around the newsagent's door, then pulled back from sight. Further up the street, a mother pushed two children under two in a pram. As Darren cursed him, Keith's fingers fumbled with the keys. His head felt like it had been split open and blood was trickling into the corner of his eye.

Darren snatched the keys from him and pulled open

the car door. 'What the hell d'you lock it for?' he asked, pushing Keith inside.

'Leave it unlocked outside here,' said Keith, 'some clever bastard'll have it away.'

He turned the key in the ignition and the engine fired first time; scraping the gears, he revved hard and swung the wheel. The first police siren could be heard no more than half a mile away.

'Watch the pram!' Darren called as Keith hit the kerb and skidded up over the pavement, evading the pram but striking the mother, rear bumper swiping her legs and knocking her off her feet. Swerving wildly, Keith rounded a lamppost, squealed back on to the road and accelerated away.

'Next time,' Darren said, as Keith threw the car into a right-hand turn and headed the wrong way up a one-way street, 'make sure you're not fucking late!'

# Five

'Bloody mess, Charlie, that's what it was. Beginning to end.' Skelton hung his overcoat behind the door, automatically smoothing the shoulders along with his hands. He and Malcolm Grafton had been comparing notes over a couple of glasses of a nice Valdepeñas when his bleeper had sounded the alert. 'Bunch of professionals is one thing, but this – couple of cowboys without a brain between them...'

Distaste showed clearly on the superintendent's face as he settled behind his desk, careful first to unbutton the jacket of his double-breasted suit, a soft grey wool-mix smelling faintly of the dry cleaner's.

'Walk in off the street and ten minutes later there's an old boy fighting for his life in intensive care, one woman with a suspected broken leg and another under sedation for shock.'

Sitting across from Skelton, Resnick nodded. He had spoken to the doctor at the hospital himself; Harry Foreman's condition was touch and go. The injured mother's two children were being looked after by the Social Services Emergency Duty Team until contact could be made with either the estranged father or the grandmother, living out at Heanor.

'Week before last,' Skelton was saying, 'went to this seminar at Loughborough, Department of Criminology. Pair today would have given them a field day. Deprived area. Disadvantaged youth. Striking at a building society

34

because it symbolizes the property-owning class that is still presented as the desirable norm.'

Resnick looked past Skelton's head towards the window, the red brick of factory buildings that had either been left to crumble or were slowly being turned into architect-designed flats with central saunas and swimming pools that no one had the money to rent or buy. Out there, the norm was mornings at the job centre, signing on, filling in forms for housing benefit; afternoons among the bright lights and plastic plants of the shopping centres, trying to keep warm. Whatever language the professor might have couched it in, Resnick thought, as far as he was concerned the economic theories about the causes of crime held more water than most.

More so than those of the Secretary of State for Education, who had recently blamed the increasing crime rate on the church's failure to preach the perils of hellfire and damnation. Over half the churches in Resnick's patch had been pulled down or deconsecrated and turned into sports centres; of the rest, at least two had been set on fire themselves.

'Banks and building societies,' Skelton said, 'hundred per cent increase in robberies in the last two years. Mostly armed.' He pinched the bridge of his nose between forefinger and thumb. 'As we know all too well. At least those two today only went in with a hammer.'

'I don't suppose Harry Foreman'll be thankful for that,' Resnick said.

'If it had been a gun,' Skelton said, 'he might not have been so keen to get involved.'

'And if he had?' Resnick asked.

Skelton shook his head, dismissing the thought. 'Members of the public, situations like that, best keeping their heads down, eyes open. No place for heroes.'

Do that, Resnick thought, not going to be a great help

as witnesses, aside from remembering the colour of their own shoes.

'Interviews proceeding, Charlie? Your team.'

'Yes, sir.'

'Keep me up to date. Anything that looks like a positive ID. Should be in a better position when we get prints in tomorrow.'

Resnick was on his feet.

Skelton lifted a memo from his desk. 'Two calls already from the local union rep, Banking, Insurance and Finance. Requests an urgent appointment. Why aren't we doing more to protect his members?'

He sighed and straightened the family photographs on his desk and Resnick, sensing his own stomach about to rumble, managed to keep it under control until he was on the other side of the door.

The CID room was in chaos. Four days before, the station's heating system had gone on the blink and, despite having the central boiler overhauled, there were still parts of the building to which no heat had returned. This was one of them. Cold enough, in Mark Divine's words, to freeze a witch's tit.

Some of the desks had been hauled out into the corridor, others piled on top of one another while the source of the trouble was tracked down. Several lengths of floorboard had been prised up and now rested precariously against a well-marked street map of the city. Pieces of piping lay on most available surfaces and a workman in grey overalls lay on his stomach, hammering cheerfully while his mate sipped cold tea and laboured over the previous day's quick crossword.

'Is it always like this?' Lorna asked, the tempo of the hammering increasing.

Kevin Naylor, interviewing her about the robbery, shook his head and smiled. 'Not always.'

'You are busy, though? Plenty to do.'

'Oh, yes. Pretty busy.'

Lorna crossed her legs: soft, between hammer blows, the faintest swoosh of nylon over nylon. 'You're lucky,' she said.

Naylor looked at her: how come?

'What happened today, first bit of excitement in weeks. Months. Since before Christmas.' She leaned forward just a little. 'What it was, this chap come in, red nose and top hat, tinsel all over it, collecting for charity. Children in Need, one of them. Anyway, there he was shaking his bucket under Marjorie's nose and he keeled right over. Started kicking his legs, nineteen to the dozen against the floor, having some kind of a fit. Marjorie put her Bic in his mouth, stop him swallowing his tongue, and he bit right through it.'

Naylor was still looking at her, questioning now, and she stared right back at him, eyes unwavering behind her glasses. 'The pen, not his tongue.'

'Our Kev,' Divine said quietly, leaning over Lynn Kellogg as she sat questioning Marjorie Carmichael, 'on to a good thing there. Dip his wick before the night's out.'

Lynn scowled and refused to turn her head to as much as look at him, while close beside her Marjorie pretended that she hadn't heard.

'All right, Marjorie,' Lynn said, as Divine walked off chuckling, 'why don't we try and concentrate on the hair?'

They had been sitting for close to half an hour, turning the sections of a spiral-bound book back and forth. Facial types: heads divided into three. A game, the object of which was to match up the most likely combination. She had had one similar as a girl, Lynn remembered, but that had been the whole body, top to bottom, a picture-book blonde for whom you chose from different sets of clothes.

'Oh, Lynnie,' her mother had exclaimed, 'just look at you. You can't put them colours together, pink and green.'

'Why not?' Lynn had asked.

'Because they just don't go. Anyone tell you that.' And she had stopped briefly to brush Lynn's straight dark hair with her fingers and stroke her cheek with the palm of an oven-warm hand.

'There,' Marjorie said, pointing. 'I'm sure that's right.'

Lynn looked at the high forehead, generous mass of curly hair.

'Isn't that the one I picked before?'

'No. Not exactly.'

'Oh, dear. I am sorry.' Marjorie turned towards Lynn, disappointed, wanting so much to please.

'Don't worry,' Lynn said, smiling faintly. 'It's not easy.' Shifting a little in her seat, more cramped than usual, telling herself that women Marjorie's size were prone to problems with perspiration, it wasn't really her fault.

'You weren't frightened, then?' Kevin Naylor was saying.

'Not at first,' Lorna said. 'It didn't seem real. You know, the way he come over to the counter, taking his time. Posing, almost. I didn't think he was serious . . .'

'No.'

'Then, later . . .' She was trying not to make it too obvious, the way she was angling her head, trying to look at Naylor's left hand, tucked under his notebook, not certain whether she'd seen a wedding ring or not. 'Later, when he started going a bit wild, I suppose I was frightened then. Well, anyone would be.'

'Of course.'

'Anyone in their right mind.'

Kevin Naylor nodded.

'I mean, look at what happened to poor Mr Foreman.'

'He was trying to stop them, was he, from getting away?'

'I don't know. I suppose so. Tell the truth, I didn't really see. I was still behind the counter, ducked down out of the way.' She smiled and he moved his hand and there it was – damn! – thick and gold and looking as if it could do with a bit of a shine. Third finger, left hand.

'You didn't actually see, then, what happened? Which one of them hit him?'

'Had to be him, didn't it? The one who did all the talking. I mean, he was the one with the hammer. The other one, the little bloke, he just stood there like a spare part, never done a thing.'

'Do you think either of the others would have seen – the manageress, for instance – do you think they would have seen the blow being struck?'

'I don't know, I doubt it. I mean, Marjorie might, ask her. But Becca . . .'

'That's the manageress?'

Lorna sucked in her cheeks and put on an accent. 'Rebecca Astley. Little Miss Hoity-Toity. Real mardy, she was. Scraightin' and carrying-on.'

'Lots of people panic, situations like that.'

'Even so.'

'You were the one sounded the alarm, though.'

'That's right.'

'Not easy, thinking what to do.'

'Thanks.'

'No, I mean it.'

For a second, Lorna touched her hand to the frame

of her glasses. 'So noisy in here, isn't it? Hardly hear yourself think.'

Naylor glanced over his shoulder and saw Divine grinning right back at him. 'Been like this for a couple of days,' he said.

'There isn't anywhere else . . .' She waited until he was looking at her again. 'There's nowhere quieter we could go? You know. Somewhere else?'

'Yes,' Naylor said, standing, feeling himself starting to go red. 'We could try.'

Lorna was on her feet already, noticing the way he was blushing and not caring, thinking it sweet. So what if he did wear a ring, that didn't have to mean so much, did it? Not these days?

'What'd I tell you?' Divine called above the sound of hammering. 'Over the side and no messing.'

'Your trouble,' Lynn Kellogg sang back. 'Judge everyone by your own standards. Least, you would if you had any.'

Divine was still laughing when Resnick came into the room. 'Busy, I see, Mark?'

'Yes, boss.'

'Best take a rest, then. Tea break.'

'No, you're all right . . .'

'Get yourself over to the deli, fetch me a couple of sandwiches. Ham and cheese and a chicken mayonnaise and salad. Mustard on both. Right?'

Divine took the proffered five-pound note and headed for the door.

'How's it going?' Resnick asked, pausing alongside Lynn and Marjorie.

'Slowly,' Lynn replied. And feeling Marjorie's sagging disappointment, added, 'But I think we're getting there.'

'Good.'

Resnick opened the door to the partitioned section that formed his own office and willed the phone not to ring until Divine had come back with his sandwiches, at least until he had got as far as sitting down. He had his second wish by as much as five seconds. Graham Millington was calling in from somewhere between Stapleford and Sandiacre where what might have been the getaway car had been found abandoned.

'If wrapped around a Keep Left sign constitutes being abandoned,' Millington added.

'Hang fire,' Resnick said into the phone. 'I'll be right out.'

'Got mysen a packet of crisps,' Divine grinned when Resnick intercepted him on the stairs.

'Your money, not mine,' said Resnick, taking hold of the bag containing his sandwiches, pocketing his change. 'Come on, you're driving. I'll eat these as we go.'

# Six

Graham Millington had been Resnick's sergeant for a little over five years and was beginning to think that six would be too long. Not that he had anything against his immediate superior, far from it. When some of the others started grumbling into their pints and calling Resnick for being too soft by half, too airy-fairy in his ideas, Millington always squashed them with a firm word. Any reflections he might have about Resnick's appearance – surely someone of his rank and salary could afford at least one decent suit that seemed to fit, one white shirt with all of its buttons intact? – or his eating habits – if Millington saw him fumbling his way through one more over-stuffed sandwich, he might just go out and buy his boss a voucher for the nearest Berni Inn, prawn cocktail, nice bit of steak and Black Forest gateau to finish, that was what you called a meal – like the loyal sergeant he strove to be, Millington kept them to himself.

No, it wasn't six years in Resnick's shadow that weighed heavily upon him, it was the prospect of six years beneath anybody.

Especially when a vacancy had come up and before Millington had been able to dust off his CV or fill in his application form, they'd whisked that woman in without her feet touching the ground this side of landing.

'Tough luck,' Resnick had commiserated. 'She's on her way to a Top Apco post and there's nothing you or I can do about it.'

'Another time,' Skelton had said, scarcely stopping to speak, 'you're still a young man.'

Not, Millington had replied soundlessly to the super's back, for much bloody longer.

'Assert yourself more, Graham,' his wife had said. 'Let them know if you don't get promotion next time, you'll put in for a transfer.'

In his more paranoid moments, Millington imagined Jolly Jack Skelton writing him a glowing reference and offering to pack his bags, shipping him east to Cleethorpes with an engraved tankard and a digital watch that would stop the second he crossed the Lincolnshire border.

'Not inspector by the time you're forty,' Reg Cossall had said, 'might as well curl up your toes and crawl into the body bag.'

'You know what they say about water,' Malcolm Grafton had smirked, 'finding its own level.'

Maybe his wife was right, the thing to do was march into Skelton's office with an ultimatum and if the result was moving somewhere else, well, why not? Except, for all her talk, he knew the last thing his wife wanted to do was move from where they'd settled. The local WEA group had just voted her on to the steering committee, the amateur dramatic and choral society had promised her something big in next season's *Iolanthe* and she was just getting to grips with the new border they'd put in alongside the *Caryopteris*. And that was without Level Two Russian.

He re-angled the interior mirror and checked his moustache. Annoying the way those little hairs at the top kept poking themselves into his nostrils. He was using his fingernails to tweak one or two away when Divine brought the unmarked Ford to a halt behind him and Resnick climbed out of the passenger seat, brushing the last of his sandwich down the front of his raincoat.

'Right across there,' said Millington, pointing towards the intersection. 'Tow truck's on its way.'

Directions had scarcely been necessary. The stolen car had three wheels on the pavement, one several inches above the surface of the road. The street sign seemed to have bent to meet it, scoring a deep groove through the roof and buckling the near-side rear door, shattering the window.

'What makes you think it's the one we're looking for?' Resnick asked.

Millington gestured towards the motor supplies shop along the street. 'Bloke in there, heard the crash and saw two white youths haring up that side road, round the back of that building. One tall, he thinks maybe curly hair, the other either a runt or just a kid.'

'Any other description?'

'Taller of the two had this loose coat on, apparently. Brown, possibly grey, anorak-type of thing. Jeans, the pair of them. Couldn't give us a lot else.'

Resnick shrugged. 'Other witnesses?'

'Not so far.'

'Cut along and knock on a few shop doors,' Resnick said to Divine. 'Before they all lock up for the night. Someone else must have heard what happened. Take a statement from the bloke Graham spoke to; might come up with a little more this time.'

Divine nodded and hurried away.

'Checked the registration,' Millington said. 'Reported stolen from that car-park out at Bulwell, sometime between twelve and two.'

'Doesn't sound as if they bothered with gloves at the robbery,' Resnick said. 'If this is down to them, likely be prints on the car as well.'

'I'll make sure they go careful shifting it, see it gets checked thoroughly soon as it gets back.'

Resnick had stepped away and was staring down the narrowing street. 'Ought to be a reason they came this way.'

'Throw us off the scent?'

Resnick shook his head. 'Everything we know about them this far, that kind of thinking seems a bit out of their league.'

'Heading for home, then?'

'Could be.'

'Run it through the computer. Likely got a bit of form anyway. Live round here, shouldn't be too difficult to find.'

Resnick pushed his hands down into his pockets. Evenings like this, the temperature dropped as soon as the light began to fade. 'Hope you're right, Graham. Quick result here'd be a good thing. Concentrate our energies where they're more needed.'

'Back among the big boys.'

Resnick nodded. 'It needs sorting, Graham. Before somebody gets killed.'

# Seven

The way Keith felt about his old man, one of those old jossers get on the bus in the morning and suddenly you're staring out the window, hoping against hope they won't lurch over, sit down next to you. Clothes that reek of cider and cheap port wine. Open their mouths to speak and the next you know, they're dribbling uncontrollably.

An exaggeration, of course, but not much of one. The way his dad had gone since the divorce, starting his drinking earlier and earlier in the day, not finishing till the money or the energy to lift the bottle failed him. Last time Keith had called at the house, two in the morning, unannounced, his father was curled asleep on the kitchen floor, arms cradled around the legs of an upright chair.

It hadn't always been like that. As a young kid, Keith remembered his dad getting smartened up of an evening, loading his gear into the van, swinging Keith round by his arms till he screamed with excitement. Early hours of the morning, Keith would wake to the sound of car doors slamming in the street outside, called farewells, his dad's footsteps, less than steady, on the stairs, his mother's warning voice, 'Don't wake the boy.'

His father would sleep till two or three, wander down for a sausage-and-egg sandwich and pots of tea. Wash, shave, do it all again.

He had been drinking, Keith realized, even then; more, probably, than had been clear at the time. Clear to Keith,

46

at least, though he could still hear his mother's shrill sermons echoing up and down the narrow house. And as the work had dried up, the bottles and the cans had appeared on every surface, lined the chair where his dad would sit, not watching the TV. 'One thing,' he would say, over and over, 'one thing, Keith, I regret – you never knew me when I was big, really big. Then you might've felt different.'

Keith fished the key from his pocket and turned it in the lock. Found the light switch without thinking. Strange how long this had been home.

'Keith, that you?'

No, it was Mick Jagger, Charlie Watts'd finally decided to jack it in, old Mick couldn't think of anyone better to take his place.

Around when Keith had been twelve and thirteen and you didn't have to be a genius to see how far things had fallen apart, that was the kind of guff his dad would sit him down, make him listen to. How he could have played with the Stones, back in the early days, Eel Pie Island, before Mick started on the eye make-up, all that poncing about. Back when they were playing real music.

Playing the blues.

'Keith?'

'Yeh, it's me. Who d'you think?'

All the bands his old man could have played with if things had only fallen right: the Yardbirds before Jeff Beck, John Mayall's Blues Breakers, Graham Bond, Zoot Money's Big Roll Band. The night he should have depped for Mickey Waller with the Steampacket, some big festival – instead of sitting behind the drums, his dad had popped too many pills and spent the set in the St John Ambulance tent throwing up.

'Keith, you're coming down here, fetch us a beer.'

As far as Keith knew, his father's only substantiated

47

nights of near-glory had been back in sixty-four when he gigged with Jimmy Powell and the Five Dimensions, joining them in Nottingham when they were on the Mecca circuit and sticking it out until they were hired to back Chuck Berry on his British tour. First rehearsal, Chuck stopped short in the middle of his duck walk and asked who the motherfucker was trying to play the drums. That was it: beginning and end of his old man's big career. For sale, one pair of Zildjian cymbals, one mohair suit, scarcely worn.

'Keith, I thought I asked you to . . .'

'Here. Catch.'

The can bounced out of Reg Rylands's hands and rolled across the basement floor.

'What you doing down here?' Keith asked, snapping open the Carlsberg he'd fetched for himself.

'Oh, you know, pottering around.'

Keith grunted and snapped open his can.

'What's that you've done to your eye?'

'That?' Keith said, gingerly touching the swelling, the bruise. 'That's nothing.'

The house was two-storey, flat-fronted, an end-terrace in the Meadows – one of those streets the planners overlooked when they ordered in the bulldozers on their way to a new Jerusalem. Keith had been born here, brought up; his mum had moved out when she divorced, lived now in a semi in Gedling with a painter and decorator and Keith's five-year-old stepbrother, Jason. Keith's father had stayed put, letting out first one room, then another, sharing the house with an ever-changing mixture of plasterers and general labourers and drinking mates who dossed down for free whenever their Social Security ran out.

'What's this?' Keith asked, pointing at the Z-bed

opened out along the wall. 'You sleeping down here now?'

'Just for a bit. Coz's got my room.' He drank some lager. 'You remember Cozzie. Some woman with him this time. Tart.'

Keith didn't know any Cozzie, but he could guess what he would look like: tattoos across his knuckles and scabs down his face. 'Hope he's paying you.'

'Course.'

Which meant that he was not.

'So what you doing here?'

Keith shrugged. 'Come to see you, didn't I?'

'You weren't thinking of staying?'

'Thought I might.'

'What's wrong with your mum's?'

'Nothing.'

'Haven't had a row?'

'No more'n usual.'

'So?'

'Change, that's all. Couple of nights.'

'You're not in trouble?'

'No.'

'You sure?'

'Yes.'

'Cause if it's anything like before . . .'

Keith hurled his half-full lager can at the floor and stormed towards the door.

'No, Keith, Keith, hold on, hold on. I'm sorry, right?'

Keith stopped, feet on the cellar steps.

'You want to stay, that's fine. Got a mattress I can bring down here, you take the bed.' Keith turned and came back inside. 'Just for tonight. Bloke up top, moving out next couple of days. I'll explain. Give him a nudge. It'll work out, you see. Here . . .' He bent down and

49

picked up the Carlsberg and handed it back to his son. 'Like old times, eh?'

'Yeh.'

'Might go out later, couple of pints. What d'you think?'

Keith sat down on the Z-bed and it rattled and squeaked. In an old chest opposite, fronts missing from two of the drawers, were his father's clothes – those that weren't draped anyhow across a succession of cardboard boxes or hanging from the back of the cellar door. A pile of shoes from which it might be difficult to find a decent pair. Bundles of old newspapers and magazines, yellowing copies of the *NME*. An old Ferguson record player with only one speaker: a radio without a back. Two snare drums, not on stands, but lying side by side, skins patched and slack. A pair of wire brushes, bent and tangled at the ends.

'Yeh,' Keith said. 'Yes, sure. Drink'd be fine.' He looked quickly at his father from the corner of his good eye. 'You might have to pay.'

# Eight

Resnick had arrived back at the station in time to find three uniformed officers hauling a seventeen-stone West Indian up the steps and backwards through the double doors.

'Argument with a taxi driver, sir. Reckoned he was charging him over the odds. Jumped on the roof and dented it. Stuck his boot through the rear windscreen. Driver tried to pull him down and got a kick in the head for his trouble.'

Resnick held one of the doors open as, finally, they succeeded in lifting him inside. A good bollocking from the custody sergeant, a night in a cold cell and an agreement to pay restitution to the cab driver and that would likely be an end to it. Summary justice: there no longer seemed to be a lot of it about. Back when Resnick and his friend, Ben Riley, had been walking the beat, so much could be settled with a warning look, a word, the right intervention at the right time. All too often now, the first sign of police intervention brought about an immediate escalation of trouble. A violent response. Unthinking.

A WPC, out of uniform, on her way home from the cinema, stops near a fiercely quarrelling couple, the man shouting at the top of his voice, the woman yelling back through her tears. When the police officer goes closer, asking them to calm down, asking the woman if she was all right, the pair of them rounds on her, the woman spitting in her face.

A young constable, six months on the job, steps between two groups of youths, squaring up to one another on the upper floor of the Broad Marsh Centre. Set upon, forced back towards the top of the escalator, he calls for help which only comes when he has tumbled to the bottom. Three cracked ribs, a dislocated pelvis, he would suffer intermittently from severe back pain for the rest of his life.

'Call for you, sir,' said Naylor, passing Resnick on the stairs. 'DI Cossall. Left the message on your desk.'

'Thanks, Kevin.'

'Couple of us going over the road for a pint if . . .'

'Yes, maybe. Later.'

Resnick squeezed past the furniture that had been moved out into the corridor and pushed open the door to the CID room. Loose boards were still stacked against the wall and from the temperature nothing had been achieved setting the heating to rights. A lamp burned over Lynn Kellogg's desk, her coat still hung from the rack in the corner, but there was no sign of her. Divine would be in the pub already, getting them in.

Scarcely a time in the last months, Resnick had walked into that office and his eyes had not flicked towards the far wall where Diptak Patel used to sit. Now there was a space, a gap in the floor, lengths of piping running through shadow. Coldness. What was it Millington had said about Patel and death? Scatter rose petals and sit around wailing where he comes from, don't they?

Well, wailing there had certainly been, that cold Saturday when the wind had whipped off the Bradford hills and cut across Resnick's back like a stick. Flowers, too. Roses. Patel's father had shaken his hand gravely, thanked Resnick for attending, never looked him in the eye. Never understood. No. What was there to understand?

'Don't,' Patel's girl friend had begged, that evening in the city centre. 'Please don't get involved.'

'I have to,' Patel had said.

Moments later, the blade with which one youth had been attacking another was turned on him. Another fucking Paki. Another fucking Saturday night. Blood from the artery spread wide and the best you could say, the only good thing, the only consolation you could find: it had not taken Patel long to die.

'Sir?' Lynn Kellogg said quietly.

Resnick had failed to hear her come in behind him.

'You all right?'

He turned his head and looked at her, slowly nodded.

'I sometimes think,' she said, 'that he's – well – that he's still here.'

'Yes.'

'But he isn't ... He's ...'

For the briefest of moments, Resnick put his hand on her shoulder and she rested her cheek sideways against it and closed her eyes. Resnick's breathing seemed unnaturally loud in the darkening room. And then she got her bag and her coat and said good night and Resnick said see you in the morning and after the door had closed he went into his office and read the note.

Reg Cossall was standing at the bar – no, more leaning – face round and broken-veined and wreathed in smoke. Angled above his head the highlights of a women's soccer match were being played out, rise and fall of the commentator's voice barely audible beneath the whir of the cash register, blur of voices.

Other faces Resnick recognized, greetings offered and shared.

'Message got through to you then?'

Resnick bought him a pint of Kimberley and a large Bell's, shaking his head at the offer of ice. For himself, a ginger ale.

'Not drinking, Charlie?'

'Not tonight.'

'Bad news, then, is it?'

'Likely. You tell me.'

One word had been written on the slip of paper, other than the details of where and when Cossall wanted to meet.

Prior.

'Up for parole, Charlie. Two-thirds of his sentence down the pan.'

Resnick glanced up at the screen. A woman with fair hair pinned close to her head was writhing on the ground, tackled from behind. Some things changed, some remained the same.

'He'll not get it,' Resnick said. 'He'll be turned down.'

'Not what I've heard. Not this time.'

'Offences like his. Violence . . .'

'Not automatic, but like I say . . .'

Resnick swallowed down the ginger ale and before the glass had been set back on the bar, Cossall had beckoned the barman, ordered him a vodka, double. The bank of video games beside the entrance jingled and hummed. From the adjoining bar, the click of pool balls and a juke box recycling the Jam.

'How long, Charlie? Ten years?'

'Nearer eleven.'

*I have no doubt that the reaction of the public to these offences of which you have been convicted is one of the gravest horror and disgust. Motivated solely by greed and with an absolute lack of compunction*

*towards anybody who stood in your way, prepared to
threaten and use violence with a callous disregard for
the safety of others, you and the men convicted with
you terrorized sections of the community in the pursuit
of personal gain. As the undisputed ringleader of these
men, I have no alternative other than to punish you
with the full force of law at my disposal.*

The public had been so disgusted that sales of the
Sunday paper to whom one of his accomplices sold his
story showed an increase of twenty-three per cent.
Prior's mother, convalescing in a nursing home after a
stroke, was interviewed by both major television news
programmes; a photograph that showed him as a child,
receiving his school's annual prize for good citizenship
and endeavour, was widely syndicated. A prostitute, who
claimed to have been his lover, auctioned her kiss-and-
tell exposé to five bidders.

'You think he'll come back here?'

'Would you?'

'No,' Cossall said, chasing his whisky with a long swallow of beer, 'but then I'm not a nutter.'

'That what you think he is?'

'Don't you?'

Face to face in the garage, the two of them, himself
and Prior, both near to breathless, the garage doors
partly open, the car ready to go. Resnick had followed
him through the house, the side door from the kitchen,
Prior's hands disappearing behind the open boot of the
car and when next Resnick saw them, they were holding
the shotgun steady, angled towards his chest and face.

Outside were voices, torches, shouts of inquiry, warning. All Resnick saw was the narrowing of Prior's eyes,
the tensing of the forefinger of his right hand. There

were things he had been trained to say in this situation but he said none of them.

The tension in Prior's eyes had relaxed a little as he brought the shotgun up towards his own body and for a moment Resnick thought he was going to rest the barrels beneath his own chin, take his life. Instead he had reversed the weapon fully and handed it across the roof of the car for Resnick to take hold of, stock first.

'No,' Resnick said. 'He's not that.'

'Happen you're right,' Cossall shrugged. ''Sides, maybe all that time inside taught him a lesson. Back out a changed man, anxious to become a useful member of society. That what you reckon, Charlie, eh?'

'Get you another, Reg? I'm going to be on my way.'

Cossall shook his head, opened his hand over the top of his pint glass. 'Shouldn't be too difficult to find out where he's likely to head for, what his intentions are. That's if it happens. Still, best forewarned, eh? Make plans.'

'Thanks, Reg.' Resnick offered his hand. 'Owe you one.'

'Yes,' Cossall growled. 'You and the rest of the sodding world.'

Over his head one of the teams had just scored what looked a lovely goal, only to have it disallowed.

Pip Hewitt came into the kitchen after speaking to her mother on the phone, to find her husband, Peter, sitting at the broad oak table, account books open near him, drinking black tea laced with rum.

'You're worried, aren't you?' she said, resting an arm along his shoulder. 'Losing that last milk order.'

Hewitt squeezed her hand. 'It's not that.'

She pulled round one of the chairs and sat close beside him.

'The parole review committee's meeting tomorrow and . . .'

'If you can't go, phone them. After all the work you've put in, they should understand.'

Hewitt drank from the thick stoneware mug, holding it out first to his wife, who smiled and refused. 'One of the men I interviewed – Prior – he's serving fifteen years, armed robbery . . .'

'Was anybody hurt?'

Hewitt nodded. 'The last raid before they were caught, a security guard . . .'

'Shot?'

'Paralysed down one side.'

Pip Hewitt's eyes reflected shock and pain. 'And this man . . .'

'Prior.'

'He was responsible? He shot him?'

'He says no, claims it was one of the others. Two weapons were discharged, but the police were never able to establish who fired which gun. Not without a shadow of a doubt. The shotgun Prior had with him when he was arrested, ballistic reports don't match it up with the injuries to the guard.'

Pip took the mug from between her husband's hands and slowly sipped the laced tea.

'I wish I knew what to do,' Hewitt said.

She gave his hand a squeeze. 'You take everything so seriously.'

'It is serious.'

'I know.'

'What's left of a man's life . . .'

'Darling . . .' Still holding Hewitt's hand, she got to her feet. '. . . finish your tea, come to bed, let's have an early night. You'll do the right thing. You always do.'

# Nine

Music – Darren had never understood what all the fuss was about. Loud or soft, fast or slow – how much else did you need to know? Keith, now, if he wasn't out hot wiring some car, he was walking around with his Walkman on, tinny little sound leaking out, mouthing the words as it went along. Rap. Who gave a rat's arse about rap. Keith, for one. Outlaw. Gang Starr. X-Clan. Caveman. Least the names were okay, cool. What had he been playing the other day? Arrested Development. Darren laughed: Keith to a T.

Outside Michael Isaacs's nightclub, he gave himself a quick once-over in the glass: chinos, white shirt pulled out loose above the waist, sleeves rolled back, silhouette of hair tinged purple in the light.

The dance floor was three-quarters full, blokes leaning back against the downstairs bar, suits some of them, carelessly watching him as he climbed the stairs.

As the DJ upped the tempo, Darren leaned over the balcony, nursing a lager top, checking out the talent. Two black blokes getting all the attention down below, buckling their legs and doing all that fancy stuff with their hands, kung fu sign language in overdrive.

There, over by the steps, big girl with reddish hair, a blue top which jiggled when she moved. Black trousers, loose at the hip. She might do the trick.

Darren shifted his position to get a better look.

According to the news, that old idiot he'd whacked

58

was still hanging on. Arsehole! Why couldn't he mind his own business? Keep his hands to himself? Still fighting the tossing war. Saved this country for the likes of you. Yes, well, right, Grandad. Thanks very fucking much!

Sodding Keith today, as much good as a johnny with a hole at both ends. If he was going to get anywhere, he'd have to find a better partner than that. Late with the car, forgetting to guard the door.

A youth in a suit jostled Darren's elbow and Darren straightened, giving him a look. The youth mumbled something to the slag he was with and the two of them wandered away.

One thing Darren had to give Keith – once his nerves had steadied he'd got them out of there like there was no tomorrow. Three police cars after them at one point and still Keith had lost them. Everything going great until he'd misjudged that turn going down towards Sandiacre. Legging it then, they'd been: till they'd found that van on Longmoor Lane. Some lame brain, who'd nipped into the paper shop for a *Post* and a packet of fags, left the sidelights on, indicator flashing, keys in the fucking steering column!

Back from there, through Long Eaton and into the city.

The tempo slowed and Darren figured it was time to head downstairs, see what was what at close hand.

That range, she was a lot bigger than he'd first thought, not that there was anything wrong with that. Some of them so skinny, he might as well have been back inside, putting it to some youth in the shower while a mate kept watch for the screws.

Face that wasn't about to win any prizes.

Her mate, the one she was dancing with, she was a lot prettier and *knew* it. Aware that Darren was standing there now and watching them, thinking he had to be watching her. Toss of the head and yes, here comes the tongue, wetting both her lips.

Saying something about him, heads close together, laughing under the music. When the record changed again, they hesitated, then started to leave the floor.

As he intercepted them, the good-looking one smiled at Darren with her eyes and he gave her a quick grin back, moving past her, hand reaching out to touch her mate on the arm.

'Come on. Can't be packing up already.'

Leading her back on to the floor, out into the middle where it was more crowded, a few minutes half-heartedly dancing round her, before hauling her close, didn't matter about the music now, whatever was happening was slow inside Darren's head. Press of her breasts against his chest, fingers of her hand against his back, his own cupping the curve of her arse, sliding up and down. Flesh there in plenty, knickers no more than a strip of material at either side.

'Where we going?' she said, almost to the door.

There had been the usual quick consultation with her friend, trip to the loo, queuing for her coat, Darren looking at himself reflected in the poster on the wall, not letting his impatience show.

'Back to my place.'

'I can't stop long.'

He looked at her, questioning.

'My mum, she'd worry.'

Darren looked back towards the interior. 'Say you're staying with a mate.'

'I can't.'

'That's okay,' Darren said, moving towards the exit. ''S'not far.'

Out on the street he suddenly stopped. 'Wait here,' he said. 'Be right back.'

Surprised, she watched him as he walked back inside, mass of curly hair outlined against violent light.

There were two men at the urinals when he went in and he stood in line, taking his time until, laughing, they went back outside. Neither of the toilets seemed to be occupied.

Less than a minute later the music went loud and then quiet. The youth who came and stood one place down from Darren was Asian, blue suit, no more than eighteen.

Darren pulled up his zip and walked behind the youth as if to wash his hands. Turning fast, he grabbed him by both arms and threw him forward, cracking his head against the wall; brought his knee up fast into the base of his spine and struck his head against the wall a second time. A kick between his legs as he pulled him round; an elbow in the face.

There was a wallet in the inside pocket of his suit: two notes, a twenty and a ten, folded in his top pocket.

'Better call the manager or something,' Darren said to the man entering as he left. 'Some bloke in there's fainted. Done himself a bit of damage.'

'Sorry,' he said to the girl with a smile. 'Caught short. You know how it is.'

'Come on,' he said, once they were on the pavement. 'Get down to the corner, we can pick up a cab.'

Darren's room was an upstairs front: curtains at the window that neither met nor matched, bed, table, wardrobe, chair. He kissed her and asked her name, offered her coffee and she offered him a cigarette.

'Milk's off,' he said, coming back with two mugs. 'Have to have it black.'

'It doesn't matter,' she said.

Darren sat beside her on the bed. 'I want you to do something for me.'

Oh, yes, she thought, though there was something about the way he said it that made her think that might not be exactly what he meant.

'Hang on,' he said and disappeared a second time. When he came back from the kitchen there was a pair of scissors in his hand.

# Ten

The black cat sprang on to the stone wall at the sound of Resnick's footsteps, purred and paced and turned as soon as he was in sight, stretched his head towards the passing touch of Resnick's hand. Inside the front door, a second cat trilled and ran towards the kitchen, while Resnick stooped and scooped up the usual unappetizing batch of mail. Gas bill, electricity bill, a personal computerized letter from his bank manager offering to make him a loan on the most friendly of terms. The third cat was sitting on the hall chest, opposite the stairs; the fourth . . . there was a metallic clunk as Resnick entered the kitchen, a saucepan lid wobbling across the floor, a bewhiskered face peering from inside the pan.

'One of these days,' Resnick said, 'you'll wake up in there too late. End up as stew.'

The cat jumped out, unimpressed, and rubbed himself against Resnick's legs.

Dizzy, Miles, Bud, Pepper.

A letter with handwriting he recognized but couldn't place. Inside its clear wrapper, this quarter's copy of *Jazz FM*. More reviews of reissues he would love to buy but the technology was failing him. You could count the vinyl albums in Virgin or HMV on the fingers of both hands. Cassette or CD. Oh, well . . . perhaps next month he'd take the plunge. Have a word with Graham Millington – he'd have a CD player, bound to; chosen by his wife after a careful perusal of *Which?*; something that would bring Andrew Lloyd Webber's *Greatest Hits* into their home with all the sterility they deserved.

Impatient, Dizzy jumped up on to the work top and Resnick, not unkindly, pushed him down. He opened a tin of kidney and beef heart and forked the contents into the four coloured bowls, sprinkling a little KitEKat Supercrunch with liver and game over the top.

*OPEN this envelope NOW and read all about your FREE holiday in the Algarve.* Resnick tore it in two and tossed it in the bin. The way Dizzy kept pushing Bud out of the way and chomping his food as well as his own, it was no wonder Bud stayed so thin.

The coffee beans were dark and shiny in the palm of his hand and he brought them, momentarily, to his face to savour the smell. Stocks were running low; tomorrow or the next day he must remember to call in at The White House and buy more.

While the water was dripping through the filter, he arranged thin slices of Gruyère cheese, slivers of smoked ham, halved black olives, onion, several pieces of sun-dried tomato and, finally, some crumblings of blue Stilton on top of two thick slices of light rye bread. Careful to keep them level, he set both pieces on the grill pan and slid them beneath the flame which was already burning.

Taking hold of Dizzy firmly and holding him in one hand, he unlocked the back door and released the black cat into the garden. If he was still hungry, he could forage out there.

When it had become clear that Resnick's marriage was over, his wife of six years setting off for pastures new, his first reaction had been to sell the house, find a flat, make a statement that now he was on his own. But the kind of energy required to go through that process had been lacking. Whatever else it was, the house – big and rambling for two, absurd for one – was comfortable.

He called *Family First* and made them a present of the three-piece suite from Hopewell's that had almost cost a second mortgage, took himself down to the auctions at the cattle market and replaced it with something older, broken in, the shape of other lives already impressed into the upholstery.

So he had stayed there and got on with his life and, opening the door one day to say no thank you to a pair of neatly suited young men who wanted to interest him in attending a class in non-denominational readings from the Bible, a skinny young black cat had wandered in, ribs visible through falling fur. Resnick had fed him with chicken scraps and cheese and warmed milk. The cat had bolted the food, all the while glancing round nervously, and as soon as both saucers were licked clean, dashed to the door and demanded to be let out.

Three days later, he was back.

Then the second day.

Then every day.

The first time the cat jumped on to Resnick's lap and allowed himself to be stroked, Resnick was listening to the Prestige album, *In the Beginning*. You know, the blue fold-out cover with the beautiful picture of a handsome Dizzy Gillespie boxed in red. 'Oop Bop Sh'Bam' with Sonny Stitt on alto, Milt Jackson on vibes. Dizzy's solo taking them into the final theme, vocal coda, slurred notes at the end.

'Dizzy,' Resnick had smiled, feeling the new weight beneath the cat's improving coat, and the animal had looked back at him with wide green eyes.

A few months later, a younger cat had appeared.

Miles: who else?

The following year, Pepper and Bud had strayed and stayed. Resnick fed them with little fuss and they grew used to his odd hours, demanding as little of him as he did of them.

He drank some more of the black coffee and started on the second open sandwich, olive oil from the sun-dried tomatoes sliding into the cracks of his fingers and making small stains to join those he was already wearing on his tie. Last time he had tried, the assistant in Sketchley's had given him a you-must-be-joking look and handed him his ties back.

The letter lay on the small table alongside the easy chair, beside the telephone, resting on the cover of the Spike Robinson he was now playing. The stamps, the air mail sticker, he could only think of a couple of people who might be writing to him from the States, but neither of them from – where was it? – Maine? Pete Barnard was a jazz fan he knew, a dermatologist who was now working in Chicago, and Ben, Ben Riley, he hadn't heard from Ben in ages, seemed to have lost touch, but when he had, Ben had been out in Montana somewhere, wearing a deputy's hat and driving a jeep. Surely that wasn't Ben Riley's writing?

Of course, it was.

*Here I am, Charlie, out in Ellsworth, Maine, enjoying the good life and working none-too-hard for the County police department.*

The first of the Polaroids Ben had enclosed showed him with his hat and badge and holstered gun and, those aside, it wasn't only the handwriting that the intervening years had changed. Ben was a lot fuller in the face, something akin to jowls hanging down towards a neck that showed a tendency to spread over his shirt collar. Gun belt and trouser belt served to support a sagging stomach that would have been more alarming had it not been for the expression of contentment on Ben Riley's face.

*Getting myself across to the east of the country has worked out fine, especially since I met Ali, my second wife.*

Resnick wasn't sure that he had known about the first. *Mentally, she's made me face up to a few things, knuckle down, cut back on the drinking and learn to take myself more seriously. Of course, young Max has had a lot to do with that.*

Alison was a broad-faced blonde who stared straight at the camera lens as if daring it to talk back. She looked thirty-four or -five, ten years younger than Ben, arms folded across her chest, wearing a check shirt and blue jeans. Max had her hair, his father's eyes and looked pretty steady on his feet for the two years Ben assigned to him elsewhere in the letter.

*Put together some of that holiday time you're never using and get out here and see us, Charlie. There's this little restaurant right by the Grand cinema, serves the best Thai food outside the Pacific. I guess, whatever else has happened to you, you do still enjoy your food.*

The music clicked off and the cat that had wandered on to Resnick's lap jumped down again and ate the fragments of ham that had dropped to the floor. Resnick slid the letter and the photographs back into their envelope and walked across the room, poured himself a drink. In 1981, when Resnick had been standing in that garage, staring into Prior's face, reaching out to take his gun, Ben Riley had been the first officer through the door.

# Eleven

'What the hell happened to you?'

'Nothing. What d'you mean?'

'I hardly recognized you.'

They were in the café on West End Arcade, opposite the bottom of the escalator, Darren and Keith, the place in the city where they met, mornings, table close against the window. Every now and then there'd be some woman, short skirt, ascending in front of their eyes.

Keith was still staring at Darren, gone out. 'How much't cost, get it done?'

Darren ran a hand over his close-cropped hair. 'Nothing.'

'How d'you mean, nothing?'

'Got someone to do it for me.'

'What someone?'

'Some girl.'

There was an old boy in the corner, chewing his way through two of toast, careful to break off the ends of brittle crust rather than risk his teeth. A young mum with a tired face was dipping her baby's dummy into sweet tea and pushing it against the child's squalling face. Couple of retro-punks waiting for the record shop back down the arcade to open, rifle through the racks of rare singles they couldn't afford to buy.

''Nother tea?'

Keith nodded. 'Yeh, ta.'

'Anything to eat?'

Keith shook his head. 'Skint.'

'I'm buying.'

While they were waiting for the sausage cobs, Keith marvelled at the difference Darren's haircut made to his face. Suddenly it was sharper, harder, his nose seemed larger, jutting out from the centre of his face; and the eyes ... Keith didn't think he'd ever noticed them before, not really, blue-grey but bright, dead bright, as if for the first time they'd been let out from under a cloud.

'So what d'you think? Suit me?'

'Yeh. Yes. It's good. Really is.'

'But you didn't recognize me, right?'

'Well, I ...'

'When I come in, you said ...'

'I knew, but not straight off.'

'It's the hair, right?'

'Yeh, of course ...'

'Anyone as saw me before, just *saw* me, that's what they'd pick on, what they'd say – hair, he's got all this curly hair.'

'Yes.'

'That girl yesterday ...'

'The one you got to cut it off?'

'The one in the building society. Lorna.'

''S'that her name?'

'Lorna Solomon.'

'What about her?'

'I was wondering ...'

'Yeh?'

'If she walked in here now ...'

'Which she won't.'

'But if she did.'

'What about it?'

'If she'd know who I was.'

Keith watched Darren lift the top off his cob and smear the pieces of sausage with mustard, shook tomato sauce over his own until it lay in it, like a puddle. Darren had been likely to go off at half-cock before, quick fits of temper: dangerous, though he hadn't looked it. Now he did. As Darren bit down into his cob and grinned across at him, Keith saw again that new-found glint in his eyes and felt a chill slide over his skin because he knew then that Darren was capable of anything.

Anything.

'Shouldn't take that long,' the workman said at the door to Resnick's office. 'Hour or two at most.'

Resnick nodded and picked up a cluster of files from his desk, resigned to losing the use of the room for the rest of the day.

'Just got a call from forensic,' Millington called over the noise of furniture being dragged across bare floorboards.

'And?'

'Seems there's some kind of log jam. Lucky to get anything this side of tea time.'

'Managed to dig out three more witnesses, boss,' said Divine. 'Out at Sandiacre. Couple stuck their heads out after they whacked into the road sign, nothing new there, but this . . . Marcus Livingstone . . . had his motor nicked from outside a newsagent's less than quarter of a mile away. Heard this engine revving like crazy, realized it was his own. Got to the door in time to see them driving off down Longmoor Lane.'

'And we're certain it's the same pair?'

'Likely.'

Resnick nodded. 'Which direction, Longmoor Lane?'

'South.'

'Double back this side of the rec,' said Millington,

'Junction 25. Once they're on the motorway, any place from Chesterfield down to Leicester in half hour.'

''Less they carry on going,' Kevin Naylor said, 'swing round Chilwell and Beeston and back into the city.'

'This car,' Resnick asked, 'it's been reported missing?'

'Yes, boss. Vauxhall Cavalier, D reg. Not turned up as yet.'

Resnick nodded. 'Let's put some pressure on. Have a word with Paddy Fitzgerald, Graham, make sure uniform patrols keep their eyes skinned.'

'Right.'

Resnick turned back to Naylor. 'That witness yesterday . . .'

'Lorna,' Naylor said. 'Lorna Solomon.'

Divine sniggered.

'How good a description could she give of the youth who threatened her?'

'Pretty good, sir. Detailed.'

'It agreed,' said Lynn Kellogg, 'with what I could get from Marjorie Carmichael. Not that I'd like to rely on her in court.'

'But from the pair of them – if we needed to – there's enough to bring an artist in, get a composite?'

Naylor and Kellogg glanced at one another before answering. 'Yes, sir,' said Naylor.

'Yes,' said Lynn.

'Kevin, this, er, Lorna . . .'

'Solomon, sir.'

'Did you take her through the pictures we've got on file?'

'Not really, sir. Wasn't time. And I thought anyway, you know, by now we'd likely have prints and . . .'

'Bring her in. Sit her down. Can't do any harm.'

'Specially,' whispered Mark Divine behind Naylor's head, 'if you can get her to sit on your face.'

'Something else, Mark?' Resnick said.

'No, boss,' Divine said, wiping the smirk from his face.

'Anybody?'

'I thought I'd see if I can talk to the manageress,' Lynn Kellogg said. 'If she's not turned in at work, I've got her home address.'

'Right. And Mark, call the hospital, check the situation with Harry Foreman. Long as he's out of immediate danger, find out when we might be able to have a word. We still don't know conclusively which one it was clobbered him.'

Harry Foreman's X-rays suggested several hairline fractures of the cranial cavity and damage to the ossicles of the middle ear. He was sedated, mostly sleeping, being fed by means of an IV drip. In one rare moment of apparently clear consciousness he asked a student nurse what had won the 3.30 at Southwell; in another asked why his wife, Florrie, wasn't there to see him. When the ward social worker made inquiries, she discovered that Florence Foreman had died in 1973, having contracted pneumonia after a fall in which she had dislocated her hip.

Rebecca Astley had been prescribed an anxiolytic by her doctor, which she had purchased in the form of Diazepam from her local Boots. Now she was lying on the settee in the living room of the flat she shared with a management trainee from Jessops, a duvet wrapped around her to keep her from getting cold as she alternately watched an old John Garfield film on Channel 4 and re-read the Barbara Taylor Bradford she'd bought for the flight to Orlando. She didn't think anyone from head office would be round to see her so soon, but just in case they did, she had put a little make-up on her face and made sure her best dressing gown, the one with the lavender braiding, was close to hand. She only hoped that neither Marjorie nor Lorna had taken the opportunity to make her look bad; Marjorie she could trust, but Lorna ... she made it a rule never to speak ill of anyone, but Lorna Solomon – it wasn't just that she was common, that wasn't altogether her fault, what she didn't have to be was such a bitch.

'Where d'you get it all?' Keith asked.

'All what?'

'All this money, what d'you think?'

After spending the best part of an hour and more change than Keith could count on video games in the place above Victoria Street, they were sitting in Pizza Hut, waiting for the waitress to bring their order.

Darren winked. 'Got it from the girl, didn't I?'

'The one you picked up in Michael Isaacs?'

'Which other girl is there?'

'What'd she want to give you money for? She cut your hair, you should have paid her.'

Darren reached under the table and cupped his crotch in his hand. 'She got paid all right. Couldn't get enough.'

The waitress, trying not to notice the way Darren seemed to be fondling himself, put down their Meat Feast Supreme and left them to it.

'Then you wouldn't know a lot about that, eh, Keith?'

Keith made a face and lifted a slice of pizza on to his plate, reached for a tomato from the help-yourself salad Darren had piled high as he could, gluing the ingredients together with blue cheese dressing.

'Day comes, you get your cock out of your hand and up some slag's twat she'll think she's been stung by a gnat and start to scratch.'

'I'd be pleased if you'd moderate your language,' said

a woman in a red hat, turning round from the booth behind. 'There are young children here who don't want to hear that kind of talk.'

'Oh, yes,' said Darren, on his feet to get a better look at the family scene, mother and grandma and a couple of kids under ten wearing school uniform. 'And where d'you think they came from, then, if it wasn't some bloke slipping a paper bag over his head, getting you bent over the bed and fucking you rotten?'

The trainee manager was keen, only her second week in the job, there in a flash. 'Sit down, please, sir. If there's some kind of a problem . . .'

'What it is, Della,' Darren said, reading her name off her badge, smiling, 'my friend and I, we ordered two portions of garlic bread to go with the pizza, the garlic bread with the cheese topping. Seems to be a long time coming.'

# Twelve

When Lorna saw Kevin Naylor come through the door of the building society office something inside her gave a clear and definite lurch. Mind you, something like that had been happening pretty much every time anyone came in, right from when they'd first opened. Her mum had told her last evening when they'd talked on the phone, take a few days off, you shouldn't go straight back, not after what happened; her friend, Leslie, when she'd called round, see how Lorna was, she had said more or less the same. Even Mr Spindler had wondered if she oughtn't to take one of her statutory sick days.

But, no, she'd felt all right, no bad dreams, nothing like that. After all, it wasn't as if anything terrible had actually happened.

Still, there it was, this roll of her insides whenever she heard the door ring open, whenever she saw it begin to swing back. It was just that, well, when she realized it was Kevin her insides gave it that little extra. Nothing wrong with that: only natural.

'I was wondering,' Kevin had said, 'if you could spare a little more time.'

It had been Lorna's idea to stop off on the way and pick up some lunch.

'We have to eat, don't we? I mean, no law against that.'

She suggested the Chinese takeaway just across from the lights on Alfreton Road, more or less opposite the garage. From there it was easy for Kevin to double-back around the block, park on the Forest, the broad swathe of concrete where weekends they did Park and Ride.

This time there were no more than a dozen or so cars there, mostly parked close together. Funny how people tended to do that, as if there was safety in company. Kevin had drawn up away off from the others, facing up towards the trees.

'This is nice,' Lorna said. 'How's yours?'

Chewing, Kevin mumbled something that might have been, 'Fine.'

Lorna had chosen prawn crackers, sweet and sour pork; Kevin the spare ribs. She leaned a little against the inside of the car door now, watching him lick the sauce from his finger ends.

'We should do this properly some time.'

'What's that?' Kevin asked.

'Eat Chinese. You like it, don't you? Chinese food?'

'I like this.'

'That's what I mean. Only one evening, in a restaurant, what do you think?'

'I don't know.'

'You mean because of your wife?'

Kevin shook his head. 'She doesn't like Chinese. Says it's too salty. Makes her ill.'

Lorna was lifting a piece of pork towards her mouth with a plastic fork, grinning.

'What?'

'I wasn't thinking of asking her,' Lorna said.

Kevin looked up through the windscreen towards the cluster of trees; someone in an off-white sheepskin coat was walking a pair of Sealyhams, holding their leads unnaturally high, the way he'd seen owners do on television, at Cruft's Dog of the Year Show.

'Where do you go?' Lorna asked.

'You mean to eat?'

'With your wife, yes.'

'I don't know as we do, much.'

'But, like, something special?'

'Like what?'

'Anniversary.'

For their last anniversary, their third, Kevin had sent a card, bought flowers, stood in line at Thornton's for one of those little pink boxes for which you chose your two special chocolates before the assistant ties it up with pink ribbon. The lights had been off at Debbie's mother's house when he'd arrived, all save for the one that was always left on in the porch to put off burglars. After waiting three-quarters of an hour, Kevin had left the flowers on the doorstep with the chocolates, gone home and taken a bacon and egg pie from the freezer, sat down in front of *Eastenders* and eaten it out of the foil, not quite warmed through.

'Nothing special,' he said.

Inside the car it was getting warm, the windows beginning to take on a film of steam. Lorna offered him the last of the prawn crackers and when he shook his head, broke it in two with her teeth, biting with a light crunch, slowly. A fragment of cracker, white, stuck to a corner of her mouth, white against the fine, dark down of hair.

She was looking at his hands, resting on his lap. 'You ever take it off?' she asked. 'You wear it all the time?'

She was staring at the wedding ring on his hand.

'Sometimes,' he said.

Lorna nodded. 'My sister's husband – they've been married eleven years – she's quite a lot older than me – would you believe it, I'm the youngest? – anyway, he claims, her husband, he's never removed his wedding ring since they got married. Not for one second. D'you believe that?'

'I suppose . . .'

'But you, you said sometimes. Meaning . . .?'

'It's a little loose. Not quite as tight as it should be. Sometimes if I'm washing my hands . . . in the shower . . .'

She thought about Kevin taking a shower; standing there, his back towards her, water splashing over him. His backside.

'We ought to get going,' Kevin said, looking at his watch.

Lorna raised an eyebrow the way she'd seen Julia Roberts do it once, that movie.

'To the station,' Kevin said.

'Look at some photos, that's what you said.'

'That's right.'

'If it's there, I'll know it. I mean, the way he came over to me first off, not a care in the world. The look on his face when he pushed through the bin bag and told me to fill it. No way I'm going to forget that.'

Kevin switched on the engine, but Lorna wasn't through talking.

'You know what gets me?' she said. 'What really gets me?'

He looked at her: no.

'When Spindler came in this morning, that's the area manager, oh, he was nice enough to Marjorie and me, good job well done, all the flannel – not that he was going to give us any money for it, no bonus, nothing like that. All the thousands we saved them. But, no, what's he droning on about all the time is Becca, poor Becca and what a terrible shock she had, how it's affected her. Makes me sick. It's not as if anything happened to her. Wasn't her that got a hammer aimed at her head. No, there she is hopping up and down on one leg, practically weeing herself.' She stopped, reading the expression on his face. 'Sorry, I'm boring you, rattling on.'

'No, it's not that. It's just . . .'

'We ought to be going.'

'Afraid so.'

Kevin released the hand brake and slipped the car into gear.

'What you ought to tell your wife,' Lorna said, as they were turning right on to Forest Road West, 'next time she goes Chinese, ask them to leave out the monosodium glutamate. You can do that, you know. Tastes a lot less salty.'

# Thirteen

By midway through that afternoon, they had what looked like a breakthrough. Forensics had finally come up with a couple of prints, forefinger and thumb, plumb on the hand brake of the abandoned car. Whoever had been driving had known enough to wipe around the steering wheel with a cloth – probably the one smeared with engine oil stuffed beneath the front seat – had thought of the gear handle too, but somehow missed the brake. There were a couple of partials on the chrome handle, driver's side, one of which was a near match for those inside, the other from a different hand altogether.

Even better, scene of crime had found a beauty smack in the middle of the side wall of the building society, where the flat of the hand had gone slap against it. The officer, dusting it down, had scarcely been able to believe his luck. Three fingers, close to perfect, almost as clear as if whoever left them had been in custody – 'Now roll it lightly, one side to the other, even pressure. Good.'

Somewhere short of six o'clock the match came through, faxed back up the line. Keith Rylands: eighteen years of age, five feet five and a half, nine stone six pounds. Six months, youth supervision order, 1988–9, theft from a motor vehicle; four months on remand, 1990, taking and driving away without the owner's consent; six months, Young Offenders Institution, Glen Parva, two more charges of TDA, one associated charge of stealing from a vehicle dismissed through lack of evidence. Last known address: 29, Albert Avenue, Gedling.

Divine showed Rylands's picture to Marjorie Carmichael, who tutted and sweated and finally agreed, yes, it could be him, could be the one. Lorna Solomon wasn't a great deal more definite. 'Thing was, you see,' she told Kevin Naylor, 'I never saw him much more than out the corner of my eye. It's the other one I was looking at, the one with the hammer.' Becca Astley was sorry but she had a terrible headache, a migraine really, she couldn't concentrate at all, no way she could be sure.

'What d'you reckon?' Millington asked. They were sitting in an otherwise unoccupied interview room, Resnick's office, as he had suspected, resembling a YTS convention of young plumbers.

'No trace on the other print, the one on the door?'

Millington shook his head. 'Not so far.'

What they did have was an artist's impression, a narrow-faced young man with a mass of tightly curled hair: it would be in the evening editions of the *Post*, screened on both *Central News* and *East Midlands Today*. Not exactly *Crimewatch*, but it might yield results.

'Nothing on file about this Rylands's known associates?' Resnick asked.

'Doesn't sound as if he had any. Pathetic little bugger.'

'Okay,' Resnick said, pushing back his chair, 'I'll get Lynn to drive me out there. See what's what. Sooner that than hanging around here without a place to call my own. Mooching about the corridors. Starting to feel like the Ghost of Christmas Past.'

'Okay, okay,' Darren called. 'Stop the car, stop the car. That's it. Here, right here.'

Keith had driven the Cavalier into the NCP car park near the Rutland Square Hotel and swopped it for a silver-grey Honda Accord with a rusted rear off-side wing and two pairs of walking boots wrapped in old newspaper down by the back seat.

Keith wriggled himself up to his full height. 'Hey, this is . . .'

'I know where it is.'

'You're not going to try knocking it over again?'

Darren gave him a look that warned Keith there was such a thing as having too much to say – what he ought to do, stick to the driving and leave the thinking to him.

'Then why are we . . .?' Keith persisted.

'Shut it!' Darren hissed and pointed at the clock on the car's dashboard. 'That working? That right?'

'Far as I know.'

Twenty-eight minutes past five.

'Right, then.' Darren said, opening the car door. 'Wait here.'

The office was due to close at five-thirty – ten, fifteen minutes for sorting stuff out, finishing up, they ought to be coming out. Darren remembered the slight hesitation when he'd spoken her name, but nothing more, real cool – 'How may I help you?' Looking back at him through those big glasses, blue-framed. He'd liked that. 'This gentleman has a query. Perhaps you should deal with it yourself.' Took nerve, that. Not a sign of wobble in her voice. Different situation, Darren thought, she and him would get along. Him and Lorna. He'd wondered sometimes what it'd be like, going with a tart as stood up for herself, not just someone to be poked and pushed around.

Resnick was pleased to sit back, let Lynn Kellogg get on with the driving. When he'd been younger, not long joined the force, he'd evinced an interest in cars because it had seemed the thing to do. What you talked about in the canteen when it wasn't how many pints you'd swilled down the night before, how many times you'd got your leg over. As he'd got older, got promoted, he'd gradually felt able to let it drop. It was a while now since he'd talked about all three.

'Called round to see Rebecca Astley this afternoon,' Lynn was saying. They were heading down Carlton Hill, about to pass St Paul's school.

'Bit of a wasted visit, I hear,' Resnick said.

Lynn smiled. 'Don't know what they think they're doing, giving her branch office to manage. Couldn't even manage to get out to the kitchen, fetch a glass of water to take these pills. Expected me to do it for her.'

Resnick laughed, imagining the expression that would have been on Lynn's face when she'd walked back into the room, handed her the water.

'On and on about this migraine. That was the way she said it – mee-graine. As though it was some rare disease. Instead of a posh name for a headache.'

Lynn slowed behind a self-drive van, signalled to turn left into Gedling Road.

'All she was interested in talking about was what a shock it had been. That and the bunch of flowers been sent to her from head office. "I don't want to brag," she said, lying there on the sofa, "but it does show what a lot they think of me." '

'Didn't tell her what you thought of her?' Resnick asked.

'Tempted,' Lynn grinned. 'Wouldn't have been worth wasting my breath.'

Twenty-nine, Albert Avenue had a newly fitted wooden door with a circle of bottle glass at normal head height. The windows poked out from the front of the roof; a satellite dish was attached to the wall. *Stuart Bird*, read the sign to the side of the small front garden, *Painter & Decorator – Estimates Given Without Obligation.*

'You must want my husband,' Christine Bird said. 'He'll not be back while seven, maybe later. He's got a job on over Newark way.'

Resnick assured her she was the one they wanted to see and she showed them into a front room that smelled of furniture polish and Windolene. A small boy lay on his stomach in front of the TV, watching a cartoon video, pausing it every time the black cat went flying into an old-fashioned kitchen dresser, swallowing plates and bowls and cups before crashing to the ground with them inside him.

'This is Jason,' Christine Bird said.

Jason rolled on to his side, stuck out his tongue, then rewound the tape and played the section through again. Christine went over and turned down the sound, turned up the flame behind the fake log fire and took a cigarette from the packet of Players Extra Mild which lay on the marble shelf above the stone surround.

'It's your other son we're interested in,' Resnick said.

It took her five attempts to light her cigarette. 'He's not here,' she said.

'Do you know where Keith is?' Lynn Kellogg asked.

'I haven't seen him, not for a couple of days.'

'And you don't know where he might be?'

'I didn't say that,' tapping away ash nervously with her finger.

'We have reason to believe . . .' Resnick began.

'Don't,' Christine Bird interrupted him. 'I don't want to know what it is he's done. Not this time. Not any more.'

'You don't happen to know where Keith was yesterday afternoon?' Lynn asked.

Christine Bird got to her feet and crossed the room.

Reaching down she switched off first the television set, then the video, and when her five-year-old started to whine and complain she gave him a look that said, not this time, and he read it well. 'Why don't you go out into the garden?' she said. 'Or upstairs to your room?'

'If I do, can I . . .?'

'One,' she pronounced emphatically. 'One only. Go on. You know where they are.'

'Twix,' she explained, as Jason left the room.

Neither Resnick nor Lynn Kellogg said a thing.

Christine Bird fidgeted with the blinds, the kind that have scalloped edges. She stubbed out her cigarette and immediately took another from the packet, sliding it back before she could light it.

'My husband . . .' she started.

'Stuart, he's been very good . . .' she tried.

'Keith . . .' she began.

This time she lit the cigarette, pushed a hand up through her hair. There were lines tracking away from the corners of her eyes, slender pouches of skin below them; the eyes themselves were grey, narrowed against the plume of smoke that coiled upwards past her face.

'When we started going together, Stuart and me . . . you see, he'd been married himself, still was, legally. I mean, their divorce, it hadn't come through. One of the things he felt bad about was the thought of leaving his kids. That was the way he saw it, though I don't think it really was like that. Not as if, anyway, she'd have agreed to let him take them with him and even if she had, well, it's difficult to see how he would have managed. Three of them, you see. The youngest just eighteen months, much younger than his other two.' She drew on the cigarette deeply; stared at her hands. 'They had her as a way of trying to sort things out, keep them together.'

Rings. Clear polish on her nails.

'When it became clear that we were going to live together, get married, I know – I know, though he never, not in as many words, although he never said it – I know what he wanted was the two of us living together. Starting fresh. Room for his kids to come over, stay weekends or whatever, of course. But nothing more. What he didn't want was, well, what he didn't want, though again he never came right out and said it, was Keith. Living with us. Here.'

Three people's breath in the double-glazed room.

'Apart from anything else, he could never understand, you see, why Keith's dad didn't want him there, why Keith didn't want to live with him. To be fair, I think he would have kept him, been happy enough to, but by then they were having these awful rows, Reg was drinking more and more, no real job, and Keith just kept on at him, on and on, prodding away till, of course, Reg – his dad – struck out and, I mean, they just couldn't go on that way, so I said to Stuart, Stuart, after we're married and we've moved into the new house, he's got to come and live with us. Keith. Till he's old enough, maybe, to have a place of his own.'

Ash drifted towards the pleats of her skirt and, absent-mindedly, she brushed it away.

'Keith hadn't been in any really serious trouble by then. Oh, there'd been, you know, silly little incidents, shoplifting, sweets and things, nothing to write home about. Just the way kids do. And truanting. One term he'd skipped off almost as much as he was there. On account of bullying, that's what he said. He's small you see, Keith, small for his age. Not that he used to be, not when he was little; well, they all were then, little. Around ten or eleven, though, when the other lads started shooting up, Keith, he seemed to stay the same.

'And they teased him for it, beat him up, you know

what they're like. Keith, he found the only way to get them on his side was act the fool, make everyone laugh, clown around in class. Which meant, of course, getting in trouble with the teachers instead. Clever, he'd been, back in the juniors. All his reports, lively, that's what they say. Bright. That all changed.'

She stubbed out her cigarette in the ashtray on the mantelpiece; stayed for some moments, staring at the wall.

'When we came here and we asked Keith if he wanted to live with us, he jumped at it like a shot. Stuart was very good with him, took him off to one side and talked to him about how it was important to turn over a new leaf, do well at school.'

She glanced at the door before going on.

'When Jason came along, he was lovely with him. Keith, at first; playing with him, parading him up and down. I think it changed when Jason was able to get out of his pram, his cot, move about. Crawl and then walk. Stuart was working more, further and further away, having to, no choice about that, and I was busy with the house, one thing and another. Little Jason, he was really quick, into everything; and before either of us knew it Keith was up to all sorts, only this time it was serious. Cars and the like. Always mad about cars. First we knew, three o'clock one afternoon, I go to the door, two police-men standing there; in uniform, not like the two of you.

''Course, when Stuart heard about it he went wild, really lost his temper. Hit him. After that it was never the same. I think Keith would have moved back with his dad, but Reg was having troubles enough of his own.

'Last time, when Keith was sentenced, Stuart said if he gets in trouble once more after this, I'm not having him back inside the house. No matter what.'

Christine's fingers fumbled out another cigarette.

' "Even it means the end of us?" I asked him and he just stands there, you know, looking me flush in the face and says, "Yes, even if it means that." '

Resnick noticed, as if for the first time, the even ticking of the clock.

'He'll be with his dad,' Christine Bird said. 'Over in the Meadows.'

Keith sat hunched forward in the Honda, fidgeting with the tuning of the radio. Five minutes back, he'd caught a snatch of M. C. Mell'O', but since then it was Gem-AM or static, difficult to decide which was worse. Darren was still leaning against the wall opposite the small parade of shops, shifting his weight every now and then from one foot to the other.

Keith watched him now, stepping away from the wall suddenly, getting ready to move. And there, back across the street, the building society door opened and the girl with the blue-framed glasses, the one they'd tried to hold up, stepped out on to the pavement.

# Fourteen

'I did think that was nice of Mr Spindler, didn't you?' Marjorie said. 'Considerate. Calling round in person, to make sure we were all right.'

'About the least he could do,' Lorna replied, watching the older woman turn the key in the lock once, then twice.

'He is a busy man,' Marjorie said.

'And we just saved several thousand pounds of his company's money.'

'You know, Lorna,' Marjorie said, dropping the keys down into her bag, 'you really ought to do something about your attitude.'

'My att–'

'I sometimes think it's the only thing holding you back.'

Lorna half-turned, vaguely aware of someone walking towards them across the street. Where the hell's it got you, Marjorie? she felt herself wanting to say. All those years of back-pedalling and going out of your way to be nice?

'Look at Becca, for instance.'

'What,' asked Lorna, more than a little steel in her voice, 'has Becca got to do with it?'

'Look at the way she's got on as fast as she has. I know she's intelligent, degree and all, but why do you think she's got where she has?'

Lorna stared at Marjorie's dough-like face, waiting to be told.

'It's because she knows how to behave towards people; especially people like Mr Spindler. She's nicely spoken and she's always well-turned out . . .'

'And if it would help her career, she's not above taking Spindler into the back office and giving him a quick wank.'

'Lorna, really!' Marjorie flushed bright red from the nape of her neck to the roots of her hair. 'I can't imagine what you . . . I can't believe . . . I'm going to pretend I never heard you say that.'

'Fine,' Lorna said. 'Believe what you like.' And, turning fast on her heel, she came close to colliding with Darren, who had slowed his pace on hearing raised voices, but continued, nonetheless, towards them.

'I'm sorry, I . . .'

''S'okay.' Darren said, chirpily. 'No harm done, eh?'

For a moment they were stationary, Darren close enough to see his new face reflected in the curved lenses of Lorna's glasses. Lorna looking at him, this tall, skinny youth with the shorn head and the beak-like nose and those protruding grey-blue eyes.

'Closed up?' Darren jerked his head sideways towards the door.

'Half-five.'

'Well,' Darren shrugged, 'call in another time, eh?'

And he was walking on down the street, hands in his jeans pockets, whistling.

'You don't know him,' Marjorie said. 'Do you?'

'I don't think so,' Lorna said, watching as Darren began to cross back to the other side of the pavement, lower down. But, somewhere inside, she felt that, yes, she did.

*

Resnick contacted the station, told Graham Millington to get Divine and Naylor down to the Meadows sharpish. If Keith Rylands was there, no sense letting him slip away because nobody was watching the back door. The sky seemed to darken abruptly as Resnick and Lynn Kellogg passed over the railway bridge on London Road, the carriage lights of short sprinter trains standing out clearly – commuters waiting to be shuffled back to Langley Mill, Attenborough, Alfreton and Mansfield Parkway. Ahead of them the traffic slowed almost to a standstill. In the car alongside, a thirtyish executive in a white shirt, sleeves rolled back just above the wrist, added another Benson Kingsize to the pollution levels and listened to the up-to-the-minute traffic report on the local radio, confirming where he was and why.

'Heart attack before he's fifty,' Lynn said caustically, glancing sideways.

'Maybe he takes long healthy walks,' Resnick said. 'Off into Derbyshire. Couple of squash games a week and visits to the health club.'

'And I'm about to get put up to sergeant,' Lynn responded.

'You will. All in good time.'

'Meanwhile I'm still at the bottom of the pecking order, counting through my cheque stubs each time I go to Safeway.'

'You're not doing so bad.'

'Aren't I?'

'You're still only twenty-five.'

'Twenty-six.'

'You'll get there.'

Lynn eased the car forward a whole fifteen yards. 'How old were you, when you made sergeant?'

Resnick could remember being summoned to the old man's office, stomach bowling googlies all the way along the corridor, not being able to get the grin off his face afterwards, so that four hours later when Elaine opened the door to him she knew. 'Nigh on thirty,' he said.

'And that was CID?'

Resnick shook his head. 'Transferred back into uniform to get the promotion.'

'Can't see me doing that. Rather stay where I am.'

'It wasn't so bad. Good experience, really. And I was back in CID inside two years. Jack Skelton had just got bumped up as well; he was my DI.'

Lynn laughed. 'I can just see him, briefings every morning, checking how you were all turned out.' She shot Resnick a quick look. 'Smart suit, well-ironed shirt and tie.'

Resnick joined in with the laughter. 'He tried.'

A gap appeared ahead in the traffic and Lynn accelerated smartly into it.

Divine was hard up against the back door, hoping against hope the suspect would try and do a runner; a strained groin had kept him out of the rugby squad for the past three games and he'd dearly love an excuse for landing a couple of good right-handers. Naylor sat behind the wheel of the second car, end of the alley. Resnick pulled on his raincoat and headed for the front, Lynn half a pace behind.

Before Resnick could try the bell, or use the knocker, the door opened and a bald man stumbled out, ripe with the smell of ammonia which comes from clothes steeped in stale urine and alcohol.

'Hey up!' Resnick stepped sideways swiftly, halted him with the flat of one hand.

'Wha-?'

'Reginald Rylands?'

'Na.'

'He does live here?'

The man's head moved forward and back as his eyes tried to focus. 'Downstairs. Try down . . . stairs.'

But, by then, Rylands was in the hallway, the head of the cellar steps, and walking forward. 'You looking for me?'

Resnick showed his warrant card, identified himself and Detective Constable Kellogg.

'You'd best come in,' Rylands said.

'Be on m'way,' slurred the bald man, stepping between Resnick and Lynn Kellogg and on to the street.

'Is he okay?' Resnick asked.

Rylands nodded. 'Long as nobody stands too near him with a lighted match.'

Inside the kitchen, Resnick turned down the offer of tea, took in the empty quart cider bottles on the floor, several days of unwashed pots and plates. Lynn hung back in the doorway, careful for the sounds of anyone making a dash for the front door.

'Something about the house?' Rylands asked. 'One of the lodgers? I'm properly registered, you know, approved. Least, till the EEC start in on toilet bowls and sinks.'

'It's not that.' Resnick shook his head.

'Then it's Keith.'

'You tell me.'

Rylands eased a finger inside his mouth, scraped away at something stuck between his teeth with a nail. 'Got to be, hasn't it?'

'How's that?'

'Always in trouble, isn't he? This thing and the other.'

'And recently?'

Rylands shook his head. 'No idea. 'Less it's motors, is it? Cars. Can't keep away from them. That what it is?'

From one of the upstairs rooms came the strangulated tenor of Josef Locke and Resnick grimaced: popular films sometimes had a lot to answer for.

'You do know where your son is?' Lynn asked.

'No.'

'We understood that you did.'

Someone of similar musical tastes to Resnick opened a door above, shouted loudly and then slammed it shut. Josef Locke faded back into insignificance.

Rylands looked with interest at the white fibre from the heart of last night's chicken tikka, suspended from his finger end. 'And who'd that be from?' he asked.

'We've just been speaking to Keith's mother.'

'Oh, yes, the former Mrs Rylands, light of my life.'

'She seemed certain that Keith was here, staying with you.'

'And I thought he was staying with her and old Stuart, the handy man *par excellence*. Funny, isn't it?'

'She said she hadn't seen Keith for a couple of days.'

'Me neither.'

'You haven't seen him?'

'You heard right.'

'Since when?'

Rylands shrugged. 'Thursday, Friday last week. You sure you wouldn't like a cup of tea?'

Resnick's expression suggested that he was.

'Well, I'll just make one for myself, if you don't mind.'

He was on his way towards the sink with the empty kettle, but Resnick was standing in front of him, blocking his way.

'We have reason to believe your son might have been involved in a serious matter.'

'I daresay. Now if you'll . . .'

Resnick took the kettle from his hand and set it down. Lynn stepped to one side in the doorway to let Divine through. 'Sorry, boss, getting dead bored out there. Thought I'd get to where the action was.' Reading the question in Resnick's face, he added, 'Kev's out back, not to worry.'

Rylands had retrieved the kettle.

'Tea up, then, is it?' Divine grinned.

'No,' Resnick said. 'It's not. Not till we've got a few more answers.'

'Well, that's it then, stand-off. Afraid I can't tell you what you want to know.'

Resnick could just smell the alcohol on his breath, not insistent, but there. Steady drinker now, he thought, controlled. Likely doesn't start till eleven, eleven-thirty of a morning, no acceleration till late on, eight or nine at night.

'You know it's an offence,' Divine was saying, 'withholding information.'

'How can it be an offence if I don't know anything?'

'You'll not mind,' Resnick said, almost casually, 'if we search the house.'

'Should I?'

'We'll see, shan't we?' Divine smiled.

'If you've a warrant. You did think to bring a warrant?'

'Too cocky by half, boss,' Divine said, nodding towards Rylands. 'Been here before.'

'Have you ever been in trouble with the police?' Resnick asked.

'Who hasn't?'

'Recently?'

Lynn Kellogg responded to footsteps on the stairs and moved out into the hallway; a man wearing stained khaki trousers and a Fair Isle jumper two sizes too tight was carrying a nondescript brown dog towards the door, one hand round the animal's mouth. Before his objective was reached, the dog wriggled out of his arms and barked.

'No animals,' Rylands said to Resnick. 'It's in the rules. Plain. So daft he thinks I don't know he's smuggling it in and out.'

'This trouble . . .' Divine began.

'Let's get back to your son,' Resnick said.

Rylands's shoulders slumped and this time Resnick allowed him to fill the kettle, set in on the gas. 'You any of your own?' he asked Resnick. 'Kids?'

Resnick gave a quick shake of the head.

'If you had, maybe you'd understand. I don't suppose you ever stop caring for them, feeling something, but . . . the rest of it, the day to day, the way they're fucking up their lives.' He stood with his eyes closed for as much as twenty seconds. 'If I knew where he was I'd tell you. Time inside, real time, he might learn a lesson. If not, least happens, he'll be out of harm's way. Not able to do anything stupid.'

'You think he might?'

'Only every sodding day.'

'Then you would tell us where he was?'

'If I knew,' Rylands said. 'Like a shot.'

'You'll not mind, then, if we take a look around?' Divine said. 'Warrant or not?'

'Forget it, Mark,' said Resnick, beginning to turn away. 'He's not here, it's okay.' And to Rylands, turning in the kitchen doorway, 'If you do see him, what you might do, persuade him to come in. Own accord, go better for him.'

Rylands nodded.

'Barring that, give me a call. Resnick. Detective Inspector.'

Rylands nodded again. 'I'll remember.'

Behind him, the kettle was starting to boil.


'You get a whiff of him?' Lynn asked. They were outside

on the pavement, the opposite side of the narrow street, looking back at the house. 'Like he worked in a brewery.'

'Starting to feel a bit sorry for him,' Divine said, 'way he was going on about his lad.'

'You and Kevin,' said Resnick. 'I want you keeping the place under surveillance. All night if necessary. My guess, the youth's been staying here and he'll be back.'

# Fifteen

He hadn't recognized him at first, not for certain; only later, watching Rylands fake his way through sincere parenting, had Resnick been able to slip the younger face over the old. A trick of memory. Tighter, eyes screwed up against the smoke, the lights. Sweat that slid down the channels of Rylands's face, sprayed from nose and forehead as he jerked his head from side to side. Slow smile that would glide into place, when on the stage in front of him, either tenor or guitar would strike a serious groove. The way he would arch back on his stool, sticks a blur as patterns and paradiddles grew from his hands.

Drinking even then, but didn't they all?

Pints of best bitter slopping across the boards: quarter bottles of scotch or vodka passed from hand to hand.

Pills.

Without effort of imagination, Resnick was there, too many bodies crammed fast, rhythmic thump of dancing feet, sweat that seemed, like raindrops on a windscreen, to rise directly up the walls. Girls you walked back along the Trent, whose interest waned when finally you told them what you did, whose hands eased free from yours, who moved a pace apart.

*Walking all over me like that. It's a wonder I didn't go flying back down the stairs.*

Elaine.

Resnick had looked for her again, other evenings when the band was playing 'In the Midnight Hour', 'My

98

Girl', 'I've Been Loving You Too Long'. Scanning the crowd for that half-serious face, angry, mocking eyes. When next he did encounter Elaine, it would be another place, another circumstance.

The music had changed, too. Instead of soul, rhythm and blues, it was slim young men decked out with purple eyeliner, stars glittering on their cheeks, songs about ancient forests or stars in the skies. Resnick stopped going.

Rylands had beaten him to it: one week Resnick had walked in, together with Ben Riley, and there had been someone else behind the drums.

Rumour was a name band had made Rylands an offer, a group, and he was back on the road, up and down the M1 more times than Peter Withe and Tony Hateley combined. There was talk of a record that should have been a hit. To the best of his knowledge, Resnick had never heard it.

He wondered how many years Rylands had been back in the city, if he still played? A pub, maybe, on the outskirts, requests from customers, keyboard and drums. Draw for the raffle, roll on the snare and a cymbal crash. Blokes pushed up on stage, half-pissed, by their mates, dropping the mike midway through some half-remembered song.

Wondered what Rylands really thought about his son.
*Any of your own? Kids?*

Without realizing what he was doing, Resnick had climbed the stairs to the top of the house.

*All those times I'd walk in here and see the expectation rise and fall in your eyes. Fancy a cup of tea, Charlie? Not what you wanted to hear. What you wanted was for me to walk in and say I was pregnant.*

Through windows that needed cleaning, Resnick looked down on muted streetlights, the road that curved away in front of the house, the road not taken, not by him.

What Elaine had finally said when she had walked in: *Charlie, we need to talk*. He knew then – the tone of her voice, the look in her eyes – that she was leaving him. Just not when.

Downstairs he checked with the station: Divine and Naylor were still on obs, no sign of Keith. It was a little shy of eleven p.m.

Resnick realized that his instincts could have been wrong. He set aside the idea of going back out there and mooched into the kitchen, began opening and closing cupboard doors. Appetites excited, cats pushed at his ankles, slid their sleek heads across his feet. It wasn't simply finding himself face to face with Rylands for the first time in – how many? Twenty? – years. It was more. Other bits and pieces of the past were nudging their way back into his consciousness, rubbing themselves against the back of his mind.

Rylands.

The Boat Club.

Ben Riley.

Elaine.

Prior.

Ruth James.

In the front room he rooted through the shelves of records, albums he'd collected since he was in his teens. After a first, and a second, search he still hadn't found it, wondered if he could have lent it to someone long ago, if maybe Elaine had taken it, memories of that first time they had met.

He doubted that.

He finally found it inside the sleeve of another record, Serge Chaloff's *Blue Serge* – not bad, Resnick thought, for an impromptu overcoat. A four-track EP with a laminated cover, soft-focus picture of the singer, head bent, before the microphone. *Ruth James .& the Nighthawks.* 1972.

Resnick slid the record on to his hand: a memory of her hand struggling to push back the air. The pallor of her face, auburn of her hair. He dispensed the worst of the dust and set it on the turntable, changed the speed. The stylus stuck near the start and when Resnick eased it gently on the vocal had already begun.

> *All those dreams and wasted tears,*
> *Every minute, every second,*
> *The worst of all my fears*

He had been called to a burglary, January seventy-four, one of those big houses off the Mansfield Road, divided into flats and then divided again. A warren of rooms in which clothes hung drying in front of a two-bar electric fire and every squeak of conversation came through the partition wall. Cooker behind a screen in one corner, the bathroom down the hall – only hot water enough to cover your knees, the plug hole circled round with other people's pubic hairs. A rusting fire escape that climbed up from the overgrown garden at the side. Too many windows with a faulty catch. One man, working alone; he had got through four rooms before Elaine came out of hers to go to the toilet and there he was, trying the door across the hall.

'What the hell d'you reckon you're about?' she'd shouted, grabbing at his arm.

The burglar – dark shirt, jeans wearing gloves – had bolted for the stairs, out through the main door, the lock of which he'd slipped as soon as he'd got inside.

'Sure you're okay?' Resnick had asked, self-conscious inside her room, Elaine sitting on the only chair.

'Um? Oh, yes, I'm fine. Fine.'

'You were lucky.'

She looked at him then, questioning.

'When you reached for him, that he didn't react.'

'He ran.'

'I know. What I meant, he might have felt provoked. He might have hurt you.'

She smiled. 'Like you, you mean?'

Resnick's eyes had smiled back. 'I didn't know if you'd remembered?'

'Someone your size? All over me? I had a bruise on my instep that lingered for weeks. Not to mention my big toe.'

'Bruised, too?'

'Worse.'

He gave her an inquiring look.

'It came off.'

'The toe?'

'The nail.'

'Oh.'

She continued to sit there and he continued to stand where he was, watching. Somewhere above, a cistern was noisily refilling.

'Shouldn't you be looking for clues?' she finally said.

'That fire escape,' Resnick said, embarrassed, 'it's like an open invitation.'

She smiled again; it was a good smile, strong, not ingratiating. 'Sooner burgled than burned.'

'What I was thinking, window locks . . .'

'We've been on to the landlord for months.'

'Maybe now he'll pay some attention.'

She got to her feet. 'And maybe not. Anyway, who cares? By then I'll have moved.'

'By when?'

'Week after next.'

She could read the disappointment in his eyes: just when I've found you again.

'Do you think you'll catch him?' she asked at the door to her room.

'Honestly?'

'Of course.'

'If he's a regular, if we pick him up for something else . . . otherwise, no. Probably not.'

He stepped out into the middle of the corridor and she looked at him again. 'Are you always that honest?'

'I hope so. I try to be.'

'Don't you find that a hindrance in your work?'

He couldn't tell from her expression whether she was teasing him or not. He couldn't think of anything else to say. Before he had reached the head of the stairs, she had gone back inside her room and closed the door. Three weeks later a card arrived, the envelope forwarded from Central Station. On the front was a photograph of a saxophone, black and white; on the reverse Elaine had written *Maybe you'd like to call round and check the security arrangements?* along with her new address.

Elaine.

And Ruth James.

This was their story, too.

> *Empty arms and empty promises*
> *And ten more wasted years*

# Sixteen

'Doner kebabs,' Darren said. 'Two Cokes. Cold ones.'

The assistant shook his head. 'Sorry, closed now. Everything switch off.'

'Closed,' Darren observed. 'What we doin', standing here?'

'Everything switch off...'

'Yeh, you said. So either switch it fucking on again or find us somethin' to eat quick, 'cause we're fuckin' starving.'

With a slow shake of his head, the assistant lifted the lid from one of the metal containers. 'Meat,' he said. 'No pitta, no bread.'

'So stick it in something else,' Darren said, being reasonable. At least now they were getting somewhere, talking the same language, almost.

'I don't know if I want...' Keith began, watching the slices of grey meat being lifted into two polystyrene trays.

'Course you fucking do,' said Darren. And to the man: 'Some of the chilli sauce on there, right? Come on, Jesus, shake the bloody thing! And how about the Cokes? Christ! Call this cold?'

Darren emptied the contents of his pocket out on to the counter in a clatter of coins. 'Have that. 'S'all I've got. And, hey! You really want to smarten up your act around here, you know? Sweep all this shit up off the floor and do something about that thing you're wearing –

more stains than Keith's jockey shorts. And hey, hey! First thing tomorrow, go to one of them places up the market, get a badge cut with your name on, stick it right there, on your lapel. People know what to call you.'

'Tony,' the assistant said.

'Tony, yeh, right.' Darren leant an elbow on the counter and patted him none too lightly on the cheek. 'Tony. You remember what I said, huh? Better than having them walking in off the street, Stavros, Stavros, all the time.'

'Not a bad bloke,' Darren said through a mouthful of meat. 'For a Greek.'

'I think he's Cypriot,' Keith said. They were walking along Lower Parliament Street, strolling really, taking their time.

'Same thing,' Darren said.

Keith shook his head. 'I think he's Turkish.'

'That's what I said. Same fucking thing.'

A black and white cab came towards them, signalling to turn right down Edward Street, and Darren stepped out into the road and waved him down; then, as soon as the driver slowed, he waved him on again.

'Forgot,' Darren explained. 'Skint.'

Keith nodded and looked at his watch; new battery just last week and it had stopped again. It had to be well past two. 'I ought to be getting back,' he said.

'What's the rush?' Darren lifted the last of the meat with fingers and thumb, tipped up the container so that the chilli sauce ran into his mouth, belched, and sent the container skimming across the street into the doorway of the gas showrooms. 'Tell you what, fucking doner tastes like shit.'

Keith thought he was going to be sick.

'Stay over at my place,' Darren said. 'Sleep on the floor.'

'Thanks,' Keith said. 'My old man, he'll be . . .'

'What? Waiting to tuck you in?'

Keith thought, chances were, if his old man was up at all, a good bollocking was all that was on the cards.

Darren took Keith's silence for assent. 'You know what I hate?' he said. 'Walking round without money in my pockets. Where's the nearest cash machine?'

They waited until a punter in a loose grey suit, late from one of the clubs, punched in his personal number and withdrew a hundred pounds.

'Got a light?' Keith said, blocking his way.

Darren hit him from behind: twice was enough, the third one just for fun. Five crisp twenties, never saw the inside of the bloke's wallet. Thank you for your custom, please come again.

A little after four, Keith woke on Darren's floor with a sore back and a stiff neck and the certain sure knowledge that he was going to die. An hour later he was still cuddled up to the toilet bowl, head resting on the chipped enamel. There can't be any more, a small long-suffering voice told him. But there always was.

Divine and Naylor were parked along the street from Rylands's house; two or three people had entered, lodgers most likely, none of them any chance of being Keith.

'Know what we ought to do when we're relieved?' Divine said. 'Get ourselves out on the old Nuthall Road. See if there's any talent hitching a lift back Heanor way.' Divine winked. 'Help 'em out, right?'

Naylor looked through the windscreen towards the soft glow of lights that hung over the city centre.

'How long's it been, Kevin?'

'Since when?'

'Since your precious Debbie took herself off to her mum's? Your kid along with her.'

Naylor shook his head. 'I don't know.' Only the months, weeks, days.

'Hardly makes you a married man, then, does it?'

'That gives me the right to go picking up sixteen-year-olds?'

Divine winked. 'Give you the right to a bit of fun.'

'Your idea of fun, not mine.'

'Jesus, you're a miserable bugger. No wonder she upped sticks and left you.'

'Look . . .' Divine was really getting his rag '. . . she hasn't left me. That's not the way it is.'

'No? How is it then?'

'She's staying at her mum's while we work things out.'

Divine laughed in his face. 'Never sodding talks to you. How can you be working anything out?'

'That's rubbish.'

'Is it? Go on, then, you tell me. When were you last round there? See the kiddie? Talk, the pair of you, without her old lady gobbing and gawking?'

Naylor got out of the car and mooched up the street towards Queen's Walk. As if it wasn't bad enough his father having a go at him over the telephone, his mother writing those letters: *Kevin, she is our granddaughter* . . .

'Tell you what,' said Divine, when Naylor climbed back into the car. 'All the women I've had since joining the force. Names, vital statistics, likes and dislikes. And, hey! Outside the knickers don't count, okay, Kev?'

By the time Millington and Lynn Kellogg took over it was the coldest part of the night. Lynn had brought a large Thermos of tomato soup and Graham Millington

107

had four spinach pasties his wife had bought from Sainsbury's, reheated and handed over wrapped in foil. The car engine they ran intermittently, needing the heater to stop all feeling from leaving them below the knees.

'The wife's talking about Corsica this year,' Millington said, 'but I'm not so sure.'

'You know that bloke I used to go out with?' Lynn said.

'The cyclist?'

'Yes, that's right. Had a card from him the other day. Heard nothing in over a year. Did I have anything fixed for my holidays and, if not, what did I feel about the Tour de France?'

'Too hot, that's what concerns me.'

'France?'

'Corsica.'

Lynn gave the Thermos a shake before pouring out what remained. Her mother had been angling at her, nothing direct but making it clear all the same, next leave Lynn got she should spend it at home with them. *It's your dad, Lynnie, he's not what he was ...* What he was was a stick of a man, old before his time, wandering between the hen houses instead of sleeping. Likely as not, out there at this moment, checking for foxes, flicking his torch on and off and all the while talking softly, as if his presence not only scared off predators, it kept the birds safe from salmonellosis, aspergillosis and blackhead.

Outside the light was flirting with the sky.

'Come on,' Millington said, firing the engine, 'he'll not show now. Let's get back to the station. Get a decent cup of tea.'

They'd been gone scarcely fifteen minutes when Keith

came round the corner, walking slow. Darren had got fed up with the sounds of Keith throwing up and when the diarrhoea had kicked in that had been enough. 'Here,' throwing him some Ajax and a balding lavatory brush. 'Clean that mess up and then fuck off. I'll see you tomorrow.'

Keith let himself into the house quietly but not quietly enough. His father was on the cellar stairs with a jack-handle in his hand. 'Figured you for a burglar.'

'Figure again.'

'Christ, you look awful!'

'Thanks,' Keith mumbled and just got to the toilet in time.

'Thought you'd like to know,' his dad said through the door, 'police were round earlier, looking for you. I don't know what you've been up to, but when you get out there, I've a good mind to give you the hiding of your miserable life.'

What happened later that morning meant that, as far as the police were concerned, Keith Rylands was all but forgotten.

# Seventeen

The time switch on the main safe was activated to open at nine-fifteen. Road works, caused by the need to replace thirty metres of sewage piping, had brought about a traffic bottleneck and the security van delivering cash for the start of business was slightly delayed. It finally appeared at nine-thirteen, three minutes late. The bank guard set aside his copy of the *Express* and moved to unlock the outer door. Two men wearing blue-grey uniforms and sky-blue protective helmets climbed down from the cab of the van, called out a remark about the traffic and proceeded to unlock the rear doors.

A bottle-green Granada drew up across from the security van and a woman wearing a high-collared wool coat got out of the passenger seat and began to walk towards the bank.

The first security man was inside the van, passing down sacks of coins to his colleague, who was loading them, side by side, into a low wooden trolley.

The bank guard set the ramp against the stone step and used the side of his shoe to edge it into place.

'I'm sorry, madam,' he said, turning towards the woman in the woollen coat, 'I'm afraid we're not open till half-past nine.'

The woman, who was a man, pulled a sawn-off shotgun from inside the folds of her coat and jabbed the barrel ends hard against the guard's neck, beneath his jaw.

One of the security men was wheeling his laden trolley across the pavement.

'Move,' the armed man said clearly, 'and this one's dead.'

The Granada was reversing towards the front of the van, two wheels on the pavement, two on the road. A second car, a grey Volvo estate, swerved around the corner and headed towards the rear of the van fast. Before it had come to a standstill, three men, wearing track suits and costume masks, had jumped out.

The security man inside the van had started to leave, one leg over the tail, and now he was back inside, struggling to lock the doors. A blow with an iron bar fractured his wrist, a second, across his shins, fetched him to his knees.

The man in woman's clothing forced the guard to walk backwards into the centre of the bank. Two masked men sprinted past them, heading for the safe. The cashier nearest to them was barged aside.

'If anyone tries to be a hero, they can be the second to die. After this one here.'

Shotgun forcing back his head, the guard kept both eyes clenched tight.

Inside the security van, both men, helmets removed, back to back, had their mouths and eyes taped shut.

The contents of the safe were being emptied into double-strength polythene sacks.

By nine-nineteen it was over: a yield, per person, somewhere in excess of three thousand pounds per minute.

Resnick was on his way to a meeting with the Home Office pathologist. The remains of a middle-aged man's body had been found in some woods north-east of the city and the possibility was that they might correspond with a missing person case Resnick had been working on. They were almost there when the news came over the radio. He leaned forward and touched his driver on the shoulder, instructing him to turn round. Parkinson and his corpse would have to wait.

'Boss, you want Kev and me back out at the Meadows or what?' Divine was on the first landing of the police station, eager and open-mouthed.

'Get a couple of uniforms round there,' Resnick said, hurrying past. 'You'll be needed on this.'

In the CID room phones were ringing, some being answered. The furniture had been replaced, the boards – save those in Resnick's office – had been relaid. It was as cold as before, if not colder.

Lynn Kellogg rose from her desk to intercept him. 'Just had a call from the hospital. Harry Foreman, seems he's out of danger.'

The concern that had leaped to Resnick's eyes faded almost as fast. 'Thankful for that, at least. Make a note to get out there and take a statement.'

'Today?'

Resnick was already moving on. 'I doubt it.'

Reg Cossall appeared alongside him in the long corridor, matching Resnick step for step. 'What I hear, this is the same team, buggers've changed their MO. Christ knows what we're dealing with now. Bunch of bloody transvestites wearing Mickey Mouse masks. Next we know, sodding students'll be putting their hands up, stunt for charity. Rag week. Awareness of tossing AIDs.'

Resnick pushed open the door to the incident room and let his fellow DI enter before him. Most of the chairs were already taken and the air was thickening with smoke. An officer was pinning Polaroids of the two abandoned cars, the Granada and the Volvo, to the board on the side wall, beside the map showing the route of the gang's escape – that which was certain, that which was conjecture. On a second map the location of the robbery had been newly flagged, joining the five others.

Out front, Malcolm Grafton was shuffling through his desk of six-by-four cards prior to the briefing. Alongside him, Jack Skelton was rehearsing what he would say in front of the TV cameras in an hour's time, wondering if he had made the correct decision in going with the double-breasted blazer instead of the suit.

The door opened again and Detective Inspector Helen Siddons came into the room, acknowledging both Resnick and Cossall with a nod, before moving towards the far end of the rows of chairs.

'Looking for a bloke in drag,' Cossall muttered, 'there's our man.'

Malcolm Grafton coughed a few times and brought the meeting to order. Jack Skelton got to his feet and began to speak.


'Hundred and twenty thousand,' Darren said. 'More, depending which version you heard.'

Keith's face showed no understanding; his skin was the colour of old putty and his eyes were glazed over.

'What's up with you?' Darren said. 'Don't you ever listen to the news?'

Keith shook his head: not quickly, not far.

'Over a hundred grand in the time it takes you to wipe your arse.'

Across the kitchen, Rylands turned his head, but decided to say nothing. He hadn't taken to Darren the first time he set eyes on him, less than five minutes ago when a hammering had brought him to the front door, Darren standing there like a skinhead with a serious personality problem.

'Hey, look,' Darren said now. 'You got a radio over there. Switch it on, bet there's some bulletin. Something new.'

He was staring at Rylands, pointing at the portable Sanyo on top of the fridge.

'It doesn't work,' Rylands said. 'Needs new batteries.'

It had needed batteries for weeks and he'd bought a fresh set, EverReadies, last time he'd been to the corner shop, but he'd be buggered if he was going to let Darren know that. Ordering him around in his own house. He wanted to find out the news, let him spend his own money, buy a paper.

'Less than ten minutes,' Darren was saying to Keith, 'and they were out of there with over a hundred thousand quid. You know how come?'

Keith squinted up at him. ''Cause they planned it?'

'Course they planned it, lamebrain. That's not what I meant.'

'Less of the names,' Rylands said.

'They got away with it,' Darren went on 'because they didn't go in empty-handed. They were tooled up. They had a gun. Shotgun. No one argues with that.'

'Who d'you think you are?' Rylands said. 'You ever stop to listen to yourself? Something out of *The Untouchables*?'

'What the fuck's that when it's out?'

'See what I mean? Don't even know you're born.'

'Come on,' Darren said, moving back towards the kitchen door. 'We're getting out of here.'

'Keith's not well,' Rylands said. 'He's not going anywhere.'

'Bollocks.'

'I am feeling rough,' Keith said.

Darren took hold of the front of his sweater and hauled him to his feet. 'Let's go.'

'You,' Rylands said. 'Let him alone.'

Darren's face tightened, eyes suddenly tense and dark – then he laughed. 'C'mon, Keith,' he said, still looking at Rylands with the cocky grin the laugh had become. 'We're off.'

'Keith . . .' Rylands started.

''S'all right, I'll be fine.'

Rylands turned back to where he was washing dishes at the sink. The water was already turning cold, the surface swimming in grease. Bits of bacon rind and fragments of eggshell nudged against his fingers. If that was the sort Keith was knocking round with, no wonder he was in trouble.

'Did you hear what happened at that bank?' Marjorie Carmichael said to Lorna as she was unlocking the front door after lunch. 'Shotguns and everything. We were lucky that didn't happen to us.'

It was only then that Lorna realized who it was had come up to her the previous evening, asking if they were still open, promising that he would be back.

# Eighteen

'You weren't serious, were you? What you said before?'

'Before what?' Darren was concentrating on getting his score over eleven thousand, his previous best on this machine.

'You know, 'about . . . well, you know.'

'Look, either spit it out or stop going on and on. You're putting me off.'

'I meant,' Keith said, 'about the gun.'

'Hey! Why not yell it out a bit louder, might be a couple of blokes over the back never heard what you said.' Concentration shot, game over, Darren had been well and truly zapped. 'There, see. See what you done?'

Back on the pavement, blinking at the light, Darren ran a hand across the top of his head; his hair had a nice feel to it now, not brittle but soft, a soft fuzz less than half an inch thick.

'Something you got to understand,' he said, 'I'm not going to spend the rest of my life just hanging round, pulling jobs for a few quid. That's what you want you better say so now. Me, I'm going to do something with my life. Get some money, real money, get noticed.'

With a quick hunch of his shoulders Darren headed off towards Slab Square and, after a few moments' hesitation, Keith hurried after him.

'So what do you think, Marjorie? Do you think I should get in touch with the police and tell them or what?'

It had to be the fourth time Lorna had asked – more or less the same question, more or less the same words – fourth or fifth time in the last hour. Lorna, not wanting to appear too anxious, too nervous either. 'Lorna,' Marjorie had said, 'I don't want to be rude or anything, but you don't think you're being a little paranoid?'

Is that what she was? Or was it the opportunity to spend some more time with Kevin Naylor that had her seeing the would-be robbery merchant in otherwise innocent people?

'It's a shame Becca isn't here,' Marjorie said. 'She'd know what to do.'

Becca knew what to do all right: stay home, send in a sick note and work hard for the sympathy vote. Good riddance, Lorna thought; she and Marjorie could manage the branch fine without her pernickety assistance.

No matter how hard she tried, she couldn't conjure up the youth's face, not exactly – the hair and the nose and the eyes but not a whole face. The walk, though, she could picture that, the slow, cocky strut along the pavement – wasn't that the same walk as the one towards her counter, only the day before?

*Here, fill that. Don't keep me waiting.*

*Well, call in another time, eh?*

'I'm going to do it,' Lorna said, and reached for the phone. The number was on the card that Kevin Naylor had given to her.

'I'm sorry,' Lynn Kellogg said, responding to the call. 'He's not here at the moment. Can I take a message?'

'Yes,' Lynn said, when Lorna had finished. 'I'll be sure that he gets it. I can't promise when he'll be able to get back to you, though. It's pretty hectic here today.'

Lorna put down the receiver, looked into Marjorie's fleshy, inquiring face and forced a smile. 'Well, that's that. Nothing else I can do now.'

117

Naylor had been thinking about his conversation with Divine, Mark sitting there in the car, giving advice for all the world as if, where relationships were concerned, he knew something about it. And then parading this scuzzy lust of one-night stands and knee tremblers as some kind of proof that he understood women. What Divine knew about women could be written on the inside of a toilet door and usually was.

'Be hard,' Divine had said. 'Stand firm, it's the only way. Whatever you do, don't let on you care.'

Yes, Naylor thought, and see where that's got you.

The longest relationship Divine had ever had with a woman likely came in short of ten minutes.

It seemed likely that after abandoning the Volvo and the Granada, the gang had doubled back on themselves, possibly using as many as four other vehicles. The only one not wearing a mask was variously described as a slim male, aged between eighteen and twenty-five, and an attractive young woman wearing rather heavy eyeshadow and with the faintest suggestion of a moustache. The masks the others had worn had been stolen from a party wear and fancy dress shop the night before and comprised Mickey Mouse, Michael Jackson, the Amazing Spiderman and the Sheriff of Nottingham. The charred remains of what appeared to be several track suits and trainers, together with what could previously have been polystyrene masks, had been found on a patch of waste ground close to the A60, north of Loughborough. The ashes were on their way to the forensic laboratory without a great deal of hope attached.

The possible identity of the young villain not averse to disguising himself as a woman was currently testing the resources of the Home Office computer.

When Resnick came into the CID room, the remains

of a toasted ham and cheese sandwich in the paper bag clutched in his left hand, Graham Millington was slumped back in his chair, overcoat on, hat on, feet on his desk, asleep. Even the first two rings of the telephone failed to wake him.

'Resnick. CID.'

Of all the people it might have been, one of the last he would have expected was Rylands.

'No,' Resnick said, after listening for several moments. 'No, that's okay. I'll come to you. Half-hour to an hour. Yes. Goodbye.'

When he set the receiver down, Millington was stirring, embarrassed to be discovered asleep.

'Sorry, I don't know what . . .'

'Doesn't matter, Graham, one of those days. Why don't you get off home? Nothing much else any of us can hope for tonight.'

Millington, who, one way and another, had been on duty since before four that morning, didn't need to be asked twice. 'Reg Cossall said to pass on a message, reckoned you know what it was about. Bloke you were talking about the other night, word is, he's likely to get his parole.'

Well, so Resnick had been wrong.

'Bad news?'

'Maybe not,' Resnick said. 'I'm not sure.'

Millington resettled his trilby on his head. 'Get back now, might be able to watch a bit of snooker before the wife gets back from Russian.'

'Taken against it, has she?'

'Not that so much. She'll have me taking off the tiles in the bathroom. Reckons on changing them for that Italian blue.'

'G'night, Graham.'

Resnick rustled around for what remained of his

sandwich, listening to Millington's whistling the 'Dance of the Sugar Plum Fairy', fading and off-key.

The pub used to be crammed full of medics from the nearby hospital, laughter and large gins and well-honed accents that cut through the ambient sound like scalpels. Now the health authority had shut the place down and sold the site to a consortium of developers whose plans ranged from high-income architect-designed flats to a covered piazza. It not only left the pub quieter, it made it quicker to get in a round of drinks.

Lynn Kellogg's turn, spotting Naylor enter before she'd finished her order and asking for an extra pint.

'Message for you,' she said, passing Naylor his Shipstone's. 'Lorna Solomon. The building society raid. Will you get back to her. Here, she left her home number as well.'

Struggling not to blush, Naylor took the piece of paper and, without looking, pushed it down into his breast pocket. All he would have had to have done, that lunchtime sharing Chinese in the car, was reach over and she would have slid into his arms. Was that what he wanted to do? The way he'd talked about himself and Debbie, as if there was nothing there, nothing left. What was the truth? He sat forward, moving in on the conversation, trying to forget the slip of paper folded inside his pocket, sipping his pint.

# Nineteen

Rylands had vacuumed the house, the landings and the stairs, from top to bottom. The carpet from the hall he had ripped out and temporarily replaced with some lino offcuts he'd been storing in the cellar. He had borrowed a ladder from a neighbour and cleaned the outside windows, scraping away grime which had gathered for years. For a tenner, another neighbour had lent him a five-hundredweight van for long enough to cart seventeen bags of rubbish, mostly old bottles and cans, to the household tip. The hall carpet, sodden and stained, had been hauled away, together with a battered suitcase of old clothes and two cardboard boxes of burnt pans, chipped and cracked china and packets of food long past their sell-by date.

The clean-up had begun half an hour after Keith and Darren had left: too early for Rylands to have begun drinking and he hadn't had a drink since. Shaving, he observed it was the first time in months the razor hadn't shaken in his hand and nicked neck or cheek. Before his shave he had taken a bath, long and hot; after it, he dressed himself in clean clothes – a pair of grey trousers that had once belonged to a best suit, a white shirt he ran over with an iron, grey pullover with a V-neck in need of a little darning. Black shoes with leather uppers that he had polished and buffed. His hair he trimmed as best as he could before brushing it flat.

Only when all that had been done did he dial the station and ask for Detective Inspector Resnick by name.

Now he and Resnick sat across from one another in Rylands's cellar room, Resnick on the slightly sagging easy chair Rylands had dragged down earlier.

'Nearly got shot of that lot today,' Rylands said, pointing at the piles of yellowing music paper on the floor. 'Must go back twenty, thirty years. Couldn't in the end – stupid, isn't it, what you cling on to?'

Resnick nodded over his mug of coffee, neither as strong nor as dark as he would have liked. Rylands was drinking the same, smoking a hand-rolled cigarette, thin as a baby's finger.

'I recognized you,' Rylands said. 'Oh, not exactly who you were, don't suppose I ever knew that and if I did, well, I'd forgot, but the face – yes – all those nights standing there, close to the band.'

Resnick nodded, remembering.

'Most men just went there for the girls. The beer.'

'I met my wife there,'

Rylands gave a rueful smile. 'There you go.'

'Stepped all over her feet.'

'Dancing?'

Resnick shook his head. 'Just being clumsy.'

'They say that, don't they? About coppers. The old joke.'

Resnick was looking at him.

'Big feet.'

Resnick continued to wait, guessing that whatever Rylands had invited him there to hear, it wouldn't be easy to say. There were things itching at the edges of Resnick's mind, too, demanding attention; memories he was unwilling to scratch. Leave it alone, his mother had been forever saying to him, you'll only make it worse.

Well, as far as the sundry blemishes of adolescence, that was likely true.

'You still listen to much?' Rylands asked, not ready yet for the conversation to go where it had to go.

'Now and again. When I get the time. Sundays at the Playhouse; the Arboretum, sometimes. Here and there.'

'Some of the old band are still playing . . .'

Resnick nodded.

'Straight ahead jazz now. R and B, thing of the past where they're concerned.'

'And you?'

Rylands was looking at the snare drums gathering dust on the floor. 'No,' he said, and then, 'Last night, when you were here, looking for Keith. All what I said . . . wasn't necessarily true.'

'No.'

'He had been here, I had seen him. Said he was going to stay. I don't know – daft really, I know if you wanted him bad enough you're always going to find him – still, I couldn't just, you know, say. Would've been like . . . shopping him, I suppose. Grassing your own.'

'Yes,' said Resnick. 'I understand.' The mug of coffee, lukewarm now, he set on the floor.

'What I said . . .'

'Mm.'

'About him being better off back inside . . .'

'Yes.'

'I didn't mean that . . .'

'No.'

'Not the way it sounded.'

'No.'

'All the same . . .' The cigarette had gone out and Rylands relit it, wisps of tobacco sizzling to nothing. 'What he's been in up to yet, cars and that, nothing serious . . .'

'Serious enough.'

Rylands looked at the floor between his polished shoes. 'This bloke he's running with now, mouth on him like a sewer, treats Keith like shit and all the while Keith looking up to him, lapping it up. I hate to see that.'

When he should be looking up to you, Resnick thought.

'How much of it's talk, I don't know. Like I say, the mouth on him. But what he was on about, earlier today, here in the kitchen, what he was talking about was getting a gun. A shooter.'

A moment's silence wavered between them.

'Did he say what for?' Resnick asked.

'Not right out, but that bank job, today, he was full of that. How they got away with it on account of the gun.' Rylands let the nub end of his cigarette fall into his mug of coffee. 'Might all just have been chat, showing off . . .'

'The reason we want to talk to Keith,' Resnick said, 'there was an attempted robbery, branch office of a building society. Two youths, one armed with a hammer. Something happened, all went wrong; ran off without getting a penny. We found Keith's prints – what might be his – on the car they used to get away.'

'A hammer,' Rylands said thoughtfully.

'Like to have broken this old boy's head for getting in the way.'

Rylands nodded. 'If it was this Darren, I'd believe it. The way he looked at me, just for a second, today. If he'd had a gun in his hands then . . .'

The rest lay between them, unsaid. Resnick thinking about walking in on Prior, shotgun in his hands.

'Keith knows where he lives?' Resnick asked.

'I suppose so.'

'And he's coming back here tonight?'

'Keith?'

124

'Yes.'

'Probably. As far as I know.'

'We could pick him up, charge him . . .'

But Rylands was shaking his head. 'There's got to be another way.'

Resnick leaned back, crossed one leg over the other and waited to hear what that was.

At the top of the cellar steps, Resnick said: 'Last night, after I'd been here, I found an old record of "Wasted Years".'

'Ruthie . . .'

'Yes.'

'Great voice.'

'Agreed.'

'Not still in touch, I suppose?'

Rylands shook his head. 'Haven't seen Ruth in years. Scarcely since that bloke of hers got sent down. What was it? Twelve years?'

'Fifteen.'

'Jesus,' Rylands said softly.

'Rumour has it,' Resnick said, 'he's on his way back out.'

'Prior?'

'Yes.'

'Jesus,' Rylands breathed again.

'I'd best be off,' Resnick said, moving away.

'What I heard, you know, back then, be a few scores to settle when he's back on the street.'

Resnick nodded. 'Possible.' He stopped close to the front door. 'Ever hear anything, where Ruth is now, give us a ring, okay?'

'Yes, right. Though, like I say, don't suppose . . .'

'This other business, your Keith, let me have a think about it. One way or another, I'll be back in touch.'

Resnick held out his hand. 'Be good if we could work something out, between us, old times' sake.'

His eyes held Rylands's for a long moment, not wanting him to escape his meaning.

'Yes,' Rylands said. 'Sure. I'll do what I can.'

'Good.'

Rylands stepped back and watched the inspector out on to the street; when he had closed the door, he leaned his head against the hardness of the wood, eyes clenched shut. He would stay there, exactly as he was, until the urgency to find a drink had passed.

The night was clear and the moon three-quarters full, Resnick needed to walk. Ten, fifteen minutes he would be in Slab Square and could pick up a cab if he wished. Hands in pockets, coat collar pulled up, Resnick walked away.

# Twenty

In the square, a fifty-year-old man, trousers rolled past his knees, was paddling in one of the fountains, splashing handfuls of water up under the arms of his fraying coat. A young woman with a tattooed face was singing an old English melody to a scattering of grimy pigeons. Resnick stood by one of the benches, listening: a girl in denim shorts and overlapping T-shirts, razored hair, leather waistcoat with a death's head on the back, standing there, oblivious of everything else, singing in a voice strangely thin and pure. 'She Moved Through the Fair'.

When she had finished and Resnick, wishing to say thanks, tell her how it had sounded, give her, perhaps, money, walked purposefully towards her, she turned her back on him and moved away.

On the steps, in the shadow of the lions, couples were kissing. Young men in shirt sleeves, leaning from the windows of their cars, slowly circled the square. Across from where Resnick was standing was the bland brick and glass of the store that twenty years before had been the Black Boy, the pub where he and Ben Riley would meet for an early evening pint. The glass that ten years ago was smashed and smashed again as rioters swaggered and roared through the city's streets.

No way to hold it all back now.

Inside the house, he showered, turning the water as hot as he dared and lifting his face towards it, eyes closed; soaping his body over and over, the way he did after being called out to examine some poor victim, murdered often as not for small change or jealousy, being in the wrong place at the wrong time. Steam clouded the bathroom, clogged the air, and still Resnick stood there, back bent now beneath the spray, content to let it wash over him.

In the kitchen, he felt the smoothness of coffee beans in the small of his hand. He knew already which album he would pull from the shelves, slide on to the turntable from its sleeve.

The purple postage stamp on the cover, Monk's face in profile at its centre, trilby hat sloping forward, angled away, the thrust of his goatee beard rhyming the curve of the hat's brim. Riverside 12–209: *The Unique Thelonious Monk*. 'If only they'd take away the blindfold and the handcuffs,' Elaine had used to say of Monk's playing, 'it might make all the difference.' Resnick would smile. Why play the right notes when the wrong ones will do?

Resnick set his coffee on the table by the chair and cued in the second track.

Monk picks the notes from the piano tentatively, as if it were a tune he once heard long ago and then, indistinctly, through an open window from an apartment down the street. There is more than uncertainty in the way his fingers falter, sliding between half-remembered chords, surprising themselves with fragments of melody, with things he would have preferred to have remained forgotten. 'Memories of You.'

Moments when it is easy to imagine he might get up from the piano and walk away – except that you know he cannot, anymore than when the solo is finally through he can let it go. When you're sure it's over, probing with another pair of notes, a jinking run, a fading chord.

At the track's end, he seems to hear her feet walk

across the floor above: door to dressing table to wardrobe, wardrobe to dressing table to bed. If he went now and pushed open the door into the hallway would he hear her voice?

'Charlie, aren't you coming up?'

The final weeks when they lay beneath the same sheets, not speaking, not touching, catching at their breath, fearful that in sleep they might be turned inward by some old habit or need.

'Christ, Charlie!' Ben Riley had exclaimed. 'What the heck's the matter with you? You got a face like bloody death!'

And in truth he had – because in truth that's what it had been like: dying.

A long death and slow, eked out, a little each day.

Fragments.

'Don't you see, Charlie?'

Once the blindfold had been taken away, it made all the difference.

# 1981

# Twenty-One

'That the post, Charlie?'

'Mm?'

'I said, is that . . .? Oh, never mind. I'll get it.'

Resnick slurped down more coffee, half an ear on the local news report, mother and her two children narrowly escaping a house fire out in Bilborough, half on what Elaine was shouting from the hall.

'That lad,' Elaine said accusingly, coming down the steps into the kitchen.

'Which one?'

'The boy who delivers the paper.'

'I thought it was the postman?'

Elaine shook her head. 'The paper.'

'What about it?'

'Him. It's him. Rides that bike of his right up to the door, hardly time to stuff the paper through the flap and he's off again. Four times out of five, see what happens.'

She dropped the *Mail* on to the table where Resnick was sitting. On a torn and buckled front page he glimpsed something more about the new princess.

'Why not have a word?' Resnick said. 'At the shop.'

'I have.'

'And?'

She pointed at the newspaper. 'You can see for yourself how much good that did.'

'What d'you reckon, then?' Resnick grinned. 'Lurk in

the shrubbery, flash my warrant card at him? Performing wheelies in a confined space?'

'Go on, make a joke out of it.'

'I don't see what else I can do.'

'You don't pay for it, that's why.'

'I don't read it.'

'You don't read anything. Aside from the back pages.'

'Better than page three.'

'The *Mail* doesn't have page three.'

'Shouldn't mind missing bits of page one as well, then.'

'God! Something has got into you this morning.'

Resnick reached for her hand. 'Part of my new image.'

'Oh, yes?' Allowing herself to be pulled gently towards him. 'What's that then?'

'Ooh, you know. Light-hearted, silver-tongued.'

'Yes?' A smile brightening Elaine's face. 'Well, I don't want to disappoint you, but you've still a way to go. And, no, I am not going to spend the next few minutes dallying on your lap.'

'Why not?'

'Because it's way past time I finished getting ready for work.'

'You look ready to me.'

'I said for work.'

Resnick's kiss missed her mouth and landed between neck and cheek.

'Do you know how long I spent putting on that make-up?'

'To the second.'

'Then you know I haven't got time to do it over again.'

Resnick grinned.

'Charlie!' She wriggled to her feet and stood over him, trying hard to look annoyed. 'If that's what you're interested in, you should have said so an hour ago.'

'I did.'

For a moment Elaine's expression changed. 'Why didn't I hear you?'

Resnick shook his head and looked away. 'I don't know,' he said.

The news had finished and Neil Diamond was sounding beefily cheerful in its place. Elaine walked across the room and switched off the radio. Resnick bit into cold toast. There were times when this house they had bought could feel strangely barren and still.

'Can you drop me off?' Elaine asked.

'Sure. I'm in court first thing. Shirehall.'

'How long've I got?'

Resnick looked at his watch. 'Ten minutes.'

'Fine.'

Toast in hand, he turned to watch her go and in the doorway she swung back towards him, a smile slipping back to her face.

'Be careful, Charlie.'

'What?'

But before he could follow the direction of her gaze, the marmalade had slid from the edge of the crust down on to the welcoming width of his tie.

A little under six months ago, Elaine had taken a new job with an advertising agency which had opened new offices in one of the Victorian factories in the old Lace Market. Open-plan premises, green plants, partners with turned-back cuffs who encouraged everyone to call them by their first names. 'It's a good opportunity, Charlie. They've got big plans for expansion and they're really keen to promote from inside.'

Her desk was close to one of the beautifully proportioned arched windows and, aside from her keyboard and printer and VDU, held a pair of trailing ivies, a scarlet geranium, a photograph of herself and Resnick at the party celebrating his promotion to detective sergeant, a small furry animal she had had since a baby, a pocket calculator and a large glass ashtray – not that she smoked herself, but her boss did and since quite often he stopped by her desk rather than calling her over to his, it was only sensible to be accommodating.

'Not that there's anything wrong with the way you dress,' her boss, the sales director, had said, tapping ash from the end of his cigarette, 'but if we saw our way to giving you an advance on your first bonus, d'you think you might see your way clear to spending it on something a little more, well, something with a little more flair?'

She hadn't said anything about the conversation to Resnick. She'd taken the money, spent it, lied about the cost, cutting it by more than fifty per cent and still had to live with the look of incredulity on his face. 'What? You spent how much? On that? To sit around at work in?'

Clothes, Resnick thought, were what you put on so as not to appear naked. They were what you covered with paper suits before stepping into a scene of crime.

For that much money they could have hired someone to repaint the outside of the house, replaced the carpet on the stairs, booked that holiday in New Orleans instead of spending a week in a self-catering cottage in Northumbria or risking coming face to face with half the rest of the local force on Majorca.

'This do you?' Resnick asked, drawing into the kerb on the corner of High Pavement and Stoney Street.

'Fine.' She leaned across the front seat to kiss him deftly on the cheek. 'You're not going into the witness box in that?' she asked looking askance at the stain on his tie.

'Don't worry. I'll hold my notebook in front of it.'

Elaine kissed him again and slid from the car. Resnick

watched her in the wing mirror, a crisp-looking woman with good legs and brown hair, small leather bag swinging from one shoulder. When it was clear she wasn't going to turn and wave, Resnick pulled away from the kerb and continued along High Pavement towards the Shirehall.

An hour and a half later he was giving evidence against a nineteen-year-old who had walked into a second-hand jeweller's on Castle Gate and tried to negotiate a price for a dozen items which were on the list regularly circulated by the police. The jeweller requested time to give an accurate estimate, asked the youth to come back within the hour. When he did so, Resnick and DC Rains had been waiting in the back.

'Good stuff,' Rains had said, examining a diamond clip through the jeweller's glass. 'Shame to let it go to waste. Owner's likely claimed on the insurance already.'

Resnick chose not to hear.

'And at any time, sergeant, when you and Detective Constable Rains were taking my client into custody, were you aware of the detective constable threatening my client?'

'No, I was not.'

'You neither saw nor heard the officer propositioning my client at all?'

'I'm not sure what you . . .?'

'You were not in the police vehicle when Detective Constable Rains said to my client, "There's half a dozen more down to you and you're going to cough for them or I'll see how your balls fit inside a pair of garden shears"?'

'Those exact words?'

'Did you hear your colleague utter those words, sergeant?'

'No, I did not.'

'Not anything like them?'

'Not to the best of my knowledge.'

'But Detective Constable Rains and yourself did question my client about other alleged offences?'

'In the course of our interview with him, yes.'

'This interview, sergeant, would this have been held in the police station?'

'Yes.'

'Not in the car?'

'I'm sorry?'

'The police car taking my client back to the station, the interview did not take place there?'

'I told you, the . . .'

'What was said to my client in the car?'

'I'm not sure, I mean, not exactly. But very little of consequence. As far as I remember.'

'Perhaps you would like time to refer to your notes?'

'Thank you, but there's nothing in my notebook about any such conversation.'

'It was silent, then, the journey?'

'For the most part, as I recall, yes.'

'You were driving?'

'Yes.'

'And Detective Constable Rains?'

'Was in the passenger seat alongside me.'

'Leaning over that seat to talk to my client, who was handcuffed in the back?'

'He may have, I don't . . .'

'You don't recall, yes, sergeant, we're getting used to your convenient lapses of memory . . .'

'I . . .'

'I put it to you, however, that you must have been aware that your colleague was leaning over towards the rear seat in which my client was travelling, both his wrists

138

handcuffed behind his back, leaning over and telling him in no uncertain terms that if he refused to own up to at least six other cases of burglary, he would personally emasculate him?'

'I have no recollection of any such conversation.'

'Nor of the detective constable reaching into the rear of the vehicle and grasping my client's testicles in his hand and twisting them so viciously that my client cried out and kicked the back of the seat and, finally, almost lost consciousness.'

'No.'

'You were not aware of any of these things I have described taking place?'

'No.'

'In which case, sergeant, my client must be lying?'

'It seems possible . . .'

'And the doctor who examined my client at the police station and found signs of severe bruising on and around the area of his testicles, he was lying too?'

'That's not for me to say.'

'You are not saying very much at all, are you, sergeant?'

'I am giving evidence as to what happened as best I remember . . .'

'So you keep saying. And, as the court is becoming distressingly aware, your memory, sergeant, is not of the best. Neither, apparently, are your powers of observation.'

Smarting, standing there in the witness box in his slightly shabby suit and his freshly stained tie, looking neither directly at the barrister questioning him nor at the judge, but directly in front of him, Resnick made no reply.

'You were *in* the vehicle?' the barrister asked.

'Yes.'

'Sleeping.'

'Driving,' Resnick said. 'I was driving. My attention was on the road, the other traffic. I was concentrating on what was going on outside the car, rather than the inside.'

'How convenient!' The barrister made no attempt to contain his sarcasm.

'Well,' Resnick said, 'it meant that we reached the station without accident.'

'In which case, sergeant, I suppose we should congratulate you on a job well done. I'm sure that after this, your superiors will look favourably on any request you might make to continue your career in traffic control.'

Resnick's eyes narrowed and, behind his back, his hands clenched and unclenched several times.

'Thank you, sergeant. I have no further questions. You may step down.'

Half an hour later, Resnick was across the road in the County Tavern, washing down a cheese and onion cob with a pint of draught Guinness. He'd already had two whiskies at the bar to catch his nerves and his head was still throbbing. Rains was the last man he wanted to see coming through the door and there he was, bouncing up the steps to where Resnick was sitting, flashing a smile to match the watch strapped to his wrist.

'Owe you one, Charlie. Several, in fact.' His open hand pounded Resnick on the back. 'Word is you stonewalled in there like the best. Place in the next Test if you don't watch out.'

He held out his hand and Resnick ignored it, bit down into what was left of his cob.

'So, then, Charlie, I'm buying. What's it to be?'

'Nothing.'

Rains pressed both hands together flat, as if praying,

raised them till they were resting against his mouth: a familiar gesture. 'Okay, have it your own way.' He took a step back. 'That supermarket blag – we've got a meet tonight, half-seven.'

Resnick watched him go, a tall man, an inch under six foot, slim-hipped, expensive suit, dark hair professionally styled and cut, twenty-nine years old.

What Rains had actually said to the terrified youth in the car was: 'There's half a dozen more down to you, you pathetic little arsewipe, and if you don't cough for the lot of them, I'll whip your grungy little bollocks off with a pair of secateurs.'

# Twenty-Two

The gang had robbed a Securicor van of eight thousand pounds, give or take the small change. They had driven a Transit into its path in the loading area outside the new Sainsbury's superstore and three men with stocking masks had jumped out of a BMW which had skewed to a halt hard behind it. Shoppers had scattered towards safety, leaving laden trolleys abandoned. If the youngest of the security guards had not taken it into his head to be a hero, it would all have gone as smoothly as the two similar raids the gang had carried out in the preceding months.

But, for whatever reason, misguided or noble, the twenty-five-year-old part-time archaeology student had hurled himself at the legs of the nearest robber, bringing him down, the money sack that he'd been carrying tumbling clear.

In the confusion and clamour that followed only these things are certain: the robber who was rugby tackled suffered a damaged kneecap, which, when the atmosphere was damp, bothered him to this day; the money sack somersaulted into the path of a small girl, little more than a toddler, who was running from her mother, stopping her in her tracks, causing her, in fact, to topple against it, her young body keeping it secure and reducing the gang's haul by approximately one-fifth; the nearest of the other masked men to the incident, immediately and without hesitation, brought the sawn-off shotgun he was carrying to his shoulder and fired both barrels into the guard's face and body. Several hours of surgery succeeded in removing almost all of the Double Nought pellets from his neck and cheek, shoulder and chest, and he was deemed fortunate to be left alive.

Fourteen detectives and numerous uniformed officers had been devoting most of their waking hours ever since to tracking the gang down. A lot of overtime and a lot of shoe leather and, for those of them with wives or lovers, a lot of broken promises and recriminations.

'Elaine, look, I'm sorry . . .' Resnick said into the phone.

'What?'

'I'm going to be back late.'

'Why are you telling me, Charlie? Late's what you always are.'

'This might be later.'

She made no attempt to suppress the sigh. 'If you're any later than quarter to eight in the morning, I'll have left for work.'

Resnick saws Reg Cossall watching him as he set down the receiver. 'Bastard, i'n't it, eh, Charlie?'

Resnick slowly shook his head.

'After my third time,' Cossall said, lighting another Silk Cut, 'I thought as how I'd got it sussed. Never give 'em a reason to expect owt, they won't be disappointed.' He blew smoke at the ceiling and laughed low in the back of his throat. 'Cow shoved off anyhow. Took one of my suits, that good Crombie coat I had, shirts, socks, trousers, piled 'em all up in the back garden, chucked a can of paraffin over and burned the bloody lot. Women! Different bloody race, Charlie, and it don't pay to forget it.'

'All right, gentlemen. Settle down now. Let's see what we've got.' Jack Skelton, two years an inspector, transferred up from Stevenage and still pretty much an outsider, was on his feet and looking round the room expectantly. A nice result here was what he needed to get his feet under the table and he was going to push everyone as hard as it took until it was over.

What they had, Reg Cossall reckoned afterwards, was about as much use as a eunuch in a brothel. They were in an after-hours drinking club on Bottle Lane, crowded round a table in the last of a succession of small rooms, Cossall and Resnick and Rains and four or five others. Any pretence at moderation, just a pint before hitting the road, had long since flown out the window. Now it was spirits, doubles, Resnick dodging the occasional round, wanting to pace himself, knowing all he had to do was get up and leave, knowing that once you'd passed a certain point it's the hardest thing in the world.

Skelton had been with them in the pub earlier, his shout, a few pleasantries and then the suburbs awaited. But Jack Skelton had rank for reason, had a young kiddie, a girl named Kate, waiting for him to kiss her good night; he had a wife, something in hospital administration, professional woman. Expectations he had to fulfil.

When Resnick made inspector, things would change; like Skelton he could make his excuses and leave, knowing full well the men were glad to be shot of him, free to talk, to call him names behind his absent back.

When he and Elaine had a child . . .

'What d'you reckon then, Charlie?'

'How's that?'

'What Rainsey here was saying, these blaggings down to Prior.'

'I thought we'd been through all that?'

'We have.'

'Checked him out.'

Rains leaned forward, jabbing a finger at the air. 'Pulled him in twice, brief right alongside him, all through interrogation, every step of the sodding way.'

'The way it's meant to be,' Resnick said.

'Bollocks!'

'Alibied to the armpits, wasn't he?' Cossall said.

'In bed with his old lady, middle of the afternoon . . .'

'I should fancy!'

'Not if you'd seen her you wouldn't. Face sour as last week's milk. Real scrubber.'

'What's his form again?' Resnick asked, interested almost despite himself.

Rains eased back in his chair. 'Couple of stretches, aggravated burglary. Fancied him for a post office job, eighteen months back, his face all over it but nothing we could prove. That time, reckoned he and the wife had driven her mother up to Harrogate, bit of shopping, afternoon tea.'

'Family man,' said Cossall quietly. 'That's nice.'

'Villain, that's what he is,' Rains said. 'Nothing else.' He leaned forward again, looking into their faces. 'What d'you think he's been up to this last eighteen month, filling in his Spot the Ball coupons?'

Cossall shrugged and Resnick checked his watch and Rains downed his Scotch and got to his feet. 'Another of these and then I reckon we go round and knock him up, see what he's got to say.'

'What grounds?' Resnick asked.

Rains winked. 'Information received. Reasonable suspicion. Probable cause. Who gives a toss? Scotch, Reg? Charlie? Vodka?'

Resnick shook his head.

'Suit yourself.'

'Jesus, Charlie,' Cossall said, watching Rains disappear

in the direction of the bar, 'most of us get tireder as the night gets longer – each hour he's awake he gets bloody brighter.'

'Think there's anything to what he says?' Resnick asked.

'Prior? He'll be into something right enough. His sort always are. That's not counting shagging his missus the wrong side of *Blue Peter*. Maybe it wouldn't hurt to give him a tumble at that.'

Resnick shook his head. 'Not like this. Not now.'

'Be off his guard.'

'For how long? No warrant, we're not going to find anything. Get him down the station and he'll be back on the street before breakfast. Besides, state Rains is in, no telling what he might get up to.'

'What, Charlie?' Cossall laughed. 'With you there to hold his hand?'

'You'd go along with it then?'

'Like hell as like! Way Rain's getting himself pumped up, time he gets there, be near enough out of his skull.'

Rains arrived back with doubles all round, setting one down in front of Resnick as if he'd never said a word; from the gleam in Rains's eye he'd slipped in an extra one while being served.

'Here's to us, then.' Rains raised his glass in front of his face. 'And here's to a life of crime.' He downed the whisky in a single swallow. 'What d'you say, then, skip?' He rested a hand on Resnick's shoulder. 'Time to see if Prior's all tucked up?'

Resnick got to his feet, leaving his drink untouched. 'Time we all went home. Got some sleep.'

'Bollocks!'

'Come on,' Resnick said.

'Keep your hands off me,' Rains said. 'Leave me a-fucking-lone.'

'Quietly,' Resnick said. 'I'll walk with you down the square, cab it home.'

'I don't need a cab, I've got my sodding car.'

'Leave it where it is. You don't want to drive.'

'Who says?'

'You're drunk.'

'Who's fucking drunk?'

Reg Cossall stood up heavily, taking hold of both their arms. 'This isn't so good. People are starting to pay attention. What say we hold it down?'

Rains swung himself clear of Cossall's grasp. 'The rest of you can do as you like. Just don't try and fucking interfere.'

Resnick caught up with him near the foot of Bottle Lane. Rains was leaning forward against the wall, urinating on to the uneven cobbles and his own feet. The car keys were in Rains's right-side coat pocket and Resnick had found them and fished them out before Rains could react.

'You can have these back in the morning. Now get home and sober up. And don't go within a mile of Prior. Clear?'

Rains's eyes were glazed and he shook his head from side to side, bringing Resnick into focus.

'You've got no . . .'

The index finger of Resnick's right hand stopped no more than two inches from the centre of Rains's face. 'Don't tell me what I can or can't do. Not you. I spent one of the worst mornings of my life in court today, bending over backwards to keep the shit off your shoes. I'm in no mood to do the same thing twice. Now get home and get yourself sorted out.'

Resnick let the keys fall into his own pocket as he turned away; glancing back from the corner of

Bridlesmith Gate, he saw Rains had not moved. Resnick hailed a cab rounding the square and gave his address.

'Good night?' the driver asked pleasantly.

'Yes.' Resnick said. 'Terrific!'

Only the front-hall light was on and Resnick switched it off as he went through to the kitchen. There was a piece of Stilton in the fridge and the remains of some pasta Elaine had made in a covered bowl. He shook some Worcestershire Sauce on to the pasta, cut slices from the cheese and sat at the kitchen table with the local paper. Fifteen minutes later, shoes in hand, he climbed the stairs to bed.

Elaine was tucked in on herself, most of the covers dragged over to her side. Resnick undressed quickly, sliding in alongside her, finding some space beneath the sheet.

'Charlie,' she said softly. 'Is that you?'

'Yes.'

'Charlie,' Elaine said, turning towards him, 'you smell of drink.'

# Twenty-Three

Resnick had his feet behind his desk before eight and by eight fifteen Rains was standing in front of him with an apologetic grin.

'Way out of line last night, sorry.'

Resnick drew breath.

'Try not to let it happen again, eh?'

'Right,' Resnick said.

'No hard feelings?'

Resnick shook his head. 'No.'

Rains held out a cupped hand and Resnick dropped his car keys into it. Rains smiled. 'Tell you something interesting,' he said. 'Bloke got picked up this morning, Rossi. Early hours. Shinning down a drain pipe out near the castle. Neighbour got up to let out the cat, spotted him, phoned in. Your mate, Ben Riley, got out there in time to help him to the ground. Once he got him talking, hardly get him to stop. Put his hand up for twenty break-ins going back two years. Says there's more but he wants to cut a deal.'

'Go on.'

Rains shrugged. 'Usual kind. Not so keen on going back inside. Something about four walls, not good for his nerves. He wants to trade.'

'Information?'

'What else has he got?'

'You know what we stand to lose? Lies and half-truths,

149

God knows how many hours chasing after things we can't make stick.'

'All the same,' Rains was nodding, 'one little titbit – reckons he knows something about the Sainsbury's job. Reckons he knows the driver, friend of a friend.'

'Name?'

Rains shook his head. 'Not yet. Not so easy.'

'Okay,' Resnick said, 'get him in an interview room. I'll have word on high.'

Rains went off smiling.

On his way back from talking to Jack Skelton, Resnick ran into Ben Riley on the stairs; Ben, still in uniform, sergeant's stripes in place. When Resnick had applied to return to CID, his friend had opted to stay put. 'Not me, Charlie, all that hanging about in pubs, rubbing shoulders with the scum of the earth. Rather keep them at a distance – close as the end of this truncheon, that's about as close as I want to get. And besides, I like the uniform. Smart. Lord alone knows what you'll look like when you're back in civvies. Without you get Elaine to sort you out every day and I can't see her being much in the way of that.'

'Just off to have words with the chap you arrested,' Resnick said.

'Tried to kid me he was from Visionhire,' Ben Riley laughed. 'People had complained about trouble with their picture; he'd gone out to sort out the aerial.'

'Four in the morning without a ladder?'

'All part of the service, he reckoned. That was before I got him to turn out his pockets. Three picklocks, a chisèl and a six-inch metal rule.'

Resnick grinned and continued up the stairs.

'Pint later?' Ben Riley called after him.

'Doubt it.'

'You'll be at the match Saturday?'

'I'll try.'

'Don't bloody try. Be there.'

Melvyn Rossi was a shortish man with a weepy left eye and skin like chalk. Son of an Italian father and a Scottish mother, he had fetched up in the Midlands by default. Seven years of hard graft in his father's ice-cream business in Dawlish had ended when his father had discovered he was unsystematically skimming off the top. His mother, who had returned to her native Inverness long since, had never had much time for him anyway. Melvyn had met a man on a long-distance coach who had told him you could pick up women in the city like fruit from the trees. True, Melvyn discovered, though his fellow-traveller had neglected to point out that you were expected to pay for them.

Rossi would break into the back of a house in St Anne's or by the Arboretum, steal what cash he could find, fifteen minutes later hand it over for the dubious pleasure of taking his clothes off in an upstairs room with a single-bar electric fire, a narrow bed and a red light bulb.

It was the crabs that cured him of that particular habit.

Now he spent his money on horses and beer and an ever-growing pornographic video collection. There were times he wished he'd never turned his back on the world of 99s and Orange Zooms and water ices in five identical flavours and this was one of them.

When Resnick entered the interview room, Melvyn Rossi was sitting at the plain wooden table, Rains standing close behind him, patting Melvyn benevolently on top of the head.

'Melvyn's decided to be a good boy,' Rains said. 'Melvyn's going to tell us everything we want to know.'

Which wasn't exactly true. As Resnick had suspected, what he told them in the space of almost four hours didn't amount to a great deal. Aside from the burglaries that Rossi had carried out single-handed, the rest was a mixture of insinuation and evasion. Rumour and counter-rumour, most of which could not be substantiated, none of which would have stood up in court, always assuming Rossi would have agreed to repeat his allegations under oath, which was almost certainly not the case.

And if he had, what judge, which jury would believe him?

Melvyn Rossi leaned first on that elbow, then on this, dabbed at his weeping eye with the corner of a handkerchief, smelled his own sweat.

'The Sainsbury's robbery,' Rains prodded again, 'where the guard got shot. You know the driver.'

'I told you.'

'Tell us again.'

Melvyn had been in a pub on Alfreton Road when the landlord locked the doors from the inside and proceeded to throw a party. Melvyn had almost certainly got himself invited by accident. Some time later he was squashed up in a corner with a red-headed woman he knew was on the game, feeding her gin and thinking she was better-looking by the minute. He had one hand on her leg, the other fingering her fleshy shoulder like it was Plasticine when she started telling him about the time she'd been paid for a foursome by two real villains, hard nuts the pair of them, fivers all over the bed, the one of them bragging about how he'd taken close to ten thousand from a security van outside a supermarket.

'Name?' Resnick asked.

'That's what I can't remember.'

'Name!' Rains shouted, leaning hard into Melvyn's face.

'Honest, I can't remember. Maybe she never said.'

'And the woman?'

'Mary, Margaret, I don't know.'

'Perhaps,' Rains said slowly, looking across at Resnick, 'you could let Melvyn and me have a few words in private. See if that wouldn't help his memory to come back.'

Resnick stared back at him. 'Not such a good idea.'

'In that case, why don't we push him back in the cells and let him stew? All right, Melvyn, you decide you've got something more to say to us, something serious, you let us know. Otherwise . . .'

Rains made a gesture of wiping his hands clean down the lapels of his jacket and moved towards the door.

'Look,' Rossi said, 'I'm doing my best.'

Resnick nodded. 'The trouble is, Melvyn, it isn't good enough.'


An hour later Rains had a quick word in the custody sergeant's ear and let himself into Rossi's cell. Less than a quarter of an hour after that, he was back in the CID room, hovering close to Resnick's desk, waiting for the sergeant to get off the phone.

'Frank Churchill, otherwise know as Chambers, also Frank Church. Address in Basford.'

Resnick looked at the smile toying at the corners of Rains's mouth. 'Funny thing, isn't it,' Rains said, 'memory? Way it comes and goes.'

Frank Churchill had gone, too. 'Manchester,' the woman who came to the door said. 'Hope the bastard gets washed down the drains where he belongs.'

153

'You'll not mind if we come in, love?' Rains said. 'Take a look around.'

'Help your bloody selves.'

They found several pairs of Y-fronts, odd socks, a striped tie that looked as if it had been used as a belt; a plastic tube of hair gel and an empty deodorant spray; a ticket-stub from the Odeon; several dog-eared western paperbacks written by an ex-postman from Melton Mowbray.

'If you find him,' the woman called out on to the street after them, 'tell him not to bother coming back bloody here!'

'We could phone Manchester CID,' Resnick said. 'Ask them to keep an eye out. Chances are he might be known up there, too.'

Rains nodded, checking the rear-view mirror as he backed the car away from the kerb. 'Vice squad, I'll see what they know about a red-headed tom called Mary.'

'Or Margaret.'

'Whatever. See who else was taking part in this little foursome, who else had reason to celebrate. Working it back, I'd say it couldn't have been more than a couple of days after the Sainsbury's job went down.'

# Twenty-Four

Mary MacDonald had been out since eight o'clock that evening. Short black skirt, black tights, high heels that pinched, a once-white blouse that hung open over the tops of her breasts. The fake fur, hip-length, she wore unfastened. By ten, Mary had been approached seven times, the car slowing as it neared the kerb, window wound down, face – always white, usually middle-aged – leaning towards her.

'Looking for business, duck?'

It was as far as the transaction had progressed. Head withdrew, window up, the car pulling sharply away, looking for what? Someone younger, slimmer, sexier, closer to their damp and furtive little dreams?

Mary watched the same cars driving round and round the circuit, some of them never going beyond the first exchange, discussion of terms – 'Any place to go? Strip? How about the night? Have you got a friend?' Mary lit a cigarette although she was supposed to be giving it up, leaned back against the stones of the high wall, paced slowly up and down.

From the corner of Gedling Grove along Waverley Street, hang about on the edge of Raleigh Street then back again, heels clicking on the pavement as she climbed back up the hill. Across Waverley Street, the trees of the park were dark and losing shape and through them she could just see the lights of the Arboretum Hotel. Some nights the landlord would let her sit at a table near the bar, sipping at a rum and black, slipping off her shoes, now and again reaching down to rub her feet. Other times, the look on his face would be enough and if she were thirsty enough, fed up enough, she would walk the other direction, up on to the Alfreton Road, where the publicans were less fussy about their trade.

The car came round again, maroon, she'd noticed it before, gliding slowly past the railings, slowing down, smoothly accelerating away.

This time it stopped.

No movement.

Then the window winding down.

Whiteness of a face.

Mary MacDonald walked across the street.

'Charlie, have you seen this?'

'What?'

'On the box. Right now. The news.'

Resnick wriggled awkwardly backwards and withdrew his head from beneath the sink: if anything was guaranteed to make him feel incompetent it was being bent over double with a full set of washers and an adjustable spanner.

'Charlie!'

'All right.' Resnick rinsed his hands beneath the tap, looked for the towel, couldn't find it; he was wiping his hands down his trousers as he stepped into the living room. On the screen an overturned bus had been set ablaze and was blocking a city street; the lights of other, similar, fires burned in the background. A youth, scarf half-masking his face, ran towards the camera and hurled a bottle. The microphone picked up the crash of glass, the whoosh of flame.

'Belfast?' Resnick asked.

Elaine shook her head. 'Brixton.'

Resnick moved closer to the set and sat down.

Mary MacDonald rented a room on Tennyson Street: three-quarter bed and wardrobe, melamine table, chair, fixed unsteadily to the wall a gas fire that made a small explosion whenever she bent towards it with a match. On the tiled shelf above it were a couple of buckled postcards sent by an aunt in Derry, a plastic flower in a slender china vase, a photograph of herself and her friend Marie at Yarmouth, holding up ice creams and wearing funny hats, laughing so much they were forced to cling on to one another so as not to fall down.

'Mary, is it?' the man said.

'I never said . . .'

He was younger than the average punter, not fat either, tall, not bad looking. What did he want with her?

'Mary, then?'

'I never . . .'

'I know, you never said.'

'Then how . . .'

'Do I know? Well . . .' smiling '. . . you look like a Mary to me. Good Catholic girl. Perhaps we met at mass.'

'I never go.'

'Nor me.'

Mary's throat was strangely dry. 'I don't understand.'

'No need. Now, why don't you take off those clothes?'

She held out a hand. 'Pay me first. You've got to pay me first.'

'Oh, yes, don't you worry. I know the rules. Rituals. Better than most.' Reaching into his coat pocket for his wallet. 'Now what did we agree? Fifteen?'

'Twenty.'

The pink of his tongue showed at his mouth as he smiled. 'All right, then, Mary. Twenty it is.'

*

Police in uniform, some still wearing their blue jackets, others down to shirt sleeves, stood in the otherwise deserted street, amazed. A young officer, twenty-one or -two, looked up into the camera's lens and one side of his face was dark with blood. Stones, half-bricks and bottles continued to land. Sirens and fire engines could be heard, overlapping, continuous. Smoke filled the edges of the screen.

'I can't believe it's happening here,' Elaine said.

'Here?'

'This country.'

Resnick nodded. London seemed far more than a hundred and twenty miles away.

The telephone rang and Elaine picked it up, listened for a moment and held the receiver out. 'For you.'

'Are you watching?' Ben Riley asked at the other end of the line.

'Unbelievable, isn't it?'

'Is it?'

'How d'you mean?'

'How long,' Ben Riley said, 'before it spreads up here?'

On the screen, police were holding shields over their faces, slowly advancing down a tree-lined street under a hail of missiles. 'Hold your line!' a hoarse voice shouted. 'Hold your line!' A man Resnick's age, who had already lost his helmet, staggered back, struck on the side of the head, and the line broke. Youths, black and white, surged through.

The newsreader's voice tolled over the scene. 'Our community relations are as good as can be expected,' said the Metropolitan Police Commissioner, Sir David McNee.

*

Backed away by the fire, Mary held her tights bunched up in one hand. Aside from the shoes he had told her to put back on her feet, she was naked. The man had removed his jacket, hung it over the back of the chair; loosened his tie.

'Don't want to get over-personal, Mary, but that body of yours, bit of a bloody disaster area if you ask me. What I mean, must've seen better days.'

She was beginning to wonder whether any of the other girls had seen her get into the car, if any of them knew the man and might have had good reason to have noted his number. Wondering whether, naked or not, she could get past him and out of the door, down the stairs and into the street. Wondering how much she would get hurt.

'What I think, Mary, way I look at it, what we're here for, looks don't so much matter. If they did, well, they wouldn't come trolling out here, would they? They'd be back in the middle of town in some hotel, waiting for the discreet knock on the door. None of your cheapskate twenty-pound job there.' He pinched the loose flesh of her arm between finger and thumb. 'No, bloke comes out here, all he wants, something to slop around in.'

'Bastard!' she spat at him, automatically flinching from his reply.

What he did was smile. 'Frank,' he said. 'Frank Churchill, that how it was with him?'

She blinked and stuttered her feet. The fire was starting to burn the backs of her legs. A piece of her skin was still tight between forefinger and thumb.

'You remember Frank? The night of the party. Just the four of you. Pissed on cheap champagne.'

She remembered her and Marie giggling so hard they liked to have wet themselves. The blokes hollering and grabbing and finally one of them fishing out some cocaine and insisting on sniffing it off Marie's backside, sniffing it up through a fifty-pound note. Her and Frank and Marie and . . .

'Who was he, Mary?'

'Who?'

Finger and thumb twisted just a little, not too much, enough. Tears came to her eyes and the backs of her legs were red and tender and the insides of those bloody shoes biting into her ankles.

'Who, Mary?'

'I don't know.'

'Don't make me . . .'

'Swear to God, I don't know.'

'Mary!'

'Ow!'

'Mary.'

'He never said, I . . .'

'All that time, you must've heard his name. Must've called him something. Frank. He must've . . .'

'John.'

'What?'

'John. I think that's what he called him.'

'John.'

'Yes.'

'You're sure?'

'Yes, I think . . .'

'You're sure.'

'Yes. Yes. John.'

'John Prior.'

'I don't know.'

'That's who it was.'

'If you say so. I said, I don't know. He never said his other name. I don't know.'

'John Prior, that's who it was.'

'You know already.'

'I know.'

'Then why all this . . .?'

'Confirmation, nothing more.'

'Oh, shit!'

'What?'

'Shit!'

'What now?'

'You're police, aren't you?'

'Am I?'

'Police, you rotten bastard!'

'Steady.'

'Pig!'

She thought he was going to punch her in the breast but the fist opened up and he stroked his fingers around the deep brown of her nipple. 'Maybe later, we can have some fun, eh? For now, why don't you get over on the bed, take the weight of your feet, take a look at these pictures, see who you recognize. Okay, Mary? Okay?'

Resnick was in the front room, transfixed by the ten o'clock news. A half-cup of coffee sat close by him, cold. A virtual no-go area had been hewn out of that part of South London, roads blocked off by vehicles overturned and set on fire. Rubble and glass were strewn across the streets. All along Brixton High Road, shop windows had been smashed through, allowing youths to loot at will. Discarded as too heavy, the settee from a three-piece suite lay on its back across the kerb.

The sky at the upper edge of Resnick's TV set burned with an orange glow.

Elaine stood behind him, hand resting on his shoulder. 'Poor Ben,' she said.

He turned to look at her.

'If it happened here you'd be all right. Now. He'd be out there, in the front line.'

Resnick nodded.

'I could never understand,' Elaine said, 'why he didn't move into CID, same time as you.'

'Fondness for regular hours. That and being out on the street.'

Elaine looked past him towards the television. 'These days, I should have thought last place anyone'd want to be. Any of you.'

Resnick got up and switched off the set. 'Bed?' he said. 'Early night?'

'All right.'

Within fifteen minutes, the rhythm of Elaine's breathing had changed and she was asleep, leaving Resnick to replay the images of the evening. How long before it spreads up here?

On the corners of Hyson Green and Radford groups of men were congregating, hands in pockets, heads down. By the early hours, well before light broke in the sky, the first crates of empty milk bottles had been taken.

Mary MacDonald sat alone in her room, squatting down before the gas fire in her pink candlewick dressing gown, praying that her friend Marie would never have to go through what she had that night; praying that what he had forced out of her would not end up in the papers, be read out in court. Simply praying.

And Rains?

Fast off the moment his head touched the pillow, sleeping the untroubled sleep of the just.

# Twenty-Five

'Time to get out, Charlie,' Ben Riley said. 'That's what it is.'

Resnick laughed. 'Just see you behind the counter of some pub, running a little newsagent's somewhere. You'd be in your grave inside a twelvemonth.'

'Better like that than hit over the head by some yob with shit for brains.'

'I don't know.' Resnick shook his head.

'Christ, Charlie, you saw them. All that talk about police harassment, racism, that was just an excuse. Smashing things for the sake of it, looting. Don't tell me that's political. That's theft. That's greed.'

Resnick sighed and bit into his bacon sandwich. When Ben's shift matched, they would meet there at Parker's, eat breakfast, talk. More often than not about the way Chedozie had run the opposition ragged the week before. But not today.

'I'm serious, Charlie. I'm leaving. Not the force. The sodding country.'

Resnick looked at him. 'You've never said.'

'Not mean I haven't thought.'

'But you'd have said. Something anyway.'

'Would I? Don't you have any pipedreams nestling away in that head of yours? Things you wouldn't even tell Elaine?'

Resnick shook his head: his problem, where Elaine was concerned, was that he made his dreams all too clear. The day he'd spotted alphabet wallpaper in Texas Homecare and told her it would look just right in the small bedroom; the way he glanced at her expectantly when she came in from the bathroom, those times of the month when he knew her period was due.

Ben Riley folded the slice of thin buttered bread in half, then half again and began, slowly, to wipe it round his plate. 'You don't think there are things she doesn't tell you?'

'I don't know.'

Riley looked at him quizzically, not quite believing.

'Well, she's ambitious at work,' Resnick said, 'I know that. Wants things for the house . . .'

'And that's all?'

Resnick finished his coffee, too weak as usual, nodded over at Ben Riley's empty cup. 'Another tea?'

'Best not. Time, almost, we weren't here.'

Outside the café, the traffic entering the city from the south and west was thickening. Pretty soon the island would be jammed tight. A fireman, wearing a red and white Forest shirt above his uniform trousers, walked past them towards the fire station alongside. The two policemen watched him till he had disappeared through the broad entrance, neither one wanting to be the first to walk away, each sensing there were still things left unsaid without recognizing what they were.

When Resnick finally arrived, the police station was humming with the previous night's events in London. He had scarcely shown his face in the CID room before being summoned to the inspector's office. Rains was already sitting there, relaxed in a chair beside Skelton's desk, one long leg crossed casually over the other.

'Looks as if we've a break in the Sainsbury's job,' Skelton said, pressing the tips of his fingers together in front of his irreproachable ironed shirt. 'Witness prepared to swear she heard Prior and another man...'

'Churchill,' Rains interrupted, 'Frank Churchill.'

'Heard Prior and this bloke talking about carrying out the robbery, bragging about it.'

'More than that,' Rains prompted.

'Using the gun.'

Resnick looked away from the inspector, staring at Rains hard. Rains recrossed his legs and smiled disarmingly back. 'Who was this?' Resnick asked.

Rains shrugged. 'Some tom.'

'They spoke about the shooting in front of her?'

'Sure.'

'It seems they were clear which of them had fired the gun,' Skelton said.

Resnick still hadn't moved his eyes from Rains's face.

'Prior,' Rains said quietly, leaning forward slightly as he mouthed the word. 'John Prior, what happened to that poor bastard of a guard, it was down to him.'

'And she'll swear to that, in court if needs be, the woman?'

'She'll swear to it all right,' Rains smiled. 'On her life.'


Prior lived in a nondescript suburban-looking house overlooking Colwick Wood Park. Some mornings it was quiet enough to hear the kids singing to the teacher's piano in the nearby Jesse Boot Junior and Infant School. Step across from the house and there were the bowling green, the recreation ground, the reservoir. At the far side of the park lay the greyhound stadium and the racecourse. There were roses here and people quietly walking their dogs; men and women wearing white sitting on the steps of the bowls pavilion comparing notes about the bias of the green.

One car swung round into Ashworth Close and

parked, three men to watch the rear of the house. The other cars, two of them, came from opposite directions, slowing to a halt at either side of a milk float making late deliveries.

Skelton waited until the milkman had cleared before giving the order to move in. Prior's wife was in her dressing gown at the door, bending down to pick up the two pints, when the detectives raced up the path, Rains at their head, Resnick not far behind.

'Just right,' Rains said, pushing past. 'Tea all round.'

'John!' Ruth Prior screamed. 'John, it's the police!'

Heavy men shouldered her aside and one of the bottles slipped from her hand, glass shattering to a hundred tiny pieces on the step.

Prior was half out of the bedroom, pulling on a pair of jeans, when Rains charged up the stairs.

'What the fuck's going on?'

Like the card in a magician's trick, Rains's warrant card was in the palm of his hand. 'John Edward Prior, I am arresting you in connection with the theft of . . .'

Already, other officers were starting to search the premises.

'Get out of my house!' Ruth Prior shouted at the man pulling clothing from the hall cupboard. 'You bastards, you've got no right.'

'I'm afraid that's not the case,' Jack Skelton said, holding the magistrate's warrant in front of her eyes.

'Fuck you!' she said, anger contorting her face.

'Why don't you get yourself in the kitchen, love?' said one of the detectives. 'Mash tea.'

'And fuck you too!'

Aside from the fact she was older, her hair had darkened into chestnut brown, there'd been some thickening around the waist and legs, she wasn't so very different from when, as Ruth James, she had flailed her arms in front of the band at the Boat, moaned and sung the blues.

They hurried Prior up the steps and into the station, laces of his brown shoes still undone. 'I'm not opening my fucking mouth till I've seen my solicitor.'

''Course not,' the custody sergeant said agreeably. 'As it should be. Now if you'll just empty your pockets out on to there.'

Ruth walked into the bedroom without expecting anyone to be there and found Rains feeling through the contents of the chest of drawers that had been tipped across the double bed.

'I thought you bastards had all gone.'

'Clearly not.' Straightening, smile curling from one corner of his mouth. 'Some of us bastards are still here.'

She watched his hands smooth across the pale shades of her underwear, almost delicate.

'Does something for you, does it?'

Rains's smile became a question.

'Women's knickers?'

'Depends who's inside them.'

'Go round pinching them from washing lines?'

'I said . . .'

'I heard what you said.'

He lifted a pair of her pants, white, lace at the front, plain and shiny at the back; all the while he was fingering them he was looking at her.

'Still appreciates you, does he? Touches you? Like this? After all these years?'

She grabbed a bottle of moisturizer from the dressing table and threw it at his head; tore the garment from his grasp and hurled it back across the room; aimed a blow

167

at his leering face and he caught her wrist as her fingers were only inches from his cheek.

'Got to be compensations, though, married to a villain. Second-hand excitement. Holidays in Malta, the Costa de Sol. Never knowing where he is at nights. Who he's with. Jumping every time the doorbell rings.'

She pulled hard and he let her go and she stood there close to him, her breathing loud in the quiet room. Car doors slammed in the street outside. A voice calling Rains's name.

'You know,' Rains said softly, 'I did you a misservice. Took you for a slag. But I was wrong. You're not that at all. Here.'

And before she knew what he was doing, he had seized her hand and pressed it between his legs, laughing when the surprise jumped in her eyes.

'Not many women,' Rains said, stepping round her, around the end of the bed towards the door, 'can make me feel that way. Not without even trying.'

Ruth was still standing there, staring across at her reflection in the dressing table mirror, when she heard the front door slam shut, the last car drive away.

'What I'd like to do,' Skelton said, 'is ask you to take us through it once again.'

'No way.'

'To be certain we have the details . . .'

'No.'

'No room for any doubt . . .'

'No!'

'I think, inspector, my client has answered your every question as fully as you could wish. I'm afraid I can really see no further purpose being served here, other, of course, than an attempt at intimidation.'

'Investigation,' Skelton corrected him mildly.

'Investigate my arse!'

Just perceptibly, Jack Skelton flinched. Sitting beside him, Resnick leaned forward, drawing Prior's attention. 'What can you tell us about Frank Churchill?' he asked.

Prior shrugged and shook his head.

'Does that signify a no?' Resnick asked.

'It means I've got a dose of Parkinson's – what d'you think?'

In his notes, the young DC wrote: Prior gestured no, nothing.

'How about Frank Chambers?' Resnick asked.

Prior turned aside in disgust and a look from his solicitor told him to respond. 'No,' Prior said.

'Frank Church?'

'Never heard of him.'

'What about,' asked Skelton, apparently studying the marks on the table top with interest, 'Mary MacDonald?'

'Was she there?'

'Where?'

'Up that supermarket, wherever? That's what you've got me here for, isn't it? So I want to know, what's she got to do with it, this . . . Mary whatever-her-name-is?'

'Miss MacDonald,' Skelton said, 'was present on an occasion when you and Frank Churchill . . .'

'I told you, I don't know any . . .'

'Ssh!' Prior's solicitor said, raising a hand in warning. He knew from experience it was when they lost their temper that his clients gave it all away.

'When you and Frank Churchill,' Skelton was saying, 'talked about the raid on the security van, openly admitted taking part . . .'

'Don't waste your breath!' Prior said with scorn, leaning his chair back on to its rear legs.

'And when you admitted being the one in possession of the gun which seriously injured one of the guards.'

Prior's chair rocked forwards fast and he was on his feet, arms braced against the table's edge, glaring into Skelton's face.

'Mr Prior,' his solicitor said, alarmed, half out of his seat. 'John.'

Resnick and the DC had moved near enough simultaneously, closing on Prior from either side, the constable's notebook spilling on to the floor. Skelton blinked and little more, his hair still brushed back and perfectly in place, tie knotted with deft correctness at the neck of his cream shirt.

By whatever mechanism Prior brought himself under control, it took forty, possibly fifty seconds to work. Time-a-plenty, Resnick thought, to have squeezed back on the trigger of a gun.

'My client would like a break,' the solicitor said. 'A drink.'

No one seemed to hear him.

'If you're going to talk about firearms,' Prior said, once he had sat back down, 'people getting shot, I've got nothing further to say.'

But when neither Skelton nor Resnick responded, he said, 'This woman, fetch her down here. Let her say that to my face. Stick me up in an identity parade. Anything. 'Cause I tell you this, either one of you's made her up or she's lying.'

When Rains and two other officers arrived at the furnished room in Tennyson Street, all the signs were that Mary MacDonald had gone. The clothes, the personal knick-knacks, even the sheets from the bed had all disappeared, leaving a thin stained mattress and a box of kitchen matches close by the gas fire.

One of the postcards of Mary and her friend Marie

had slithered almost from sight, wedged against the cracked lino by the door.

For the best part of two hours they knocked on doors, rang bells, came no nearer to knowing where Mary MacDonald might have gone. All they could do now was show the picture of Marie to the Vice Squad in the probability that Marie was also on the game, hoping against hope that she hadn't done a bunk at the same time.

The CID room was oddly quiet, the click and hiss of cigarette lighters, irregular sounds of men breathing. Jack Skelton sat on one of the desks, shirt sleeves rolled evenly back upon his wrists. 'House, garage, garden – we turned up nothing. The only witness we might have had has disappeared. We don't seem to be any further along with Prior in this business than we were a week ago.'

Rains lifted his head as though to intervene, but, under the inspector's eyes, ducked it back down and continued examining his shoes.

'We're going to have to kick him loose.'

'Any point hanging on to him till morning, sir?' one of the detectives asked.

'If you can give me one,' Skelton responded.

He could not. Nobody could.

'Right,' said Skelton, levering himself to the floor, 'Release him. Now.'

# Twenty-Six

Resnick had returned home around seven that evening to find Elaine engrossed in the spread sheets she had on the dining-room table, the radio defiantly tuned to Radio Two. Computerized figures and Barry Manilow: for Resnick an eminently resistible combination.

'Anything to eat?' Resnick said over her shoulder.

She didn't look round. 'Cold chicken in the fridge.'

'You?'

'I had lunch.'

'It's supper.'

'I'm not hungry.'

Resnick opened a pot of Dijon mustard and dipped pieces of three-day-old chicken into it, eating absent-mindedly as he scanned the local paper, the urban ghetto scare stories in the *Mail*. In the front room he put a record on the stereo, realized he wasn't listening and switched off.

'How about the Club? I wouldn't mind a drink.'

Elaine turned slowly. 'The Polish Club.'

'Where else?'

'I thought you'd allowed your membership to lapse?'

Resnick shrugged. 'A chance to rejoin.'

'You go. I ought to finish this.'

For some moments Resnick struggled to summon up the interest to ask what *this* was. 'Maybe meet me there later?' he said.

'Maybe.'

'I shan't be late,' he called from the hall.

If Elaine responded, he failed to hear.

Somewhere in his teens, for reasons he would have found difficult now to clearly remember or define, Resnick had turned against his parents' Polish culture. Perhaps it was no more than what teenagers did. The young Resnick as James Dean. He recalled seeing the film, *Rebel Without a Cause*, most of his sympathies flowing to Dean's father, poor Jim Backus, wearing an apron and embarrassed, standing mortified upon the stairs, flinching from the anger of his son's tirade.

For Resnick it had been less dramatic, more gradual; little by little he had stopped answering his parents in their native tongue, speaking in his own instead. The boys at school had rechristened him Charlie long since and Charlie he had been happy to become.

Sitting now with an iced glass of lemon vodka, he felt he was visiting a strange country, stranded in the past. Photographs on the walls of men in uniform, decorations for lost wars. The bartender in his neat white jacket looked along at him and smiled. At round tables heads were lowered in desperate conversation. Suddenly standing, he swallowed down the remainder of his vodka and pushed through the doors into the street.

The city was soft red brick, broken by green trees. For more than an hour he walked it aimlessly, nodding to people whenever they passed.

The phone rang a little shy of four a.m. and Resnick reached mistakenly for the alarm. By the time he had propped himself on one elbow and lifted the receiver, Elaine was awake as well, looking at him reproachfully from her side of the bed. Resnick listened, grunted a few times in agreement and broke the connection.

173

'What is it?' she asked as he swung his feet towards the floor. 'This time of night.'

'Morning,' Resnick said, beginning to assemble his clothes. 'It's morning, more or less. They found a woman, Mapperley Plains, out on the golf course.'

Resnick read the question in her eyes.

'No,' he said. 'She's alive. Pretty badly beaten, apparently. They've taken her to Queens.'

'Why phone you?'

Without looking in the mirror, Resnick was fastening his tie. 'Case I'm involved in. Some chance there's a connection.'

'Charlie,' she said, when he was at the door.

'Yes?'

'Nothing. It doesn't matter. You'd better go.'

Car headlights cut soft channels through the slight mist; the surface of the grass was bright with dew. Unseen, birds stirred up the day. There was still an indentation where the body had been found, midway to the seventh hole, nestling the edge of the rough. Yellow tape marked off the spot.

The uniformed officer who had found her was still there, peaked cap circling round and round between his fingers, Panda car parked close with the others, static and occasional voices from its radio spilling out across the green.

'Caretaker rang in,' he told Resnick, 'reckoned how he'd heard this car. Couple of break-ins past month or so. Worried this might be another. Drove out and checked around like. Just on my way when I heard this sound.' His gaze flickered away to the markings on the ground. 'It were the girl.'

Resnick nodded, understanding the startled expression that survived at the back of the young officer's

174

eyes. He and Ben Riley had been that young once, stumbling upon their first assault victims, pretending that it didn't affect them, needing to show they didn't care.

'No doubt who she is?'

The constable shook his head. 'Bag was off in the bushes. Must've got thrown, no telling who by.'

Versions of the scene were already playing themselves out in Resnick's mind.

The handbag was plastic, creased shiny black. Inside were several tissues, crumpled and used, a lipstick labelled Evening Rose, three Lillets, a packet of condoms with two remaining, a small tan diary in which little had been written – entries Resnick recognized as the names of pubs, a handful of names – at the front, on the page headed Personal Details, she had written Marie Jacob, five foot three, brown eyes, brown hair, no birth date, an address in Arnold.

Resnick remembered the photograph Rains had brought in from Mary MacDonald's empty room, two women on the front at Great Yarmouth, smiling, squinting their eyes against the sun. Mary and Marie.

'She'd been cut,' the constable said. 'Across the face. Here.'

With the tip of his index finger he drew a line diagonally down from below the lobe of his ear, almost to the cleft of his chin.

'And beaten. Knocked around pretty bad. Time I found her, this eye, it were good as closed.'

Resnick nodded, picturing it clearly. 'No sign of any weapon?'

The young PC shook his head.

'Give the light half an hour, maybe a little more. Then get a search organized. Thorough. Every blade of grass. If the weapon's here, we want it found.'

They could wash away the caked blood and the dirt, replace the blood, lessen the pain; what they could not do was remove the fear.

'I don't know,' Marie said in an accent so soft that Resnick had to lean over her face to hear. 'I don't know who he was.'

Her lips were swollen and cracked.

'I met him, earlier, you know. We were on the golf course for a bit of business when he started in hitting me, no reason at all.'

She motioned that her mouth was dry and Resnick lifted the glass from the bedside table, was gentle as he could be, one hand raising her head so that she could drink through a bendy straw.

'No,' she said, voice fading near to nothing. 'I never knew him. Never saw him before.'

When Resnick held photographs before her she blinked her eyes and barely shook her head. She cried. Resnick sat there till the staff nurse tapped him on the shoulder and then he left.

'Believe her, Charlie?'

'No, sir. Not really. Could be telling the truth, of course, but no, I don't think she's giving us all she knows.'

'Just a feeling, or have you got something more?'

'Just a feeling.'

Skelton stood by the window, looking out. Below, a line of lock-up garages, factories with raised roofs and a few neat streets of council houses beyond. In the middle distance the floodlight towers of both soccer grounds pushed up against the sky. Further still, the green of a solitary hill. 'Prior,' he said, turning back into the room. 'You think Rains could have been right.'

Right as Rains: it didn't even raise a smile.

'Don't want to, do you, Charlie?'

'Maybe not.'

'No more your methods than mine.'

'No.'

'But within hours of us lifting him, both women Rains says might have dropped him in it . . .' Skelton shook his head. 'One's in hospital, terrified half out of her wits, and the other . . . Well, we don't know where she is at all, do we?'

'Manchester,' Resnick said. 'They're still checking.'

'Let's hope with some success.'

Resnick thought about Marie Jacob's face and prayed the inspector was right.

'Couple of uniforms checked her address,' Skelton said. 'Nothing useful there at all. But then, they wouldn't look with your eyes.'

'I'll get out there,' Resnick said. 'Poke around.'

Skelton nodded, giving each of his shirt cuffs a little tug before turning back to the window. When he had applied for the transfer, accepted the promotion, he had failed to realize how different it would be, less than a hundred miles north and close to the Trent. How hard to slot in. He hoped that, as his wife was in the habit of suggesting, he had not perpetrated one of the major miscalculations of his life.

# Twenty-Seven

Resnick spent forty minutes with a sixty-eight-year-old man who was convinced he had come about his stolen bike. 'Locked the bugger up in the entry an' everything. Right t'the bloody fence. Side entry, along of the house. Safe enough you'd say, aye, so did I. But it weren't, you see. Some clever sod's snuck round there with bolt clippers, right through bloody lock, less time than it takes to crack an egg. Wouldn't mind so much, but I've had that bike – Raleigh, good 'un, made good 'uns in those days – had that bike, must be – what? – well, dozen year at least. Maybe more. Who'd want to steal a bike like that? Spite, that's what I put it down to. Spite or cussedness, 'cause they'll not get much for it. All them fancy coloured jobs with half-assed handlebars and great thick frames, that's what they want nowadays. Not solid and dependable, like mine.'

He looked across his back kitchen at Resnick, a wiry man with a shiny bullet head and a neat greying moustache, braces hanging down either side of his trousers.

'Got so,' he said, 'you can't leave anything out your sight more'n a minute or it's gone. Thieving bastards'd have the shirt off your back if they thought as they'd get away with it.' He shook his head. 'That bike, my lifeline were that. Now it's bloody gone.'

Resnick phoned through and checked the crime number, established that no progress had been made. Truth was, though they might catch the thief, the bike would already have been sold intact or stripped down for parts.

He accepted several cups of tea, each stronger than the last, sipping from a thick china cup, the inside of which was stained with overlapping rings of orangey brown. Trying hard not to look at his watch, he listened while the man talked about his son in Australia, the grandchildren he had never seen, the stroke that had taken his wife – God rest her – early from the world. Agreed that Tommy Lawton was the best centre forward this country had ever had – bits of kids nowadays with these flash cars, won't as much as kick a ball without there's someone there fanning 'em with a cheque.

Resnick had seen players in the County side the past few seasons, would have found it difficult to kick anything without the aid of an on-the-pitch injection.

'I don't want you to think,' the man said, showing Resnick to the door, 'as I'm one of those who can't keep up with the times, forever rattling on about how much better everything was when they were young, 'cause I'm not. Not by a long chalk. But I'll say one thing and I know you'll bear me out, folk were a lot more honest in them days, folk round here, ordinary folk I'm talking of now, like you and me. Why, twenty year back, I'd gone off down the shops, I'd not so much've bothered to've locked this front door, never mind bike. Now – well, you know about now well as I do.'

Resnick thanked him for the tea and walked past the bushes of roses that needed pruning, out of the gate and on to the street. The house was three doors down from Marie Jacob's address and the old man thought he might have seen her once or twice, but couldn't be sure. 'Time I might have looked at a bit of skirt,' he'd said, 'now you are going back a fair while. Not that I wasn't above a thing or two when wind were in right direction.' And he'd winked and grinned and Resnick had grinned back, men together, talking the way men did, in the old days and now.

Marie Jacob had lived with her aunt, a short, plumpish woman who was struggling to move an easy chair down the stairs and into the middle room when Resnick rang the bell. He took off his jacket and helped, finally forcing the legs past the frame of the final door with a shove that stripped away several layers of paint and the skin from his own forefinger.

'Here,' Clarise Jacob said, 'let me put a plaster on that. You'll not want it turning all gangrenous on you, sure you won't.'

Despite his protestations, Resnick found himself sat firmly down, while the woman fussed and cleaned and smeared his finger with Germolene before wrapping it in Elastoplast with a technique which leant heavily on the early Egyptians.

'I never asked her a great deal, you know, about her life. I mean, she's a grown woman.' Clarise smiled. 'More so than me. I'm only four foot eleven, did you know that? Can't even see over the counter at the bank without I've got my high heels.'

'Marie,' Resnick prompted. 'You don't know who she might have been meeting last night?'

Clarise Jacob pursed her lips. 'Like I say, I was never one to interfere. As long as, you know, she came across at the end of the month with her little bit of rent.' She looked at Resnick directly. 'Family or no, bills've got to be paid. Either that or we'd all be out on the street.'

Exactly, Resnick thought, where Marie was earning her money in the first place.

'You'd know, though, what time she left?'

'I would. I would. You're right. It couldn't have been

before ten, on account of I was still watching the box. I made a habit of turning it off, you know, right at the start of the news.' She studied Resnick's face seriously again. 'It's not good for you, that's the thing, too much of it, you see.'

Whether she meant television or news, Resnick wasn't clear. 'I wonder . . .' he began, getting to his feet.

'If you can see her room. Oh, sure. Though those two boys earlier, they did the same.' She escorted him up the stairs. 'I'll not speak ill of her behind her back, specially after what happened, but, you'll see, the tidiest soul on this planet she was not.'

The walls were covered with posters of rock stars and the previous Pope; almost every available surface was covered with a riot of clothing, garments of all designs and colours.

'The officers who searched earlier,' Resnick asked, 'they weren't responsible for this?'

'Oh, no. They did a bit of tidying up.'

'Did you ever hear her,' Resnick asked, 'mention a man by the name of Prior? John Prior?' He was back downstairs now, towering over Clarise Jacob in her tiny hall.

'I'm sorry,' she said. 'I'm not being a lot of help at all.'

Resnick slipped the lock on the front door. 'Anything you think of later that might be relevant, give me a call. I've left my name and number.'

'All right. And, ooh, when you're making out your report, it's Clarise with an S, R-I-S-E. Everyone always gets it wrong. Bye-bye.'

Eleven minutes past two: if I were a social worker, Resnick thought, I might consider I'd had a pretty good morning. The Fiesta in front of him swerved outwards to avoid an ageing pigeon and Resnick braked hard, then swore as the engine stalled. He had vaguely intended to call in at home, but that was enough to change his mind; if he took one of these turnings to the right, that would bring him down on to the Mansfield Road. He was humming one of those Parker tunes with unpronounceable names, beating his fingers against the wheel, when he saw a woman walking out of a house a little off to the right. The house was quite substantial, thirties probably, set back from the road; the woman, wearing a blue suit, smart, turned her head to look back at the man who was now locking the front door and she was smiling. It was Elaine.

Resnick accelerated clear, took the next road to the left, a narrow street curving back up the hill, swung in between two parked cars, switched off the engine and applied the brake. Suddenly, in the sealed space of the car, he could hear his own breathing, smell his own sweat. He was starting to shake.

Elaine, leaving the house, low heels clipping the flagged path beside the gravel drive. A suit that had cost a month's wages and more. Graceful turn of the head and slow. A smile he had seen before. Beside the front garden shrubs, the low stone wall, a sign which read *For Sale*. The man at the front door, pocketing the keys. Volvo parked at the kerb, dark blue. It had been a long time now since Resnick had seen that smile.

When his breathing was back to normal and his hands steady, he continued up the sloping road, circling an irregular block.

The Volvo had gone.

Slowly, Resnick slid into its place.

*Viewing Strictly by Appointment Only* across the bottom of the sign.

The garden was orderly, just the grass perhaps in need of a trim. The curtains at the upstairs windows had been drawn a uniform third across. Below, the ruched blinds had been set to deny any nosy passer-by an easy glance. Resnick sat there for a quarter of an hour and nobody walked past in either direction, there was no sign of movement from inside the house, no sound.

He got out of the car, locked it, and walked up to the front door. Two locks, a Chubb and a Yale. The gate beside the garage was bolted, but a tall man could reach the bolt end on tiptoe. It took seconds, not minutes, to slip the back door lock with an Access card he rarely, if ever, used. Two glasses had been rinsed and left on the drainer to dry; they were not dry yet. Nothing else in the kitchen suggested recent occupation. The air was flat and smelled faintly of lavender; the central heating had been switched off.

Faint, he could see the marks their feet had made upon the stairs.

The toilet had recently been flushed, a fragment of paper flat against the inside of the bowl, a single curl of hair floating dark upon the water. The taps of the hand basin were slightly damp to the touch, bubbles of lather on the purple soap.

In the second bedroom, at the back of the house, the pillows bulked unevenly against the quilted headboard. Resnick lifted up the floral duvet and eased it down towards the foot of the bed, lowered his face towards the imagined indentations at the centre of the sheet. Careful, they had left no marks. What remained, unmistakable, was the sour-sweet smell of sex: another scent, the natural odour of Elaine's body, clinging to it lovingly.

# Twenty-Eight

Rains had half of a chicken rogan josh in a plastic container and he was offering it round the CID room when Resnick came in. 'How 'bout you, Charlie? Never known you to say no to some free grub.'

Resnick said no.

He went over to his desk and sat shuffling through meaningless pieces of paper, applications for courses, arrest forms, incident reports. Back across the room someone got the most from the punchline to an old joke and someone else laughed. Phones rang and were answered. Business as usual.

Rains dumped the container in the metal bin, wiped his fingers on a pocket handkerchief, lit a cigarette. 'That woman, Charlie, Prior's wife. Knew her, didn't you? Some time back.' He perched on a corner of Resnick's desk, leg swinging. 'Know her well?'

Resnick opened one of the drawers and took out a notebook, spiral bound.

'Anything I saw may be taken down?' Rains grinned.

Not for the first time, Resnick caught himself wondering how it was that Rains managed to dress the way he did on a DC's salary. According to gossip from officers who claimed they'd been there, the interior of Rain's flat looked like something out of an ad for expense-account living. The car he had parked downstairs was a two-year-old Golf GTI.

'You do know her?' Rains said. 'Ruth Prior?'

'Not really. Not personally. Who she is, that's all. Who she used to be.'

'Some singer, right?'

The last time Resnick had heard her, or maybe the next to last, she had done a version of 'I'd Rather Go Blind', so slow, he thought, listening, time must have stopped.

'Yes,' he said. 'She was a singer. Local, mostly. Blues, soul, stuff like that.'

'Sort of Tina Turner?'

'If you like.'

'Without the tan.'

Resnick said nothing.

'And she gave it up to marry him, Prior?'

'I suppose so.'

'No kids, though, eh?'

'Not as far as I know.'

Rains let himself down from the desk. 'How long d'you reckon it is, then? Since she jacked it all in for a life of domestic bliss?'

'Must be five years at least. Six?'

Rains grinned. 'No wonder.'

Resnick's expression: what?

Still grinning, Rains cupped his crotch in one hand. 'Ready for a taste of something fresh.'

'Is she?'

'Yeh. See it in her eyes. Just might not know it yet herself, that's all.' Midway between Resnick's desk and the door, Rains looked over and winked. 'Married women, they're a cinch.'

When Elaine got home a shade after six-thirty she assumed Resnick had not yet returned. It was only after making herself a pot of tea and opening the tin of lemon creams that, wandering between rooms, she noticed his jacket on the bannister rail.

'Charlie! Charlie, are you here?'

It was quite likely that he could have been in and gone out again; certainly, his car hadn't been outside.

'Charlie?'

She sat in the comfort of their new settee – the arguments there had been before she'd felt able to go into Hopewells and put a down payment on *that* – drank her tea and leafed through a magazine. Unable to concentrate, she knew that something was troubling her: she didn't feel that she was alone.

'Charlie? You're not in bed, are you?'

The bedroom was empty, her dressing gown diagonally across the foot of the bed where she had left it. A pair of discarded tights on the floor near the wardrobe and she scooped them up, dropping them in the laundry basket as she walked out of the room towards the last flight of stairs.

'Charlie, whatever are you doing here?'

He was sitting in an old easy chair that had come from his parents' home, the fabric along the arms worn smooth until the original pattern had all but disappeared.

'What are you doing up here?'

There was new wallpaper on the walls, an old carpet on the floor, a whitewood chest pushed into one corner of the room. Cartons and boxes that had never been emptied since they had moved. Some of them – God! – Elaine knew were stuffed full of rubbish she had kept since leaving school: reports, magazines, pocket-sized diaries crammed with spidery writing, fevered accounts of first kisses and half-conjured dreams. In there somewhere was a scratched Parlophone single: the Beatles' 'I Want to Hold Your Hand'.

'What on earth are you doing?'

186

'Thinking.'

'What about?'

It was too dark in the room for her to be able to clearly see his face. Only the light from the stairs lengthening Elaine's faint shadow.

'You don't normally come up here.'

'Sometimes I do.'

It occurred to her that were she not able to see him, she might have had difficulty in recognizing his voice.

'What are you thinking about?' she asked.

'Work.'

'That girl, the one on the golf course?'

'Yes, that.'

Elaine took a pace back towards the door. 'I've not long made some tea.'

Resnick nodded. 'I'll be down.'

She hesitated a few moments longer before going back downstairs. When Resnick eventually followed the tea had grown stewed and cold and Elaine was washing salad to go with the grilled chicken breasts they were having for their meal. As Resnick crossed in front of her, taking a beer from the fridge, she didn't say anything more about the incident and neither did he.

'Ready in about half an hour, that okay?'

'Yes,' Resnick said, pouring the beer over near the sink, 'that'll be fine.'

Prior was channel-hopping, switching between the highlights of the Eurovision Song Contest, a studio discussion about law and order in our cities and an interview with Spurs' Argentinian midfield player, Osvaldo Ardiles. 'If they win the Cup, it'll be down to that little bastard,' Prior said over his shoulder. 'Lawyer, too, back home.' Prior laughed. 'Ever end up in court, reckon I'll ask for him. Ossie for the defence. Good, eh?'

187

'Wonderful.'

He reached out and caught her by the wrist. 'Christ, Ruth! What is it with you lately?'

'Lately?'

'Every time I open my mouth all I get's this great put-down.'

Ruth pulled away, rubbing at her arm. Sometimes he didn't know his own strength; sometimes, she thought ruefully, he did, and knew enough to hit her where the bruises didn't show.

'Jokes,' she said. 'The same old jokes. Maybe I'm fed up with them.'

'Yeh? What else you fed up with?'

'Oh, you know. Life. Think I'll go and stick my head in the oven, end it all.'

'North Sea gas,' Prior smiled. 'Don't work no more. Better off locking yourself in the garage, leave the car engine on.'

'You'd like that, wouldn't you?'

'Don't be stupid.'

'I'm not stupid.'

'I know, I know.'

'Stuck round here all the time, I might as well be.'

'Get out then?'

'Oh, yes? And do what?'

'Get a job.'

Ruth laughed. 'Only place you'd let me do that'd be a convent.'

'Not likely. Let them nuns get a look at you.'

'Stop it! Just stop it!'

'What? Ruthie, what?'

'Going on. This joke, this fantasy. As if I was some kind of sex queen.'

'You still get blokes turning their heads after you in the pub, in the street.'

'Yes?' She moved close against him, her hip brushing him as she sat on the arm of the chair. 'If I'm so sexy, how come I'd need to be on *Mastermind* to remember the last time we made love?'

From the sudden change of expression on his face, she thought he was going to take a swing at her, but the phone rang and she jumped to her feet. 'I'll get it,' she said.

She recognized his voice straight off and it was like him grabbing her hand again and pulling it against him, although she pretended that she didn't.

'Come on,' he said. 'You know who it is?'

'You want to speak to John?' she asked.

Rains laughed. 'I wondered if you fancied meeting for a drink?'

For some time after she had broken the connection, Ruth stood in the still quiet of the hall, staring at the way her fingers curved around the sharp red of the receiver, the tarnished gleam of the ring biting tight below the knuckle. From the living room came the sound of Prior's mocking laughter, the oompah bass and fractured vocal of the Icelandic entry.


Resnick had watched the discussion, the Police Commissioner's assertions that he would never countenance No-Go areas in the capital; the search for an appropriate police response which veered between a return to community policing, ordinary coppers on the beat, to the advanced technology of CS gas and the riot shield.

'What do you think?' Elaine asked as the programme came to an end.

'I don't know,' Resnick said, 'but Ben reckons we'll soon get the chance to find out firsthand.'

'Want anything before bed?' Elaine asked. 'Tea or anything?'

Resnick shook his head. 'Think I'll sit up for a while. Listen to some music.'

Elaine thought about offering to sit with him, till she saw which record he was pulling from the shelf. That bloke who played piano like a man with no arms.

'Don't sit too late then.'

'I'll be all right. You get some sleep.'

Resnick poured a vodka and took it over to his chair; found the track he'd been hearing, off and on all day, inside his head. Ten, eleven single notes, seemingly unconnected, fingers jabbed down against the keys, till suddenly, the steady rhythm of the bass, swish of brushes against the snare and the vibraphone takes over, finding a line, a melody where none had existed before. July second, nineteen-forty-eight, New York. 'Evidence'.

# Twenty-Nine

The main office of Hilton, Lockett was on Trinity Square, where the fumes from the waiting buses and the cars waiting for spaces in the National Car Park were enough to lessen life expectancy a good five years. Resnick walked into the square past the Post building, pausing to look at the special offers on art paper in the stationer's window and buy a packet of mints from the newsagent's. He hoped he wasn't developing a sweet tooth.

There was no mistaking the man he'd seen leaving the house with Elaine. Leaning now over one of the young women at her desk, smiling as he made some remark. He was several inches shorter than Resnick himself, slim; the suit, dark blue with a narrow stripe, was the same as he'd been wearing then. The same or similar. The young woman laughed and the man moved across the office to his own desk near the rear.

There were several people inside, couples, browsing the property details: houses under £40,000, houses under £65,000, houses under £85,000; £85,000 and above. There was a photograph of the detached house on Richmond Drive in the window; save for the two figures who had been outside, it was exactly as Resnick remembered. And well above the £85,000 mark. Good: he was pleased Elaine wasn't selling herself cheap.

Resnick pushed open the door and stepped inside. Three faces looked up at him expectantly. Ignoring them, Resnick went to the appropriate section and lifted a

191

sheet detailing the Richmond Drive property from the rack.

'A very fine house, sir.' He was blocking Resnick's path, professional smile in place, scent of violets faint on his breath. 'Excellent value.'

Resnick nodded and took a step to the side.

'Was it that particular property you were interested in, that particular area? We have a number of others . . .'

Resnick knew if he stayed there another minute he would hit him, full in the face. 'No,' he said, pushing past, 'this is fine for now.'

Out on the street he screwed the paper down into his jacket pocket and hurried between heavy green buses towards the lower edge of the square. One hand against the railings outside Jessops, he caught his breath: not since he had been in uniform, confronted by a gang of youths shouting abuse and spitting in his face, had he felt such a need to lash out, strike back. Although he hadn't admitted it at the time, almost certainly hadn't been aware that it was so, this had been one of the reasons that had nudged him into CID and out of the front line. The urge to strike back – more than that, to hurt, actually hurt. It frightened him.

Inside the Victoria Centre, he skirted round the mothers and toddlers, mothers with prams, climbed the central stairs to the upper floor. Passing between the stalls laden with vegetables and fruit, the rows of hanging plants and cut flowers, he took his stool at the Italian coffee stall. One espresso, full. He had scarcely received his change before ordering a second. And a third. He withdrew the property details from his pocket and smoothed them out upon the counter. *This substantial property provides an excellent opportunity for purchasing a large and established residence in this exclusive and much sought-after area of the city.*

'Thinking of moving?' Maria asked, settling his third espresso in front of him.

'Something like that.'

She moved away to serve another customer as Resnick turned over the sheet of paper. *Viewing earnestly recommended*, it said in thick letters across the bottom of the page.

The police car was parked across the street from the station and Ben Riley slid from the passenger side when Resnick approached, Ben not in uniform, wearing the same sports coat and flannels he stood in on the terraces deploring another County attack gone wrong.

'Where the hell've you been?'

'Why?'

'Nobody seemed to know where you were.'

Hands in his pockets, Resnick shrugged his heavy shoulders.

'You all right?' Ben Riley was craning back his neck, looking at Resnick keenly. 'Okay?'

Under his friend's gaze, Resnick looked away. 'Fine. Why?'

'You look dreadful.'

'Thanks.'

'All the more reason for lunch,' Ben urged him.

Resnick shook his head, glanced towards the station. 'I can't.'

'I'm paying.'

'I've got things to do.'

'And you have to eat lunch.'

'I'll get a sandwich.'

'And indigestion.'

'Sorry, Ben.' Resnick stepped into the street. 'Some other time.' Ben Riley's hand reached for his shoulder, holding him back. 'Work, Charlie. This is work. Believe me. This is stuff you'll want to hear.'

'Excuse me, sweetheart. Love. Miss. Another couple of pints, please.' Ben Riley beamed and offered the waitress his glass.

Resnick flattened his palm over his and shook his head.

'Half?' the waitress asked.

'Thanks.'

They were in Ben Bowers at the top of Derby Road; if you angled your head round sharply enough it was possible to see Canning Circus police station through the window. Ben Riley was eating his way through a steak, T-bone, medium rare, French fries, broccoli, new season's peas. Resnick had ordered the lemon sole, sauté potatoes, salad. The only other diners were on expense-account lunches from the insurance company offices along the road.

'So picture this,' Ben Riley was saying between mouthfuls, 'there we are, eleven-fifteen, eleven-thirty, whatever, on our way out of the pub, taxi waiting, all of a sudden there's this commotion across the street. Two couples, blokes in their Friday-night suits, women wearing dresses so thin you can see the goose pimples on their arms from where we're standing . . .'

He broke off as the waitress set the glasses on the table; used the blade of his knife to dab English mustard on to the reddish end of his steak.

'Where are we?' Resnick asked. 'This pub?'

'Woodborough. You know, the country and western nights.'

Resnick didn't like to think about it. He had never understood how a grown man, otherwise fully in control of his faculties, could break down and cry at the sound of Hank Snow singing 'Old Shep'.

'Anyroad, there I am, few more sheets to the wind than rightly I care for, looking over there, hoping it'll all calm itself down, storm in a biryani, when one of these blokes knees the other one right in the groin. Woman I'm with, instead of hauling me off, she's all for a bit of action. "Go on, then. You can't turn your back. Go over and get them sorted." ' He cut off a wedge of meat and chewed at it thoughtfully. 'I get half-way across the road, bloke who's been hit, unlocks the boot of this car parked at the kerb and comes up with a gun.'

If he didn't have all of Resnick's attention before, he had it now.

'Bloody shotgun!'

Resnick set knife and fork quietly down and pushed away his plate.

Ben Riley grinned. Two insurance executives across the aisle were hanging on his every word. 'Where there'd been a lot of shouting and commotion, everyone was suddenly quiet. Three of them staring at this shotgun and the chap with it looking ready to take the other bloke off at the knees.'

By now the entire restaurant was silent, wanting to know how it had worked out.

'He was so engrossed in what he was doing, didn't seem to hear me at all. Got right up behind him, tapped him on the shoulder. Jumped half a foot in the air, dropped the gun.' Ben Riley was smiling broadly, enjoying the audience. 'Got a foot on it, showed him my warrant card, that was about that.'

You could hear breath being released around them on all sides, click of utensils on china, conversations resumed.

'Seemed the car he was driving wasn't taxed, his driving licence had been withdrawn six months previous and, of course, he didn't have a licence for the gun. I get the names and addresses of the others, make sure my woman gets a taxi, me and him go back inside the restaurant – pretty fair tandoori, by the way, specially when it's on the house – anyway, we get to talking, he's worried about this motor thing, needs it to get around, can't believe he was so stupid as to threaten this bloke with the gun. Been mates – what? – four years, but that's not what's really putting the shits up him, what is, he had that gun earmarked for somebody else. One of the things he's into, a little buying and selling on the side. It's in police custody, how can he sell the gun?'

Resnick could feel the small vein vibrating at the side of his skull. 'Did he say who he was going to sell the shotgun to?' Hoping against hope, not really believing what Ben's reply was going to be, but knowing all the same.

Ben Riley leaned forward across the table and lowered his voice. 'Prior. John Prior.'

Resnick picked up his knife and fork and cut across the fleshy section of lemon sole. His appetite had come back.

The man's name was Finch, Martin Finch, and they didn't talk to him in one of the interview rooms at the station; they talked to him in Ben Riley's Vauxhall, parked in a lay-by on the Kimberley-Eastwood by-pass, east of Junction 26. The temperature was such that the windows were steaming over, three men in that confined space the best part of an hour, Finch's sweat holding his shirt flat and wet to his back, running into his groin. Finch wanted to reach down and scratch, wriggle and set himself to rights. Except for small movements with his hands, he sat quite still, leaning back into the rear corner of the car, grey tongue dabbing at his drying lips. Softly, the four-speaker stereo was playing one of Ben Riley's compilations of Country hits.

'The gun that was used in the Sainsbury's job,' Resnick asked, 'did that come from you?'

Finch mumbled something that could have been yes or no.

'Again,' Resnick said.

Audible this time, Finch staring at the condensation on the window as traffic, like blurred ghosts, swished by outside. 'Yes.'

'You knew what it was for?'

'No.'

'You must have had an idea?'

'No. Never.'

'The person you sold it to, that was Prior?'

'Not direct.'

'Explain.'

Over the whine of a steel guitar, George Jones was preparing to get hurt all over again.

'I met up with Frank ...'

'Frank Churchill?'

'Yes. Through him I met Prior. After the deal'd gone through.'

'They talked about the robbery?'

''Course not.'

'But you knew?'

'No.'

Resnick wiped his hands along his thighs. 'You thought they were going out to shoot rabbits?'

'Maybe.' A flick of the tongue. 'Why not?'

'You know now,' Ben Riley said from behind the wheel. 'After last time, no way you can't know.'

Finch lowered his face into his hands. Count to five

hundred in tens and when you look they'll all have gone away.

Resnick leaned closer along the back seat. 'This time, Prior contacted you himself?'

'Yes.'

'Why not Churchill?'

Finch shrugged. 'Maybe he's not around. Who knows?'

'When,' Resnick said, 'were you supposed to make delivery of the gun?'

'I don't know.'

'Don't lie.'

'Honest to God . . .'

'Yes?'

Finch's eyes left Resnick and found Ben Riley instead. His temples were beginning to throb; it was increasingly difficult to breathe. 'Tomorrow, day after. He's supposed to get in touch.'

'How?'

'Phone.'

Resnick glanced towards Ben Riley, who gave a quick, almost imperceptible nod. 'Go through with it. Go through with the deal. Soon as Prior's in touch, arrangements are in place, you call us.'

An articulated lorry went past so fast along the bypass it made the car vibrate. Sweat dropped from Finch's nose on to his mouth and chest. Tanya Tucker asked to be laid down in a field of stone; Billy Joe McAllister jumped off the Tallahachee Bridge. 'All right,' Finch breathed eventually. 'Okay. Yes. Yes.'

# Thirty

'Whatever's the matter with you, Charlie?' Elaine was leaning against the living-room door, a glass of white wine in her hand.

What's the matter with you? Resnick felt like asking. Since when did you start drinking at home, this side of seven o'clock especially. Resnick was listening to Charlie Mariano, thumbing through back issues of *Jazz Monthly*, the omelette he'd made earlier balanced cold on its plate at the edge of his chair, largely untouched.

'I don't know,' he said, looking at her steadily. 'Is something the matter?'

Elaine held his gaze for several moments, clicking forefinger against thumb as she turned away.

When Resnick appeared in the kitchen fifteen minutes later he was wearing his grey raincoat, unbuttoned and unbelted. 'I'm going to the match.'

'What match?'

'Reserves.'

Without humour, she arched back her head and laughed. 'Christ! Is staying in the same house with me suddenly that bad?'

He stood on the County Road side, near the half-way line. Rain began to fall in swathes, darkening his coat, seeping through to his shoulders. On the pitch a bunch of youngsters and the odd gnarled professional hoofed the ball out of defence in the hopeful direction of their opponents' goal. Tackles slid fast across the greasy turf and, with so few people in the ground, you could hear, all too clearly, the crack of bone meeting bone.

'Here! Here! Here!' a player called, arms like semaphore. 'Get the bastard thing upfield!'

Gripping the metal rail before him, Resnick failed to notice that his fingers had whitened, his knuckles were purple. So many times since the previous afternoon the words had lain on the back of his tongue, waiting to be spoken and each time he had swallowed them whole and unsaid. *Whatever's the matter with you, Charlie? Is staying in the same house with me suddenly so bad?* He could smell something strange and sweet and it was the scent of violets, filling nostrils and mouth, making him retch. *Married women*, Rains had said, smug and handsome and knowing, *a cinch*.

When, less than five minutes from the end of the match, County's reserve striker latched on to a weak back pass and toe-poked the ball past the keeper for the game's only goal, Resnick could scarcely raise a cheer.

It was a drinking club near the Forest, as unlike the one where he'd been with Resnick and Cossall as it was possible to be. The DJ at the far end of the main room was playing reggae and Rains's was the only other white face at the bar. 'Scotch,' he said, 'large. And a large gin.'

He slid a note across the bar and pocketed the change, picked up the glasses and carried them to the far end where Ruth was sitting.

'I told you . . .' Ruth began.

'It's a free country.'

Ruth laughed bitterly. 'Is it?'

Rains sat himself on the stool beside her, tasting his Scotch. Ruth lit another cigarette and poured the gin into her own glass.

'We can't talk here.'

'Why not?'

'I'm known. Besides, he might come waltzing in any minute.'

'Okay, my car's outside. We could go for a drive.' He drained his glass and began to get to his feet. Ruth scowled and looked straight ahead but otherwise she didn't move. Rains settled back down and gestured to the barman for a refill. He thought if there were any real danger of Prior arriving she would have left the moment she'd recognized him at the door.

Ruth held the glass by the stem, tight, wondering if some kind member was in the entrance hall already, letting Prior know his wife was sitting there, taking drinks from a sodding copper. She could see Rains's reflection mirrored above the bottles, so fucking good-looking it made you want to throw up.

'Another?'

She didn't answer and he took her silence for agreement and bought a large gin. Ruth waited for him to start in on Prior's activities, how did it feel being married to a villain? He surprised her by asking her how it felt, not being able to sing any more.

'Not able? How d'you mean?'

'Don't suppose he takes to the idea much, does he? Wife up on stage, on show? Bit old-fashioned about things like that, I should imagine.'

Before they were married, Prior had gone everywhere to see her. Step out on to the stage and there he was, somewhere at the back of the room, leaning, smiling. Later, it was, 'Jesus, Ruthie! You have to start that cater-wauling, every minute of the bloody day?' At first, career going nowhere, bands breaking up around her, record contracts not materializing, she had found it difficult to mind. The joy had gone out and all that was left were torn vocal cords and hard work.

'Don't you wish,' Rains said, 'you could do it again, now and then, just for the hell of it?'

Ruth stubbed out her cigarette, automatically reaching for another. 'It's been too long. Any voice I might've once had's gone.'

He put his hand over the one that was bringing the cigarette to her lips. 'Maybe then you shouldn't smoke so much?'

She shook him free. 'My father, that's what you want to be? My agent? You're short of an act for the police smoker? What?'

Rains waited until she was looking full into his face. 'I like you. Talking to you, it's good. I like that. Paying you a bit of attention, I reckon it's too long since anyone's done that. You deserve better. That's all.'

Ruth sat there, you cocky young bastard, you're so full of shit; but listening all the same, knowing he was lying, enjoying every word.

When he arrived back at the house all the lights were out and Resnick assumed that Elaine had got tired of her own company, caught a cab to someone welcoming. But she had gone to bed early, her face blinking back at him from the pillow when he switched on the light. She covered her eyes and he snapped it back off.

'Coffee? Tea?'

'No, thanks.'

The usual courtesies.

Resnick spread the coffee beans across the palms of both hands, lowering his face towards them. Even so, it lingered: sweet-sour smell of the sheet, oil of violet on the breath. In the living room he thought of playing Parker's 'Lover Man', one of those bruised ballads Billie

Holiday sang with Lester Young. Either, he realized, would reduce him further into self-pity. He fetched a notebook from the desk by the window and wrote up that day's conversation with Martin Finch. If anything went wrong, he was going to need all the accurate documentation he could muster.

Almost an hour later he called Ben Riley on the phone.

Ben's voice was quiet and Resnick wondered if there was someone there with him, the woman who had witnessed the incident with the shotgun or someone else. 'What's the matter, Charlie? Can't sleep?'

'Sorry, I didn't realize it was so late.'

'Not to fret. What can I do for you?'

'That deal today, with Finch? You think it was all right?'

'Will he follow through, you mean?'

'Yes,' Resnick said.

'Depends who he's more frightened of, us or Prior.'

They talked some more, Resnick reluctant to put down the phone.

'You know what I was on about the other day,' Ben Riley said eventually. 'About getting out.'

'Leaving the force?'

'Quitting the whole bloody lot, lock, stock and barrel. Well, I'm serious. Maybe didn't think I was at the time, but I am. I'm getting out, Charlie. Started looking into it, serious. Got an appointment to talk to the union rep later this week.'

Resnick's stomach was hollow and chilled. 'Where the hell'd you go?'

A pause and then, 'The States, perhaps.'

'Don't be daft. Whatever it is you're running from here, ten times as bad over there. New York. L.A. You'd be . . .'

'Big country, Charlie. Not all cities, you know.'

'If it's a quiet life you want, what's wrong with Devon? Cornwall?'

At the other end of the phone Ben Riley sighed. 'It's not a quiet life I'm after, Charlie. It's a new one.'

Not knowing what to say, Resnick said nothing. 'Get to bed, Charlie,' Ben Riley said. 'Maybe see you first thing? Breakfast, eh?'

'Maybe,' Resnick said and rung off.

There was a half inch of coffee cold in the bottom of the cup and he tipped enough Bell's into it to make it half full. Drank it standing at the foot of the stairs. At the bedroom door he listened to the sound of Elaine's breathing and knew that she was deep in sleep. In the bathroom, he switched on the shower and stood under it for a long time, head bowed. Then went to bed.

# Thirty-One

'Chancy business, Charlie. Can't say it's the way I'd have played it.'

'No, sir.'

Skelton was in the midst of compiling the duty roster, coloured pins and stickers strategically placed at the four corners of his desk, each ready to be slotted into place. He reminded Resnick of those elderly men at the BR Travel Centre, just aching to be asked the quickest way to get from Melton Mowbray to Mevagissey on a Sunday, calling at Wolverhampton and Weston-super-Mare on the way.

'Conspiring to provide a known villain with an illegal weapon, that's the way the courts might see it.'

'Yes, sir.'

'Still, now it's set in motion, best let it play itself out. But I want a close eye kept, Charlie, understood? A close eye.'

Resnick turned towards the door.

'Can't remember, Charlie – squash, that your game or not?'

'Not exactly,' Resnick said.

Skelton nodded. 'Bit of difficulty finding partners.' His gaze drifted down in the direction of Resnick's gently spreading stomach. 'Could do a lot worse than give it a thought. Getting to the age when it pays to look out for these things – health, fitness – doesn't pay to let them slide.'

Resnick gave it some thought while he was enjoying a smoked ham and brie sandwich, light on the mustard, heavy on the mayonnaise. That and other things. Brushing his fingers free of crumbs, he crumpled up the empty bag and dropped it in one of the black and gold litter bins around the square. Time to do a little more house hunting, he thought, crossing towards the old post office building dividing King and Queen streets.

The young woman at the first desk had a complexion like sour milk. 'Oh, that would be our Mr Gallagher,' she said in response to Resnick's inquiry. 'He's just stepped out of the office for a moment. Is there anything I can do to help?'

Resnick was in the middle of declining when the bell above the door sounded and Gallagher returned, different suit today, a charcoal grey. He had the early edition of the local paper under one arm, a bar of Cadbury's Fruit and Nut and a packet of twenty Benson Kingsize in his hand. He handed the chocolate to the young woman and slipped the cigarettes into his own pocket. He seemed to recognize Resnick, but not the exact connection.

'Richmond Drive,' Resnick prompted him.

'Ah, yes, of course. You're interested then?'

Resnick nodded.

'Good, good. Not been on the market for long and already we've had a lot of interest.'

'It is empty, though? Vacant possession?'

'Oh, yes. People that lived there moved abroad. France, I seem to remember.' He gave Resnick a professional smile. 'Do you have somewhere to sell?'

'Yes.'

'Perhaps we can help you there. Handle both ends. But first things first . . .' He reached for a leather-bound appointment book. 'You'll want to view the property.'

'No, that's not necessary.'

'But surely you can't . . .'

'My wife's already been round the house.'

'Oh, I see. I'm sorry, you didn't say. I . . .'

'Yes. Matter of fact, you showed her round yourself.'

Gallagher was thumbing back in his book. 'I don't remember . . .'

'Well,' Resnick said, a pace closer, 'I'm sure you do a lot of that kind of thing.'

Gallagher glanced up with a quick, uncertain smile; he was still turning, back and forth, from page to page. 'I'm afraid I still don't . . .'

'Probably no reason you should. My wife, come to think of it, she didn't have a lot to say about it either.'

'If I could have the name?' Gallagher said.

'Oh, Resnick. Mrs Resnick. Elaine.'

The appointment book slipped from his hand and he caught at it, steadying it against his body at the second attempt. Much of the colour seemed to have left his face. He made a guttural, stuttering sound that never threatened to become real words.

'If there's anything else,' Resnick said, 'you can get in touch at the station. I expect Elaine mentioned I'm a policeman. Detective sergeant. CID.'

'What the hell were you doing, Charlie?'

Elaine had been waiting for Resnick the moment he turned the key in the front door; not waylaying him exactly, but there at the centre of the hall, close to the foot of the stairs. He wasn't sure, but he thought she might have had a drink or two to steady her resolve.

'What the hell did you think you were doing?'

He gave her a what-do-you-think? look and made to go past her into the kitchen.

'No, Charlie. No, you don't. We're having this out, here and now.'

He tried again and physically she blocked him, pushing her hands against his arms. 'Talk to me, Charlie. Talk.'

He looked into her face. 'I don't think I've anything to say.'

'Really?' Head to one side, sarcastic. 'You surprise me.'

'I'd like to think you'd surprised me.'

She hit him, fast and unthinking, her open hand smack across his cheek, the edge of her ring catching his lip. When he moved his tongue, Resnick could taste blood.

He walked around her and this time she made no attempt to stop him. Resnick got as far as the back door and realized he didn't know what he was doing there.

'Running out again, Charlie? Another football match to go and see?'

He turned to face her. The anger had scarcely diminished in her eyes.

'You went into where he worked and threatened him.'

'He?'

'Philip.'

So: Philip Gallagher. Phil. 'I didn't threaten him.'

'No? Well that was certainly the way it felt to him. I'm a police officer. Sergeant in the CID. Christ, it's like a bad film.'

'I wouldn't know.'

'No, you wouldn't. Not on your social calendar too much these days. Films. Nor a lot else, for that matter. Forgetting the football, of course. Late-night drinking, no danger of forgetting that.' She laughed, shrill and short and bitter. 'We used to go to the pictures, Charlie, I don't know if you remember. Cinema. Dancing. Even the theatre once or twice, although you did have a tendency to fall asleep after the interval. Still – used to do a lot once upon a time, you and me.'

'Why do I think this is turning into some kind of an attack on me?'

'Is it? Maybe because that's the way you feel. Catholic guilt, Charlie. All that stuff you thought you'd disowned.'

Resnick leaned away from the door. 'I should've thought if there was any guilt around . . .'

'I should have the monopoly?'

'You were the one sneaking off in her lunch hour.'

'Sneaking off?'

'Making love to another man.'

The bottle that she'd opened was close to where she was standing and she poured herself another glass of wine. The bottle was nearly empty. 'We weren't making love, Charlie, Philip and I. What we were doing was fucking. There's a big difference.' Slowly, she carried her glass of wine towards him. 'What you and I do – used to do – that was making love. Tender, Charlie. Careful. Solicitous. What we do, myself and Philip, other people's beds, we fuck!'

He swung his arm and she saw it coming, trying to block him and not quite succeeding, the heel of his hand catching her at the front of the left temple, alongside the eye. The glass she had been holding shattered against the floor. Elaine stumbled backwards, the worktop saving her from falling.

Resnick moved towards her, arms outstretched, apologizing; instead of flinching, she lifted her face towards him, daring him to strike her again. Resnick wrenched the back door open and slammed it behind him, unable to see where he was running, half-blinded by the tears of shame and anger in his eyes.

# Thirty-Two

'If you were going to hit anyone,' Ben Riley said, 'you should have had a crack at him.'

'Wouldn't do any good,' Resnick said.

Ben Riley shook his head. 'I'm not so sure about that. And, by my reckoning, nine out of ten people's think the same.'

'That doesn't mean they're right.'

'Come on, Charlie. It's a bit late to be bloody reasonable. And he was, if you'll pardon the expression, screwing your wife.'

'Not a crime.'

'Isn't it?'

Resnick got up from the table and started to pace haphazardly about.

'For God's sake, Charlie, have a drink.'

'Better not.'

'Some coffee then.'

'All right.'

'I've only instant.'

'Never mind. Forget it.'

Ben had been ironing shirts when his friend had arrived, bending over the board with a bottle of Jameson close to hand and a celebration of George Jones's ten years of hits in the cassette deck. He'd switched it off when the door bell had rung and hadn't felt moved to turn it back on. He doubted if Resnick was ready for 'Nothing Ever Hurt Me (Half as Bad as Losing You)', never mind 'If Drinkin' Don't Kill Me (Her Memory Will)'.

'What are you going to do?' he asked.

'I don't know.'

'You want me to go round, talk to her?'

Resnick shook his head.

'You're sure? 'Cause I will.'

'Thanks, no. It's hard to see how it would help. It's something we've got to sort out for ourselves.'

'Yes, I suppose you're right.' He pointed at the bottle and Resnick shook his head. 'Just give it a little time, eh?'

'Yes.' Resnick sat back down, shaking his head. 'I suppose that's the thing to do.'

'D'you want to stay here tonight? You know there's plenty of room.'

Resnick accepted gratefully, realizing that it was no more than temporary respite: a night on the couch away from what still had, painfully, to be faced.

They ate breakfast at Parker's, Resnick sure he would have no appetite, but something – the smell of bacon? – making him ravenous the moment he walked to the counter. Ben Riley settled for tea and a sausage cob, looking on amused as Resnick tackled black pudding, back bacon, tinned tomatoes, double egg, chips and beans.

'Jesus, Charlie. Good job you don't get cuckolded often. You'd be over eighteen stone.'

'It's not funny, Ben.'

'I know that. What d'you think I'm cracking jokes for?'

Resnick sawed off a slice of black pudding, wiping it round in the tomato juice before transferring it to his

211

mouth; one of those things, if you didn't think what it was made from, it could taste wonderful.

'Happen we'll hear from Finch today,' Ben Riley said without much conviction.

Four firemen, just off night watch, came in talking about a fire on the industrial estate they were all persuaded was arson.

'What worries me,' Resnick said, 'drifts on too long, Skelton might get cold feet, have him pulled in before Prior's in contact. That happens we're back to square one.'

'He'll allow forty-eight hours, got to.'

Resnick shook his head, forked up the last of his beans. 'No got to about it.'

'Should have played squash with him,' Ben Riley grinned. 'Sweat your way into his good books.'

'Yes.' Resnick eyed his empty plate. 'Can just see me chasing a little green ball after that lot.'

'If you want to stay over again,' Ben said when they were on the pavement.

'Thanks. Best not. Sooner or later it's got to be faced. Sooner's the better.'

'Who you trying to convince, Charlie? Me or you?'

One question Resnick did know the answer to.


Resnick had to take a statement from a thirty-year-old curate who'd witnessed a mugging on his way back from a parochial visit. Another case he was working on. They sat the best part of an hour in a draughty church hall decorated with Sunday School paintings and posters advertising a fund-raising dance for the end of Lent. As he sat listening, taking notes, asking questions. Resnick tried to imagine Elaine and himself visiting someone like this to discuss their problems. That or a marriage guidance counsellor. Was that what you did when you could no longer speak to one another? Talk through a third party? He was only now beginning to realize they hadn't been communicating: what they'd been doing, opening their mouths, pronouncing words.

'I'm sorry,' he said to the curate. 'Could you just say that again?'

When he got back to the CID office there was a sheaf of messages on his desk, the last of them, written hastily in blue Biro, *Finch* and a six-figure number. At the bottom, the initials, barely legible, RC.

Reg Cossall was out interviewing a remand prisoner at Lincoln Prison. Resnick dialled the number on the paper and after thirty rings no one had answered. He tried again on the quarter-hour for an hour and when somebody eventually picked up it was a girl of around nine or ten who told him he was calling a public call box on Valley Road.

Resnick thought about driving out there and decided against it. Chances were Finch might ring in again and if he did it was better if he were there to take the call. So he did paperwork, tried not to look at his watch, kept an ear open for Cossall's voice on the stairs.

When Cossall finally returned, he was unusually subdued. The young man he'd been out to see, two days short of his twentieth birthday, had tried to kill himself that morning by puncturing his wrist with the broken end of a fork he'd stolen from the dining hall. When that hadn't worked he'd broken it again and pushed the pieces down his throat. 'All the bastard'd've got was six month suspended. Likely probation.' But something about it had got even to Cossall – that degree of self-inflicted pain.

'Reg,' Resnick said, approaching. 'You took this message. Finch.'

'Yeh. Wants you to ring him. Regular cat on hot bricks, sound of it.'

'I tried. Call box. No one there.'

'That's 'cause you tried at the wrong time then, isn't it?'

Resnick showed him the note. 'How was I supposed to know the right one?'

Cossall took the slip of paper from his hand. 'Sorry, Charlie. Must've forgot to write it down.'

'You haven't forgotten what it is?'

'No way. Three o'clock. Four o'clock. On the hour.'

It was seven minutes past four. Resnick dialled the number, held his breath, willing the receiver to be picked up.

'Yeh?'

He thought he recognized the voice as Finch's, but he wasn't sure. 'Martin Finch?' he said.

'Who's that?'

'DS Resnick,'

'Why the hell didn't you phone before?'

'Never mind that, I am now. What have you got?'

'He's been in touch. I'm meeting him tonight.'

'He still wants to buy?'

'There's something coming up. Pretty soon. Wants it bad. Tried putting him off, tomorrow, but no, got to be tonight or he'll go someplace else.'

'Tonight's fine. Where's the meet?'

Finch's voice was like a leaf. 'I'm going to be all right here, aren't I? You're not going to get me mixed up in this? If Prior ever susses . . .'

'Listen, I've told you. You won't even be involved.'

'Involved to the sodding eyeballs, that's all!'

'Relax. We won't go near him when he's with you. Anywhere near you. Nobody ever has to know . . .'

'He'll know.'

'Just tell me,' Resnick said, letting the firmness back into his voice, 'where the meet's arranged for, place and time.' Nodding into the telephone then, 'Uh-huh, uh-huh,' writing the details carefully down.

Skelton was not long off the squash court; his hair, prematurely starting to grey a little, was brushed back flat upon his head and his face was flushed. He was wearing a navy blue track suit and white Adidas shoes with green piping. 'One thing I'm not prepared to countenance, letting him take delivery of a weapon and then using it to commit a robbery. It's not on.'

'Our information suggests whatever's going down, it'll be pretty soon. That time, we can keep him under observation, twenty-four hours. As soon as he moves, we move too.'

'And all that needs to happen is we put one foot wrong, someone gets shot, maybe this time they get killed, where does that leave us? I'm sorry, Charlie, the risks are too high. Walk into the super's office with that and I'm as like to walk out again with a flea in my ear as anything. No, we'll do the simple thing and we'll do it right.' Skelton looked at his watch. 'Incident room, eight o'clock. Make sure everyone knows.'

Back in the CID office, Resnick phoned Elaine.

'Look,' he said, 'tonight, something's come up. I'm sorry. I've no idea what time I'll be back.'

'How convenient,' Elaine said and hung up.

# Thirty-Three

Ruth climbed out of the bath, water streaming down her thighs. She'd lain in there too long, idling with her thoughts, the skin on her fingers ridged and puckered. Reaching for a towel, she rubbed a circle on the steam-covered mirror with her fist. Jesus! Like waking up and discovering you'd turned overnight into your mother. She wound a white towel about her head, began to pat her legs dry with another. *How's it feel, then, after all that time, not being able to sing*? Cocksure bastard with his hands round the glass, nails even and smooth like they'd been manicured, long fingers. *How's it feel*?

'Ruthie, you going to be all night?'

The look in his eyes when he took her hand and pressed it against him. Bastard! Excited, she hated him for that.

'Ruthie!'

*Every night I'm kept waiting*, she started singing to herself, face blurred in the mirror, gaunt and unfocused. *All those dreams and wasted tears* . . .

Prior knocked loudly on the door. 'There's other people in this house, you know.'

'Couple of minutes.'

'You better be.'

There'd been other people, right enough, same old faces along with a few new ones; conversations that petered out the minute she walked into the room. Phone calls that would be terminated at the least chance of being overheard. Something new was in the offing, something big, and he wouldn't say anything about it till it was over. Then there'd be the bragging – 'Ought to've seen their faces' or 'Like a bleeding dream, Ruthie, clockwork wasn't bloody in it' – the celebrations with champagne swilled down like water and holidays to exotic places. The lies. 'Papers. Ruthie, you know what they're like, blow it all up out of proportion. Hardly laid a finger on them.' And last time: 'All an accident, never should've happened. Wouldn't've done if he hadn't took it into his head to be a sodding hero. Me? Ruthie, come on! When did you ever know me as much as touch a gun?' God! The lies. How she hated the same old, senseless lies.

'Ruth!'

'All right!' She wrenched the door open and moved quickly past, into the bedroom, Prior's voice trailing behind her.

'Jesus! What you been up to in here? Like a bloody sauna!'

Ruth closed the door and unwound the towel from her body, draping it over the end of the bed. In the full-length mirror her breasts were getting smaller, the flesh over her hips and around her thighs was thickening. Sighing, she closed her eyes. *All those lonely wasted years.* Rain's face, wide-eyed with honesty even as he lied. *I like you. Talking to you.* The beginnings of a well-trained smile edging his face. *You deserve better, that's all.* Well, she wasn't going to get it if she stayed where she was now with Prior forever breathing down her neck.

Resnick was to be in the lead car with three others, Hallett and Sangster and a new lad called Millington. Skelton would be in car two with Maddoc and McFarlane and Terry Docker. 'Your show this, Charlie, I'm just

217

along for the ride.' The third car contained Rains and Cossall and Derek Fenby. Uniforms were providing extra back-up, sealing off the area around the Prior house once the time was ripe. Resnick had asked for Ben Riley and got him. One officer in each car was armed.

The first car alone would stand close watch on the pub, where two plain clothes officers were already stationed, borrowed from outside the city so there was less chance of them being recognized. As soon as the deal had gone down, the other cars would close in.

'All right,' Skelton said, 'nobody loses their head. We want a result here, not gunfight at the OK Corral.'

A couple of officers politely laughed.

'Charlie? Last thoughts?'

Resnick was on his feet. 'Thanks, sir. I don't think so. We all know what we've got to do.'

'Yes,' said Reg Cossall, 'make sure that bastard Prior goes down for a long time.'

There were cheers for that.


'Ruth?' He'd changed into light blue slacks, dark crew neck sweater under a brown leather coat. Tan shoes with tassles. Where's the gold chain, Ruth thought? 'I'm off out. Shan't be long.'

She swung her legs down from the settee. On the TV an off-duty surgeon was performing an emergency operation with the assistance of one of the night cleaners and a hastily sterilized Swiss army knife.

'Going to the club?'

'No,' Prior said and winked. 'See the well-known man about the well-known dog.'

Ruth looked back at the screen. 'Is this the dog that takes a .38 calibre bullet or the one that prefers shotgun shells?'

Prior laughed as he closed the door; over the sound

of the TV she could hear him doing a really bad Presley impression down the hall. Now or never, Ruth thought, might be just about right.

The pool tables in the side room were crowded round with onlookers, the occasional shout at a lucky shot or a bad miss rising above the general noise. At the back of the main bar a woman in a floral dress was plying coins into the electronic fruit machine as if feeding a long-lost child. The juke box cut in with a sudden burst of eighties' techno-pop, fighting it out with the landlord's tape of Western theme tunes which was playing through the speakers above the bar.

'What the hell's the matter with you?' Prior asked as Finch made his second return from the gents in fifteen minutes. 'Got the runs or what?'

'This ale,' Finch said, holding up the glass. 'Goes through me like nobody's business.'

'So stop bloody drinking it,' said Prior, who was sticking to Scotch and water, nibbling his way through a packet of nuts, shells overflowing the metal ashtray. 'Anyway,' he said, pulling back his jacket sleeve to see his watch, 'almost time we weren't here. Got the wife to get back to, know how they are.'

'Give her one,' Finch laughed nervously.

Prior scowled and pushed back his chair. Coins spilled from the fruit machine so liberally that the woman couldn't hope to catch them in her hands. 'Parked round the back?'

'Yes,' Finch said. 'Hang about while I finish this.'

Prior took the glass from his hand and set it down. 'In your own time. Let's do this now.'

They walked out past the pool players, half of them sixteen at best. There'd been something in the *Mirror* that morning about underage alcoholics, Esther Rantzen or Anneka Rice or one of them setting up a telephone helpline. 'Any kid of mine . . .' Prior had started over his scrambled eggs, but the look on Ruth's face had shut him up. Far as the pair of them knew any kid of his hadn't been born yet.

'Just left the pub,' the detective said into his two-way radio. 'Rear car-park, the pair of them.'

The shotgun was wrapped in a length of wool blanket, sheathed inside thick plastic; the notes were in fifties, rolled tight and held in place with a rubber band. The exchange took less than forty seconds. 'Okay,' Resnick said into the handset. 'We're on.'

Fed up with TV, Ruth had climbed on to a dining chair, scrabbled about in a box on the top shelf in the alcove, above Prior's Brian Ferry albums, his Rod Stewart and his Elvis Presley. Paperback books by Wilbur Smith and Jeffrey Archer. The corners of the cover had got bent, one of the edges torn. 1972. She could remember going into the recording studio still. Manchester. Driving up there with Rylands, through the Peak and along the Buxton Road. Four tracks and it had taken them the best part of a day. Cold in the studio and she'd found it difficult to pitch in key, sent Rylands scurrying out from behind his drum kit to buy a quarter-bottle of brandy.

Ruth wiped away dust with the side of her hand and set the record down. Play it now before he came home. The rawness of the sound took her by surprise, the echo, her voice. Well before the first song was over, she lifted up the stylus, slotted the record back in its sleeve. That moody, soft-focused picture, head down by the mike like she was Janis Joplin. Well, lighting a cigarette, she wasn't Janis; she was alive. Just. Without bothering to get back on to the chair, she tossed the record back up into the box.

*Ruth James & the Nighthawks* RIP.

Hallett drove, enjoying this part of the job, good at it. Followed a stolen Sirocco once, all the way from Exeter to Chesterfield, five different motorways, never spotted once. Now he ghosted eighty yards behind Prior's car as it swung down Southdale Road, turning south through Bakers Field towards Colwick Wood park. In the back Graham Millington began to whistle, tuneless and unrecognizable, until the others stared at him and he shut up.

The other cars were slowly closing, east and west.

The palms of Resnick's hands were dry and beginning to itch. Since making his call several hours before, he had not thought of Elaine once.

Ruth had intended to be in bed before Prior arrived back, but she had switched the set back on and a programme about prisoners' wives had caught her attention. Talking to camera, some of their faces had been electronically distorted to avoid recognition. Story after story of impossible journeys by bus and train, often with kids in tow. Month after month, year after year. Stand by your man. If mine gets nicked, Ruth thought, he can sod that for a lark!

Above the television sound she heard the car draw up outside, switched off and went quickly up the stairs.

'Ruth? Ruthie?'

No reply. Prior switched on the TV and flicked through the channels. Highlights from tonight's top of the table promotion battle. He broke off a piece of mature cheddar with his fingers, popped open a can of beer. If this is the top of the table, he thought after a few minutes, God help the rest of them.

He was lolling back against one corner of the settee, feet resting on the coffee table, when Sangster swung a sledgehammer at the door, the second time enough to splinter the hinges clean away.

Resnick was first inside, calling, 'Police!', Hallett and Millington on his heels. Prior raced from the front room, shouting Ruth's name as he passed the stairs. 'Charlie!' Hallett yelled. 'Go! Go!' Prior wrenched open the kitchen door and slammed it shut behind him. Ruth, pulling on a robe over her nightclothes, stepped out of the bedroom into a chaos of chasing feet and harsh voices. Prior leaned his weight against the kitchen table and rammed it against the door; through the window he could see the shadowy figures of men at close intervals between the roses.

'Bastards!'

Rains looked up at Ruth from the well of the stairs and winked.

Hallett shoulder-charged the kitchen door and his ankle turned under him, but the door budged back far enough for Resnick to squeeze through. A quick look towards the rear windows, which were still closed. He guessed the side door led into the garage and he was right.

The offside door to the car was open and so was the boot. Prior partly screened behind it, bending low. The only light was that which came through the kitchen but it fell across Prior's back and face.

'CID,' Resnick said breathlessly. 'DS Resnick. I . . .'

Prior moved to his right as he straightened and when he did he had the double-barrelled shotgun in his hands. Something banged against the garage door outside, but the hands didn't falter; they were holding the gun quite steady, angled towards the upper part of Resnick's chest.

Peripherally aware of other voices, outside and behind, Resnick could only concentrate on Prior's eyes as they narrowed down, the slight tightening of the finger behind the trigger guard.

The breathing of both men was ragged.

Resnick took a pace forward and cautiously, very slowly, began to open the fingers of his empty right hand.

Something inside Prior changed, like a switch being thrown; his eyes widened and blinked and he began to reverse the shotgun, the barrels towards his own head. Christ! Resnick thought, he's going to kill himself. But the swivelling movement didn't stop until the stock was pointing towards Resnick and he went quickly forward, hand reaching across the roof of the car, to take the weapon from Prior's loosening grasp.

The garage doors slid quickly up into the roof and Ben Riley stepped out of car headlights, concern on his face. Hallett and Millington moved either side of Resnick, turning Prior around, reading rights and warnings as they fastened cuffs about his wrists.

'Did well, Charlie. Star performance.'

Resnick turned at the sound of Rains's voice and there he was, grinning from the kitchen doorway, Ruth at his side. Rains had a police-issue pistol in his right hand.

'Thought for a minute there I was going to have to use this.'

Resnick pushed past them, back inside the house, Ben Riley following him through.

# Thirty-Four

Summer in the cities.

Prior was refused bail, on the grounds that he might skip the country or attempt to interfere with potential witnesses, and jailed on remand. Martin Finch was persuaded to testify that in addition to the shotgun Prior had surrendered to Resnick, he had supplied the weapon that had seriously wounded the Securicor guard and that Frank Churchill had told him it was to be used in a robbery Prior was organizing.

When Churchill stepped off the Manchester train, officers were waiting to arrest him.

Resnick was officially commended for bravery and the object of several late-night celebrations in the local force. He found himself celebrating again when the soccer season ended and County were promoted to the First Division of the Football League for the first time in fifty-five years.

He sat in front of a television set with Ben Riley, watching Spurs' other Argentinian, Ricky Villa, plough his way through a maze of players in the Manchester City penalty area and score the winning goal in the FA Cup Final replay. When it was over, Ben told him that he'd written an exploratory letter to the Montana State Police.

One of Prior's fellow prisoners came up to him in the exercise yard and told him his wife was getting her leg over with a copper. It took four men to prise Prior away; by the time they'd succeeded, the other prisoner had a broken nose and a ruptured spleen.

Resnick and Elaine were talking again, being civil at least; she said she had stopped seeing Gallagher, needing to think things through. There was still a great deal that went unspoken, neither of them willing to prise open what each, in their different ways, was apprehensive to examine.

In June there was more rioting in London and in July the attempt by police to arrest a black youth for stealing his own motor bike resulted in violent confrontations which lasted for three days. Petrol bombs were hurled at a beseiged police station in Manchester and riots threatened to tear apart the decaying hearts of many other inner-cities: Birmingham, Blackpool, Bradford, Cirencester, Halifax, Huddersfield, Hull, Leeds, Nottingham, Preston, Reading, Sheffield and Wolverhampton. The Prime Minister, Margaret Thatcher, refused to accept either swingeing unemployment or bad housing as causes, putting the violence and looting down to criminal greed.

Police used water cannon, CS gas and plastic bullets to quell the disturbances. And Ben Riley applied to the American Embassy for his visa.

The fag end of July, Resnick, with four days' leave and time hanging wide on his hands, bought white gloss paint and set to work on the skirting boards in the unoccupied top bedroom.

The first time Elaine came up the stairs she brought biscuits and a mug of tea; the second she stood, arms folded, and said: 'Charlie, we need to talk. Charlie, I want a divorce.'

# 1992

# Thirty-Five

'Pam Van Allen?' people would say. 'What kind of a name is that?'

'My husband's.'

'Your husband's called Pam?' same old jokes.

Either that, or it was assumed she'd got herself married to a Dutchman, like, you know, that detective on television.

Truth to tell, his name had been one of the most attractive things about him, just the right amount of seriousness and mystery; so much more interesting than her own name, the one she'd be born with, born into, which was Gold. Pam Gold: it didn't exactly have a ring to it. It made her sound, Pam thought like the wife of a dentist or a lawyer or a psychotherapist, spending her days listlessly shopping for things she already had.

All right, she knew that was a stereotype.

But that was the way people thought. If she weren't careful, she caught herself falling into the same trap – despite the fact that her dentist was called Adams and the lawyer she'd consulted about the divorce had been Mitchell of Haywood, Turner and Mitchell. She had never, knowingly, met a psychotherapist. Though her husband had suggested it on numerous occasions towards the end of their five-year marriage.

Five years, two months, thirteen days. After the usual healthy mudslinging, she'd walked away with fifty per cent of the resale value of the house and its contents and her husband's name.

'It doesn't make sense,' her friends at work said, disappointed. 'All that's over. You should go back to who you really are.'

But Pamela Van Allen was who she felt she was; it didn't make her think of him at all. Little did. Dandruff and *Mastermind* and pee stains round the toilet bowl. And Pam Gold was a stranger who had once bopped around to Paul McCartney and 10CC, believed in silly love songs and the things we do for love.

Pam Van Allen was a probation officer in the city, thirty-five years old, six years' experience, responsible single woman with a responsible job, showing her identification as she slowed to a stop at the prison gates.

She had worked out a strategy for visits like these. Next to no make-up, just a touch around the eyes, loose cotton jumper under a check wool jacket, plain skirt, three-quarter length. Female, but not flaunting it, no kind of a come-on; clearly feminine, not a dyke. Careful about gesturing with the hands, crossing legs, being over-generous with the smiles. Know what you wanted to say, questions you had to ask. Firm, not over-friendly, but all the same, what you wanted was their trust.

The first doors rang shut behind her and an internal clock automatically switched on, counting the minutes till she would walk back out again. The man she was going to see had been imprisoned for a decade of his life.

Since that night he'd last called on Rylands and they had talked about the prospect of Prior being released, Resnick had tried to push it to the back of his mind. With the burglary rate taking a steep hike and a spate of quick and savage underpass muggings, that wasn't so difficult. And, of course, the investigation into the highly organized series of armed robberies was, as the phrase went, ongoing. In this connection, Divine had taken to flexing his muscles at a health club in the Lace market, swopping confidences afterwards with a pair of likely lads who seemed to have more disposable cash than four nights a week as club bouncers would account for. Graham Millington was doing his drinking in Sneinton, hobnobbing with a snout who'd put some good tips his way in the past and just might be about to do so again if the price was right.

The atmosphere in the CID room was tense, simmering, waiting, if not to explode, at least to let off a head of steam. The workmen had finally got the central heating system working again, floor boards had been replaced, furniture dragged from corridors and odd corners; Resnick had his office back to himself. Space to think, plan, enjoy a deli sandwich without being looked at askance. He was polishing off a salami and gorgonzola on light rye when the phone rang.

'Resnick. CID.'

'Neil Park.'

Neil was a senior probation officer, a fair-weather County fan, a man whom Resnick trusted and might have liked had not the ambivalent relationship between the police and the probation service stood between them.

'You were interested in who's been assigned to Prior.'

Resnick waited.

'Pam Van Allen. D'you know her?'

Resnick had an unclear picture of a woman in her mid-thirties, not tall, darkish hair – not worn long, he remembered, cut quite close to her head. 'I think so,' Resnick said. 'Who she is, anyway. I don't recall speaking to her.'

'She's good,' Neil Park said. 'Reliable. Doesn't take any pushing around.'

'Will she talk to me?'

A hesitation at the end of the line, longer than Resnick liked.

'She might.'

'But you'll not suggest that she does?'

'That's right.'

Thanks a lot, Resnick thought. 'Didn't see much of you this season,' he said.

Neil Park laughed. 'Work's bad enough without suffering on my day off and paying for the pleasure.'

Resnick thanked him and rang off. Twenty minutes later, shuffling through the past few days of incident reports, he remembered that Pam Van Allen's hair wasn't really dark at all: it was that shade of grey that in some lights looks almost silver.

What must he had been thinking of?

Prior hadn't reacted to her name. Sat there and answered her questions, briefly, not impolitely, never avoiding her eye. His face was sallow, lines curved from his mouth, his cheeks were lightly sunken in. The accent wasn't local, Pam thought. Oh, there was an overlay, words and phrases; but below all of that it was harsh, southern, London or close.

'You appreciate it'll be difficult,' she said. 'Readjusting.'

He glanced up at her quickly, keeping his head angled down. It was almost mischievous, that look wrinkling his eyes.

Pam hurried on. 'Being in here, it's hard not to get . . .'

'Institutionalized.'

'Yes.'

He spread one hand upon the table, the other resting, loosely clenched, upon his knee. 'You'll help me.'

She nodded. 'Yes. As far as I can.' The room was

suddenly small and short of air. Sweat ran in a single line along Prior's face, running from his short hair to his close-shaven chin. 'Certainly, we'll find you somewhere to live. At first. While you get sorted.'

'Somewhere?'

'A hostel. A place in a hostel, that's the most likely.'

Prior looked round at the walls. 'I thought I was getting out? Released.'

'On parole.'

''Course.'

'The hostel,' Pam said, 'it probably won't be as bad as you think. Not too many rules. Only common sense. Anyway...' Was that her perspiration she could smell or his? '... it's only temporary.'

'You said.'

'While you find your feet.'

'Yes.'

'Find work.'

Almost lazily, Prior shifted position, leaning one shoulder towards her. 'You'll help with that too.'

'Of course. Yes. As far as we can. There are contacts we've built up and if they don't pan out, there are workshop places. Retraining. Learning new skills.'

Prior fixed her with his gaze. 'Sounds great. Can't wait.'

Pam began to push her papers together, putting them back in her case. 'Well,' she said, rising to her feet, 'I shall come and see you again. With any luck I'll have more definite news about the hostel place. And we'll have a chance to talk in more detail about your plans.'

'Good,' Prior said flatly. 'I'd like that.'

As she made a move to leave, he stood quickly and offered her his hand.

# Thirty-Six

Keith had to hand it to his dad – ever since the day he'd decided to stop drinking stop was what he'd done. If Ladbroke's had been offering odds, Keith would have been down there with every penny he could muster, happy to put it all on his old man to be back on the bottle before the week was out. After all, hadn't he grown up hearing his parents lob promises like hand grenades between them? *Listen, you've got my word . . . That's the last time, I swear . . . I'll never ever . . . Cross my heart and hope to die.* 'Promises,' his gran had said once, her sour commentary on the whole affair, 'are like pie crusts – meant to be broken.'

But here it was, not yet ten in the morning, his father had already stripped the paper from three of the walls in the bathroom and was moving in on the fourth. Consistently, the house was being transformed. The last of his dodgy lodgers had found his belongings, such as they were, stacked against the front wall. Instead of stale beer and puke, it smelled of disinfectant and fresh paint.

'Set the tea to mash,' Rylands called from the bathroom door. 'I'll be down in a minute.'

In the kitchen, Keith delved his hand into a packet of Honey Nut Cheerios and started eating them dry.

'Why don't you sit down, have a proper breakfast?' Rylands said, rinsing his hands beneath the tap.

'Not hungry.'

'There's plenty of bread. You could make yourself some toast.'

'I said . . .'

'Okay, okay.' The kettle coming to the boil, Rylands made the tea himself, swilling hot water round the inside of the brown earthenware pot and emptying it out before dropping in two tea bags, thinking about it, adding a third. 'What you going to do today?' he asked.

Keith pushed the cereal packet back in the cupboard and shrugged.

'I could use a hand in the bathroom. Those tiles . . .'

'No thanks.'

None of the cups and saucers seemed to match and all of the mugs were chipped or cracked: he would have to chuck them out, get himself to the market and get them replaced.

'How about work?' he asked, pouring the milk.

'Huh?'

'I thought you said this week you were going to look for a job?'

'There are no bloody jobs.'

'Pork Farms, they need people on the night shift.'

'Don't think I'm working in some factory, coming home stinking of meat.'

Rylands poured the tea. 'Suit yourself.'

'If you don't like it, I'll move back out.'

'That wasn't what I said.'

'Well . . .'

Rylands passed Keith his tea, sat at the kitchen table and started to leaf through the *Mirror*. 'Sure you don't want any toast?'

'Sure. Have some yourself, I'm not stopping you.'

'Had mine a couple of hours ago.'

'What d'you want, a medal?'

Rylands looked at his son, sipped his tea; all that

235

belligerence in the boy's face, clenched fists, his stance. A young lifetime on the defensive, warding off those who were bigger, older, stronger. From the first day Keith had stepped into the secondary school playground he had been bullied, made fun of, an easy mark. The few friends he had were usually lower on the pecking order than he was himself: a timid boy, part-Indian, part-Chinese, with silky skin and long dark eyelashes that curved; an asthmatic lad with glasses thick as the bottoms of half-pint mugs. Either that, or they were using him for their own ends.

'Seeing that Darren today?'

'Maybe.'

Rylands nodded and turned to the sports pages.

'Why d'you want to know?'

'No reason.'

Keith was standing close against his father's elbow. 'Don't like him, do you?'

'Do you?'

'What sort of a stupid question is that?'

Rylands took hold, not roughly, of his arm. 'One it wouldn't hurt for you to think of an honest answer to.'

Keith shook him free and stood away. 'I'm off out.'

'All right,' Rylands said. 'I'll be here.'

Darren had been watching her, Lorna. Nothing regular or consistent, not methodical, just whenever it came into his head, if he was at a loose end, didn't have anything better to do. So he knew the route she took to work, the corner shop where she would stop off to buy a paper and occasionally a packet of cigarettes, more often than not some magazine; he knew the way she walked back, sidetracking sometimes to call at the minimarket and pick up something for her supper – frozen calorie-counters meals and Slimma soups, she went in for a lot of that. Not that Darren could see why.

He'd sneaked up close to the house once, the one where she had her flat; shinned over the wall and stood in the back garden, not really a garden, more of a yard. Leaned against the flimsy shed and watched her undress. Not all the way, not before she'd crossed the room to switch out the light, but far enough to see the last thing she had to worry about was being overweight.

Maybe he should tell her, casual like, in the news-agent's when she was picking up her copy of *Today*. Helpful words from a friend. No. Let it wait until he was ready to put right what went wrong before. Drift in off the street and saunter over to the counter. Lorna Solomon? You've got a really good body, you know that? Oh, and while you're doing nothing, just empty all of that cash you've got there into this sack.

Real cool: he liked that.

Standing in front of the boarded-up shop down the arcade from the building society, he looked at his reflection in the darkened glass and grinned at himself as he repeated the words. Practice makes perfect.

Taking his time, Darren wandered towards the building society office and looked through the glass door. Fat woman who worked there – now if anyone needed her calories counting, she did – explaining something to this old couple, expression on her face suggesting that she was going through it for at least the third time. And Lorna alongside her, laughing suddenly at something the man in front of her had said; counting the bank notes out carefully before passing them under the glass. For an instant she looked towards the door and in that instant Darren instinctively dodged back so that neither of them was ever sure – Darren whether he had been spotted, Lorna if she had seen who she had thought she'd seen.

The square was riddled with bikers and hippies and punks with swastikas tattooed on to their faces with blue Biros or shaved into the top of their close-cropped hair. The same old woman stood amidst the same grubby pigeons and scattered them with bird seed and stale crumbs.

Keith and Darren sat on the low stone wall, sharing a piece of flabby pizza, Darren taking drags from a bummed cigarette. What Keith wanted to do was walk into the Park Estate and nick a car, one of those Ferraris or Mercs with personalized number plates that were always so invitingly there. Get on to the motorway going north and see what it really could do.

But Darren wasn't having any. Stupid, he reckoned, to take the risk. Get caught over a bit of fun when they had serious plans. Keith kicked his heels, unable to extract from Darren precisely what these plans were.

'You don't worry. You'll know what you need to know soon enough.'

He would never have dared say so, but there were times when Keith doubted Darren had any real plans at all. Except for the gun. That was the one thing it always came back to, almost the only thing he ever talked about now, aside from that woman who worked in the building society and how he wouldn't mind giving her one, how any day now he was going to get hold of a gun. The look on Darren's face when he said it, as though somehow that was going to change everything, change the world.

'Got any cash?' Darren asked. 'I fancy a Coke.'

Keith shook his head.

'Jesus!' Darren said, flicking away the butt of his cigarette as he stood clear of the wall. 'I hate that. Not even

238

enough between us for a drink when you want one.' He jerked his head in the direction of the nearest underpass. 'Come on,' he said.

# Thirty-Seven

Millington was peering at the screen of the VDU, chewing at the bottom of his moustache and pondering the wonders of modern technology, the overlap between what he'd gleaned from his informant and the facts as known. He still couldn't decide if he were being taken for a ride.

'Anything to go on, Graham?' Resnick said, pausing at the sergeant's desk.

Millington scowled. 'Sometimes reckon we'd be as well off with crystal balls.'

Across the room a phone rang and Kevin Naylor picked it up. 'CID, DC Naylor speaking.'

Resnick remembered there was a call of his own he wanted to make; he went into his office and closed the door. Down through the window, he could see the track-suited figure of Jack Skelton jogging past the lock-up garages below the main road.

'Yes, of course I know who it is,' Naylor was saying. With a half-guilty glance across the room, he angled his chair towards the wall.

'I called before,' Lorna Solomon said. 'Left messages. You never phoned back.'

'I know. I'm sorry. Things have been busy.'

'I thought . . .' she hesitated.

'What?'

'You were avoiding me.'

'Like I said, it's been busy.'

240

There was an uneasy silence between them and Kevin sensed rather than heard her breathing at the other end of the phone. He wondered where she was calling from, work or home? Behind him, one of the other officers swore lightly and slammed shut a drawer. Graham Millington was whistling something vaguely classical, the music from some advert or other.

'Kevin?'

'Yes?'

'I wasn't sure if you were still there.'

He was thinking of sitting close alongside her in the front of the car, the warmth of her arm whenever she moved it accidentally against his, Chinese food and perfume.

'That youth, I've seen him again.'

'The one from the robbery?'

'Yes.'

'Where?'

'Right outside. Just today.'

Naylor swivelled the chair back round towards his desk. 'You're sure?'

'Yes. At least I think so.'

'It couldn't have been someone else? I mean, a bit like him? After what happened . . .'

'He was outside the door, staring in. When I saw him he jumped away.'

'He didn't come in?'

'No.'

There was a pause and then Lorna said, 'Kevin, it's not the first time. I'm sure I've seen him before.'

'He spoke to you, on the pavement outside.'

'No, other times. And not just at work, here at the flat. Kevin, I think he's watching me.'

Naylor reached for a ball point and flicked open the pad on his desk. 'You at home now?'

'Yes.'

'Best let me have the address.'

It wasn't a place that Resnick knew, not the inside of anyway, a wine bar-cum-restaurant on Barker Gate, across the street from the snooker club. The entrance was down a flight of steps off the pavement, the room that you stepped into had a bar away to the left, a few small tables pressed against the right-hand wall, plenty of space to stand in between. Through an archway there appeared to be a second room for more serious eating.

Most of the people near the bar seemed to have strayed in for a drink after work and stayed. Grey suits and cigarette smoke and braying conversation. Pam Van Allen was sitting at the first table, a white wine spritzer in front of her, reading a paperback book. In that light her hair was a metallic grey.

Her eyes lifted from the book as Resnick came towards her.

'Hello. Charlie Resnick.'

'Pam Van Allen.'

She held out her hand and her grip was brief but firm.

'Can I get you another drink?'

'Thanks, I'm fine.'

He went to the bar for a glass of house red and she read another page of her book, a novel about college friends who spend a summer together in middle age, the first time some of them have seen one another in ten or more years. Pam could only think of two people she still knew from university, none from school. All those friendships you're sure will be so important the rest of your lives.

'It's good of you to meet me.'

She gave a slight shrug and waited for him to settle down. He was a big man, bulky, the kind who could do with all the exercise he didn't get. A roundish face with serious eyes. Dressed like that, he'd be less conspicuous in the side bar of a pub.

'If you're hungry,' Pam said, making conversation, 'the food's pretty good. Snacks. Hummus. Things like that.'

'Maybe later.'

She glanced at her watch, then folded down the corner of the page and closed the book.

Resnick drank some wine. 'John Prior. You've been to see him.'

Pam said nothing, waited.

'You're happy about the fact that he's going to be released?'

'You don't expect me to answer that.'

'All right, then. Let's put it this way. How much do you know about the circumstances of his arrest and trial?'

She turned her glass around on the table. 'A little.'

'He was convinced some of the information against him came from his wife. That there was some sort of arrangement between her and the police.'

'And was there?' Self-consciously, Pam smiled. 'I don't expect you to answer that either.'

From the adjoining room came the sound of breaking glass, the ironic roar of approval, applause.

'Look,' Pam said, 'I don't know where we're going to go with this. Anything that passed between my client and me, that's confidential.' She lifted her spritzer, thought better of it and set it back down. 'I don't know what I'm doing here.'

'You came.'

'Go and meet him, my boss said. A favour to me. Hear what he's got to say.' She looked sideways at Resnick and then away. 'I thought what else I might be doing, decided it wasn't so important, and came.' She blinked her eyes closed and pushed one hand up through the side of her hair. 'I'm not so sure it was a good idea.'

Resnick tried a little more of the wine. 'What else would you have been doing?' he said.

'Tonight? Warm bath, hot as I can stand, glass of wine . . .' Her fingers drummed lightly on the cover of the paperback. 'A book.'

Resnick's turn to smile. 'Everything except the bath.'

Pam pulled her shoulders back, making her posture more professional. 'All I can do, inspector, is listen to whatever it is you want to tell me. I can't promise it's going to affect my actions one way or another.'

'All right,' Resnick said, 'it's this. Remarks Prior made, at the trial and after, they were heavily vindictive. The most frequent, the most violent, were directed towards his wife. I'm concerned that after his release he might try to carry those threats out.'

Pam was looking at him evenly, paying little attention to whatever was happening around her. 'Prior's wife,' she said, 'do you know where she's living?'

Resnick shook his head. 'No.'

'It could be anywhere?'

'It could be.'

Pam finished most of her drink and opted to leave the rest. When she was on her feet, Resnick pushed back his chair ∕ d followed suit and it occurred to her that he was ╰ ╷g clumsily polite.

'When you were talking to him,' Resnick said, for a moment his hand resting on her arm, 'did he mention his wife? Give some indication of how he feels about her?'

What Prior had said was: 'Last thing I wanted was her traipsing out here, week after week, another of those poor bloody prisoners' wives. Not that I didn't want to see her, mind. But, look at it this way, ten years minimum, just not on. Best never to start than have to get less and less, once a week, once a fortnight, once a month. Then again, if we'd had kids, might've been different. No, what Ruth had to do, live a life of her own.'

'I've told you,' Pam said, 'anything that passed between my client and myself . . .'

'But he did talk about her?' Resnick persisted.

Pam's mouth was feeling suddenly, oddly dry. All those people. The tobacco smoke. The wine. 'A little,' she said. 'And when he did he was very calm, very reasonable. Now I do have to go.'

Resnick nodded and stepped back. Beyond the far curve of the bar, a group started to sing 'Happy Birthday'. He stayed on his feet to watch Pam Van Allen walk away, the final glint of her hair silver as she passed through the light.

# Thirty-Eight

Lorna hadn't spent as much time in front of the mirror since she was fourteen and worried about spots. Five times she had changed her entire outfit, five times, everything from those little blue bikini pants she'd bought on sale at Knickerbox to the vaguely see-through cream blouse from Dorothy Perkins. And make-up! She'd put it on, wiped it off, finally decided on a little light eyeliner, a touch of blusher, the new lipstick she'd bought at Boots last Saturday, South Sea Coral.

Of course, she ought to have run round with the Hoover before getting herself all clarted up, but first things first and anyway it wasn't like her mother making one of her scheduled visits. Kevin Naylor wasn't going to be lifting up the glass Dalmatian on the mantelshelf to see if she'd moved it when she was dusting, or surreptitiously running his finger along the top of the cupboard in the bathroom.

'Doing anything special tonight?' Marjorie had asked when they were cashing up.

'No, I don't think so. Probably stay in, watch telly, get an early night.'

She wished!

She'd nipped out in her lunch hour and bought a few nibbles – pistachio nuts and bacon-flavoured crisps – which she'd emptied into cereal bowls and left casually around.

The most difficult decision had been about what to

drink. Kevin, she thought, was probably a beer man, but, for all that, there was something nice about the idea of sitting on her freshly plumped-up settee with a bottle of wine. In the end, she'd gone to the corner shop. Had four cans of lager cooling in the fridge and a bottle of that red wine they were always advertising, the one where these old men go off into the fields at daylight to check on the grapes. She hoped it would be all right. She'd had half a mind to ask Becca's advice, Becca not being above dropping the names of fancy restaurants she'd been taken to – 'Dinky little portions, so beautifully presented!' – but in the end she'd decided against it. Another patronizing lecture from Becca about the last thing she could cope with.

Lorna looked at her watch, checked it with the clock over the oven, peeked between the living-room curtains down into the street, slipped her tape of Lionel Ritchie's Greatest Hits out of its box and into place and slotted it into the machine.

She was ready.


Maybe, Resnick thought, Pam Van Allen was right about Prior. Prison had calmed him, all those hours alone with four walls had helped him to see things in their true proportion, rationalize. Maybe whatever grudge he'd had about Ruth had faded into relative insignificance. Out of sight, out of mind, wasn't that the way things worked?

He had stayed in the wine bar long enough to finish his glass of house red, okay, he supposed, but what it had given him a thirst for was a real drink, which was why he was sitting at the bar in the Polish Club, his second bison grass vodka of the night on the point of disappearing.

What probably happened, Resnick thought, was the more you brooded on things, the more significant they became. Of course, he didn't know what it had been like for Prior, spending all that time inside. Except, he guessed, the last thing he would want to do was get back in again. Resnick remembered, as clearly as if it had been days and not years, the look on Prior's face when they had stood, the pair of them, face to face in that garage: the look in Prior's eyes. Fear that had locked Resnick's muscles, knotted his stomach. The only time in his life he had been threatened with a gun. And Prior, thinking more clearly, pragmatic, weighing up the odds. The sounds of other officers outside. The way he had reversed the weapon and handed it across the roof of the car, what might almost have been a smile lighting up his eyes.

Resnick downed his vodka and pushed away the glass: there had to be a risk the prison review committee and the parole board had erred in their judgement, that Pam Van Allen, however experienced, had had the wool pulled over her eyes. It was a risk he had to minimize.

He slipped a coin into the phone box in the hall and dialled Lynn Kellogg's number from memory.

Lorna had opened the bottle half an hour back, eaten half the nuts. The crumblings of cork that had gone into the glass she had picked out with her fingernail, sliding them over the rim. She drank it without concern for the taste, gulping it down as if it were cherryade. No way he was coming now. She was midway through her second glass when the door bell rang and she jumped, startled, spilling it on to her hand and arm, tiny splashes across the front of her cream top.

Damn!

Kevin Naylor stood on the top step in a dark suit, pale blue shirt, maroon-and-grey striped tie, an apologetic look upon his face. 'Work,' he said. 'Last moment, something came up. Sorry I'm late.'

He wasn't about to confess to sitting round the corner in the car the best part of twenty minutes wrestling ineffectively with his conscience.

'That's okay,' Lorna smiled, reaching for his arm as if afraid he might run away. 'Come on inside.'

The room was warm and comfortable-looking, two small lamps burning, knick-knacks that Lorna had been attracted to dotted around on odd surfaces, a pair of stuffed yellow bears pushed together on a low bookshelf in the alcove.

'Don't sit there,' Lorna said, as Naylor began to lower himself into the one armchair. 'This is a lot more comfortable,' patting the cushions of the settee. 'I was just having a drink,' she said. 'What can I get you?'

'No, it's okay, thanks.'

'There's wine or beer. Cold lager in the fridge.' Standing in the kitchen doorway, Lorna smiled at him and wished now she'd stuck with her new button-through skirt instead of the black trousers she was sure emphasized her hips.

'Lager's fine,' Naylor said.

Lynn pulled into the car park at the front of the Polish Club moments before Resnick extricated himself from a one-sided conversation with a committee member and stepped through the door.

'Hope I'm not dragging you away from anything important,' Resnick said as the car slowed for the roundabout at the foot of Sherwood Rise.

'Writing to my mum,' Lynn said with a resigned smile. 'Been putting it off for over a week. Another day or so's hardly going to matter.'

'How are things?' Resnick asked. 'Your dad any better?'

Lynn shook her head. 'Still not sleeping. Fretting himself half to death about his chickens. Mum keeps trying to get him to go to the doctor but he refuses. Claims there's nothing wrong with him.'

'Any chance he's right?'

'Lost nearly two stone in four months. He wasn't big to begin with.'

'Maybe you should take some time off? Go home.'

'Yes, I expect you're right.' She lost her patience with the driver in front and swung wide to overtake before the lights. 'That's what my mum says, anyhow.'

'So how many times is it you've seen him?' Kevin Naylor asked. He was leaning back against one arm of the settee, Lorna facing him, one leg tucked beneath her, the other one inches away from brushing his own.

'Four or five,' she said. 'That at least.'

'And that's definite? I mean, each occasion, you're positive it was him? The same bloke came into the office that afternoon?'

'I'm not going to forget that in a hurry, am I?'

'No, I suppose not.'

'That poor old boy, the way he got hit round the head.'

'When you've seen him,' Naylor asked, 'he hasn't, well, he hasn't threatened you in any way?'

'No, but you see that's what I don't like about it. Not that I want him to, you know, threaten me or anything. But it's the way he looks at me, this sort of grin, as though there was some big secret between us and I knew what it was.'

Naylor lifted the can from the table and realized it was empty.

'I'll get you another.'

250

'No, you're all right.'

But she was already on her way, hand smoothing along his shoulder as she squeezed between the edge of the settee and the low table.

'The worst thing is,' Lorna said, coming back into the room, 'I get this feeling he's watching me, other times as well. Even here, in the flat.'

'Inside?'

She shook her head. 'Out there, I suppose. Like he's watching me come in and out.'

'But you've not seen him? Hanging around?'

'Only at work, nearby.'

Naylor smiled reassuringly. 'Likely you're getting all worked up over nothing.'

'Am I?' Lorna handed him the can, fingers accidentally pressing against his.

She sat on the arm of the settee and he shifted along but not far. Through the thin material of her trousers, he could feel the warmth of her leg against his side.

'Kevin?'

'Um?'

'Your wife, what time's she expecting you home?'

'She isn't.'

Lorna reached for his hand, width of her fingers easily masking his ring.

Rylands had been down in the cellar when Resnick and Lynn Kellogg had arrived; someone had told him that old copies of music papers were selling for a pound a throw down in London and he was sorting through his copies of *Melody Maker* and the *NME*, thinking to make an accurate list of exactly what he had. He led Resnick and Lynn into the kitchen and made a pot of tea.

'This matter we talked about before,' Resnick said.

'Which one?'

'Ruth first.'

'I still don't know anything definite.'

Resnick wasn't sure if he was telling the truth or hoping to bargain. 'Prior's a lot closer to getting out. Could be any time.'

Rylands half-turned. 'I'll do what I can.'

'Your son,' Lynn Kellogg said, 'you do want us to do what we can to help him?'

'Yes, of course. Like I said, he's not really a bad lad, it's more . . .'

'You've spoken to him?' Lynn pressed. 'You know he's willing to co-operate?'

'Not in so many words, no. Not exactly.'

Resnick was quickly to his feet, Lynn following suit. 'If you don't want him back inside, Keith, I shouldn't waste a lot more time. If he goes down again . . .'

Resnick moved towards the door, letting the sentence hang.

'Thanks for the tea,' Lynn said.

They were at the end of the narrow hall before Rylands called them back. 'About Ruth, I did hear something. Just a whisper. Nothing definite.'

Resnick felt himself relax; he was close to smiling as he turned. 'Check it out. Be sure. You know the deal. I get to Ruth in time, we'll go easy as we can on your Keith. Just as long as he's prepared to talk to us.'

'Yes,' Rylands nodded. 'I know.'

'DC Kellogg here,' Resnick said, 'that's who Keith will be dealing with.' Lynn reached out and opened the front door. 'Twenty-four hours,' Resnick said, 'I think that's all we can afford.'

# Thirty-Nine

'Hey up, kid!' Divine exclaimed the moment Naylor entered the office. 'You look shagged out, you.'

'Give over, Mark,' Naylor said. 'Just for once.'

'Didn't know you and your Debbie were back together again,' Divine grinned.

'We're not.'

'Oh, hey. Clocked that, everybody? Our Kev's been getting his leg over in the line of duty. Not.'

'Leave it alone, Mark,' Lynn Kellogg sang out from the far side of the room.

'Who was she?' Divine goaded, leaning over Naylor, who had that second slumped behind his desk. 'That bird you were taking a statement from? Right tasty that. Shouldn't mind having a go at that meself. Two's up, eh?'

Naylor's chair went flying as he sprang to his feet, squaring up to Divine, ready for all the world to take a swing at him then and there and to hell with the consequences.

'Come on then,' Divine said, stepping back to give himself room. 'Any time you reckon you're man enough to try it.'

'Try what?' Millington asked from the doorway, freezing the action before it had started. 'Well? Kevin? Mark?'

Naylor shook his head and sat back down, leaving

Divine with his fists clenched, adrenaline pumped and nowhere to go.

'Get down the health club last night?' Millington asked him.

'Yes, sarge,' Divine said.

'Anything useful? New?'

'I think so. Maybe.'

'Good. On account the super wants to see us, ten minutes sharp. Any notes you've got, best make sure they're to the point. He'll not thank us for wasting his time.'

Divine nodded and headed back to his desk. Millington waited until he was settled before bending close to his ear. 'I don't know who started that little lot . . .'

'All I did was . . .'

'Don't know and don't want to know. But hark to this: what you're doing, walking a very thin line. There's them as'd be well pleased to see you fall off it. Carry on the way you're going, likely they'll get their wish. Right?'

Without looking round at the sergeant, Divine nodded.

'Understood?'

'Yes, sarge.'

'Good.' Millington straightened. 'Nine minutes and counting. Buckle to.'

Naylor kept his head down, accepted the mug of tea Lynn Kellogg offered with a nod, he'd tried to get this incident report filled out three times now and still couldn't get past the first few lines. One of those days it was difficult to spell your own name. Three o'clock when finally he'd got back last night. Who was he kidding? It had been a lot closer to four. And then he'd scarcely been able to sleep. Roaming round the house, rolling the breadth of that empty bed. 'Stay,' Lorna had said.

'What's the point in going home now?' He'd tried to explain without ever himself knowing why. 'You've said, your wife's stopping over at her mum's. So who's to know?' What he hadn't told her, his wife had been stopping over at her mum's the best part of a year.

Light of six this morning, he'd been in the kitchen mashing tea, eating toast with raspberry jam; replaying the night over and over in his mind. My God! One thing he'd always thought, Debbie and himself, their sex life had been pretty good, up till she'd fallen for the baby at least. What he now realized was how much, in their ignorance, they'd been missing. Or maybe it had just been him who'd known no better – his experience hadn't exactly amounted to much. Red-faced fumblings upstairs at the Savoy; tussles in the car park up the street from Madison's and once on a patch of grass in Wollaton Park overlooked by a small herd of grazing deer. Debbie had been the first woman he'd slept with, the first he properly made love to, just as he'd been the first for her.

He hung his head and sighed.

Most likely Debbie did know a lot more about it than him, all those articles in magazines, orgasms, arousal – what was it? – G-spots? Maybe she'd lain there night after night, waiting for him to do stuff he'd barely thought of; wanting him to but too shy to ask.

Unlike Lorna: an education in herself.

And nice. The way she said nothing about his inexperience, though it must have been obvious enough. Funny, too. Stories she'd told him about the people at work.

Why then had he left there thinking of Debbie, more so, more seriously than in a long time? He'd made his gesture a long while back, left a message asking her to call and he hadn't heard a thing. What if Divine was right and it was really over, had been for months though neither of them was admitting it? But then they weren't denying it either; they weren't even talking.

He screwed the form into a ball and dropped it in the bin, pulled another one towards him. If he and Debbie no longer had a marriage, why the guilt that he'd been feeling creeping home? How much did that guilt bring to the excitement of what he'd done?

'Now then, Charlie,' Skelton said. He was retying the lace of his Nike Air Tech shoes, the ones with pockets of inert gas in the soles to help with shock absorption. Nigh on a hundred pounds and worth every penny. 'Seems these lads of yours might be on to something. Whispers young Divine's been picking up about some kind of French involvement in these robberies, didn't look to be panning out at first. Sight too fanciful, aside from anything else. But rechecking passenger flight lists into East Midlands, back from Birmingham, could be something to it.'

Resnick nodded, increasingly conscious that mayonnaise was beginning to seep through the brown paper bag in his hand.

'Thought we might let the pair of them fly over, Paris. Little gentle fraternization. See if they can tie things together.'

'Millington and Divine?' Resnick said with vague incredulity.

'Bound to happen more and more. Just wait till that bloody tunnel's up and running.'

'Even so.'

Skelton decided to do a little gentle limbering up on the spot. 'They'll cope right enough. Besides, Graham Millington, got a bit of a thing for languages, hasn't he?'

'I think that's his wife.'

'Oh, well, he's no fool. He'll cope.'

Resnick transferred the sandwich from one hand to another; set it down on the ground and Skelton was likely to land one of his size tens on it. 'I was more concerned about Divine. My guess, he travels about as well as the average English soccer fan. Out of his head before the plane's started circling Orly Airport.'

Skelton was bracing himself against the wall, stretching his hamstrings. 'He's the one put in all the spadework, Charlie. Credit where credit's due.'

Resnick shrugged and stepped back. 'Your decision, sir, not mine.'

'Yes, well, I'll give some thought to what you say. Any movement on this other business you've got yourself stuck on? Prior, is it?'

Resnick nodded. 'Due out any day. I'm keeping an eye.'

Skelton lifted first one foot then the other hard against his buttocks. 'Bit of a sideshow, isn't it, Charlie? My way of thinking. Wouldn't want to explain away too many man-hours boxing with shadows. Chasing old ghosts. Eh, Charlie?'

The superintendent moved off with a sprightly step, leaving Resnick to walk heavily up the stairs towards his office. As Resnick knew, ghosts could be real enough and you ignored them at your peril.

'Wondered if you'd spoken with your Pam Van Allen?' Resnick said, when he'd raised Neil Park on the phone. 'Since she and I had a chat.'

'Only briefly.' Something about the connection made it sound as if the senior probation officer were standing in a deep hole. 'I got the impression she resented the degree to which you were putting her under pressure.'

'I didn't think that's what I was doing at all.'

'Come on, Charlie. You're male, more experienced, high-ranking, used to telling people what to do and

257

expecting them to do it. Other ways of applying pressure than waving a big stick.'

'It wasn't what I intended,' Resnick said.

'I daresay. All I'm saying is, whatever you were hoping for, you might just have pushed her the wrong way.'

'It shouldn't be to do with any of that,' Resnick said. 'All I want is for her to be aware of the risks . . .'

'What you want is for Prior to stay locked away.'

'It'd make life a lot easier all round.'

'But not for him, eh, Charlie? Not for Prior.'

'Look . . .'

'Sorry, Charlie. Rushed off my feet. Got to go.' The voice fell lower into the pit and finally disappeared, leaving Resnick staring at a dead telephone and a half-eaten chicken and Jarlsberg salad sandwich.

Kevin Naylor had walked around in his lunch break, window shopping in Saxone's and the Camera Exchange and what had once been Horne Brothers but was now a bizarre floating market offering T-shirts, three for £5.00, assorted CDs £2.99 each. When he finally convinced himself to make the call, he was so worked up the coins fell between his fingers and rolled across the floor.

'Debbie?'

He knew if her mother answered he was sunk and the pleasure at hearing his wife's voice would have been hard to fake.

'Kevin?'

Debbie was surprised to hear his voice at all, never mind the tone; surprised to the point where she came close to seeming pleased herself. 'I don't think it's such a good idea, though,' she interrupted him, 'you coming round.'

'That wasn't what I meant,' Kevin said, taking the bit between his teeth. 'What I thought was, you could ask

258

your mum to look after the baby, I'm sure she wouldn't mind. Meet me in the city. Go somewhere for a meal. Somewhere nice.'

There was a silence at the other end of the line and Kevin braced himself for the worst, but 'All right,' Debbie said, still sounding doubtful. 'I'll have to check with Mum, though.'

'I'll meet you in Yates's,' Kevin said, quick before she could change her mind. 'That upstairs bar. You know, looking out over the square. Debbie? Okay?'

'Yes, I suppose . . .'

'Eight o'clock. See you. Bye.'

He rang off before she had a chance to say anything more. In the small rectangle of glass at the centre of the box, he could see his eyes were unusually bright and there was perspiration on his skin. He knew, without having to look, that his hands were shaking.

# Forty

Something about the Citroën DS had always rated Keith's attention. Not that there was anything special about the performance; plenty of run-of-the-mill motors would whip you along the fast lane of the motorway in half the time. It was more the look of it, that smooth front which helped to make the whole machine seem longer than it really was. And the suspension. Keith had read up on it once, a wet afternoon going through the motoring magazines in the library on Angel Row. What had it been now? Hydrophonic? No. Hydromatic? Anyway, hydro-something, one of those, Nitrogen gas and fluid, he remembered that. Like riding on air.

He'd come close to nicking one before, this great DS 23 Pallas, right-hand drive, 5-speed manual gearbox; he'd spotted it gliding off the ramp from the NCP car park at the top of Barker Gate. Practically wet himself, hadn't he? Hung out there morning and afternoon the next five days, hoping to get close to it again. No such stinking luck.

But today, sheltering by the bus stops below the Broad Marsh from a sudden shower, he'd seen another, black with whitewall tyres, queuing to get into the multi-storey opposite. DS 21, fuel injection, semi-automatic. High on the top floor, sandwiched between a Fiat Uno and a Metro, that was where he found it. Smooth to the touch. Half an hour and the floor would be full, few motors driving in and out. Keith gave it a quick kiss on the roof for luck and scurried away to the stairs to wait.

All Darren could do that morning, sitting across from Keith in the West End Arcade, not to tell him to fuck off out of his life and have done with it. Keith, fussing around with the ketchup bottle, jinking little dollops of it over the inside of his sausage cob, forever trying to talk him out of it. Too risky. Too close to the last time. Too likely to end up getting caught. That was what Keith was pissing his pants about, getting sent back inside. Knowing they'd be after his arse the moment his feet hit the floor. Miserable little bastard, days like this, Darren was forced to think it served him right. Days like this he thought he should have let Keith go ahead and hang himself, no great loss to the world.

Finally, Darren had had enough. 'Listen,' he'd said, grabbing Keith by the front of his jumper, 'half-two, top of King Street, you be there.'

'With a motor?'

'No, what d'you think, going to give me a piggy-back, all the way to Bestwood.'

'Where you going now?' Keith had asked, almost plaintively, watching Darren heading for the exit.

'Never you mind, I've got things to do. Just do your side, right? And this time, don't be late.'

One of the things Darren had to do, collect a few supplies. The assistant had been too preoccupied in trying out some new computer game to pay him much attention. Little green men who either changed into trees or else were eaten by dragons, zapped by spears.

'Hey mate!' Darren had finally called. 'You work here or what?'

The name on his tag read Robert, pinned to the front

of his navy blue long-sleeved sweater. From the look on his face, Darren was more of a nuisance than anything else.

'You remember hearing about that robbery?' Darren asked, casual as you like, choosing to ignore the salesman's indifference. 'Where they all wore those Mickey Mouse masks, like, sort of disguise?'

'Oh,' the assistant said, already bored, 'happens all the time.'

'Yeh? Well, you got any like that? Here?'

'Life-size masks?'

'Yes.'

Stifling a yawn, Robert wandered off, to come back some minutes later with a selection that ranged from an over-jolly Friar Tuck to Cruella de Ville. 'This sort of thing?'

Darren slipped Catwoman over his close-cropped hair and adjusted it so that he could focus through the slotted eyes.

'How about guns?' Darren asked, having to shout through the mask to make himself heard.

'What kind?'

'Pistols. Something that looks pretty life-like.'

Robert brought him a black plastic Colt .45 and a metallic grey snub-nosed .38 with NYPD in relief on the butt.

'Okay,' said Darren, taking hold of the Colt and pointing it at him. 'Empty the till into one of these bags.'

'What is this? Some kind of joke? You know as well as I do that's just a toy gun.'

Darren reversed it and slashed him hard across the face, cracking the plastic and tearing the skin alongside the eye. In seconds he was reaching over the till, loosening the cash drawer, grabbing bank notes, fives and twenties and tens, from beneath the roller clips that held them down.

The assistant called out and made a grab for Darren's leg. Swivelling on the ball of one foot, Darren kicked him in the throat. 'Like you say, Robert,' Darren said, voice muffled through his Catwoman mask, 'this kind of thing happens all the time.'

When he ran past the baked potato salesman, the newspaper seller advertising *Viz*, the old boy playing 'K-K-K-Katy' on his harmonica, back up the steps that took him towards the Playhouse and the old General Hospital, nobody as much as looked twice.

'Where the hell d'you get this?' Darren asked, throwing himself into the front seat.

'Broad Marsh, why?'

'If you wanted to advertise, wonder you didn't hi-jack one of them buses with slogans all over the sides.'

'It's a DS,' Keith said, striving for the proper respect. 'Collector's item. Give an arm and a leg for one of these.'

Darren gave him a quick flash of the Colt .45. 'Let's hope it don't come to that, he grinned.'

The building society office was close to a cinema whose final programme had been a double bill of Jerry Lewis in *The Bell Boy* and Elvis Presley as a half-breed American Indian in *Flaming Star*. Since then it had been a cut-price furniture store, a Kwik-Save supermarket and a Fast-Fit tyre centre. Now it was standing empty, boarded up. Keith swung the Citroën smoothly on to the forecourt, applied the handbrake and left the engine running. So quiet, it was like listening to a CD between the tracks.

'Don't go anywhere,' Darren said.

'Sure you don't want me to come with you?' Keith

asked, hoping the answer would be no. He was enjoying this less and less.

'After last time?' Darren laughed. he had the mask stuffed inside his zipped-up jacket, the broken handle of the toy gun poking out of his trouser belt. 'Second you see me come back out that door, that's when you move. Right?'

Nervously, Keith nodded.

There were two people queuing inside the building society, a man in plasterer's overalls and a woman with a shopping trolley, waiting in front of a video monitor that was entertaining them with a tape loop testifying to the virtues of borrowing to your credit limit. Own a yacht. A time-share in the Scottish Highlands.

At the counter an Afro-Caribbean woman was checking that her wages had been credited to her account that month. Darren waited until she moved away and slipped into her place, circumventing the queue.

'Hey up!' said the plasterer. 'Think we're stood here for us health?'

'There is a queue, sir,' said the clerk. It was only when she looked up properly that she realized the person who had pushed to the front was wearing some kind of mask.

'All the cash you've got,' Darren said. 'Hand it over.'

'Here!' the plasterer made a move forwards and Darren pulled the pistol from his belt and waved it in the man's face.

'Oh, dear God!' the woman with the shopping trolley exclaimed and wavered sideways, colliding with the television set and knocking it from its stand on to the floor.

'Eunice,' Darren said, reading her name from the badge attached to the apricot uniform blouse, 'don't bother counting it, just push in through here. The lot.'

Another employee came through from the back, wondering what all the commotion was about. A quick look and they ducked back from sight.

'That's not a real gun,' the plasterer exclaimed. 'It's only a chuffing toy!'

'Eunice,' Darren said, seizing the last bundle of fifties and stuffing them into his pocket, 'anyone ever told you you're a darling?'

Later on, giving her account to the reporter from *East Midlands Today*, Eunice had to giggle; the last time she'd been called darling had been by a mechanical parrot at Goose Fair. Made her jump half out of her skin it had. 'D'you know,' she confided in the camera, 'gave me more of a turn than what happened this afternoon.'

Keith saw Darren dart through the door and eased his foot on to the accelerator. 'What on earth you wearing that for?' he asked as Darren sat there, chuckling to himself beneath the mask.

'Video cameras,' Darren said.

'What?'

Darren pulled the mask over his head and pushed it under the seat. 'Video cameras. On the ceiling. Got them in that branch haven't they?' He laughed. 'What d'you reckon, I want to see myself like a fool, plastered all over every TV in the country, next edition of *Crimewatch*?'

Sweating more than a little, Keith bit gently into the inside of his lower lip as he tested the engine's acceleration along a clear stretch of the ring road.

'Know what?' Darren said happily, counting the notes into his lap. 'Lot more here'n I bargained for.' Reaching across, he gave Keith's leg an enthusiastic squeeze. 'Our luck holds, soon be able to buy yourself one of these.'

# Forty-One

Jeans? Debbie used to say how much she liked him in jeans; about the only time he didn't look like a policeman. Trouble was, he never really felt comfortable in them. Not the pair he was wearing now, Levi Silver Tabs he'd bought eighteen months back at Bankrupt Clothing Company, nor the ones he'd got in the Gap sale. Simply, they didn't feel right. Like going out on an under-cover and being spotted within the first few minutes. He pulled them off and draped them over the back of the chair. Where were those beige jobs he'd worn to the last police smoker? Those and the dark jacket, the blazer, at least he felt smart in that without being dressed up like a dog's dinner. All that was left now was the tie, yes or no, finally deciding no, much too formal, definitely not, then slipping it into his side pocket in case he felt like changing his mind.

Any minute now the taxi would be here.

Watch, credit card, cash, keys.

Kevin hesitated by the bathroom door; the aftershave with a tang of lime – was that the one brought Debbie out in a rash or not?

Divine had stopped off at WH Smith no more than ten minutes before closing. 'These tapes,' he'd asked, pointing towards a boxed set of *French in Five Easy Stages*, 'they any good?'

The assistant thought Divine looked more the type for

Club Med, somewhere with a beach and sun enough to show off a good body. 'We do sell a lot,' she said hopefully.

'Yes, but do they work?'

She giggled lightly. Not bad, Divine thought, take away the crossed front teeth and surplus facial hair, fair pair of tits though, wouldn't mind giving it a pull.

'See, I'm off to Paris. Pretty soon. Business.'

'Oh. Well, there is this one here, two double-length cassettes or one CD and accompanying booklet. See? *Eurospeak Languages for Today's Businessman*. That might be more the kind of thing.'

'Thing I'm looking for,' Divine confided, leaning a well-muscled arm on the top of her counter, 'something more personal. You know, relaxing after hours. Hard day's graft. Can't enjoy the night life, no point in going. Stay here and get legless at the Black Orchid, eh?'

'Miss Armitage,' the supervisor sang out like a frost in summer, 'let's see you cashing up now.'

'What d'you reckon then?' The picture on the box showed a girl with a long blonde pony tail and a black beret, pointing excitedly up to the Eiffel Tower. 'Biggest one she's ever seen.'

Maybe he wasn't cut out for Club Med after all, the assistant thought. Works outing to Skegness, more his kind of thing. 'I'm sorry,' she said, 'but we are closing now.'

Divine settled for a pocket phrase book and a paperback visitor's guide to Paris, thumbing through the latter as he stepped out on the pedestrian precinct, stopping short at the picture of a girl in a scarlet G-string from the Crazy Horse Saloon. A mother with a pushchair ran into the back of him and most of the child's Mr Whippy ice cream slid down his leg.

'What the chuffin' heck d'you think you're doing?' Divine bellowed.

'It's you, you great lummux!' the woman shouted back. 'Parking your great backside right in front of us without a by-your-leave. What've you got in that head of yours for brains, sawdust or what?'

And she swung pushchair and wailing child around him, leaving Divine to wipe away the ice cream that was still slithering down his second-best pair of trousers.

Naylor stood close by the plate glass front of the upstairs, looking out at the groups who were beginning to swarm the square. Down the hill from the Concert Hall and the Theatre Royal, along St James Street and past the Bell opposite; from the right past the cinemas, the Odeon and Cannon, spreading the length of the old Market Square itself, past the fountains and the lions to the underground lavatories and the mobile stall selling hot pork rolls and beefburgers with glistening onions. Pushing and shoving and laughing. The police van alongside the bus stop. Listening to the plods in the canteen it got worse week by week, month by month, but Naylor remembered Resnick saying that when he'd been out there in uniform twenty years ago there'd been trouble Friday, Saturday nights just the same.

He wondered about finishing his half and going back into the bar to fetch another, maybe get one for Debbie too, save queuing later when she turned up. If she turned up. He was rehearsing her excuses in his head – my mother, the baby – when he saw her alighting from a double-decker over on Beast Market Hill. Dark blue skirt or dress, silvery top, thin blue jacket, leather bag slung over one arm. Forehead pressed against the inside of the glass, he waited for her to look up and, stepping off the crossing on to the broad curve of pavement below, and, smiling with surprise at her own pleasure, that was what she did.

Keith knew chances were if he simply dumped the Citröen, abandoned it, it would get trashed before it was found. Normally that was part of the point, only this was not a normal car. Gliding along the A52 on his way back into the city, engine close to silent, suspension like feathers, Keith thought he'd died and gone to heaven.

He knew it was a risk, but for the first time ever, he was determined to return the motor to the exact spot where he'd found it.

Our luck holds, Darren had said, you'll be able to buy one of your own. Keith chewed at a hangnail on the little finger of his right hand. Mixture of his luck and Darren's stupidity and he could see himself ending up back in court. Back in prison. Just thinking about it was enough to turn his bowels to water. Never in his miserable life had he been as serious as when he'd tried to top himself in that cell. And Darren, hollering for help, unfastening the sheet and lifting him down. What for? So that he'd have some-one to boss around the rest of his life? Someone to look up to him, run errands, steal cars, drive him from one increasingly risky robbery to another.

Hear him running off at the mouth before Keith had dropped him off. About how he was going to trade up from that pathetic toy pistol to a real one; how he was going to walk in on that Lorna Solomon and show it to her, see the look on her face, do the thing right.

Keith had felt grateful to him for saving his life, in a way at least: each day now he was less and less sure. Turning with the traffic in front of the big MGM night club, Keith indicated that he was moving across into the inside lane, looking to park.

\*

'Where are we going?' Debbie asked, as Kevin Naylor took her arm and steered her around a group of young white males in short-sleeved white shirts.

'You'll see,' he grinned. 'Surprise.'

The restaurant was quite dimly lit, tasteful, round tables with a single flower in a white vase at its centre; the menus were padded and thick and pages long.

'What d'you think?' Kevin said, looking round. He'd asked Graham Millington, who went out for a meal with his wife first Friday after payday, regular as clockwork. Lynn Kellogg too. The consensus seemed to be, of all the Chinese restaurants in the city, this was probably the best.

'It's nice,' Debbie admitted. 'Only . . .'

'Only what?'

Only you know I'm not all that keen on Chinese food, was what she'd been going to say, but instead she shook her head and gave him a quick smile and said, 'Oh, nothing.'

He had looked nice standing up there in Yates's, waiting for her, really nice, and although talking at first had been a bit of a strain, now they were both beginning to feel more relaxed.

'You watch out for him,' her mum had said, 'got to be after something, you mark my words.' Then she'd got that look on her face, the one she'd paraded when Debbie had first told her she was moving back home, smug and prophetic. 'I wouldn't mind betting he's found himself somebody else, that's what this is all about. Wanting to talk you into one of those do-it-yourself divorces. You see if he isn't.'

If that was the case, Debbie thought, he'd hardly be sitting there, wedding ring shining from the back of his hand. Without warning, she thought she might be about to cry so she picked up her bag and excused herself, went to the ladies, leaving Kevin to order.

Keith phoned his mum and his stepfather answered so he hung up; his dad was still hauling bundles of old papers and magazines up from the cellar, sorting through and arranging them in piles all over the front room floor.

Keith made himself baked beans on toast and ate it watching TV. If there had been a tape player in the first-floor room he'd taken over as his own, he would have gone up there and listened to some Luther Ingram or some David Peaston, Galliano or Dream Warriors except that he didn't have the tapes either, they were still back at his mum's. Truth was he didn't know what on earth he did want to do.

When his dad stuck his head round the door and asked if he fancied lending him a hand, Keith shrugged and said, 'Why not?'

It turned out to be simple enough. Check through the pages to make sure they were all there, nothing torn out or otherwise missing; if it was all okay write down the date and issue number.

'What's all this in aid of?' Keith asked.

'Making a few bob.'

'For this old crap?'

When his dad explained it to him, Keith was really surprised. Though he knew youths who'd lash out just about everything they had on some comic or other; ten pounds for one in Japanese and then you couldn't read the words. No accounting for some people's taste.

'Fancy a beer?' Rylands asked after they'd been working half an hour or so.

'I thought you'd given it up?'

'Doesn't mean you've got to. I'm having tea myself.'

'Tea's fine.'

While they were drinking it, Rylands sounded Keith out on his idea of hiring a stall in the market, Fridays and Saturdays at first, selling back numbers of *NME* and stuff like that, jazz magazines – kids were supposed to be interested in jazz, weren't they? – maybe other things. He'd wandered into one of the second-hand bookshops on the Mansfield Road and come across a couple of hundred mixed film magazines, copies of *Picture Post* as well, made an offer for the lot. Bloke was holding them for him till the Monday. Him and Keith trawled round a few car boot sales and the like, they'd soon pick up more stock.

'So,' Rylands said, sitting cross-legged, leaning back against the wall. 'What d'you think? Reckon it'd work?'

'Might.'

'You're interested then?'

'Me?'

'Why not? What else you got to do?'

Keith shrugged and made a face.

'Thought, you know, we could run it together.'

'I'd lose my dole.'

'Not necessarily. Depends how we work it. And anyway, what d'you want, be on the dole the rest of your life?'

'No.'

'Well, then. Why not give it a try?'

Keith shook his head. 'I don't know.'

Rylands finished his tea and pushed himself to his feet. 'Best get on. Plenty of time for you to think about it. Might be a bit of fun though. Laugh if nothing else.'

'What about Darren?' Keith asked, staring at the front page of a *Melody Maker* from 1959: '*Emile Ford and the Checkmates to Headline Moss Empires Tour.*'

'What about Darren?'

'He'll expect me to be with him.'

'Don't you worry about Darren,' Rylands said, bending to take Keith's empty cup from his hands. 'I've got ideas how to deal with him.'

'It tasted different somehow,' Debbie said.

They were standing inside the hallway of the starter home she and Kevin had first moved into, the one where he still lived.

'Least come in and have some coffee,' Kevin had said as the taxi that was meant to be dropping him off drew close. 'You can always get another cab in a bit.'

They'd got inside the front door and not much further; hadn't as much as switched on the hall light.

'What tastes different?' Kevin said, kissing her again.

When they moved their mouths apart minutes later, she could sense him grinning at her in the dark. 'Not this,' she said.

'What then?'

'The meal. Chinese meal. Find it so salty as a rule.'

'Ah,' Kevin said, grin widening, 'that's because I asked them to hold back the monosodium glutamate, I expect.'

'I didn't know you could do that.'

'Oh, yes. Just a matter of knowing what to ask.'

She laughed and reached inside his jacket, tickling him, and they ended up on the floor.

'Kevin, no.' Though there was something specially exciting, Debbie thought, about being there, so close to the front door.

'No, we can't.' The only place she and Kevin had ever made love was in bed, their own bed or a bed and breakfast.

'Kevin!'

His hand was high on her tights, ball of his thumb starting to apply pressure . . .

'No!'

'What?'

She smoothed down her skirt and drew her knees towards her chest.

'We are still married, you know.'

'I know.'

'So?'

'Kevin, switch on the light.'

'You're angry, aren't you?'

'No. No, I'm not.' She reached for his hand and held it. 'Really, I'm not.'

'What is it, then?'

Even though it was dark and she could see little more than the outline of his face, Debbie looked away. 'I'm not on the pill any more. There didn't seem to be any point.'

'So?'

'I don't suppose you've got anything with you. Any, you know, protection.'

'There's a twenty-four hour garage not far. They're bound to sell them. I could nip and . . .'

'Kevin, no. Maybe it's not such a good idea this time anyway.' He sighed and she gave his hand a squeeze. 'I'm not rejecting you, you know.'

'No? Well, that's what it feels like.'

Debbie laughed and deftly moved her other hand. 'No, Kevin, *that's* what it feels like.'

He laughed, surprised, and reached for her again, but she was quickly to her feet and they were both blinking in the sudden light. 'What about that coffee?' she said. 'While you're getting the kettle on, I'll order a taxi.'

'You could stay.'

'I know. I will. One step at a time, hm?'

Kevin grinned and kissed her on her forehead and alongside her ear and, quickly, at the corner of her mouth and, still grinning, walked off into the kitchen.

# Forty-Two

'The hostel we spoke about,' Pam Van Allen said, 'it's all fixed up.'

She waited for Prior to respond but, of course, that wasn't necessarily what he did. Most people, ordinary people, the kind you bump into at parties, supermarkets, dentists' waiting rooms, make a remark like that and they react. 'Oh, really?' Or 'That's good.' A grunt even. Something that helps the conversation along.

Whereas Prior . . .

It was enough for him today to continue to stare at her, not threatening exactly, nothing sexual the way it would be with a lot of men, locked away without the benefits of conjugal visits. Prior simply stared. And waited. Okay, you're here, doing what you're paid to do, now say what you have to say.

Pam crossed one leg over the other, automatically smoothing her skirt past her knee. 'Big, old Victorian house over by Alexandra Park. Really nice.' She paused. 'I don't know whether you know it round there?'

This time there was a grunt of kinds, not expressive enough for Pam to tell if it meant yes or no. Perhaps he'd simply been clearing his throat.

'Anyway, like I say, it is very nice. Kept up better than a number of hostels we use, I'd have to say that.' She saw his eyes shift focus towards her hands and realized that she'd been fidgeting with the silver ring she wore

275

on the little finger of her right hand. 'You will be sharing, a room I mean. Did I mention that before?'

Prior shook his head.

'Sorry, thought I had. Two of you most likely. It's the only thing about the rooms being so big. All the usual regulations, pretty much what you'd expect. No alcohol, no drugs. Restrictions about visitors, too. Up into the bedrooms, that is.' What was the matter with her? Why was she chattering on? She uncrossed her legs and eased back in the chair; held, for several seconds, her breath and returned his stare.

'As soon as you're released, we'll help you to look for work and accommodation, like I've said. Things like making sure you're on the housing list. Those flats above the Victoria Centre, they fall vacant pretty often. And then there are always the housing associations. They'll look sympathetically on your application as a matter of principle.'

The air inside the room seemed to be getting thinner and thinner. Pam wanted to dart a glance towards her watch, but didn't like to try. She seemed to have been talking for ages now, a barely assisted monologue. Prior listening, not caring; as if none of this had anything to do with him. As if she were making plans for somebody else.

'Your wife . . .' the words were out before she could stop them.

'Ruth,' Prior said.

'Yes.'

'What about her?'

'I was just, I suppose, wondering, well, if you'd thought any more about maybe trying to get in touch with her.'

'Should I?'

Pam gestured vaguely with both hands. 'I don't know.

276

I mean, no. I don't think there's any should about it. It's not a case, I mean, of obligation.'

Now he was staring again, feeling the pressure she had put herself under, enjoying it.

'Sometimes,' Pam said carefully, finding her way, 'especially when couples haven't seen one another for a long time, there's a sense of – what shall I say? – unfinished business. Things that have gone unsaid for too long. A lot of stuff that has to be cleared away before people can get on with their lives.'

'People?'

'Yes.'

'Ruthie and me.'

'Yes, I mean, I suppose . . . I just thought . . .'

'No,' Prior said. 'I don't think so. Like I said, that was all a long time ago.'

Pam got to her feet; she was feeling shaky but she would have found it hard to have said exactly why.

'Besides,' Prior said, 'I don't even know where she is.'

'I'll see you again,' Pam said, 'on the day of your release. After that, it will need to be weekly. You can make an appointment to come to the office, regular, that will be best.'

Prior nodded agreement and got to his feet, once again offering her his hand, cool and calloused and dry.

Resnick was at home when the call came. One thing and another he'd earned himself an hour or two off. For some time he'd employed a woman from up the road to come in one afternoon a week and keep the place clean, hoover and dust. Until Dizzy had nipped her ankle for the third week in succession it had worked out fine. Now there he was, lugging the old-fashioned Hoover up and down stairs, half-heartedly rubbing lavender furniture polish into the table in the dining room, working a balding squeezy mop over the kitchen floor.

Cat hairs everywhere.

He made it more palatable by playing music loud enough to be heard throughout the house. Eddie 'Lockjaw' Davis was rabble-rousing in front of the Basie Band when the phone started ringing; he didn't hear it until the first solo was over and the sound had diminished down to the sparse notes of the Count's piano.

He almost tripped over a distressed Bud, who'd been cat-napping on the landing, one paw folded over his eyes. Still mumbling apologies, Resnick lifted the receiver just in time.

'Said at the station you were there,' Rylands said. 'Thought they must've got it wrong.'

'Hang on a minute,' Resnick said. 'Let me turn this record down.'

'*Atomic Mister Basie*,' Rylands said when Resnick arrived back at the phone. 'Great record. I remember the first time . . .'

'What do you want?' Resnick asked.

'That arrangement we spoke of . . .' Rylands's voice was lower now, as though there were someone in the house he didn't want to overhear.

'What about it?'

'I think he'd be willing to talk, to that young woman, like we said.'

'Good. And the other matter?'

A slight pause and then, 'I'm not sure now, can't be positive, but, yet, I reckon I know where she might be.'

Lynn had picked Keith up several blocks away, close to the Portland Leisure Centre where she sometimes went for a morning swim, days it opened at seven-thirty, do your lengths in freedom before the first of the school parties arrived. She'd driven round on to the embankment and parked, Keith's response when she suggested walking little more than an inclination of the head. In the end, she had got out of the car and he had followed, the same as he had when she'd set off towards Wilford Bridge.

Now and again teams of rowers went past them, water splashing up in their wake, voices of the coxes clear and sharp as they urged them on. Asian families sat on the sloping grass, women together in brightly coloured saris, children playing in their midst; the men sat off to the side, dealing cards on to a rug.

She was surprised how small he was, how young his face: it was like walking with a shame-faced younger brother, a recalcitrant nephew. A son. A child, certainly. And yet she had seen his record, knew the time he had spent in YOIs. She had read the report of his attempted suicide. 'A feeble and misguided cry for help.'

'What's it like,' Lynn asked, 'living with your dad?'

'S'all right.'

'Better than living with your mum?'

'S'pose so.'

'When I was still living at home,' Lynn said, 'my mum, she always meant well, but she was forever fussing at me, why don't you do this, why don't you do that?' Lynn laughed, taking Keith by surprise. 'There I was, twenty years old, standing in her kitchen, taller than her by half a head, and she's still wetting the corner of her handkerchief with her tongue and aiming to wipe this bit of dirt I've got on my face. Got so I couldn't stand it at all.'

'Yes,' Keith said. 'I know what you mean.'

'Listen,' Lynn said, stopping to look back the way they'd come, 'why don't we walk back there to the

Memorial Gardens and sit down. Not too many people as a rule. Might be easier to talk.'

Except that the whole place was under the thrall of a monolithic tribute to Queen Victoria, it was a public garden like many another: beds of flowers carefully tended by council workmen, assorted trees and banks of shrubs, patches of lawn interrupted by gravel paths.

'You realize,' Lynn said, 'nothing that I've said's an absolute promise?'

'I'll not go back inside,' Keith said. 'I'll kill myself first.'

She laid her hand on the bare skin of his forearm and he flinched.

'Like I said, we'll do what we can. I'll do everything I can. I promise you that.' She waited until, for a second, his eyes flickered towards her face. 'As long as you keep your side of the bargain.'

'I've told you . . .'

'I know. But I have to be sure.'

Without difficulty, Keith conjured up Darren's face. That look in his eyes, that blue-grey brightness becoming brighter still as he toyed with the pistol in his hand. Next time, Keith knew, it was going to be real.

'It's okay,' Keith said quietly, staring at the ground. 'Long as you play straight with me, you'll get what you want. No mistake.'

# Forty-Three

He and Elaine had taken holidays here, Northumberland, a succession of rented cottages close to the coast – north from Amble and Alnmouth Bay, through Seahouses and Bamburgh to Berwick-upon-Tweed. The first had been the worst. The flat itself, upper floor of a smallholder's cottage, had been right enough; where it had fallen down was the panoramic view. An undisturbed vision of caravans at the rear; to the front, cabbage fields as far as the eye could follow. Somewhere beyond those acres of darkening green lay soft dunes and broad beaches, the slow roll of the North Sea.

'Take it on trust.' the owner had said. 'Me and the missus have for years. I'n't we pet?'

Resnick and Elaine had returned to other locations. The sands were largely deserted, stopped breathtakingly by castles, impressive in their decay. They had taken a boat out to the Farne Islands to see the puffins and sea birds; had walked the causeway over to Holy Island and had to run full into the wind on the way back so as not to be trapped by the tide.

They had made love in hired beds, often spurred on by a visit to the local pub, a meal eaten in unspoken anticipation. In part, it was what holidays were for.

It was difficult for Resnick as he turned east off the main road and headed towards the coast, to recall these things with pleasure.

The road narrowed and soon he was facing a T-junction

with no sign to suggest which way to turn. Stopping to use the map, nevertheless he made the wrong choice and got lost twice more before he found himself driving down the gentle hill with the sea to his left, into the village where Ruth now lived.

Fishermen's cottages had been built around a green, making three sides of a square; a low wall dividing land from the beach made the fourth. The buildings were uniform, painted white. He guessed that for the most part now they functioned as holiday accommodation, folk who wanted a week or two away from it all. At the rear end of the square there was a small pub, across from that a shop that seemed to be long closed. There were cars parked outside some of the cottages, but not most. It was far enough into the day for lights to be showing faintly at some of the windows. Smoke trailed upwards from several chimneys. Resnick locked the car and stretched his legs and back: it had been a long enough drive.

For a few moments he stood near the wicker lobster pots stacked high to one end of the sea wall. South, it was just possible to see Dunstanborough Castle outlined against a darkly reddening sky.

Ruth's cottage was at the northern corner, the first passed entering the village. There were neither lights nor smoke. Resnick began to walk towards it. No answer when he rattled at the letterbox, knocked on the door. He would ask in the pub.

Ruth was sitting in the far corner of the bar, her feet resting on another chair and a book open against the table. There was a glass by her right arm, a half of bitter it looked like, three-quarters down; a cigarette burned on an ashtray to her left. She scarcely looked up as Resnick came in.

The dog, a large pale retriever that lay curled beneath the table, raised its head and kept Resnick in its sights. When he walked towards the table, a glass of Worthington White Shield in his hand, the dog growled.

As soon as Ruth reached down and touched it gently between the ears it stopped.

'Mind if I join you?' Resnick said.

'What happens if I say yes?'

Her face had become leaner still, sucked in at the cheeks; the flesh around the eyes seemed somehow to have peeled back. There was barely a trace of red in her hair now; what there were, here and there, were white hairs startlingly strong and thick.

Resnick pulled round a chair and sat down.

Ruth continued to read. Charles Dickens. *Hard Times.* 'Decided a bit late in life to get myself an education.'

Resnick took a long swallow at his beer and waited till she'd reached the end of her chapter. A torn beer mat marked her place.

'You showing up here like this,' Ruth said. 'No accident.'

'He's getting parole. Matter of days. I didn't know if you'd heard.'

Ruth took a drag from her cigarette, finished her beer and held the empty glass for a moment in the air. The barman fetched her over a fresh one, took the old one away.

'Not so many customers this time of year,' Ruth said. 'Get treated like royalty.' She laughed low in her throat. 'Not ours, someone else's. No,' she said, after taking a drink, 'I didn't know.'

'Does he know where you are?'

Ruth shrugged. 'What difference? You found me, didn't you? And don't tell me it's your job. He's got ways of pressurizing people most of your lot only dream about.'

'You could move on,' Resnick said.

'Run?'

'You came here.'

'That was a fair time back. I like it here. Most people, one week, two, they're in and out, gone. No one knows who I am, what I was, what I was married to. Those as know bits and pieces, none of their business, they don't care.'

'He said a lot of nasty things, at the trial.'

'He was always saying nasty things. Doing 'em, too. He can't scare me. Not any more. And even if he could, I've stopped running.' She swung her feet to the floor and the dog shifted position. 'He tried anything now,' she said, stroking the animal's fur, 'this one'd let him know what for. Wouldn't you, darlin'?'

The dog twisted its head to lick her hand.

'He threatened to get even.'

'What for? Ten years? He thinks that was down to me? That was never down to me. You had evidence, witnesses – that sorry bastard Churchill turning grass. Christ, you had him cold with a gun in his bloody hands. What did it need me for?'

Resnick didn't answer; the truth was, in detail, he didn't know. How much Rains had wheedled out of the bitter wife, how much from other sources?

'You must take it serious, driving all the way up here.'

Resnick nodded. 'I do.'

Ruth laughed again, breaking off midway into a racking cough. 'What you going to do,' she said once she'd controlled herself again, 'stick around? Be my personal bodyguard?'

'No. Just wanted you to know, that's all.'

She nodded towards his glass. 'Now you'll want to be getting back. Duty tomorrow, most likely.'

Resnick took a quick drink before pushing the glass aside. 'Always sediment at the bottom; no matter how carefully you pour it.'

'Yeh,' Ruth said, 'Bit like life, eh?' She laughed. 'Christ, hark at me. Not through one Dickens and I'm talking in symbols.'

Resnick got to his feet and once more the dog growled, low in his throat. 'One thing,' he said.

'Do I still sing?'

'When did you last see Rains?'

What colour she had drained from her face. 'Not since he dumped me. Best part of ten years. Best part's been not seeing his lying face.'

Resnick placed a card with his name and number on the cover of her book. 'Any reason. Any time. The station can always raise me.'

Ruth looked up at him with a raised eyebrow. 'Regular Lazarus, eh? Something in the air, all these blokes coming back from the dead.'

By the time Resnick had reached the door, she had her feet up and was back reading. A few more of the windows were showing lights and a wind had got up from the north-east. He turned his collar up as he crossed the green towards his car. He would stop at the first place on the main road and get coffee; traffic should be relatively light and it shouldn't be too long before he was home. Though to the cats who were waiting to be fed it would seem an age.

The headlights of Resnick's car raked across the white-wash of the cottages as he swung round, but failed to pick out the figure standing deep in the shadows beside the sea wall, biding his own time.

# Forty-Four

Millington had been so chipper that morning, the idea had flirted across his wife's mind that he might be having an affair. It was partly the sparkle in his eye, partly the appetite with which he'd wolfed down his muesli and dried fruit without as much as a pulled face or an offhand reference to the tastelessness of skimmed milk. He had rinsed his bowl, brought her a second cup of tea without being asked, brushed her cheek with a kiss that was forceful enough to make clear he'd trimmed his moustache that morning.

When she wandered out into the hall, he was brushing the shoulders of his jacket on its hanger and whistling what sounded suspiciously like 'Love is a Many Splendoured Thing'.

'See that James Last's on at Concert Hall again this summer,' Millington said. 'Maybe I should get us a couple of tickets?'

'After last time, Graham, I should hardly thought you'd have wanted to go again.'

Last time, the woman behind had tapped Millington's wife on the shoulder and asked her in quite a loud voice if there wasn't something she could do about her husband's snoring.

'Oh, aye, restful, though, weren't it?' He slipped on his coat and headed for the front door. 'Possible, bit on the late side tonight. Pint or three after work. Business, like.'

'Yes, Graham,' she said, 'whatever you say.'

Blimey, Millington thought, getting into the car, what's eating her? Face like one of them frozen dinners before it sees the inside of the microwave.

He was in the CID room, close to the door of Resnick's office before his superior arrived, loitering with intent.

'All right, Kevin,' ten minutes later Resnick's voice audible from the stairs, 'first things first. Let's take a look at last night's files.'

'Sir.'

'Morning, Graham. Bright and early.'

Naylor had been in since before seven, the early shift, one of his tasks to organize all messages received during the night into national or local, another to ensure the log showing the movement of prisoners was up to date. He carried these files over towards Resnick's office now and Millington held out his hand.

'I'll take those in, lad. You could do worse than set tea to mash. Okay?'

Naylor shrugged and did as he was told.

Millington placed the files on Resnick's desk then closed the door by leaning his back against it.

'On to something, Graham?' Resnick asked with a grin. His sergeant could hang on to a secret about as long as a small boy could harbour a fifty-pence piece.

'This chap I've been meeting for the odd pint down in Sneinton. Strictly small time, like I've said, but knows a few of the bigger boys. Or likes to let on as he does.'

'Which is it?' Resnick asked. Up to the present he'd found it hard to take either Millington's low-grade grass or Mark Divine's high-flown theories about Eurovillains too seriously.

'Got a bit cheesed off last night, he were standing there scoring drinks out of me left, right and centre and what he'd offered, so much hot air. I told him, come up with something new, something we can use, or he could find someone else to do his drinking with.'

'And?' Resnick prompted. Sitting behind his desk and watching Millington's face, he could taste the anticipation.

'Rains,' Millington said, unable to prevent himself from smiling.

'He put up his name?'

'Along of one or two others.'

'No doubt about it?'

By now Millington's face was positively beatific. 'DC Rains, late of this parish.'

'DC no longer.'

'A long way from it, so it seems.'

Initial elation over, Resnick's mind was racing. 'I thought he was abroad?'

'So he was. Still is, by all accounts. Northern Spain, well away from your *hoi polloi*. According to my friend, he isn't above flying over to take care of a little business.'

'What business is he in these days, our ex-colleague?'

Millington was enjoying this enormously. 'Much the same as before, apparently, only from what would you say, a different perspective.'

Resnick was on his feet. 'Do we know this is anything more than malicious gossip? After all, easy to spread stories about someone a thousand or so miles away.'

'What made it gel for me,' Millington said, 'remember that blagger was mixed up with Prior? More than a passing interest in armed robbery himself, though he played that down at the trial. Did his best to set it all at Prior's doorstep, planning, shotgun, the lot.'

'Churchill?' Resnick said.

'Frank Churchill.'

'He's in this as well?'

288

'According to what I was told last night, him and Rains've stayed in touch more or less ever since.'

Darren had wasted half the day looking for Keith. First off, he'd waited for him at the usual café, but Keith never showed; the best part of an hour hanging around the square, wandering in and out of various amusement arcades. When finally he'd rung his old man to find out what the hell Keith was playing at, Rylands had told him he had no idea where Keith was, he had left the house about half-nine or ten, never saying a word.

Well, okay. He'd get this done on his own.

The shop was up Carlton Hill, one of those places piled floor to ceiling with stuff people have no further use for – toasters, radios, steam irons, manual typewriters, video recorders that would neither record nor play; the pavement outside boasted refrigerators and electric fires, cookers with rust-encrusted rings, a wheelchair that was chained to the wall to prevent the local kids commandeering it for joyrides down the hill.

The owner was a sixty-eight-year-old woman called Rose, whose sister had scarcely been out of the wheelchair the last four years of her life. She viewed Darren with a proper suspicion, uncertain if he was going to try to sell her something stolen or order her to empty the till.

Darren picked up an antique Teasmade and gave it an exploratory shake. The matron at the home had boasted of owning one of those, though he'd never seen it. There'd been other lads, older and bolder, who claimed they had.

'You want to buy that?' Rose asked.

'What I want to buy,' said Darren, 'is a shooter.'

'How's that?'

'You know. A gun?'

The woman opened her arms and pointed around. 'Find one among that lot, duck, sell it you with pleasure.'

Darren reached into his trouser pocket and pulled out a thick pile of twenties and tens. 'What I was told, anyone wanted something like that, you could arrange it. What's it called? On commission.'

Rose pushed her hands down into her apron and sucked her top plate back against the roof of her mouth. 'I'll have to make one or two calls. You come back here in an hour or two.'

Resnick and Millington were in Skelton's office. The elements had decided to turn the screw a little and after an oddly humid, muggy morning, rain was now rattling the window panes.

'What degree of involvement are we talking about here?' Skelton asked. He was standing with his back to the weather, the industrial landscape beyond his shoulders disappearing into mist. 'How actively involved are we saying Rains might be? Is he planning these robberies? Difficult if he's spending more time out of the country than in. Are we meant to assume he's actually taking part? What?'

Resnick looked over at Graham Millington.

'Er, afraid he's not too clear as yet . . .'

'Your informant?'

'Yes, sir. So far he's not gone into a lot of detail.'

'You think he might?'

Millington took his time in answering, 'It's possible, sir.'

'So, presumably, is the supposition that since you were pushing him hard for a name, he pulled one out of the hat? One he knew it would be difficult for us to check.'

Millington fidgeted on his chair. 'Yes, sir. It could be, only . . .'

'This informant,' Skelton said, 'you've used him before?'

'Once or twice.'

'And the quality of the information?'

Millington shrugged. 'Fair to middling, I suppose you'd say.'

Skelton resumed his seat. 'I'd prefer to say something a lot more positive than that, Graham, if I'm to stand behind this as a new line of inquiry.'

What had started out as a cracking day, Millington thought, was losing its sparkle by the minute.

'What happens if we haul him in, this bloke?' Resnick asked. 'Lean on him?'

'Might yield something. Then again, might send him back into his shell.'

All three men fell silent and there were only the muted footfalls from other parts of the building, the hiccup of telephones and the swirling beat of the rain.

'The original investigation, Charlie,' Skelton was moving paper clips around his desk blotter with the precision of a war room general, 'when Prior and Churchill were brought to book, let me see if I'm remembering straight. A lot of the preparation of evidence for the DPP, testimony and the like, Rains was responsible for that.'

Resnick nodded. It had been Rains who had come up with the dates and places that had shaken Prior's alibi; Rains who had dramatically produced details of planning meetings that had taken place in Prior's house.

'And his connection with Churchill? Enough to imagine some kind of relationship might have been formed between them then?'

'Rains visited Churchill a number of times in prison, when he was on parole. That was when Churchill agreed to corroborate allegations that were still pretty much up in the air.'

'And bought himself a light sentence in return.'

Resnick nodded. Six years to Prior's fifteen, released after less than three. Yes, Churchill had good reason to think co-operating with Rains was beneficial. Question was, how far had that benefit become mutual?

Skelton was on his feet again, pacing the room. Resnick responded to Millington's wordless question with a light shrug of the shoulders and a quick sigh.

'You knew him, Charlie. Rains. Worked with him. You were a lot closer to him at the time than either Graham or I. Serious armed robbery – do you see him being involved in that?'

Resnick leaned forward in his chair. 'The thing about Rains, one above all others, he was never afraid of pushing hard where others – myself included – would tend to hang back. No matter what else, I always had a grudging sort of respect for that.' Resnick sat back. 'About the only thing I did have respect for. Find a weakness, use people, dump them – that was Rains.'

'So if he's yet to dump Churchill?'

'He's still using him.'

'And robbery, heavily armed,' Skelton probed, 'he'd have no compunction about that?'

'If ever he reckoned the gains worth the risk, I don't think the thing's been invented Rains'd have one penny-worth of compunction about.'

The rain drummed and drummed and Skelton rested his head against the upturned fingers of his hand. Millington, sensing the way the wind was turning, allowed himself the beginnings of a smile.

'Okay,' Skelton said, hands now flat on his desk, 'Graham, lean on this informant of yours just as far as you think you safely can, your own judgement. Mean-

292

time, we'll chase Churchill up on the computer, last known addresses, whatever we can. Contact Interpol and the Spanish police and see if they can locate Rains, be nice to know where he is. If he's been travelling here regularly it's possible he's been using an assumed name, in which case it might be the one he's living under over there. Divine's been checking the flight manifests for this French caper of his, much of the information we want should either be on file, or, better still, on disk.' He looked from one to the other. 'Gentlemen, let's keep this pretty much to ourselves for the time being, but meantime why don't we run with it as far as we can?'

Both Resnick and Millington got to their feet and turned to leave.

'Graham,' Skelton said, calling him back. 'Good work. Much more of this, we'll run out of excuses to keep you where you are.'

Millington was so chuffed, he came close to colliding with the door on the way out.

# Forty-Five

When Darren had arrived back at the shop, Rose told him he would have to wait a couple of days. Darren couldn't believe it. No wonder private enterprise was going to the dogs if you couldn't get hold of a shooter without going through a lot of red tape and standing in line. It was nearly as bad as signing on for the dole.

'No,' he'd said. 'No way. Not two days. I want it now.'

'Fine,' Rose had said, 'there's somewhere else you can get the same, good luck to you.'

But Darren didn't know anywhere else.

'Look,' Rose said, lowering her voice to avoid being overheard by a couple who were mulling over the purchase of a gas fire. 'Look, don't be a stupid boy. What's so important it has to be done the next couple of days? Eh? Someone's slipping your girl friend a little something on the side and you want to catch them at it, don't you think he's still going to be the day after tomorrow? There's a post office you've got your eye on, a betting shop perhaps, it'll still be there, believe me.'

Darren felt like whacking her around the head for suggesting that he was stupid, but she patted him on the arm as if he were a recalcitrant child. 'You come by, oh, not too early, eleven, eleven-thirty, I'll have it all arranged. Okay?'

Darren had grunted that it was okay.

'Good boy!' And she patted his trouser pocket with a

laugh. 'You keep tight hold of it now. Don't go spending it on all the wrong things.'

Now Darren was waiting on a patch of disused land close by the canal, across from a disused warehouse from which the letters spelling out British Waterways were steadily peeling. Pigeons bunched on the sills of broken windows, launching themselves without warning into sudden flurries of flight. Darren tightened his hand around the iron bar beneath his jacket for comfort. Half-ten the meeting had been set for and his watch had passed that nearly fifteen minutes ago.

Not far from his feet the water lapped gently and above his head the moon slipped in and out of cloud. If Rose was setting him up, he'd go back to the shop and turn her face to mush.

Even as he had that thought he heard the car engine slowing on the road, the crunch of gravel as it turned towards him. A moment later he was caught in the uneven circle of dipped headlights and the car was slurring to a halt.

One man was black, the other white. Lethal weapon's right, Darren thought with a nervous grin. Wearing short jackets and jeans, one with Converse basketball boots, the other tan deck shoes, neither of them looked that much older than he was himself.

'Got the money?' the white bloke asked.

Darren nodded: yes.

'Show.'

Darren had a fleeting thought that they were going to mug him and drive off, pitch him into the canal.

'I've got it,' Darren said, 'you don't have to worry.'

'Okay,' the young black man said, turning back towards the car, 'we wasting our time.'

'No.' Darren lifted the roll of notes from his pocket and held it for them to see.

The men exchanged looks and made their decision. The boot of the car was unlocked and snapped open. Resting on the spare wheel was a canvas duffle bag and it was this that the black man unfastened and reached inside.

There were two guns in thick polythene, bound at each end with wide brown tape. The tape was prised loose from one end and pulled back, the weapons shaken out on to the bag.

'Pistols, right? That's what you said?'

'Yeh.'

'Okay, this one...' lifting it for inspection '... Browning. Like new, hardly been fired. Well good. This – PPK, nothing better. Here, cop a feel.'

Darren took first one, then the other weapon into his hand; they felt alien, cold, heavier than he'd expected. He didn't want them to know this was his first time, but there was no way they couldn't tell and their eyes found each other in the dark and shared their amusement at his expense. The white man lit a cigarette and the smoke from it showed light upon the air.

Darren liked the heft of the PPK in the palm of his hand. 'How much?'

'Seven hundred.'

'You're joking.'

The black one held out his hand for the pistol. 'Joking,' his companion said, 'not something we do a lot of.'

The PPK was replaced carefully inside its polythene sheath.

'The other one, then,' Darren said. 'What was it? Browning, yeh. How much for that? That can't be as much, right?'

The pistols were already out of sight.

'What we were told,' closing the boot, 'you were serious. Must've been a mistake.'

296

'Six hundred,' Darren blurted. 'I can manage six hundred.'

The white man in the deck shoes had the driver's door open. 'Six and a half.'

'Ammunition. I'm going to need . . .'

'Half a dozen shells.' He was back in front of Darren, holding out his hand. Behind him, the boot door popped up and the duffle bag reappeared.

'You won't regret it,' the man said, counting out the notes. 'Will he?'

'No,' his mate said, shaking six shells loose from a cardboard box. 'I doubt it.'

'This is it?' Prior said, staring up at the house.

Pam Van Allen nodded. 'This is it.'

A large building originally, it looked as if extra rooms and sections of roof had been added piecemeal, to accommodate unexpected children or, more likely, a live-in gardener, an undermaid. Ivy clung to the face, thick around the windows and above the polished oak door. At any one time there were a dozen ex-prisoners housed there, occasionally more.

Pam walked with Prior into a high, wide entrance hall with the original patterned tiling still on the floor. The staircase would have allowed four people to ascend it side by side without touching.

'You're lucky, you've got the room at the back. There's a really nice view.'

One of the two beds were already occupied, though not at that moment; the covers had been carelessly pulled back and there were clothes bunched on it in small piles, shirts and socks, a pair of jeans.

A transistor radio had been left playing and Pam walked over and switched it off. 'See what I mean,' she said, pointing out over a ragged patchwork of allotment gardens and unclaimed land, down towards the centre of the city.

But Prior had already blocked her out. He was sitting on the other bed, hunched forward, rolling himself a cigarette.

Darren had picked up the girl at Madisons. Outside, actually. She had been leaning up against the brick wall opposite the stage door of the Theatre Royal, forehead pressed down against one hand, while with the other she fumbled for a tissue inside her bag. She was wearing a blue dress with a high neck but a deep V slashed out of it that gave Darren a good view of her breasts.

I've seen her around somewhere, Darren thought, and as she realized he was watching her and stood away from the wall, ready to challenge him, he remembered where.

'How about,' Darren said with a grin, 'a meat feast with extra cheese, garlic bread with mozzarella and a large coke?'

'Do I know you?' the girl blinked. It wasn't long since she'd stopped crying and her make-up had smeared.

'Della, right?' Darren said, moving in closer. 'Pizza Hut. Manageress.'

'Trainee,' Della said, close to a smile.

'Not for long. I'll bet.'

Aware that he was staring down the front of her dress, Della pulled the gap together with her hand.

'How come you're out here?' Darren said. 'What's up?'

'My boy friend's in there dancing with somebody else, that's what I'm doing out here.'

'Wants his head seeing to.'

'You think so.'

'I know so.'

Della blew her nose into a tissue and dabbed at her eyes. 'Well, I might as well be going.'

'No,' Darren smiled, shifting his balance enough to set himself in her path. ''S'early yet. Why don't we go over the Café Royal? have a drink?'

I'm not stopping long,' Della said, turning on her low heels to look round the room. It reminded her of boarding houses she'd been to stay in with her parents when she was younger, Southport or Filey or places like that. It didn't look like a room in which somebody actually lived.

'How many sugars?' Darren called from the shared kitchen.

'One,' Della said.

Darren appeared in the doorway with a mug in either hand.

'I shall have to be going soon,' Della said, taking one of the mugs and standing in the centre of the room. Last mistake she was about to make, go over there and sit on the bed.

''S'okay,' said Darren, 'Lot to do myself tomorrow as it is. Tell you what, though . . .' sitting back on the bed himself '. . . 'fore you go, you won't believe what it is I've got to show you.'

# Forty-Six

Millington wanted to get out of the car and give his legs a stretch; he wanted to take a pee and not into the plastic bottle which he'd swiped before his wife could put it away for recycling, fresh orange juice it said on the label, produce of more than one country. He wondered if he weren't getting a bit long in the tooth for this kind of obs, all right for youngsters like Naylor, sitting alongside him, working his way through an old issue of *The Puzzler*.

'Hey up!' Naylor said, as a car nosed into the street from the far end.

Both men sat tense as the maroon Datsun drove towards them at a regulation thirty; when they were certain it was going to turn into the drive of Number 11, it continued blithely on past.

Naylor sighed and shook his head. Millington reached into the glove compartment for another Bounty bar, dark chocolate covering, not the milk. Kevin Naylor shook his head and popped a Polo into his mouth. It was coming up to three-thirty in the afternoon and they had been in position since morning.

'Tell me something, Kevin,' Millington said, screwing up his Bounty wrapper and transferring it to his jacket pocket. 'If you were pulling down one big score after another, all that cash split – what? five, six ways? – would you elect to live in Mansfield? In a semi three streets away from your mother?'

'Long as it wasn't Debbie's mother, I don't know as I'd mind.'

'But Mansfield . . .'

'I don't know. It's not so bad. We nearly bought a place out here, actually. When we were getting married. Starter homes on one of them small estates, lot cheaper than in the city.'

'So why didn't you?'

'It were Debbie. Didn't feel right, moving so far away from her mum.'

'Her and Frank Churchill, then – lot in common.'

No matter how much he tried, Naylor could never stop himself breaking the mint with his teeth before it was as much as half gone. If they had set up home up here, he was thinking, things might have gone a sight more smoothly for them. Without Debbie being able to nip round to her mum's every time any little thing went wrong, they'd have had to work things out for themselves more.

'How is it going now?' Millington asked. He'd heard the rumours, same as everyone else. 'You and Debbie.'

'Not so bad,' Naylor said. 'Pretty good, in fact. Thanks, sarge, yes. Looking up.' they had spent two evenings together now, met for lunch one day at Jallans and Naylor had been certain Debbie wanted to go back to bed after, but he was on duty and she was due to see someone about a part-time job.

This time the car was a Granada estate, six months old, and the driver signalled his intentions to turn into Number 11 some forty yards away. He had his head turned aside as the car swung on to the drive; the gap between the driveway and the door was no more than twenty feet and he didn't stand around to watch the roses grow, but Millington and Naylor saw enough to be convinced this was their man.

Frank Chambers. Frank Church. Frank Churchill. Probably back from visiting his dear old mum.

Lynn Kellogg had been out of the office when Keith had first called and he'd refused either to leave his name or speak to anyone else. When he tried an hour and a half later, ringing from the only unvandalized box in the Bridgeway Centre, Lynn was on her way back in with her arms full of files.

'Hello? DC Kellogg.'

His voice was so faint, she couldn't make it out, but guessed anyway. 'Keith, that you?'

They met in the Memorial Gardens, walking round and round between the beds, all that Keith could do to remain there at all, never mind sitting down.

'And you are positive?' Lynn asked. 'About the gun?'

'He showed it to me.'

What Darren had actually done was slide the PPK beneath the table in the café and jab it against Keith's balls, not so hard as to make him cry out, hard enough for him to reach down and find out what it was. It had been almost enough to make Keith wet himself then and there; something he hadn't done since he'd been shut away in Glen Parva.

'How can you be positive it isn't a replica?'

'We got into the lift in the Trinity Square car park and stopped it between floors. He showed me. Ammo, too. No way it's anything but the real thing.'

When they'd got the lift going again, Darren had walked along the roof as far as the edge and leaned against the parapet, aiming the pistol at people walking along the street outside Jessops and the Stakis Hotel, taking careful aim and pretending to fire, making clicking sounds with his tongue and laughing. 'There. See that? Right between the fucking eyes!'

'And when did you say he'd told you to steal the car?'

'Wasn't definite. Just be ready, be ready. Don't let me have to come looking for you and not find you, that's all.'

'Okay,' Lynn said, 'just do as he says. Get back to me as soon as he's contacted you. That way we'll have plenty of time to get into position.'

Keith stopped alongside a small rockery with pink and purple flowers. 'What'll happen?' he asked.

'Happen? We'll disarm him, take him away fast. Lock him up out of harm's way. Your way, too. It's all right, Keith, you're doing the right thing. There's nothing for you to worry about.'

Now I know how it feels, Lynn thought as they walked towards the embankment, lying through my hind teeth.

Skelton had decided it was time to go public. It seemed as though, after nearly nine months, Operation Kingfisher was showing signs of coming home to roost. Most of the officers involved in the inquiry were present: aside from Resnick's team, Malcolm Grafton, Helen Siddons and Reg Cossall were looking over the newly circulated reports, waiting for the superintendent to spell out the next stages.

What Skelton did was to signal twice with nods of the head, once towards the lights, once the projector. A slide showing a man standing inside a walled garden, snow-capped mountains behind him, flicked into view, to be followed by a medium shot, head and shoulders, finally a close-up, slightly blurred by the necessary use of the zoom lens.

'Rainsey,' Reg Cossall breathed. 'As I live and breathe.'

'Former DC Rains,' Skelton confirmed, 'taken in the grounds of the villa where he's been living these past six years. About seventy miles north of the town of Leon in the Cantabrian Mountains.' Skelton looked around the darkened room. 'Since these pictures were taken, Rains has disappeared. If he's flown, especially using a British passport, it must have been under an assumed name.'

'What about other modes of transport, superintendent?' asked Helen Siddons.

The car registered to him is still garaged at the villa, but, of course, that means nothing. The Spanish police had promised a thorough check of car hire firms in the area, but so far nothing's materialized.'

'Too busy enjoying their siesta,' suggested Cossall in a stage whisper.

'It's not so far to the French border,' Malcolm Grafton pointed out. 'Pick up one of those TGVs, you're talking getting on two hundred miles an hour. Ferry across the Channel, here in no time.'

'If *here* is where's he's heading, Malcolm,' Reg Cossall pointed out.

'If we're not working on that possibility, Reg,' said Helen Siddons, 'I don't know what we're doing here at all.'

Cossall sat back glowering. Reg! What did that jumped-up tart think she was at, having the bollocking temerity to call him Reg?

Skelton signalled and the slide disappeared, the lights came back on. 'There are still a lot of ifs. If Rains has been travelling to and from this country with any frequency, we've yet to establish proof of this. If he's been in this area, you might think it strange there doesn't appear to have been one sighting of him, not one solitary rumour that he was here – until the one floated by Graham's informant. Having noted all of that, what interests me most is the supposed Churchill-Rains connection. It's Charlie's opinion they could have been close; the informant's busy telling us they've become closer. And one thing we know for certain, though we've been short of a great deal that's provable in court, Churchill is a long-term villain, a professional robber with likely half a dozen scores to his name since he came out of Parkhust in eighty-five.'

'Time the bastard was back,' someone said to murmurs of agreement.

'We're keeping him under surveillance,' Skelton said. 'Round the clock. Either Rains contacts him or vice versa, we should know.'

'Have we got a tap on his phone?' Helen Siddons asked.

'What we have is an outstanding application to monitor all calls.'

A low moan ran round the room.

'One thing,' asked Malcolm Grafton, 'how does this affect the status of the French inquiries?'

'Continuing, Malcolm. Possibly a little closer to the back burner, that's all.'

'What that bugger wants to know for,' Cossall said to Resnick, who was sitting close to one side, 'reckons he's on to a Parisian bloody holiday, doesn't he? All expenses paid. Taxpayers' money to spend his nights down in the *Folies Bergère*. Waste, eh, Charlie? Going to send anyone, down to you and me.'

In the event it was to be none of them. Skelton passed the news to Resnick at the end of the meeting and it was his duty to impart the decision to Divine, who was entertaining the CID room with his impersonation of Maurice Chevalier performing a particularly lewd version of 'Thank Heaven for Little Girls'.

'Mark, my office a minute.'

Divine stood inside the closed door, hands clasped at his back.

'The, er, French connection you've been working on . . .'

Divine's eyes began to shine.

'I'm afraid it's been decided there's a need to send a more senior officer. Someone fluent in the language and of a rank which would enable them to . . .' The rest didn't need saying. The change in Divine's expression made it clear how well he understood. 'DI Siddons will be the liaison officer travelling over; seems she's more or less bilingual.'

There was a day when Divine would have tried to make a joke out of that, but this wasn't it.

'Sorry, Mark,' Resnick said, surprising himself by actually meaning it.

'Thanks, boss,' Divine said gloomily.

Instead of going back to his desk, he walked through the CID room and out at the far end without saying another word. In either language.

# Forty-Seven

Ruth padded across the tiled floor in bare feet. Why hadn't she been surprised when Resnick had walked into the pub? Recognizing him instantly from the trial and earlier – standing in the side door of the house, Rains behind her, watching Resnick and her husband face to face. Watching her husband's face, the gun; knowing that he was playing the percentages inside his head. How much do they know? How much can they prove? How much time am I going to get? She remembered how close Rains had stood to her, warmth of his breath against the side of her neck; even then, his hand reaching out for her, touching her back.

She poured nearly boiling water into the pot and swished it round as she took it to the sink and poured it down. One tea bag and one for luck. Digestive biscuits in the tin on the shelf. She poured on the water and replaced the lid, left the tea to brew.

The dog watching her all the while, clear eyes following her every move. A ritual like many others. One which Resnick's visit had left undisturbed. A couple of halves in the pub, few chapters of whichever book, back to the cottage for a cup of tea and while that was standing, she would feed the dog. Afterwards, walk him on the beach. Well, she would walk, the dog would run. Then home for a little telly, maybe the radio, another early night, the dog curled on the rug at the bed's foot.

Ruth stood with both hands to her face, pressing deep.

Resnick had walked into the pub and told her what she had always known, sooner or later, would be the case: he's coming out. *I'll get you, Ruthie. Get even with you. Pay you back, you double-crossing bastard. Cunt. You bitch.* There had been a photograph of her, front page in most of the papers, little black dress, descending the steps outside the court. Pale face. There behind her, smart in his suit, that handsome smiling face, hands raised and spread to ward photographers and press away.

*Mrs Prior will be making a statement later through her solicitor.*

*Pleased, course I'm pleased. We got a good result.*

Prior's release, so long coming, she had ceased to fear it long since. What would come would come and who was she to say she didn't deserve it? *Grassing up your old man, you slag, you don't deserve to live.* Rumour was his mum had hired some tearaway to teach her a lesson, throw acid in her face. Ruth hid herself away, down London, abroad, a spell in Glasgow, back for a while to the city, then here.

*You can walk but you can't run.*

She liked it here. The quiet. All those early years in front of speakers jacked up so high she was lucky not to have permanent damage to her ears. In Glasgow once this journalist had recognized her, a stringer for the *NME*. Begged her to let him do her story. *Not talking a magazine piece here, I mean the real thing. A book. Built around you. The history of British Rhythm and Blues.*

She hadn't told that story or any other. Not even after the trial when they'd all been round her like flies round the honeypot. The *Sun*. The *News of the World*. Money she'd been offered. My Life with a Villain. My Life with a Face. Some tart who reckoned she'd screwed him silly in her scabby little bedsit had sold this yarn about champagne and foursomes and how Prior hadn't been able to get enough. Well, after all the years of virtual abstinence he'd practised with her, maybe that was the only part Ruth had believed.

It was late. The dog had finished its food and was waiting, bemused, by the door. The tea was cold and stewed. Ruth changed her shoes, buttoned up her coat.

The roll of the sea as it folds back against the sand. If Prior walked up to me now, out of this long dark, Ruth thought, what would I say or do?

Returning, as she neared the sea wall, she heard the quick scratch of a match and, moments later, saw the soft glow of a cigarette. Just kids, she thought, doing some cold courting.

Resnick's card was still in the pocket of her skirt and she dropped it on to the kitchen table as she walked through. For fifteen, twenty minutes she sat with her feet up, listening to Radio Two: Brian Matthew more relaxing than another bout of Gradgrind.

'Come on,' she said, and with its usual enthusiasm the dog trailed her up the stairs to bed.

On the outer edge of the city, nights before, travelling back, Resnick had pulled across to the side of the road and cut the engine. Lights splayed out before him like a net. A feeling, not quite pain, had caught low in his throat. His instinct had been to slip a fresh cassette into place but inside his head Lester was already playing 'Ghost of a Chance'.

*unseen, not quite unbidden,*
*someone has just slipped in.*

Ruth was vaguely aware of the dog paddling off downstairs but it was such a familiar sound she never really woke: what did wake her was the sharp, sudden sound of tearing close to her head.

'What's that?' Jumping up with a start, blinking into the near dark.

'That,' the familiar voice said, 'was the sound of your dog's throat being cut.'

'Bastard!' she sobbed, reaching sideways for the light.

Beside the bed, Rains smiled down. 'Don't worry, Ruthie. It was only this.' One of her shirts which she'd left hanging over a chair was dangling from his hand, ripped from tail to neck.

'The dog! Where's . . .?'

'Downstairs sleeping, not to fret.'

'He wouldn't . . .'

'Hungry. Gave him a little something to eat.'

'If you've . . .'

'Just a few hours. He'll be right as rain.' Rains smiled. 'Funny that, isn't it? Always makes me smile. What's so right about rain.' Never taking his eyes from her, he sat on the side of the bed. 'Always when you least expect it. Forgot the umbrella, raincoat in the car.' He laughed, smiling with his eyes. 'Good to see you, Ruthie. You look like shit.'

He scarcely looked older; what age there was, if anything, had made him even better-looking. Too handsome for other people's good.

'No sense pretending we parted on the best of terms, is there? Even so – I thought some things were all agreed. No true confessions, no stories. No talking out of turn.'

'How did you get here? How did you find me?'

'Ruthie! Used to be a detective, remember?'

'I know what you used to be.'

Rains leaned one hand against the covers, close to her

leg. 'Followed him. Charlie. Heard he'd had the feelers out, asking questions, and I followed him.'

Ruth glanced away and when she looked back his expression had changed.

'You thought shutting yourself out here would stop people finding you; thought getting that dog would protect you if they did. Well, now you know better. And I know you won't forget.' His hand moved fast and he had hold of her jaw, fingers pressing hard against the bone. 'One thing, when he comes to see you, Prior; if he wants to know what went on between us, if I used you to fit him up, you don't tell him a thing. Don't as much as mention my name.' Leaning quickly forward he kissed her on the mouth. 'Life's good, Ruthie. Too much so to have it fucked up by some jealous bastard, fresh out of prison, harbouring a grudge.'

She stayed there for a long time after Rains had gone, allowing the warmth gradually to seep back into her skin. Only then did she put on her dressing gown and go downstairs and kneel beside the dog, unconscious on the kitchen floor; sit, with its head resting in her lap, until it stirred with the first light glinted off the sea.

# Forty-Eight

Resnick woke at two to the sound of breathing: lay there for second after second, aware of the heart pumping against his ribs, that the fevered breathing that had woken him had been his own. He was layered with sweat. The fear was not his own.

> *a tideswell like moving bone*
> *Like Monk fingering 'These Foolish Things'*
> *from broken glass*

He got up and didn't switch on the light. The cat, knowing it was too early, recircled itself at the foot of the bed and closed its eyes. Because the fear was not for himself, it was no less real. He stood beneath the shower and the sound that he heard was water dragging back across the shore. He knew that Ruth had no phone: knew that he could phone the pub and rouse the landlord, call the constabulary in the nearest town. Knew, without knowing why, without questioning, that whatever had happened, that part of it, was through.

Deliberately, he dressed, made coffee, buttered toast, broke cheese. Some of the coffee he drank, the remainder he poured into a flask. If he drove fast he would beat daybreak. His headlights cut channels across brick and stone. The only fear now was what he would find.

Ruth had stayed in the kitchen with the dog, cradling it, until, at last, its eyes rolled open and, moments later, it shuffled unsteadily to its feet. Now the animal lay curled on the battered settee in the living room and Ruth sat, trying to read, with her umpteenth cup of tea.

It snagged at the back of her mind, like a hangnail, that she should slip on her shoes and find her purse, walk the few yards towards the sea shore and dial the number Resnick had left her. She was loath to admit to herself that part of the reason she didn't do this was she was afraid to take that first step outside the house.

Yet why?

If it were Rains that she feared most he had proved to her how easy it was for him to magic himself inside her house. If he had wanted to do her physical harm he could; if he wanted to harm her in the future he could again. She had no doubt of this.

But maybe Rains was not the one she really feared.

She would call Resnick and say what? This friend of yours was here threatening me. What did he do? He tore one of my old shirts. Ruth smiled. Resnick and Rains, had they been friends? It seemed unlikely. She thought that to Rains, admitting to a friend would have been a sign of weakness, strictly to be discouraged. Friendship meant give and take and life, for Rains, was all in the taking.

She was back in the kitchen, refilling the kettle, when she heard the car approaching.

'Do you always act on your hunches?' Ruth asked. They had walked up away from the beach, on to a green knoll that never seemed to reach its peak. Off to the west woods became fields and fields became lost in hazy mist. Squinting along the shoreline into the early light they could see the silhouettes of castles, bulked against the sky.

'Not always,' Resnick said. 'Usually.'

'Doesn't it ever get you into trouble?'

'Doesn't everything?'

They walked on until the land seemed suddenly about to fall before them, tumbling sharply down to a narrow cleft, a stream of grey-green water that wound snake-like towards the sea.

Ruth patted her pockets, found and lit a cigarette, smoke from it quickly lost in the air. 'So what did you expect?' she asked. 'To find me dead?'

'I wasn't sure.'

'But that was one of the possibilities?'

'I suppose so.'

She almost smiled. 'You weren't disappointed.'

Resnick shook his head.

'But Rains,' Ruth said, 'you didn't think it would be Rains?'

'No. I mean, I didn't know. But, no, I don't think so.'

'He's out then?' Ruth said, moments later. They both knew she meant Prior.

'Yes.'

'And you're watching him?'

'No.'

'Expect me to believe that?'

Resnick shook his head. 'We haven't the reason, haven't the resources. He'll be expected to report to his probation officer once a week.'

Ruth snorted.

'D'you want to start walking back?' Resnick said.

'All right,' Ruth said, but neither of them moved.

'What you have to understand,' Ruth said several moments later, 'no one had looked at me like that in so long I swear I'd forgotten what it meant. No one had touched me, wanted to touch me. It was as if, early, stupidly bloody early, that part of my life had just stopped.

'And then there was that bastard, hands all over me, like he couldn't get enough.' She finished her cigarette, nipped the end between finger and thumb and opened the last of the paper, scattering shards of tobacco towards the ground. 'I knew he was using me, though, of course, he denied it. Knew and I never cared. I thought, Prior's going down for a long time and what that means to me he doesn't care, he doesn't give a shit. I'm just this thing that he's lived with and used to cook and clean and wipe between his legs. I felt *that* low.' She looked at Resnick and made a gesture with her hand as if she were holding something minute. 'And what Rains did, he stopped me feeling like that. Oh, Christ alone knows, not for long. But when he did . . .'

Ruth began to walk and Resnick moved into step beside her. All the while she had been talking he'd shut out the constant roll of the sea and now that she was quiet it came back the more strongly, accompanying them home.

'You haven't got any coffee,' Resnick called from the kitchen. The past five minutes he'd been through every drawer, every cupboard.

'That's right.'

He made more tea.

'What I've got,' Ruth said, wandering in followed by a still dazed-looking dog, 'is a stomach lining I'm going to leave to medical science. They'll use X-rays of it in years to come, illustrating the dangers of tannin.'

For all the jokes, she still looked lined and drawn, still jumped at the first strange sound.

They sat at the table, the dog beneath it, asleep again, snoring faintly.

'Rains,' Resnick said, 'he didn't give any indication of where he was staying, anything like that?'

Ruth shook her head. 'You'd go and talk to him? I mean, officially?'

'I daresay.'

'What for? What could you prove?' She drank some tea. 'What did he do, aside, I suppose, from breaking in?'

Resnick leaned towards her. 'There's more.'

'With Rains?'

'Yes.'

'What sort of more?'

'We're not sure, but . . . one or two things, we think he might be involved.'

'What kind of things?'

Resnick leaned back. 'When you were seeing him, did he ever talk about Frank Churchill?'

'Only questions. The usual things. Meetings, places and times. All the usual things.'

'He didn't give the impression they might be close?'

'Rains and Churchill!' Ruth gave a derisory laugh. 'Fine bloody couple they'd make! Only person Frank Churchill's ever been close to's his mother. Rains'd never got that sort of close to anything unless it was a mirror. Anyhow, why d'you want to know?'

Resnick's turn to shake his head. 'Doesn't matter.'

'No? That's what Rains'd say. Every time. We'd be lying there, you know, after making love, I'd be waiting and sure enough they'd come, the questions, on and on and if either I wouldn't answer or ask him why he wanted to know, that's what he'd say – doesn't matter. Ten, fifteen minutes later, he'd be asking the same thing. 'One thing I've never done, knowingly, give that bastard anything that'd push my husband deeper into the shit. Never. And if that's what Rains was saying, to you lot or anyone else, he was lying. He was covering up.' She released his arm and the marks of her fingers were left, pale, on Resnick's skin. 'Maybe what you were suggesting was right, maybe he did have something going with Churchill, more than was thought. As far as jobs was concerned, I shouldn't think there was anything I knew as Frank Churchill didn't. Less.' She got up and carried the two mugs, hers and Resnick's, to the sink.

'I ought to be going,' Resnick said, looking at his watch.

'Thanks,' Ruth said.

'What for?'

'Being bothered. Coming.'

'Just one thing,' Resnick said.

'What's that?'

'Why did you stop singing?'

'Fuck right off,' Ruth said, grinning.

# Forty-Nine

Darren pressed his finger full force against the bell and kept it there until Rylands, flushed in the face with anger, threw it open.

'What in God's name d'you think you're at?' Rylands demanded.

'Keith,' Darren said, ignoring his reaction. 'He in?'

'Out.'

'Out where? Been walking all over the city centre past couple of hours, looking for him.'

'He went to the job centre,' Rylands said.

'Job Centre!' Darren was incredulous. 'What the fuck's he want to go there for?'

'Here you go, sarge,' Naylor said, shutting the car door with a clean thunk. 'Jumbo sausage and chips.'

Millington's eyes lit up. Go anywhere near his wife with a jumbo sausage and you risked a lecture on harmful additives and carcinogenics. 'Get the mustard?' he asked.

Naylor fished a sachet containing a vibrant yellow from his breast pocket.

'Good lad!'

Naylor had fetched himself cod and chips. Or was it haddock? For the best part of fifteen minutes both men ate, neither spoke.

Millington was dipping the last few inches of his sausage into the puddle of mustard when the door to Number

11 opened and Frank Churchill came out. Without looking around, he unlocked the door of the Granada and climbed in.

'Probably off to see his mum,' Naylor suggested.

'Goes there,' Millington said, screwing up the wrappings of his lunch, 'he walks.'

'Maybe he's taking her for a drive?'

'And maybe I've just been eating prime beef.'

Naylor fired the engine and waited while Churchill backed out across the road and headed away from them at a good speed.

'Just make sure you don't get too close,' Millington said. 'Last thing we need, him spotting us.'

Naylor nodded, indicated right and changed down for the bend.

'Where the fuck've you been?' Darren grabbed hold of Keith by the shoulder, swinging him round so fast that Keith lost his balance and ended up on his knees.

'Get up, you prick! You look fucking pathetic!'

Keith scrambled to his feet, aware that several passersby were looking round at him and sniggering. That's it, lady, laugh your tossing head off, why don't you? He shook Darren's hand clear and said nothing.

'You avoiding me or what?' Darren demanded.

'Leave him alone, you great bully,' called an old woman with what looked like a year's supply of papers in a pram. 'He's only little.'

'Sod off, granny!' Darren yelled back.

'Yeh,' said Keith, 'sod off.'

They walked together across the road, ignoring the traffic, forcing it to stop or swerve around them.

'Gum?' Keith said, holding out a pack of Wrigley's.

'Yeh, ta.'

They sat on the wall near the gents' toilets, kicking

their heels against brickwork that was covered in graffiti and pigeon shit.

'Your old man said you was down the job centre.'

''S'right.'

'Anything there?'

'Don't bloody joke.'

'This car,' Darren said.

'Which one?'

'The one you're going to nick.'

'What about it?'

'Friday.'

'Why Friday?'

''Cause more people take money out Fridays, bird brain. Lot more cash there waiting.'

'We going to do another building society?' Keith asked.

'Yes,' Darren said. 'And this time we're going to do it fucking right!'

'On the M1, boss. Heading north.' Divine was monitoring Millington and Naylor's progress as they followed Churchill's Ford Granada. 'Reckon he's heading for a meet with Rains?'

'Any luck,' Resnick said, 'he's doing exactly that. Keep me in the picture.'

'Right.'

Resnick went into his office and dialled a number, asked to speak to Pam Van Allen.

Frank Churchill was sticking to the outside lane, keeping the speedometer between seventy-five and eighty, moving over only when some salesman, flogging his company car, came fast up behind him, flashing his lights.

Naylor kept several vehicles between himself and their quarry, alternately moving up and falling back, doing

320

everything he could to make sure his wouldn't be the vehicle Churchill habitually saw in his rear-view mirror.

'He's slowing down,' Millington said. 'Pulling over.'

Naylor had noticed already, dropped behind a lorry carrying pharmaceutical goods north from the Continent.'

'Service station,' Millington said. 'Just up ahead.'

Naylor checked in his own mirror and signalled to leave the motorway.

'I don't want you to think,' Resnick said into the phone, 'that I'm pestering you about this . . .'

There was a silence, out of which Pam Van Allen said, 'I'm trying hard not to.'

'I was interested to know how you think he's taking to being out, settling into the hostel, whatever.'

'Pretty much the way you'd expect somebody to do when they've been excluded from society for ten years. He's tense, apprehensive . . .'

'Angry?'

'I didn't say that.'

'I know. But I'm concerned . . .'

'For his wife's safety.'

'Yes.'

There was another pause, longer, and Resnick could almost hear the probation officer thinking. Through the glass at the top of his door he could see Divine's head, bobbing a little as he spoke into the telephone.'

'After what you said,' Pam Van Allen said cautiously, 'I talked to him about his wife, his feelings towards her. Everything he said suggested he sees that relationship as being very much in the past. He showed no inclination to open it up again, get back in touch. Certainly he expressed nothing like anger towards her.'

'And you believed him?'

321

'Yes. Yes, I did.'

'Good.'

'Goodbye, inspector.' Resnick had a sudden image of her as she set down the receiver, one hand pushing up through her cap of silver-grey hair, the other pinching the bridge of her nose as she closed her eyes.

'Boss!'

Alerted by Divine's shout, Resnick hurried into the main office.

'Graham,' Divine explained, holding out the phone. 'Wants to talk to you.'

Resnick identified himself down what was clearly a wavery connection.

'Good news is, it's Rains right enough. No mistaking him anywhere. Standing in line in the cafeteria waiting for Churchill to join him over chicken, chips and peas.'

'What's the bad?' Resnick said.

'Where they've sat themselves, bang in the middle of the place, can't get near 'em without getting spotted. Tried getting Kevin on to table behind, but what with all the chatter and the background bloody muzak and the cutlery, you'd need to be leaning over them with a hearing trumpet to know what they were talking about.'

'Lynn's on her way in a car. Rendezvous outside. When they leave, you take Rains, let her tag along with Churchill.'

'What if she don't get here?'

'Stick to the plan, follow Rains.'

'Right,' Millington said and then quickly, 'They're moving, got to go.'

Naylor walked down the steps from the cafeteria and ahead of him Rains and Churchill separated, neither one of them in any obvious hurry to go back to their vehicles. Churchill browsed the magazines in the shop; Rains spent a pound or so on the games machines near the exit. Churchill went into the gents and locked himself into a cubicle. Millington didn't think they'd been spotted, though there was no way of knowing for sure. What they were observing could simply be careful practice, nothing more. At least, it gave Lynn Kellogg more time to arrive. He had no way of knowing the northbound carriageway had been temporarily blocked by an accident involving a lorry and a fifteen-year-old youth joyriding in a stolen Fiesta.

Suddenly Churchill was hurrying across the parking area towards his Granada and that diversion was enough to give Rains a vital start back up the steps towards the bridge linking the two sides of the motorway.

The three blue saloons left the service area heading south in a virtual convoy and between them Millington and Naylor got the registration of one and a half. And they couldn't be sure which of the three Rains had been driving.

Frank Churchill, meanwhile, had continued his journey northwards and they could only hope that a sense of filial duty would take him back to Mansfield so that they could pick up his trail again.

'A balls-up, Charlie. A regular balls-up, I don't know what else to call it,' Skelton said after Resnick had made his report.

Alone in the CID room, smarting still, Graham Millington thought after that day's work he'd be fortunate to retain his sergeant's stripes, never mind promotion.

# Fifty

Lorna didn't know why it was, but ever since Kevin Naylor had stopped returning calls something appalling had happened to her appetite. Instead of settling down to watch *Neighbours* with a Linda McCartney low-calorie broccoli and cheese bake, she found herself reaching for the telephone and waiting, tummy impatiently rumbling, until the Perfect Pizza delivery man appeared on her doorstep. Her lunch had progressed from two crispbreads and a piece of celery to lasagne and chips at the local pub. Breakfast was no longer a single shredded wheat, it was porridge with maple-type syrup and cream, several slices of toast and marmalade and instant coffee with two spoonsful of sugar.

She had overheard Becca yesterday whispering to Marjorie in a voice that could have been heard up and down the street. 'You don't suppose, do you, that our Lorna's got herself pregnant?'

Fat chance!

'I'm sorry,' Kevin Naylor had said when she'd finally raised him on the phone, 'but there's another officer handling that now. I've been shifted on to something else.'

Shifted back to his wife, Lorna thought. She still hadn't forgotten that in the midst of their one and only night of passion, Kevin had etched a particular moment forever on her mind by digging his fingers sharply into her shoulders and shouting, 'Yes, Debbie! Yes, Debbie! Yes, Debbie, yes!'

Lorna ran her finger round the inside of her breakfast bowl, scooping up the last of the syrup and cream, before rinsing it under the tap. Oh God, she thought, next thing I'll be running out of things I can wear, having to go out and buy myself a whole new wardrobe. The one saving grace was the example of Marjorie, huffing and puffing and perspiring her way through every working day. The minute Lorna found herself rivalling Marjorie, she was enrolling in Weight Watchers, withdrawing her savings and booking two weeks on a health farm.

In the bathroom she cleaned her teeth with care, applied the finishing touches to her make-up. At least it was Friday, another week nearly over. Maybe tonight she'd go down the Black Orchid, let her hair down; dance enough she might even lose a few pounds.

The senior officers involved in Kingfisher had been in closed session ever since Jack Skelton came back from his early morning run. The consensus was this: Rains was back in circulation and his meeting with Churchill was enough to suggest Millington's information had at least a patina of truth. Rains, moreover, was aware of the possibility he and Churchill might be being watched. There was no certain way of knowing whether their tail had actually been spotted or if they were merely taking precautions. But then, as Reg Cossall suggested, you don't waste time fiddling around with a condom if all you're interested in's a quick wank. Even as he said it, Cossall thought he might get an earful from Helen Siddons, but all she did was compliment him on his awareness of the need for safe sex. All you need do, darling, Cossall thought, is carry on looking like that. What he did was smile and keep his mouth shut.

Finally it was agreed that they would maintain a careful watch on Churchill for another day, Frank having obligingly returned to his Mansfield home in time for tea. Meantime, extra officers would be assigned to the search for Rains. If nothing had developed within twenty-four hours, Frank Churchill could be brought in for questioning. If they moved quick enough, rattled him enough, they might squeeze some answers out of him before he was able to shelter behind his brief.

'Fetch us another tea, Keith. Make sure it isn't stewed, eh? More like gravy, this last cup.'

Keith could tell from the tone of Darren's voice that he was seriously on an up. Sitting by the back wall of the Arcade café, finishing his cooked breakfast and looking so sodding full of himself. At least his cropped hair had started to grow out a little, he didn't look so weird any more. Like one of them skinheads you saw sometimes round the city centre, lace-up Doc Marten's and Levis and swastika tattoos.

'Better treat yourself to something more than that,' Darren said, watching Keith with his two of toast.

'How come?'

Darren winked. 'Big day today, can't afford for you to be feeling queasy.'

'What's on, then?'

'What's on? Day trip to Skeggy, what d'you think? You and me, we've got some unfinished business to do, right?'

Keith looked at him sharply, the unnatural gleam in his too blue eyes. 'You're not serious? I mean, not after what happened last time, it's not . . .?'

'Jesus Christ!' Darren had one of Keith's hands tight inside his own and was squeezing hard. 'You know what, I reckon I'd've done us both a favour if instead of cutting

326

you down inside that cell, I'd let you swing. You're about as much good as a foreskin in a Force Ten gale.'

Tears were forming in the corners of Keith's eyes as his face grimaced with pain.

'All you got to do, be out front with the car, ready to get us out of there. I'll go in on my own.' He snorted with derision. 'Worked a bloody sight better without you last time, why not this?' And he gave Keith's hand a final squeeze before letting it go. 'Now don't take too long,' Darren said, 'it's time we were out of here.'

Keith pushed half a slice of half-cold toast into his mouth and almost choked.

'No word from young Rylands?' Resnick said, pausing by Lynn Kellogg's desk.

Lynn shook her head. 'Not as yet.'

'See if you can raise Mark or Kevin for me, will you? Maybe something's happening on the Churchill front.'

It was Divine whom Resnick eventually spoke to. The most exciting thing that had taken place was Churchill mouthing off at an old man with an orange delivery bag over his shoulder cluttering up the place with useless leaflets not worth the paper they were printed on. Chop down half a sodding forest just to keep you walking the streets.

Better kind of villain, Resnick thought, setting down the phone, not only is he nice to his mum he's worried about the ozone layer and the state of the planet.

Shivering in the call box and not from the cold, Keith was having difficulty getting his coins into the slot, pressing the correct buttons for the number.

'Oh, Miss Solomon,' Becca piped in her shrill little voice, 'could you come and help here, please?'

Lorna pushed aside the computer print-outs she'd been checking, query from an account holder about the regularity with which her salary had been paid in, and got to her feet, automatically smoothing down her skirt as she stood.

What all the fuss was about, she didn't know. There were no more than three people waiting, pretty average for this time of the day, she didn't see why Becca couldn't cope on her own till Marjorie got back from her coffee break.

'Thank you, Miss Solomon,' Becca smiled as Lorna took a seat alongside her, 'mustn't keep the customers waiting.'

Ever since she had started putting on a little weight herself, Lorna couldn't help but notice how skinny Becca really was. Like a couple of twigs in American tan tights.

'Yes, sir,' Lorna said, looking up through the glass. 'How may I help you?' And then thinking, oh, no; oh, Christ!

'Hello, Lorna,' Darren grinned. 'Remember me?'

'Becca,' Lorna started, 'I think . . .'

'Never mind about no one else,' said Darren, 'this is between you and me. Now here . . .' and he pushed a green bin liner through beneath the glass '. . . get that filled and don't piss me about.'

Lorna froze.

Becca spotted the bin liner from the corner of her eye and screamed.

Darren reached towards the waistband of his jeans and pulled out the gun.

A middle-aged man wearing decorator's overalls began to move towards the exit and Darren yelled for him to stop and levelled the pistol at his head. The man stopped.

'Lie down!' Darren ordered. 'All of you. Flat down

with your hands over your heads.' He'd seen them made to do that the other night in some film and it had looked pretty good.

'Okay,' he said, swinging the PPK round until once again it was pointing towards Lorna. 'Lorna, what you have to do, all that cash, in the bag. And Lorna, nothing clever like you tried before, none of that business with alarms.' He tapped on the glass with the barrel end of the gun. 'Reinforced or not,' he smiled, 'once I press this trigger, this isn't going to be worth shit.'

Becca had doubled forward, head towards her knees, praying for it all to go away. Lorna, scarcely taking her eyes off Darren and the pistol, was dropping handfuls of money down into the bag.

Stretched across the floor like sardines, none of the customers moved.

'Come on, come on!' Darren urged. 'Be quick!'

Lorna held up the green bin liner for him to see. 'That's all there is.'

'You wouldn't be holding out on me?'

There wasn't a patch of colour anywhere in Lorna's face.

'No, I suppose not.' He gestured with the gun. 'Back over here.'

Reaching up to retrieve the bag and the money, Darren had his face close to hers. 'Have to come round and see you some time. Easy now I know where you live.' He grinned and winked and blew her a kiss.

'Everyone stays where they are,' he called out at the door. ''Less they want to get hurt.'

Pushing the pistol down from sight and switching the bin liner to the other hand he pushed his way through the door to where Keith was waiting in the car.

Except that Keith wasn't waiting and nor was the car.

'Armed police,' said an amplified voice. 'Put your hands behind your head and get down on the ground. Do it now.'

Darren could see four vehicles, angled across the road; behind each one were men in blue overalls, arms outstretched, weapons at the ends of those arms all pointing at him.

'Keith!' Darren screamed in anguish. 'Keith!'

From the safety of the car where he was sitting with Resnick and Lynn Kellogg, a block away from the building society, Keith heard Darren's voice calling his name and brought up both hands to his ears.

'Armed police,' the voice repeated. 'You are surrounded. Raise your hands above your head now and then clasp them behind your neck. This is your final warning.'

Darren reached inside his jacket and pulled clear the pistol, bringing it round until it was held out in front of him, aiming in the direction of the nearest car.

The sergeant in charge of the tactical response team gave the order and Darren was hurled back and swayed like an off-balance skater, before falling forward with nothing to break his fall.

He had been hit once in the neck, twice in the chest and, to all intents and purposes, was dead before he struck the ground. The crash team from the ambulance did what they had to do but really it was for show. The officer who retrieved the unfired 9mm Walther PPK would testify in court that the safety catch was still on.

Inside the unmarked car at the far side of the disused home improvements store, Keith Rylands sobbed against Lynn's shoulder till his throat was sore, while Resnick stared through the windscreen and tried to blot out the sound.

# Fifty-One

The media thought it was Christmas come early: a young man, albeit armed and potentially dangerous, being shot down and killed by the police on an unremarkable city street in broad daylight was still an unusual enough occurrence not to pass unremarked. The Assistant Chief Constable gave a press conference and went into the news studios of both independent television and the BBC. The legal officer of Liberty issued a statement condemning the use of firearms in a public area as questionable and the police response as being excessive. The only one of the marksmen who had fired who could be persuaded to comment publicly, said he had simply done what he was trained to do. The dead man had aimed a weapon in his direction and he had felt his own life and that of his colleagues was in danger.

Not only the local but the national newspapers cleared the headlines, published photographs of both Darren and Keith; there were illustrators' reconstructions of the events and several pictures showing the blood on the pavement as a dark, blurry newsprint mass, akin to an abstract painting.

Local radio spoke at length to Lorna Solomon – 'brave and resourceful' – and Rebecca Astley – 'cool and elegant under pressure'. Keith Rylands's father – 'former rock star with hit records to his name' – said that his son was under sedation and too distressed to comment.

In everything but the *Express* it was newsworthy

enough to drive the constitutional problems caused by the rift between the Prince and Princess of Wales on to page two.

Resnick and Lynn Kellogg finished the afternoon at the market coffee stall, drinking strong espresso and saying very little. Earlier, Resnick had phoned Rylands to make sure that Keith was okay, giving what assurances he could that in the circumstances, Keith was unlikely to be charged.

He accepted a lift home from Lynn, eschewed his usual shower and soaked in a hot bath until it was hot no longer. He was in the kitchen feeding the cats and beginning to wonder what he was going to feed himself when the front doorbell rang.

Afraid it might be a reporter chancing his arm, Resnick opened up cautiously; of all the people it was least likely to be, his visitor was in the top two or three.

'Now then, Charlie. Big day, eh?'

It was Rains.

Sitting across from him in the living room, watching him drink the beer he'd asked for and got, Resnick was surprised how little Rains had changed. The face was fleshier perhaps, especially around the jaw; his body generally was thicker; all in all he'd probably put on ten or twelve pounds, but he was still fit. Resnick guessed he played the occasional game of tennis or squash, swam, worked out. But then he also drank and smoked.

He lit up now, asking first as a matter of course and taking Resnick's shrug as a yes.

'Anything to do with you, Charlie? That business today?'

'Something,' What the hell are you doing here, Resnick was thinking? Why have you come?

'Things've changed a bit, eh? Hardly open a paper

nowadays without some poor bastard's got himself shot by one of our lot. Your lot. Not before time, my way of thinking. That kid today, for instance, bit of a cowboy, wasn't he? Not a real pro. Nothing to get worked up about.' Rains took a long swallow from his glass. 'Not a bad drop of beer that, Charlie. What did you say it was, German?'

'Czech.'

'Good anyway.'

Get to the point, Resnick thought; if there is a point.

'We used to put a few pints away, eh, Charlie? Back when we were mates.'

'We never were that.'

'What? I've closed more pubs and clubs with you and Reg Cossall than any of us'd like to remember.'

'We were never mates.'

Rains cocked his head to one side. 'Have it your way.'

'What do you want?' Resnick asked, impatient with waiting.

'What?'

'You heard, what do you . . .'

'What do I want? Fine question, Charlie. Not seen hide nor hair of you in what? Eight, nine years. What's wrong with a social call?'

'After this time.'

'Not been around, Charlie. Been living abroad.'

'I know.'

Rains grinned and set down his glass. 'Better get me an ash tray, Charlie, or this is going to go all over the carpet.'

'Let it.'

'Elaine would never've let you get away with that.'

'Keep her out of it.'

'Like you did?'

Resnick was on his feet and for a moment Rains

thought he was going to take a swing at him; he thought
he might enjoy that. Instead Resnick walked past him
to the square bay of the window and looked out through
the partly drawn curtains into the shadows of the front
garden.

'How much do you know, Charlie?'

Resnick turned slowly. Rains was lolling back in the
comfortable chair, the one Resnick usually sat in himself,
alone there in the evenings, thinking, listening to music.
He hated the way Rains had arched his knee on to one
of the arms of the chair; hated the smug expression on
Rains's face.

'Most of it,' he said.

'Such as?'

'I know that you and Churchill had a meeting yesterday; that, one way or another, the two of you have been
associates since you persuaded him to grass up Prior.'

'Is that what I did?'

'Didn't you?'

Rains smirked. 'Maybe.'

'You got inside information from Churchill, enough
to send Prior down for a long time, and so as to keep
him in the clear, let on you'd got it from Prior's wife.

'You wanted Churchill still smelling sweet because if
his colleagues thought he was a grass they'd freeze him
out, never work with him again and that wouldn't suit
you because you wanted Churchill back in action passing
on your share of the take.

'You wanted Prior out of the way because you were
having an affair with his wife, probably because you
hoped you'd get information out of her as well, but
maybe because you genuinely liked her, fancied her at
least.'

Rains made a sound which meant don't be a fool.
'That was work, Charlie, Diddling that slag, that was

work. You don't think I could have feelings for a woman like that?'

Resnick moved away from the window, closer to where Rains was sitting. 'I don't think you could have feelings for anyone outside of yourself.'

'No?' Rains laughed. 'Never mind, eh, Charlie. Feelings enough for the both of us, you've got. Regular bleeding heart. Always were and I daresay you've got worse.'

'This is your last chance,' Resnick said. 'Say what you've got to say and get going.'

'Told you, Charlie, needed to know if you really had anything or if you were just fishing. Thought if I came to you and asked straight, you'd find it hard to lie.' Rains smiled. 'Not in your nature, never was.'

'I'm grateful.'

'Yes,' said Rains, getting to his feet. 'For once, so am I.'

'What makes you think you can just walk out of here?' Resnick asked. 'How do you know I won't stop you?'

'Arrest me?'

'Why not?'

'What charge?'

Rains moved towards the living-room door and Resnick set himself in his way. More than anything else what Resnick wanted to do was tear the smirk from Rains's face, do so with his own hands. He stepped to one side and allowed Rains to walk by. Heard the front door open and close. He stayed there, without moving, for a long time; until it was quite dark around him and the muscles of his legs were numb.

Perhaps the most pernicious thing about people like Rains was they had the power to make you behave like them.

# Fifty-Two

The first thing Ruth saw when she looked through the window that morning was the car she had heard drive up, parked now down by the sea wall, close to the first of the lobster nets. One of those removable signs on the passenger door, a minicab, car and driver for hire.

Ruth threw a coat over her shoulders, told the dog to stay where it was. 'You didn't come all this way by taxi?'

Prior gestured, palms of his hands outwards. 'I don't have a licence, Ruthie, don't own a car. What else was I to do?'

Stay away? Ruth thought, the words catching on her lips. Christ, she thought, I would hardly have recognized him. For the first time she had some insight into what it must have been like for him inside, locked away all those years.

Prior stood before her, almost sheepish. 'Aren't we supposed to kiss or something?'

Despite herself, Ruth smiled. 'Why break the habit of a lifetime?' she said.

Prior smiled back with his eyes. He wasn't going to hurt her, she could tell that. 'Why don't you come inside?' she asked. 'I'll make some tea.'

Prior looked off towards the sea. 'If it's all the same to you, I'd sooner stay out here.'

'Fancy a walk, then?'

'Why not?'

336

'Wait a second,' Ruth said, turning back towards the house. 'If I leave the dog behind, he won't understand.'

She waited until they were on the hard, damp sand, heading south, before telling him of Resnick's visit; telling him about Rains, the way he had got into her room at night, half-frightened her to death. Pretended to have killed the dog.

'Bastard!' Prior whispered.

'Rains,' Ruth said, 'there's more.'

'You don't have to tell me. I don't want to know.'

'Yes, you do,' Ruth said. 'It's why you're here.'

When she had felt married to him, living with him, imprisoned by him, Ruth had never been able to talk to him; now she had seen him again, this stranger, she could tell him anything.

She did: anything and everything.

Prior listened without interruption; said nothing for a long time. When he spoke it was almost wistful, distant – 'Makes you think, what happened to you, me, Rains running free.' There was no disguising the hurt and anger in his eyes.

'D'you want to turn back?' Ruth asked when they reached a point where the dunes came down closer towards the sea. 'We've come a long way.'

'Yes, all right. Best think about the taxi fare, eh?'

Several times walking back towards the cottages, Prior picked up a piece of driftwood, bleached white, and threw if for the dog to chase. At the sea wall, Ruth turned quickly towards him, kissed him on the face, and hurried across the green, just managing not to run, not looking back until she was inside and the car was pulling away on its long journey home.

Too late to cry now.

Prior remembered Churchill's mum, how she always

maintained he was a good son. When Prior called on her out of the blue, she was pleased to see him, invited him in.

'Frank never told me you was out.'

'Could be he doesn't know.'

'He'll be around soon. Always comes by of an evening when he can, likes to know I'm all right. Well, you can see I am. Come on in the lounge and put your feet up, some dreadful rubbish on telly, never mind. He'll be right pleased to see you, will Frank.'

He was so pleased he tried a runner, but Prior had him by the throat, face pressed hard against the paintwork on his mum's lounge door. 'I always knew you weren't worth the paper I shat on, Frank. Just give me where I can find Rains, that's all I want with you. And don't you try and warn him or I might be back.'

'Thanks, Mrs Churchill,' Prior said at the rear door. 'Nice to see you looking so well.'

Rains had more or less finished his business here, one more plan to okay, another investment to be made on his way back through London, currency to be transferred into his bank in Spain as pesetas. It was as well he'd come out to talk to Frank himself, convince him of the wisdom of riding their luck less hard. When you'd kept a good thing going this long, criminal to see it come down, all because of a little local greed. But he was happy now. Frank would pass along the world, see it all sorted. Tomorrow he'd be back on the plane, leaving Resnick and the rest of his former colleagues still floundering.

Rains took the brandy bottle over to the bed, poured a good measure into the glass and slid between the sheets. He had bought a Jeffrey Archer at the airport coming over and he read a couple more chapters now before finishing his drink and switching out the light.

In less than ten minutes he was asleep.

He was still asleep when a hand clamped across his mouth and a voice he failed to recognize spoke his name. Suddenly awake, he wriggled against the weight that was holding him down.

'Rains?'

The only reply was muffled, angry. What the hell was going on?

'It's me, Prior. This is for me. And my wife. In a way it's from Frank, too.'

It was the old coal hammer that had stood by Frank's mum's hearth more than twenty years. When her late husband had worked down the pit she'd got free coal and she'd kept the hammer there, handy, for breaking up the larger chunks. Prior lifted it above his head and brought it down between Rains's eyes as hard as he could.

Likely that blow was enough to kill him, but Prior didn't stop until the greater part of Rains's once handsome face was spread across the pillow and beyond.

He dropped the hammer down and wiped his hands upon the sheet, wiped splashes of blood from the bottle and gulped down some brandy, neat. There was a telephone in the next room and he used that to make the call.

'Hello? Who is this?' The voice was faltering, heavy with sleep.

'Is that Pam? Pam Van Allen?'

'Who is this?'

'It's me, Prior.'

'Why are you ringing me at home, and at this time?'

'You gave me your number.'

'Yes, for emergencies.'

'Right,' Prior said, 'that's what this is.'

Resnick waited a week. Prior was back inside, awaiting trial for murder. True to form, Frank Churchill had grassed on all and sundry in order to save his own hide; six men were on remand, facing five counts each of armed robbery, including Churchill himself. Ruth stayed put in her cottage, and Debbie Naylor had moved back in with Kevin and the baby, though she left some of her things at her mother's just in case. Lorna Solomon applied for a job in the principal office of the Abbey National Building Society in Sheffield and got it. Mark Divine went to France for a weekend by Hovercraft and was sick both ways. Resnick waited a week before dialling the probation office number and asking to speak to Pam Van Allen.

'I suppose you're calling to crow,' she said, when she knew who it was.

'What over?'

'Prior, of course.'

'Why? You were right. You said he had no antagonism towards his wife and you were right.'

There was an uneasy pause and then Pam said, 'Look, I'm sorry, but I'm really busy . . .'

'What would you think about meeting me some time?' Resnick asked. 'A drink or something. After work.'

He imagined her staring at the phone, surprised, maybe slightly embarrassed, maybe pushing one hand up through her silver-grey hair.

'I don't know,' she said finally. 'I'll have to think about it. I'll let you know.' And she hung up.

Resnick placed the receiver and went out into the CID room, hoping not too many people would notice the smile beginning to form on his face.

# Living Proof

John Harvey

*For Liz*


*What if I did not mention death to get started*
*or how love fails in our well-meaning hands*

ROBERT HASS: Thin Air

# One

The man running down the middle of the Alfreton Road at
five past three that Sunday morning was, as Divine would
say later, absolutely stark bollock naked. Poetic, for
Divine, if not scrupulously true. On his left foot, the man
was wearing a size eight, wool and cotton mix, Ralph
Lauren sock, a red polo player stitched on to the dark blue.
And he was bleeding. A thin line of drying blood, too light
in colour to match the Lauren logo, adhered to the man's
side, its source, seemingly, a puncture wound below his
pendulous breast.

The surface of the road was hard; it bruised his feet and
jarred his knees: his breath rasped harsh against his chest.
Promises to give up smoking, take up swimming, resume
playing squash – little in the man's past ten years had
prepared him for this.

Still, he continued to run, past the Forest Inn and the
Queen Hotel, the carpet tile shop and the boarded up
fronts of the café and the fruit and veg shop, both long
closed down; past Don Briggs Motorcycles, the Freezer
Centre and Kit 'Em Out, all closed down; on past the
Krishna Vegetarian Restaurant and Take Away and the
tiny health food shop that offered vitamins and ginseng,
athletic supports and marital aids.

Stumbling along the broken white line at the centre of
the road, he passed the boarded-up branch of Barclays
Bank, Tony's Barber Shop, the Bismilla Tandoori, the
Regency Bridal Salon and the Running Horse pub, before
finally, outside the vivid green front of Il Padrono

1

Ristorante Italiano, balance all but gone, arms flailing, he collided with a car parked near the kerb and cannoned sideways, falling heavily to his knees.

Under the changing glow of the nearby traffic light, his eyes were bright with tears. Not wanting to, he pressed his fingertips against his ribs and groaned.

The next time the light turned green, he pushed himself back to his feet and though at first his legs refused to move, he forced himself to carry on. Overweight, balding, middle-aged, a wound near the centre of his chest that had started to bleed again, the man had no idea where he was running to, only what he was running from.

# Two

Across the city, Resnick was sleeping soundly, cats curled here and there among the humps and hollows of his bed.

He had spent the weekend in Birmingham, at a conference called to address the establishment of a national police force. More silver epaulettes and high-flown phrases than he had encountered in one place since Marian Witczak had dragged him along to a revival of *The Merry Widow* at the Theatre Royal.

'I feel,' one senior officer had said, 'that we are already moving towards the formation of such a force in a very British way.' Piecemeal, ill-considered and over-cautious then, Resnick had thought, somewhere between the re-organisation of the National Health Service and the building of the Channel Tunnel.

'Y' never know, Charlie,' Jack Skelton had said, when he pleaded a backed-up schedule and sent Resnick along in his place, 'might not do you any harm, putting yourself about a bit. Letting yourself be seen. After all, don't want to stick at plain inspector all your life.'

Didn't he?

Watching all the high fliers like Helen Siddons, Home Office approved, race past him in the fast lane, didn't make Resnick feel he had a great deal of choice. Although, truth to tell, if he had wanted promotion badly enough, he would have pushed for it by now himself. Got it, like as not, for all that he had long ignored the lure of the local Masonic Lodge and had maintained a steadfast preference for watching County over chipping balls on to

3

the green, getting his handicap down below double figures.

No, the team he had working with him now – no one fussing overmuch with how he went about his job – thanks very much, Resnick liked it where he was.

The alarm aroused him a few minutes short of six and he padded, barefoot, towards the bathroom, cats, instantly alert, winding between his legs.

The shower head was in need of cleaning again and the water jetted out at him, unevenly, too hot or far too cold.

Before the cats could be fed, the caked residue of the previous day's Whiskas had to be prised from their bowls and Bud, the youngest, seized the opportunity to perfect that pathetic mew of hunger which, allied to the soulful stare of his eyes, would have served well amongst the young men begging beside the mural in the Broad Marsh bus station. What had someone at the conference called it, homelessness? A choice of lifestyle? As if, Resnick had thought, anyone would deliberately choose to sleep rough through the kind of wet winter they had just experienced.

He forked food into the four bowls, allowing the others to get a head start before letting Dizzy in through the back door, from where he had been patrolling the night. Tail angled high, the black cat stalked past him, green eyes narrowing against the extra light.

Resnick dropped a handful of Costa Rican beans into the grinder, sliced rye and caraway, set the kettle on to boil; he removed the outside layer from what remained of the Polish garlic sausage and cut thin slices from a stump of Emmental cheese. Behind him, through the glass at the top of the door, the sky was turning through purple and orange to red.

Resnick carried his breakfast through to the living room, switched the radio on low and sat with yesterday's paper on the arm of his chair, while Miles assiduously cleaned himself on his lap, pink tongue licking deep between extended claws.

It was the time of day Resnick liked best, the quiet before most of the world had got under way. Even back in the days when he had been married – before the advent of the cats – he would slide from the bed early, careful not to disturb Elaine, and wander contentedly through the empty rooms before settling with a cup of coffee and a new record on the stereo, headphones to his ears.

These days he rarely used the headphones for fear he would fail to hear that first summons, hauling him into the working day – bit of an emergency, sir, something's come up.

This morning he got as far the sports round-up just ahead of the half hour – another England bowler laid low by a strained groin – before the phone rang and he swivelled towards it, Miles jumping to the carpet before he was pushed.

Divine's voice was loud with cynicism and wonder. 'Those blokes who were attacked a few months back in the red-light district, looks like we might have another.'

'Serious?'

'Serious enough. Lorry driver picked him up by Canning Circus, not far short of running all eight wheels right over him. Stretched out in the middle of the chuffing road he was, absolutely stark bollock naked.'

'Twenty minutes,' Resnick said. 'I'll be there.'

# Three

Those blokes.

The first had been your average punter, run of the mill; confectionery salesman with a wife and kids in Hinckley and a four-year-old hatchback stuffed full with Snickers and liquorice chewing gum. Halfway along one of the alleys off Waterloo Road, lured by leopard-skin leggings and red high heels, and two men had suddenly been standing there behind him, quick and still from the darkness. Three weeks on the critical list, it had taken all the skills of the Senior Registrar and her neurosurgery team to reconstruct his skull, fragment by fragment, piece by broken piece. Every day his wife had come in on the bus to sit at his bedside, reading *Woman's Weekly*, filling in puzzles, eating his grapes. A couple of months later, one of his credit cards had turned up in Leicester, part of a job lot being offered for sale in a pub near the covered market.

The second victim had been an Italian soccer fan, jubilant after his team's victory in the Anglo-Italian Cup and celebrating on the open spaces of the Forest Recreation Ground with his friends, waving thousand-lire notes and singing Pavarotti's *Greatest Hits*. A young redhead, newly arrived on a Super Saver from Newcastle, had offered him a quick hand-job in the trees off the road, anything to stop him singing. A couple of early morning dog-walkers found him tied to a sycamore hours later, terrified, stripped of everything save his first-team replica shirt. Seventeen stitches it had taken to mend the gash in his forehead. His plane ticket had been found in a rubbish bin near the Forest park-and-ride and his passport, torn in two and two again, finally surfaced floating on the duck pond by the entrance to the Arboretum.

The most recent occurrence had been at the nub end of March, another sales rep, in the city on a roll and booked into the Royal Hotel. He had met a woman in the penthouse bar, nice looking, good clothes, nothing garish but out for business just the same. Back in his room, she had undressed him on the bed, encouraging him, he said, to talk dirty to her all the while. Call her, you know, a slag, a dirty whore, stuff like that. When he was down to his Jockey's, she had pulled a knife from her handbag and stabbed him, once in the side, once through the flesh of the upper arm. Frantically, he had pushed her clear away and she had fled, off out of the room and down the hotel corridor, leaving him in no position to chase her. The description he gave of her, detailed as it was, matched no known prostitute on the Vice Squad's books. Just another housewife, most likely, eking out the Family Support.

Three incidents, probably unrelated, and now a fourth.

Resnick crossed the street from the centre of Canning Circus, early traffic already building up on its way along Derby Road towards the city centre. Time was, he would have bumped into Jack Skelton at this hour, the superintendent setting out on his regular three-mile run. But since early spring, Skelton's exercise had been restricted to pacing the four walls of his office. Whether the superintendent's relationship with DI Helen Siddons had progressed beyond an older man's fantasy or not, Resnick could imagine only too well the tartness with which Alice Skelton would have scolded him for his folly. And Siddons' accelerated promotion to the West Country had done little to ease the situation, leaving Skelton increasingly disgruntled and grey-haired, his girth thickening at a noticeable rate.

The CID office was close to the head of the stairs on the first floor, an L-shaped room with filing cabinets ranked along the far wall, below detailed maps of the city. A succession of desks and tables ran along two of the walls and down the centre of the room. Graham Millington's desk was on its own, adjacent to the thinly partitioned office which had the words *Detective Inspector Charles Resnick* on its door.

Behind Millington's desk were the kettle and mugs and the rest of the paraphernalia for tea- and coffee-making. Most of the other surfaces were clogged with official forms in a variety of shades and colours, typewriters and VDUs, here and there foil containers harbouring the remains of the previous night's chicken korma or lamb kebab.

In the usual way of things, only the officer on early shift would have been present when Resnick arrived, busy updating the files that logged the night's activities, after which the primary investigation of the inevitable break-ins would be his or her responsibility. This morning, though, Mark Divine had been there from first light, back aching after sharing the interior of a rusting blue Transit with Kevin Naylor, the pair of them peeing into old orange juice cartons and waiting forlornly for the Home-care warehouse on the Abbeyfield Industrial Estate to be raided for a third time.

'What buggers me,' as Divine was overfond of saying, 'is who'd go to all that trouble to liberate three gross of sink plungers and a couple of dozen aluminium ladders?'

The fourth night in a row in which they were no nearer to finding an answer.

Naylor had snuck off home to snatch a quick hour snuggled up to his Debbie, while Divine, for whom home

8

offered no such luxury, had opted for a kip behind his desk. He had been snoring nicely when the duty officer rang up from below with details of a man who'd been brought in barely conscious from the end of the Alfreton Road. Soon after which, he had phoned his superior.

'Mark,' Resnick said, door swinging to behind him.

'Boss.' Divine swung his legs down from his desk and stood to uncertain attention.

'Best fill me in.'

Divine told him what little he knew about the man who was presently in a bed at Queen's Medical, barely conscious and temporarily restricted to fluids.

'This stab wound,' Resnick asked. 'Life threatening?'

'Seemed so at first, now they reckon he's going to be okay. Missed anything vital, by the sound of it.' Divine shrugged. 'Lost a fair bit of blood all the same.'

'And the nature of the attack, how much do we know about that?'

'Not a heck of a lot. I mean, when he first come round he was full of it. Tart and whore, over and over, blaming her, like, for what had happened.'

'It was the woman who stabbed him, that's what he's claiming?'

'No two ways about it. Aside from that, though, started asking him a few questions, clammed up tighter'n a virgin's arse. Wouldn't even tell us his name.'

Resnick frowned and shook his head. 'All right. Have a word with Vice, see if they had anyone on patrol last night, late. They might have noticed something that'll tie in. Minute Kevin arrives, pair of you can get up by the Forest, talk to the girls on the early shift. Meantime, I'll drop by the hospital. Maybe if our mystery man knows he's out of danger, he'll be more ready to talk.'

'Right, boss.' Divine was alert now, tiredness fallen away. It wasn't every day Resnick was prepared to trust the younger man's instincts and there was a grin around

9

the corners of Divine's mouth as he sat back behind his desk, reaching for the phone.

Lynn Kellogg was on the stairs as Resnick went down. After the traumas at the start of the year, she had had her hair cut short, making her face seem less rounded, more severe. More often than not now, there was a haunted look, hunched at the back of her eyes.

'Morning, Lynn. Everything okay?'

'Fine.'

Neither of them believed it.

Resnick made a mental note to ask if she were still seeing the police psychiatrist, and if she were, whether it was doing any good.

# Four

After circling the inner ring road twice, Resnick squeezed into a parking place at the rear of the hospital, close to the offshoot of the canal. Above, the sky showed a flat, unbroken blue, but the sun, for early summer, gave off little warmth. He thrust both hands deep into his jacket pockets as he walked.

That way in took him past the psychiatric wing and an image of his ex-wife, Elaine, slipped unbidden into his mind: the way she had looked the last time he had seen her, after spending God knows how much time in places likes this. And Lynn, he kept thinking of Lynn – two years without a relationship worthy of the name, and when she had come close to giving her trust to someone again, it had been the wrong man.

It had been a mistake that had cost her more than pride and self-esteem; it had very nearly cost her life. Resnick remembered how it ended: the mud that had sucked, thick, about his feet as he had run across the field-end, awkwardly towards her, helicopter hovering noisily above; the way the blood had pumped, jaggedly, from his heart when he knew that she was safe.

In the months since then, all conversation between them had been formal, withdrawn, as if what each had glimpsed in that despairing clutch of arms was more than they would dare acknowledge. And Michael Best was in custody awaiting trial for kidnapping and murder. His days in court – and Lynn's – still to come.

The single door which Resnick knew led through to the

rear of Accident and Emergency was directly in front of him and he pushed it open and went in.

They sat in small groups of relatives and friends or else they sat alone, staring off into that space where time, long since, had decided to stand still. For so many of the people here, Resnick thought, this was how they spent their lives; uncomfortably, on institutional chairs in institutional rooms, waiting for the number clicking slowly over to correspond to the one clutched in their hands. Social services, the housing department, medical centre, the dole; the bored clerk checking their answers, painstakingly scrawled upon this form or that. Rent rebate, clothing allowance, disability benefit. The women, pregnant, or with three kids under five who ran and chased between the lines of chairs, defying all the shouts and threats, sporadic and half-hearted, until finally they went flying, arse over tip, crashed into the wall and cried. Men with short moustaches, tattoos and sallow faces, shutting out all noise, clenching and reclenching their fists at their children's screams – the futility of dreams.

An Asian family sat off on its own, near the door, the man in a brown suit, bandage lopsided about his head, his wife in a sari, pale blue and green, carpet slippers on her feet, a small child, little more than a baby, sleeping fitfully inside her arms. Close to Resnick, a middle-aged man with tight grey hair and lined face, wearing someone's cast-off Fair Isle pullover pocked with holes and small burns, sat smoking a cigarette, after each drag carefully tapping the ash into the empty can of Strongbow cider clenched between his knees.

The nurse Resnick intercepted was wearing a sister's uniform and the badge on its lapel told him her name was Geraldine McAllister. Almost certaintly she was older, but all she looked was twenty-five or -six.

12

'Excuse me,' Resnick said. 'But you had somebody brought in earlier, a stab wound . . .'

'We had several.'

'This one . . .'

'Three, to be exact.' Resnick had expected Irish and what he got was Scots, not broad but unmistakable, musical.

'The one I'm interested in . . .' he began.

She was looking at the warrant card he held out in one hand. 'That would be John Smith, then, I expect.'

'Is that his name?'

She smiled. 'Probably not. But we had to call him something. He refused to give a name.' The smile was still there, broader if anything. 'Not very inventive, is it?'

'I'm sure you've got better things to do.'

'Than be inventive? I doubt that. Not round here.'

'Gerry,' a male nurse called from round a curtain, 'can you take a look at this a minute?'

'You,' she said to Resnick. 'Inspector. Don't go. Two shakes now and I'll be back.'

One small emergency extended into another and it was not so far short of half an hour before they were sitting in a cramped office behind the receptionist's desk. A polystyrene cup of lukewarm grey coffee sat, unwanted, between Resnick's feet.

Gerry McAllister held an X-ray in her hand, slanted up towards the light. 'You can see, the wound isn't very deep, a couple of inches at most. Even so,' she shook her head, 'a little bit higher and to the left . . .'

Her hair was not chestnut as Resnick had first supposed, but auburn, redder at the ends than at the roots. And she was older, a cross-hatch of worry lines around her eyes. Thirty-four or -five?

'Was it consistent with, I mean, did it seem to have been made with a knife?'

13

'Rather than what? A knitting needle, something like that?'

It hadn't been precisely what Resnick had in mind.

'A couple of weeks back,' Gerry McAllister said, 'we had this woman come in. She'd flagged down a taxi on the road; didn't have any money, but the driver brought her here just the same. There was a knitting needle sticking out from the corner of her eye.'

Automatically, Resnick cast his mind back, trying to recall whether the incident had been reported.

'There'd been a row at home, apparently. Things had got out of hand.'

Resnick nodded. 'Boyfriend or husband?'

The sister shook her head firmly. 'Mother. Should they go to the bingo or stay in and watch *Blind Date*.' She smiled. 'Alarming, isn't it, the way things get blown up out of all proportion? Arguing like that over something like *Blind Date*.'

'Our Mr Smith,' Resnick said. 'He didn't say anything about how he came to be stabbed?'

'My hand slipped a little on the needle,' Gerry said, 'when I was giving him his injection. Punctured the skin more than I'd intended. He didn't even open his mouth then.'

Resnick grinned and got to his feet.

'I've checked up on the ward, it's okay for you to go up and see him. Maybe he'll talk to you,' she said.

Resnick doubted that were true, but thanked Gerry McAllister and followed her out of the room. Immediately, three voices were calling her from three different directions, each as urgent as the next.

The anonymous victim had been put into a side ward which he shared with two men way past pensionable age and a nervous-looking youth whose bed was marked 'Nil by Mouth'.

14

He was lying on his side, face towards the wall, a tray of barely browned toast and soggy cereal on the bedside cabinet, untouched.

'Not hungry?' Resnick asked, pulling out a chair and setting it down close to the bed.

The man raised his head enough to look into Resnick's eyes, then rolled away.

'Whatever happened,' Resnick said, 'you were lucky. Lucky someone found you, brought you to us; lucky to be here. That whoever did this wasn't stronger.'

He reached out and, without force, rested his hand on the upper edge of the sheet, bone and flesh of the man's shoulder beneath. At his touch, the man flinched but nothing more.

'Listen,' Resnick said, 'if there's somebody out there attacking men, men who put themselves in a vulnerable position – we need to bring them in. If we don't, well, you understand what I'm saying. The next person might not get off as easy as you.' His voice was soft beneath the squeak of passing trolley wheels, the muffled inanities of breakfast television from the main ward. 'You wouldn't want to be responsible for that, would you? Someone dying?'

Beneath his hand, Resnick felt the muscles tighten through the loose flesh of the man's arm.

'Whatever you were up to, last night, no reason that shouldn't remain your business. No need to broadcast it around. Time to time, we all do things we'd rather nobody else knew. Family. Friends. It's something I can understand.'

For an answer, the man shuffled further across the bed, shrugging off Resnick's hand; sheet and blanket he pulled up until they half-covered his head.

Resnick leaned low across him, close enough to sense the damp ripeness of the man's sweat. His fear.

'Think on what I've said. Talk to us. Co-operate. You'll

find it easier all around.' Resnick raised his head and then, almost as an afterthought: 'There is a charge, you know, obstructing the police in the course of their duties.'

He took a card from his wallet and slipped it between the man's reluctant fingers.

'I'll be waiting for you to call me. Don't leave it too long.'

# Five

'Yes, madam,' the uniformed PC was saying to the old lady at Enquiries, 'of course I can arrange for the Crime Prevention Officer to call round. If you'll just let me have your name and address and phone number, then he'll get in touch with you and agree a time.'

Resnick stepped around the woman as she fumbled in her handbag for the scrap of paper on which she had scribbled all the details down. 'I've just moved, you see, and I forget . . .'

Off to the right of the stairs, a repetitive yelling came from the direction of the police cells, the same two words, over and over, deadened of all meaning. 'Hold it down in there,' came the custody sergeant's voice. 'I said, hold it down!'

Resnick grinned into the silence that followed. The newly appointed custody sergeant had been transferred from Central CID; six foot three, boots that shone whenever he was on duty and shirts that were always freshly ironed. Most Saturdays he played alongside Divine in the Force's first XV and when he said hold it down, only the most drunken or foolish disobeyed.

Resnick turned left at the head of the stairs, towards the bird-like clamour of phones.

'CID. DC Kellogg speaking . . .'
'CID. DC Naylor . . .'
'CID . . .'

'Graham,' Resnick raised a hand in greeting as he

threaded his way between the rows of desks towards his office. 'Any chance of a cup of tea?'

'Kev,' Millington said, looking across at Naylor. 'Mash for us, will you?'

Naylor drew the telephone away from his face, one hand clamped across the mouthpiece. 'Mark, you're not doing anything.'

'Lynn,' Divine began, noticing that she was on her feet, 'while you're up . . .'

'Don't,' Lynn shook her head, 'as much as think about it.'

'Chuffin' hell!' Divine moaned, heading for the kettle. 'At least when Dipak was still here, you could count on him to fall for it.'

Overhearing, Lynn treated him to a look that would have stripped several layers of wallpaper. Although off duty, DC Dipak Patel had intervened in a brawl in the city centre and been fatally stabbed for his trouble: he had been a close colleague and a good friend.

'What I meant,' Divine grinned, seizing his chance to wind her up, 'one good thing about encouraging all these minorities into the Force, they're so grateful to be here, they don't mind doing a few chores.'

'Yes?' Lynn was out from behind her desk, blocking his path. 'All these minorities? Take a look, Mark. How many can you see?'

'Aside from you, you mean?'

'All right,' Millington said, setting himself between them. 'Shut it. The pair of you.'

'The pair . . .' Lynn began.

'Enough!' Like a referee about to issue a yellow card, Millington raised a hand in the air and glared. Lynn held his gaze for ten, twenty seconds, before turning aside, and grudgingly resuming her seat.

Blowing her a kiss over Millington's shoulder, Divine wandered across towards the kettle.

'And you,' Millington said quietly, coming up behind Divine as he was flipping tea bags into the pot, 'don't be so quick with your mouth. That way you might give what you call a brain a bit more of a chance.'

There were three Home Office circulars waiting on Resnick's desk for him to read, initial and pass on; a subscription renewal form for *Police Review* and information about a forthcoming course on the computer analysis of fingerprints at Bramshill College. Resnick pushed these to one side and shuffled through his drawer, searching for the flier from the newly refurbished Old Vic – the Stan Tracey Duo were playing that season and, if at all possible, he didn't want to miss them.

'Boss?' Millington knocked and entered, two mugs of tea precariously balanced in his one hand.

Resnick reached out and relieved him of one of the mugs, found a space to set it down; was it Millington or his wife, he wondered, who'd selected that particular shade of olive green from the suit rack in Marks and Spencer's?

'Ram raiding,' Millington said, helping himself to a seat. 'Buggers have come up with a new twist.'

Resnick sipped his tea and waited; over the past eighteen months there'd been a dramatic increase in the number of robberies carried out with the aid of stolen cars. As a method it was bog simple: drive the car fast through the front window of a city centre shop, jump out, grab what you can, either slam the car into reverse and drive back out or run like fuck.

'Bloke out at Wollaton, just back in from tending his begonias – holly-leafed, apparently, not so easy to grow ... anyway, sat himself down to watch a spot of racing, wife about to do the honours with the biscuit barrel and a pot of Earl Grey, when this four-year-old Ford Escort comes steaming up his front drive, detours across the

19

lawn, smack into the conservatory at the side of the house.'

'After his prize blooms, then, Graham?' Resnick asked. But Millington was not to be diverted.

'Old boy grabbed the fire tongs and went off to repel boarders, while his missus phoned us. These three youths were into the house through the side door, knocked him flying, concussion, had the old lady tied up with the telephone wire and went out of there in five minutes flat. Half a dozen cups gone from his trophy cabinet, silver medals, jewellery box from the bedroom, her fur coat, watch, thirty-five-piece ruby wedding dinner service, didn't as much as bother with the VCR.'

'The couple, how're they doing?'

'Shook up, who wouldn't be? Keeping him in Queen's for a few days' observation. She's got a daughter, come to stay.'

'Leads?'

'Car was stolen the day before, shopping centre out at Bulwell. Found abandoned a few hours later, not so far short of Cinderhill.'

'Wouldn't be much left of it, then.'

'Four wheels and a chassis.'

Resnick had a mouthful more tea. 'Didn't Reg Cossall have something going over that way somewhere?'

'Broxtowe, yes. Still has. Urban Youth Initiative, that's the official name for it. Won't tell you what Reg calls it.'

'Have a word, then, Graham. Might tie in with something, someone he's got tabs on.'

'Right.'

'Meantime, description of what's missing . . .'

'On its way round today. Long as we can keep forgetting the photocopy budget.'

There was a knock and in response to Resnick's 'Come in,' Divine's head and shoulders appeared round the edge of the door.

'Kev and me are just off up the Forest. I was wondering, bloke in the hospital, anything useful?'

Resnick shook his head. 'Not as much as a name. How about Vice? Anything from them?'

'Low profile last night, as it happens. Promised to put the word out today, though. Turn up anything, they'll let us know.'

'Okay, Mark. Oh, and if Lynn's still there . . .'

But Lynn Kellogg was already in the doorway. 'Break-ins in the Park. Five in total. Close enough to be the work of the same team. Several reports of an old post office van in the area, could have been using it to haul the stuff away in.'

Resnick nodded. 'Cool your heels on that for an hour, will you? Fellow who was stabbed last night, he's out at Queen's, refusing to say a word. Get yourself down there, see what you can do.'

'Right, sir, will that be Mata Hari, then, or Florence Nightingale?'

Resnick looked at her carefully and she was a long way from smiling.

'Don't suppose I'm allowed to ask any more if it's the time of the month?' Millington said, after Lynn had closed the door.

'No, Graham. You're not.'

Millington shrugged inside his olive-green suit and sucked on his upper lip. 'This party I'm getting up to go to Trent Bridge, first Saturday of the Test, you've not changed your mind?'

But Resnick was already shaking his head. Watching County of a Saturday afternoon through the winter was one thing – all the speed and excitement of plant germination, but at least it was over in an hour and a half. Whereas cricket . . .

'Oh,' Millington said, a last thought as he left Resnick's office. 'Skelton wants to see you. Something about shots

21

in the park?' And he was off, wandering in the direction of the teapot, lips puckered together as he whistled thoughtfully through the opening verse of 'Sailor'. An early hit of Petula's, but a good one.

# Six

When Resnick knocked and entered, Skelton was standing behind his desk looking at the first of several sheets of fax paper which were curling around his hand.

'Charlie, come on in.'

Resnick recognised neither of the other people in the room, a man and a woman rising to greet him, the man stepping forward with an uncertain smile.

'Charlie, this is David Tyrell, Programme Director of *Shots in the Dark*. Detective Inspector Resnick, CID.'

Tyrell was tall, taller than Resnick by an inch or more, bespectacled, his already slim body made slimmer by a suit that Resnick wagered cost more than a season ticket to County plus change.

'Inspector, good to meet you.'

Tyrell's handshake was strong, the eyes behind the glasses unblinking, but his skin had the pallor of someone who has spent too long out of the light.

'This is Mollie,' Tyrell said. 'My assistant.'

'Mollie Hansen. Assistant Director, Marketing.' Her grip was quick and cool and those five words enough to mark her as a Geordie, strayed from home. She stood there a moment longer, taking in Resnick with slate-grey eyes, the pinch of blood where he had nicked himself shaving, the speck of something yellow crusted to his lapel. A widening of her mouth, not yet a smile, and she stepped back – scarlet T-shirt, Doc Martens, jeans.

'You know this festival, Charlie? The one Mr Tyrell's responsible for.'

'Not really.'

Over by the side wall, Mollie Hansen sighed.

'Why don't we all sit down?' Skelton suggested. 'See what we've got.'

Tyrell crossed his legs, drew a cigarette packet from his pocket and, almost in the same gesture, pushed it back from sight. '*Shots* has been running four years. It's a crime and mystery festival, films mainly, TV, more recently, books as well. Each year we invite special guests, stars, I suppose you'd call them, to some extent built the programme around them. You know, Quentin Tarantino, Sara Paretsky, people like that.'

Knowing neither of them, Resnick nodded. He felt the strength of Mollie Hansen's gaze, weighing him up for what she thought he was.

'This year,' Tyrell continued, 'we've got Curtis Woolfe. The director. His first public appearance in fifteen years.'

'Sixteen,' Mollie said quietly.

Tyrell ignored her and carried on. 'For the book side of things, we've managed to get Cathy Jordan to come over from the States. Which is great.'

'Except . . .' began Mollie.

'Except she's been receiving threatening letters.'

'Which is why we've come to you.'

Cathy Jordan, Resnick was thinking. *Jordan.* He wondered if he should know the name, wondered if he did. The last crime novel he'd tried to read had been an old Leslie Charteris found inside a chest of drawers he'd bought in an auction at the Cattle Market. He had never finished it.

Skelton was holding the faxed copies out towards him and Resnick stood and took them from his hand. The words were typed and faint, not easy to read.

*You know, I really do think you've been*
*allowed to pursue what is after all a very*

*limited talent altogether too far.*

*It's one thing, of course, for people who should know better to be taken to the point where they will award you prizes, quite another for you to have the brazen effrontery to accept them.*

*Remember Louella Trabert, Cathy, remember what happened to her?*

Resnick looked up, 'Louella Trabert?'

'She's in one of her novels,' Tyrell said. 'A character.'

'A victim,' Mollie said.

Resnick was watching her, the tilt of her chin, the flushing high on her cheeks. 'What does happen to her?' he asked.

'She gets dragged from a car in the middle of the night, with her children left strapped in the back seat. These guys haul her off into the woods, strangle and rape her. Next morning one of the kids gets free and finds her upside down, tied by her ankles to a tree, her body slit from neck to belly with a hunting knife. Gutted.'

'Not exactly,' Tyrell said.

'Jesus! How exact do you want it to be?'

Resnick glanced at the other letters and set them back down.

'You're taking these seriously? She's taking them seriously? Cathy Jordan.'

'Seriously enough to let us know,' Tyrell said. 'But not enough to prevent her coming.'

'They were posted in America?' Resnick asked.

Tyrell nodded. 'New York. Where she lives.'

'And she's no idea who sent them?'

'Apparently not.'

'Well,' Resnick moved back to his seat. 'Maybe she feels she'll be safer over here anyway.'

Tyrell looked over at Mollie, who was already reaching down towards the black leather bag by her feet.

'This arrived this morning,' Mollie said, the envelope in her hand.

# Seven

*Dear Cathy,*

*I keep waiting for you to make the announcement, go public, seize the moment during one of those chat shows you're always on whenever I switch on the TV. You know, one of those quiet moments, snuggled down on the settee with Letterman, or laughing with Jay Leno and then, out of the blue, leaving aside all the fun and the gossip – and you are funny, Cathy, I have to give you that – you'll come right out with it. Let me tell you something now, you'll say, looking right at us with those big, blue eyes of yours, the truth is, David, Jay, I am the most talentless bitch that ever got up on her hind legs and walked. Real talent, that is. Leaving aside self-promotion and back-stabbing – plagiarism – all the things I'm really good at. Oh, and of course it helps to have the morals of the well-known alley cat, best not forget that.*

*The trouble is, Cathy, the richer you get, the more units – isn't that what you call books nowadays, dear? – you sell, the less likely this is to happen. So I'm going to have to stop it now, myself, over here in England. Put an end to this farrago, once and for all. You do understand me, don't you, Cathy?*

*You do realise I am serious? Poor little*
*Anita Mulholland, Cathy, remember what*
*happened to her.*

The letter was on a single sheet of white paper, A4 size,
unwatermarked, undated, almost needless to say,
unsigned. At first glance, a good bubble jet or laser printer
had been used. The envelope in which it had been
delivered was self-sealing, slim and white, manufactured
by John Dickinson and with the words 'Eurolope Enve-
lopes' printed over and over in a grey diagonal across the
inside. Centred on the front of the envelope, the words
'Cathy Jordan'. No postmark, no stamp.

'You found this where?' Resnick asked.

Tyrell glanced at Mollie. 'In the office,' Mollie said.
'At Broadway. It was there with the other mail when I
arrived.'

'What time?'

'I usually get in at around a quarter to ten. This morning
it was earlier, half past nine. I was sorting through the post
and I found this.'

'Who else was in the office beside you?'

Mollie gave it a little thought. 'The cleaner would have
been and gone. If the mail arrives before she leaves,
usually she'll put it on the desk, but this was still on the
floor. The only other possibility is Dick McCrea, he's the
finance director. He's sometimes in ahead of me, but . . .'

'But today he's in London,' Tyrell put in, 'a meeting at
the BFI. He would have gone straight to the station, the
7.38 train.'

'If he'd forgotten something, though,' Resnick said, 'at
the office, something he needed . . .'

'Dick McCrea,' Mollie said, 'got his memory in a direct
deal with God. Forget is a word he doesn't admit exists.'

'Miss Jordan,' Skelton said, 'you've told her about
this?'

'Not yet,' said Tyrell. 'We thought . . . I thought first of all we should speak to you. See if there wasn't something you could do. Not a bodyguard, exactly . . .'

'Heaven forbid!' Mollie said, not quite beneath her breath.

'I don't know,' Tyrell continued, 'some kind of police presence, maybe. Low key. Something that would reassure her.'

'The last thing we want,' Mollie said, 'is for people to be put off attending because they think there's going to be some kind of incident.'

Or, Resnick thought, for one of your star guests to get back on the plane and fly home.

'When's Cathy Jordan due to arrive?' Skelton asked.

'Tomorrow,' Mollie said. 'The early morning flight. Her publisher's meeting her at Heathrow and taking her into London for lunch. She's continuing up here by train. She should arrive about a quarter to five.'

Resnick and Skelton exchanged glances. Aside from the recent stabbing, there were other serious crimes outstanding: a sub-post office that had been robbed at gun-point and the postmaster shot through the leg and shoulder when he tried to resist; a domestic incident that had left one partner with burns to the face and neck from scalding water, one of the children with badly bruised ribs and a closed eye; unsolved burglaries were up for the third year in succession, as were thefts from vehicles and taking and driving away without consent. The recruitment of new staff was on hold. Budgets were screwed down tighter than an Arctic winter. This was policing in the age of cost-effectiveness and consumer choice, when those at the top talked of minimal visual policing, counted the paper clips, put a ban on overtime and sat up long into the night massaging the crime figures. If Resnick and Skelton were in the business of selling sentences, less and less people were buying. The last thing they needed was a media celebrity in need of mollycoddling, a body to guard

29

and protect against an unknown possible assailant during a festival at which the attendance might run into the thousands.

Skelton took a breath. 'Charlie, why don't you liaise with Miss Hansen? Arrange to meet this Cathy Jordan, talk to her, try and get a sense of how serious she thinks these threats really are. Assure her we'll co-operate as fully as we can during her stay. Without making promises we can't keep.'

Resnick nodded reluctantly and glanced over at Mollie Hansen who was already drawing a card from the back of her Filofax. 'My number's on there.'

'Meantime,' Skelton was on his feet now, 'I trust neither of you will say anything about all of this to the press. If there is anything to these letters, the last thing we need is a three-ring circus.'

'Of course,' said Mollie.

'Absolutely,' said Tyrell.

Unless, Resnick thought, they reckoned that instead of putting people off, a few good rumours might do wonders at the box office.

'Here,' Mollie said, pulling a paperback book from her bag and pushing it into Resnick's hands. 'You might like to take a look at this. It's meant to be one of her best.'

## DEAD WEIGHT

### An Annie Q. Jones Mystery

by

### CATHY JORDAN

'One last thing,' Resnick said. 'The Anita Mulholland mentioned in the letter, is she another character in one of these books?'

'That's right,' Mollie said.

'Another victim?'

'She goes on holiday with her family, to Mexico. She's thirteen. One evening her parents go down to a barbecue by the hotel pool and leave her upstairs in their room. When they get back up, an hour or so later, she's gone. A few days afterwards, someone comes across this thing like a scarecrow in the hills outside the town; it's made from Anita's clothes, up high on a cross of sticks. The police get up a search and dogs find her body in a shallow grave.' The tension in Mollie's voice was tight now and undisguised. 'That's it,' she said, 'apart from the ways she's tortured before she dies.'

Tyrell was looking at her with concern, possibly anger. Quickly he shook Resnick's hand and then Skelton's. 'We should be going. Superintendent, Inspector, thanks for your time.'

'I'll expect to hear from you,' Mollie said to Resnick from the door. 'Meantime, enjoy the book. Let me know what you think.'

After she and Tyrell had left the room, Skelton fussed with a few things on his desk and cleared his throat. 'Quite partial to a bit of *Morse*, myself,' he said.

Resnick didn't answer. He dropped the paperback down into the already sagging side pocket of his coat and headed out along the corridor towards the CID room. Another task he was certain he didn't want.

# Eight

Sharon Garnett took her time walking back up Forest Road West to where she had parked her car, a four-year-old Peugeot in need of a new clutch. She was wearing black ski-pants that emphasised her height, a red and yellow scarf pulled bandana-like across her hair; in one hand she was carrying a can of Lucozade, a paper bag containing a cheese and ham cob in the other. Relaxed, Sharon moved like someone at ease with herself, strength held in reserve.

The vehicle that slowed alongside her was a Vauxhall, almost certainly a fleet car, a dark blue Cavalier. The driver pressed the electronic switch to lower the window and leaned across. 'Working?' he asked.

She put him at thirty, no more than thirty-five, dark striped suit, white shirt, tie; expensive watch on his wrist, hair brushed down and across to compensate for its early loss. Sharon wondered if she had seen him there before and decided she probably had not.

'How about it?' he tried again. 'You working or not?'

'Sure,' Sharon said, without breaking her stride, 'though not the way you mean. Now piss off before I run you in.'

The Cavalier was off up the street and turning left into Southey Street with speed enough to leave tyre marks on the tarmac. Sharon shook her head: why was it some men were content with a jacket potato at lunchtime and for some it was a quick shag?

Back behind the wheel of her car, she popped the top of

the Lucozade can and tilted back her head to drink. A pair of girls – one in a short skirt and heels, the other in tight red trousers and boots – spotted her fifty yards along the opposite pavement, turned in their tracks and began to walk briskly back the other way.

The Lucozade was warm and fizzy and the cob was ten degrees short of stale; fragments of crust splintered over her legs and the seat. The Terry Macmillan she'd been reading lay open, face down, on the passenger side. The dashboard clock told her she had a good two hours to go.

Sharon Garnett had joined the police late, in her mid-thirties, a career move she had tried not to see as a sign of desperation. All her applications to CID in London had been rebuffed and it had taken a move north-east – to Lincolnshire – before she was able to join the ranks of detectives. After the best part of a year, she had known she wanted something closer to the cutting edge than investigating poultry fraud and pig rustling in King's Lynn. Moving here to the city had meant a move back into uniform, but almost immediately she had put in for a transfer to Vice, officially uniformed still but working in plain clothes, a step on the ladder towards the real thing.

The Vice Squad in this neck of the woods comprised one inspector, two sergeants and twelve constables, three of whom were women. What they hadn't had, until Sharon joined, was an officer who was black.

Leaning sideways, she wedged the can into the pocket of the passenger door, and what remained of the cob she stuffed back into its bag and placed on the floor. A grey Sierra crawled past for the third time, slowing almost to a stop at every woman it passed. In her notebook, alongside its registration, Sharon wrote the time. As she watched, the car turned right on to Waverley and she knew from there it would make a left on to Arboretum, then left again up Balmoral or Addison, squaring the circle.

This time she was ready. As the Sierra headed back

along Forest Road East, Sharon started up the car and drove diagonally across in front of it, headlights on full beam. The driver had two alternatives: run smack into her or stop. He stopped.

Sharon was out of her car quickly enough, not running, tapping at the near-side window for it to be rolled down.

'Police Constable Garnett,' she said, holding up her identification. 'I've observed you on three separate occasions in the past half hour, stopping to speak to known prostitutes.'

In the front of the Sierra, the two men exchanged glances and the one nearest to Sharon smiled. Divine drew his wallet from his inside pocket and let it fall open close to Sharon's face. 'Snap,' he said. 'Why don't we go and get a drink?'

The table was chipped Formica, the seats were covered in a dull red patched synthetic, and the television set above the bar was showing music videos, beamed in from somewhere in Europe. Hand-drawn posters on the walls advertised quiz nights, bingo nights and karaoke. Divine sat nursing what was left of a pint of Shipstones, Naylor a half of bitter; Sharon Garnett had drained a small glass of grapefruit juice and said no to another.

They had filled Sharon in on the events of the previous night, asked her if she had heard anything that might be useful, but she could only shake her head in reply.

'The girls you spoke to,' Sharon said. 'Any of them come up with anything?'

'Seen and heard sod all,' Divine said.

'And likely,' Naylor added, 'not to tell us if they had.'

'Then why bother going through the motions?' Sharon asked.

'Because if something happens,' Divine said, 'like this bloke in hospital takes a sudden turn for the worse and pops his clogs, or a couple of months down the line there's another incident, similar, maybe proves fatal, then at least we've covered our backsides.'

'And the guv'nor's,' Naylor said.

'Who is your DI?'

'Resnick.'

Sharon Garnett smiled, remembering. 'Not a bad bloke. Give him my best.'

Divine swallowed down the remainder of his pint. 'Don't you get brassed off with Vice?' he asked when they were back on the pavement outside. 'Spending all day chatting up scuzzy tarts and warning off kerb crawlers.'

Sharon shook her head. 'Half the rest of the squad, eight hours a day for the past twelve days, watching seven boxes of videos, clocking faces, trying to decide if what they're seeing's simply gross indecency or worse.'

'Dunno,' Divine grinned. 'Got to be worse ways of earning a living then watching dirty movies and getting paid for it.'

Sharon's mouth moved into a rueful smile. 'More than a few of those, I doubt you'd think that way. Even a horny bugger like you!'

Divine grinned, taking it as a compliment. Naylor laughed and thanked her for her time and he and Divine turned right towards where they had parked their car, while Sharon walked across the street to have a word with one of the girls who was loitering there, smoking a cigarette.

'Will you take a look,' Divine said, head turned to watch Sharon walk away, 'at the arse on that.' But he was careful to keep his voice low, so there was no danger of her overhearing him.

Lynn Kellogg knocked on Resnick's office door mid-afternoon, just as he was taking a bite out of a smoked chicken, tomato and tarragon mayonnaise baguette. Late lunch. A sliver of chicken slipped out on to his fingers and he ate it as delicately as he could, not noticing the tomato seeds which had sprayed across his tie.

'Our mystery man at the hospital,' Lynn said.

Resnick looked at her expectantly.

'He's done a runner.'

Resnick lowered the baguette on to the back of an already stained NAPO report and gave a slow shake of the head.

'There was some kind of emergency down at the other end of the ward. He stole some clothes and walked out without a word. I spoke to the nurse in charge; as long as he keeps the wound clean, changes the dressing, he should be fine.'

'Well,' Resnick said, 'one way of looking at it is that it's good news. No victim, no crime.'

'But?' Lynn said.

'If the similarity to that stabbing in March is more than coincidental, we've likely got someone out there with some kind of grudge. Could turn worse before it gets better.'

'That incident,' Lynn said, 'businessman from out of town, staying at one of the big hotels, wasn't that it?'

Resnick nodded.

'We could have a quick ring round, see if there's any with an outstanding account. I doubt he went back to pay his bill.'

'Worth trying,' Resnick said. 'See what you can turn up. Oh, and if Mark and Kevin are back ...'

But he could already hear Divine's shout and raucous laughter as the two detectives entered the outer office. It didn't take long for them to make their report.

'We could have one last try tonight,' Naylor suggested.

Resnick nodded. 'Keep in touch with Vice, let them know you're around.'

'Reminds me, boss,' Divine said. 'One of theirs this

morning, one we spoke to, real looker, Afro-Caribbean.'
His tongue negotiated the term with exaggerated care, as
if stepping across a minefield. 'Wanted to be remembered
to you, Sharon Garnett.'

A memory flicked across Resnick's face. He had first
met Sharon early in the year: a cold January morning, the
ground rimed with frost, a body buried in a shallow grave.
One of the victims of the man who had held Lynn Kellogg
prisoner.

Resnick glanced over towards Lynn's desk, wondering
if she might have picked up on the name. But, directory
open before her, Lynn was talking intently into the phone.

'All right, Mark,' Resnick said. 'Thanks.'

Sharon, as she had made clear, was keen to move across
to CID; he would have a word with the inspector in Vice,
find out how she was settling in, couldn't do any harm.


'D'you know,' Millington said later. It was already well
past six and Resnick had been considering cutting his
losses, calling it a day. 'D'you know, for the price of a seat
at the Test, good one, mind you, up behind the bowler's
arm, you could see three films at the Showcase, nip into
the bowling alley for a couple of games and still have cash
left over for Chicken McNuggets and fries.'

Resnick was sure he was right. 'You read a bit, don't
you. Graham?' he said.

'I like the odd Ken Follett, Tom Clancy. Why d'you
ask?'

'Here.' He pulled Cathy Jordan's book from his pocket.
'Have a go at this. Might just be your kind of thing.'

Millington took the book, looked at the cover,
shrugged, tossed it on to his desk. 'Thanks. You coming
over the road for a quick pint?'

'Another night.'

'Suit yourself.'

It was the same old routine they went through most

evenings. Unless there was a special reason, Resnick preferred to let the team have the bar to themselves. Oh, he'd stop by for a quick Guinness now and again, buy a round and be on his way. Fancied a drink later, he would stroll over to the Polish Club, elbows on the table with a bottle of Czech Budweiser or Pilsner Urquell, listen to the gossip about who was in hospital, who had died, what Sikorski had said to Churchill in 1941.

# Nine

Millington didn't stay long in the pub. Somehow he had managed to get himself wedged between Divine, making the usual extravagant claims about his sex life, and one of those ritual bores with a four-hundred-thousand-pound house in the Park. Sooner multiple orgasms, he thought, than a voice that spoke from generations of cold showers and good breeding, boring on and on about the way the working class was intent upon undermining the country's manufacturing base.

Millington wanted to tell him we hardly had a manufacturing base any longer, and most of that was due to the government or bad management – most likely by people like him. Most of the factories Millington knew that shut their doors never got round to opening them again. To say nothing of the pits. Hell and hullabaloo there'd been above a year back, marchers on the streets and speeches in the Square, whole bloody communities on the dole. Arnold Bennett! It was almost enough to make you vote Labour.

'Another?' Divine tapped his empty glass. Embellishing the story of his night out with a couple from Annesley, mother and daughter, had left Divine with quite a thirst.

'No, you're all right. Off home any minute.'

'Come on. Early days yet, just a half.'

Millington flattened his palm across the top of his glass and shook his head.

'Suit yourself,' Divine grinned and let out a low belch to get the barman's attention. 'Hey up!' he called, 'how about some service?' Divine, anxious not to lose his audience, hadn't even got to the bit about the snake yet.

A cos lettuce and half a cucumber were waiting for him in the salad spinner, a Marks and Spencer lasagne in the microwave. Millington guessed from the spoons on the dining room table there'd be dessert, like as not that Greek yoghurt with honey.

Madeleine called down from the bedroom to say she'd not be many minutes, wouldn't he like to make them a nice cup of tea? While the kettle was coming to the boil, he wandered off into the garden; this time of the year, all you had to do was turn your back and the bloody grass wanted cutting.

Trills and worse wafted down from the upstairs window; auditions for the local amateur operatics were in the offing and Millington could sense this year his wife was nurturing ambitions beyond the chorus.

'What would you think, Graham,' Madeleine asked a while later, showing the jar of Hellmann's low-calorie mayonnaise to her salad, 'if I said I were going to try out for the lead?'

'I'd say good luck to you,' said Millington, poking around in his lasagne.

'You don't think I might be, well, wrong for it? The part, I mean.'

'Depends what it is.'

'*The Merry Widow*. I'm sure I told you.'

'And that's the part? The one you're after? The merry, er, widow?'

Madeleine set down her fork and knife and prepared to look hurt. 'Yes.'

Beneath his moustache, Millington smiled. 'Not trying to tell me something, are you, love?'

'What? Oh, Graham, no. For heaven's sake!'

'Not been slipping down to the garden centre for the

odd half gallon of weedkiller? A little arsenic in the salad dressing?'

'Graham! Don't say things like that. Not even in jest.'

Millington went back to his lasagne, wondering what had happened to good old meat pie and chips.

'What I meant was,' Madeleine began. It was later and she was spooning yoghurt into two bowls. 'The character, the one I'd like to play, she's meant to be gay ...'

'Gay?'

'Lively. Sort of sparkling, you know. Full of joy.' Madeleine paused, scraping stray yoghurt from the back of the spoon on to the edge of the carton. 'Sexy.'

'Well, that's all right, then.'

'What?'

'For the part. Sexy.'

Madeleine pushed her bowl away. 'That's what I mean.'

'What?'

'It's just a joke.'

'It's not a joke.'

'It is.'

Millington stood up from his chair, leaned across the table and kissed her on the mouth. When he eased away, some few moments later, there were honey and yoghurt in his moustache and neither he nor Madeleine knew who was the more surprised.


'I was wondering,' Millington said, turning away from a woefully unfunny situation comedy on the TV, 'if you fancied an early night?'

Across the room, Madeleine blinked across a pile of nine-year-olds' science notebooks. Thirty-seven drawings of a paramecium, all of which made it look like a hairy shoe. 'All right,' she said. 'Yes, I could. I'll just have to finish these first.' Already she was making calculations, dates and figures flying around her head, wondering if maybe it was worth checking her temperature with the bathroom thermometer.

Chipper, Millington had put on the dressing gown his mother-in-law had bought him the Christmas before last and gone downstairs to make a pot of tea. Never mind Divine and all his bragging, Millington was prepared to wager it didn't get much better than that.

Madeleine, for whom it had actually been almost as satisfying a ten minutes as her husband had concluded, sat, propped up by a brace of pillows, searching for her place in *Lives of the Christian Martyrs* and still envincing a slight glow.

Millington brought the tea back up on a tray; best cups and saucers, green padded cosy, a small plateful of rich butter shortbread and custard creams. He remembered to stop whistling 'Don't Sleep in the Subway' out on the landing, not wanting to irritate her nerves.

'Graham,' Madeleine said, all smiling reproach, 'we'll get crumbs in the bed.'

'Not to worry,' he winked. 'Be changing the sheets tomorrow anyway.'

Biting her tongue rather than telling him not to be smutty, Madeleine reached for a shortbread biscuit instead. Millington settled the tray between them, poured milk and tea, set his cup on the bedside table and reached for the book that Resnick had handed him.

Madeleine's only immediate reaction was to shift a little on to one side, leaning her weight towards the light.

*If anyone had told me, Annie Jones, you'll end up spending your seventh wedding anniversary alone in the front seat of a rented Chevrolet, outside of Jake's at the Lake in Tahoe City, I'd have told them to go jump*

*right in it. The lake, that is. But then if that*
*same anyone . . .*

'Graham,' Madeleine said, rolling towards him, 'whatever's got into you?'

'How'd you mean?'

'First, you know, and now this.'

'This?'

'You're reading in bed.'

'So?'

'You never read; not anywhere, never mind in bed.'

'I read that – what's his name? – John Grisham.'

'You bought the book when we were on our way back from Devon, read the first two pages, put it in the bag for Christian Aid and saw the film.'

'Two pages is about all I'll read of this as well, if you don't let me get on with it. Try engaging you in conversation once you're stuck into one of these doorstops of yours and I get a look fierce enough to excommunicate the Pope.'

'All right, Graham,' Madeleine said, giving it just a touch of the long-suffering. 'I'm sorry. I won't interrupt you again.'

'S'okay, love,' Millington said, fidgeting his backside against her hip. 'Not as if it's anything serious, not like yours. No one's going to set me an exam on it when I've finished.' He opened the paperback wide and cracked the spine a little, rendering it easier to handle.

*But then if that same anyone had told me, the*
*day I appeared, fresh out of law school, ready*
*to start work at the offices of Reigler and*
*Reigler, bright and full of promise in my newly*
*acquired dove-grey two-piece with a charcoal*
*stripe, skirt a businesslike three inches below*
*the knee, that I would swap what was clearly*
*destined to be a famous legal career for that of*

*a lowly private eye, I would gleefully have signed committal forms, assigning them to the nearest asylum, and tossed away the key.*

*'You know, Annie,' my mother had said, the time I plucked up courage to explain, 'you can't really be a private eye, they only have them in the movies. And books. And besides, they're always men.'*

*My mom, God bless her, always seemed to have a vested interest in remaining firmly behind the times.*

*'Sure, Mom,' I said, 'you're right.' And inched back the business card I had proudly given her, stuffing it back down into my wallet. There'd be another time.*

Madeleine turned with a start as Annie Q. Jones hit the floor with a small bump. Millington's eyes were closed and pretty soon, she knew, he would begin to snore. Leaning across him carefully, Madeleine lightly touched her cheek to his and then switched out the lamp.

# Ten

The kids outside the amusement arcade at the end of
Fletcher Gate stared back at Resnick with flat, hostile
eyes. Fifteen, sixteen, younger: high-top trainers, T-shirts,
jeans; cans of Coke and cigarettes and something in a
polystyrene box from Burger King. Maybe they knew he
was a policeman, maybe not; what they saw was someone
older than their fathers, another version of their teachers,
probation officers, social workers, another heavily built
man in a shapeless suit.

A common incongruity, the windows in front of which
they lounged or sat displayed pottery objects no one ever
bought – shire horses, vases, bug-eyed dogs – all steadily
gathering dust.

Resnick turned right towards Goose Gate, pausing for
some moments outside Culture Vulture, looking with
quiet delight at the display of extravagantly designed
shirts he would never wear, black brothel-creeper shoes of
the kind he had surreptitiously changed into almost thirty
years before, ready to go out and about with his mates.
Blown-up reproductions of Blue Note record covers hung
as a backdrop: Big John Patton, John Coltrane; trumpeter
Lee Morgan in his three-buttoned Italian jacket, neat shirt
and knit tie; Dexter Gordon, leaning back from the curve
of his saxophone and laughing on *A Swingin' Affair*.
Inside Resnick's head a Hammond organ surged and
Jimmy Smith set out on 'Groovin' at Small's', a blues
solo Resnick had long savoured, even though the album
itself had disappeared from his shelves without trace or

reason years before, the way favourite albums were sadly wont to do.

Crossing into Broad Street, the sound played on against a counterpoint of car horns and discordant voices, underscored by the insistent rap beat that came through the open doors of other hip, expensive clothing stores; only when he stopped outside Broadway's offices and pressed the buzzer did the music disappear.

'Charlie Resnick,' he said, head bent awkwardly towards the intercom. 'Here to see Miss Hansen.'

Too late, he thought Ms would have been more appropriate, awkward to pronounce as he always found it.

The door to Mollie's office was open, but Resnick hesitated long enough to catch her eye before walking in.

The scarlet had been replaced by a plaid shirt which almost matched the one on k. d. lang in the *Even Cowgirls Get the Blues* poster that was tacked up behind Mollie's desk. The desk itself held neatly labelled files, a stack of bright red plastic trays close to overflowing, several movie books, a battered A–Z map of the city, three purple mugs, each holding a residue of coffee and, at the centre, a desk-size Filofax with annotations in three colours.

'You found it all right, then?' Mollie said brightly, gesturing for him to sit down.

Resnick moved two telephone directories and eased himself down into the chair.

'Coffee? I can send out for cappuccino. You know the new deli at the end of the street?'

'If it's no trouble.'

Mollie called past him towards the open door. 'Larry, I don't suppose you've got a minute . . .'

He had.

Mollie drew a sheet of paper from one of the files and slid it towards Resnick. Her desk, he thought, lively and organised as it was, lacked the merest trace of anything purely personal – a photograph, a fading birthday card, a Post-it note reminding her to buy more flour, a pint of milk. He wondered where she kept her life and what it was like – or if this were all there was.

'This is Cathy Jordan's itinerary,' Mollie was saying. 'As you can see, we're trying to make as much use of her as we can. Some of these things . . .' leaning forward, she pointed with her finger, '. . . are arranged in tandem with her publisher. And here, and you see, here, she's taking a couple of days out. Stratford, I think, and Scotland. Or maybe it's the Lakes.'

Resnick ran his eyes up and down the page – press conference, Radio Nottingham, Radio Trent, Central TV, BBC Radio Four, several book signings, a reading, two panel discussions and her attendance was requested at a civic reception. Also there were the name and address of the hotel where Cathy Jordan would be staying, complete with telephone, fax and room numbers. He would study it all in detail later.

'Covering all of these isn't going to be easy.'

'Until we've talked to Cathy Jordan, we just don't know.' Only slightly mocking, she treated him to her professional smile. 'One thing we have to remember, she's not just our guest, she's a guest of the city as well.'

'And our responsibility.'

Mollie was still smiling. Resnick folded the list and slid it into his inside pocket.

Larry turned out to be a ruddy-faced youth of nineteen or twenty, ponytail dangling down beneath the reversed peak of his deep red Washington Redskins cap. The coffee, in white polystyrene cups, was strong and still hot. Mollie took a spoon from one of the used mugs and lifted chocolatey froth towards her mouth with such expectation that, for a moment, Resnick saw more than an efficient young woman whose life was strictly colour-coded.

'The letters,' Mollie said, 'what did you think? I mean, ought we to be taking them seriously or not?'

Resnick tasted a little more of his coffee. 'To a point, I don't see we have any choice. After all, Louella Trabert, Anita Mulholland – they may just be characters in books, but that doesn't mean the threats aren't real.'

Mollie smiled, meaning it this time. 'You've got a good memory for names.'

Resnick knew that it was true. Names and faces. There were others he could have added. Victims. Fact and not fiction. It went with the job, like so much else: a blessing and a curse.

'You don't like her, do you?'

'Who?' Mollie sitting back a little, on the defensive.

'Cathy Jordan.'

'I don't know her.'

'You know her books.'

'That's not the same thing.'

Resnick shrugged. 'Isn't it? I should have thought they must come close.'

Mollie was fidgeting with her spoon. 'Anyway, what I think's neither here nor there.' She leaned forward again, the beginnings of a gleam across the grey of her eyes. 'Unless you think I'm the one who wrote the letters.'

'Are you?'

Mollie flipped a page in her Filofax. 'If the train's on time, I could ask her to meet you at the hotel. There should be time before the opening reception. Say, a quarter past six?'

Resnick set down his cup. 'All right. Always assuming nothing crops up more urgent.'

'Good.'

He got to his feet.

'Here,' Mollie said, handing him a glossy black brochure with the *Shots in the Dark* logo heavily embossed on its cover. 'This is the press kit. There's a programme inside. And a complimentary ticket. It is a crime festival, after all. I should have thought you'd find quite a lot of interest. Especially if you like the cinema.'

For all his good memory, Resnick was having trouble remembering anything he'd seen since *The Magnificent Seven*. He took the brochure and nodded his thanks.

'I don't suppose you've had a chance to look at that book yet?' Mollie asked when he was at the door.

'No, afraid not.'

As he walked out along the narrow entryway and on to the street, Resnick noticed a freshening of the wind and when, back at the corner of Fletcher Gate, he tilted his head upwards, he felt the first drops of a summer shower bright upon his face.

# Eleven

It wasn't as though Cathy Jordan had never been to England before. First, as a visiting student, on exchange from her state college in Kansas City, Kansas, she had been catapulted headlong into the heyday of British hippydom. Carnaby Street and the Beatles and the Stones and her first toke, four girls passing it between them, cramped inside one of the cubicles in the ladies' room at the Roundhouse. Could it really have been the Crazy World of Arthur Brown out on stage, singing 'Fire'? Or maybe that was later, underground at UFO? She couldn't remember now. The way her world had spun three hundred and sixty degrees beneath her, it was a wonder she remembered anything at all. Her family ringing nightly, after watching television newscasts of the French students setting fire to the barricades outside the Sorbonne; youngsters with long hair battling with police outside the US embassy in Grosvenor Square. 'Are you okay? My God, Catherine, are you sure you're okay? What is going on over there? The whole world seems suddenly to have gone mad.' One of her dad's Eddie Fisher albums playing steadfastly away in the background – 'Oh! My Papa!', 'Wish You Were Here.'

Her second visit had been made almost ten years later, when her first husband had been stationed at a US air force base in Lincolnshire and she had opted to join him for six months. In a number of ways, it had not proved such a good idea. From time to time, women old enough to be not just her mother but her grandmother had chained themselves to the base's perimeter fence in protest at the American presence. Sometimes when she was shopping in the nearest town, angelic-faced young men wearing CND badges or brandishing copies of *Socialist Worker* would spit at her in the street.

Whatever else, her abiding impression of England was not of cobbled streets, spied through the swirl of a quaint Dickensian pea-souper; nor of some fading thatched roof idyll over which the sun barely set and where the squire and village bobby reigned supreme. England, for Cathy Jordan, represented unrest and disruption, change – not only for the country, but for herself.

Yet looking out now through the smirched window of the Intercity train as it cleaved through the flat softness of the Midlands landscape, she saw only field on field washed by a perpetual grey drizzle – cattle standing morose at hedgerows, a single tractor turning ever-widening circles to no purpose, knots of ugly houses huddled at road ends – nothing to stir her heart or energise her mind.

Three days ago it had been Holland, before that Denmark and Sweden, Germany: just another damn book tour, that's what it was. A tour she had begun alone and was ending with her second husband, Frank Carlucci, asleep on the seat alongside her.

Frank, who had got bored minding his own business back in the States and had flown out to mind hers. Except that he had forgotten what it had become like for the pair of them, on the road together – the sterile proximity of hotel rooms and polite, translated conversation. More than three days and Frank was floundering awkwardly in Cathy's wake, bored, and Cathy, unable to stop herself, was sniping at him without let-up or mercy.

This was already the sixth day.

The brittle plastic glass which held her Scotch now had no more than a quarter-inch of once-iced water slopping about at the bottom, and Cathy wondered if she had the energy to walk back through the train to the buffet car and order another.

'Do you think she'll be here on time?'

Mollie Hansen glanced up from her *Independent*. 'I don't see why not, do you?' There they were, twice on the Listings page, bare details under Events Around the Country and a boxed Daily Ticket offer – two pairs of seats for the opening night – complete with picture. Good old *Independent*! Saturday they'd promised a feature-length piece on the Curtis Woolfe retrospective, which would fit nicely with the Cathy Jordan profile they were publishing on Sunday. Coverage in the *Observer*, the *Telegraph* and *The Times*, all they needed now was the *Mail* for a pretty clean sweep.

As Tyrell watched the overhead screen, the arrival time disappeared. 'You see. Trouble.'

Moments later, it flashed back up: 5.18.

'Why are they never on time?'

'David,' Mollie shook her head. 'A minute late, I think we can live with that. Don't you?'

The woman who walked along the platform towards them was a good few inches above average in height, even allowing for the cowboy heels on the tan boots she wore below her jeans. Red hair, straight save for a slight curl at the ends, hung shoulder-length. She had taken the time to refresh her lipstick and the greenish shadow above what, even at a distance, were disturbingly blue eyes. A tweed jacket, predominantly green and tailored at the waist, hung open over a red silk shirt. She was carrying a medium-sized carpet bag in her left hand.

Rhonda Fleming, Tyrell decided, meets Arlene Dahl: though, close to, there was more than a touch of Lauren Bacall about the mouth.

Mollie was looking, not so much at Cathy Jordan, but at the barrel-chested man with cropped grey hair walking alongside her. He was carrying large, matching suitcases in both hands, a third tucked beneath one arm. Shorter than Cathy, what impressed immediately about him was his size. The bags he was carrying could have been toys.

For a moment, Mollie's face settled into a scowl: she didn't like surprises. Nevertheless, she was the first to step forward and hold out her hand. 'Cathy Jordan? Welcome to *Shots in the Dark*. I'm Mollie Hansen. We've spoken on the phone. And this is David Tyrell, he's the Festival Director.'

'Hi!' said Cathy. 'Hello.' Shaking hands. 'This is my husband, Frank.'

'Frank Carlucci. Good to know you.' His voice was pitched low and edged with something that might have been tiredness, but could have been drink.

Tensing instinctively, Mollie was surprised to find his grip so soft, not weak, almost delicate. 'We didn't know you'd be coming.'

Carlucci shrugged strong shoulders. 'Last-minute thing. Joined up with Cathy in Copenhagen. Nice little town. You know it at all?'

Mollie shook her head and they began walking towards the end of the platform, Carlucci falling in step beside her, while, immediately behind them, Tyrell was talking to Cathy Jordan.

'This hotel where we were just staying,' Frank Carlucci was saying, 'the Plaza. Oak panelling you'd kill for, leather books all round the bar, huh! They got this pillar in the lobby, names of all the celebrities ever stayed there engraved in gold. Well, maybe it was brass. But everyone, you know. Liza Minnelli, Paul McCartney, Jack fucking Nicholson. Michael Jackson. Well, maybe they'll be taking that one down. But Cathy, next time we go back,

53

hers'll be up there along of the rest. Alongside of Jack Nicholson, ain't that something?'

Mollie made a sound that was strictly non-committal; Nicholson had been all right in *Chinatown*, but after that what was he? An overpaid actor with a paunch and falling hair.

Climbing the steps from the platform, Carlucci was still talking and Mollie realised he was the kind of man whose idea of a conversation was one-sided – he talked and you listened. She moved ahead on to Cathy Jordan's free side, Tyrell on the other telling her how excited he was she could be there, how much he liked her work.

Glancing across, Mollie put Cathy's age as late forties, certainly not a day under forty-five. Her bio sheet was surprisingly coy when it came to details like age. But whatever she was, Mollie thought, she was looking good.

Outside, on the station forecourt, waiting for a taxi, Tyrell assured Cathy that the civic reception would be no big deal, nothing exhausting. So far, neither he nor Mollie had said anything to her about the hand-delivered letter or its threat.

> *You do realise I am serious? Poor little*
> *Anita Mulholland, Cathy, remember what*
> *happened to her.*

# Twelve

'Graham, you didn't get anywhere with that book, I suppose?'

Millington looked across the CID room hopefully, unable to pick out most of what Resnick had said. Two desks away, the world's noisiest printer was chuntering its way through a listing of the last six months' unsolved burglaries, broken down by the Local Intelligence Officer into location, time and MO.

Lynn set down the receiver, pushed herself up from her desk and stretched her shoulders and back. The last of her trawl around the city's hotels and she was no nearer to finding the identity of the mystery man who'd done a runner from the hospital. As one of the clerks had pointed out, with so many accounts prepaid by employers' credit cards, all some clients had to do was turn in their keys and wave goodbye.

'Sorry,' Millington said, having made his way to where Resnick was standing. 'Couldn't hear a bloody word.'

'That woman's book, the one I gave you . . .'

'How about it?'

'Thought perhaps you could give me some idea what it's about. Got to see her later.'

'Ah. Can't say I really got that far. All right, though. Not rubbish, you know what I mean. One thing pretty clear – she's not Agatha Christie, you'd have to say that.'

Resnick guessed that to be a compliment, but with Millington you could never be sure. This was, after all, the person who swore Petula Clark did a better version of

'Lover Man' than Billie Holiday. 'Not got it with you, I suppose, Graham?'

'Have, as a matter of fact. Reckoned I might give it twenty minutes in the canteen, but, of course, it never happened.'

'Best let's have it back, then. Take a look on the way down.'

'Suit yourself.' Millington shrugged and turned away to fetch him the book.

Minutes later, Resnick was on his way down the stairs, a copy of *Dead Weight* in his hand.

Cathy Jordan poured herself another shot from the one of the pair of kingsize bottles of J & B Rare they had bought on the plane. She and Frank buying silence with the usual share of booze in the usual bland hotel room, though here the walls were closer together than usual. Which meant that they were too. In a way.

Right now they were getting ready for the reception. Frank was wandering about morosely in a pair of striped boxers and a white shirt, the creases from where it had lain folded in the case pulled flat across the muscles of his arms and back; Cathy was wearing a couple of towels and a cream half slip, which she hated, but the problem with the dress she had chosen was the minute you stood in front of the light, it was the next thing to being featured in an X-ray.

For once it was Frank who broke the unspoken truce. 'So what d'you think?' he said. 'You worried or what?'

'About the reception?'

'Reception, hell. The letter.'

Examining a pair of tights, Cathy shook her head. 'Sticks and stones,' she said.

'That's it, sticks and stones?'

One leg in, one leg out, Cathy looked across at him. 'That's it.'

Frank breathed out noisily and shook his head. 'You're not scared? Spooked? Not even one little piece?'

Turning away, Cathy shook her head. Of course, she was scared. Not all the time, not even often, but, sure, step into a lift and there's a guy standing there, looking over at you in a certain way – walk out into the street to catch some air and the window of a slowing car slides down – who wouldn't be scared. The world was full of them, God knows, it wasn't just the pages of her books. Sociopaths. Psychopaths. Whoever was writing those letters wasn't *Dear Abbey*.

But admitting it to Frank, that was something else. The way it had become between them, everything was a statement of strength, not of weakness, neediness. It wasn't in her nature to be the one to back off.

'It's why you're here, isn't it?' Cathy said. 'Reason you changed your mind, flew over. Look out for me. Protect me.' She made *protect* sound like a dirty word.

Frank was having trouble with the knot of his tie. 'And if it is?'

'You needn't have bothered. They've got professionals for that.'


Resnick arrived at the hotel later than he'd intended and Mollie Hansen was already waiting on one of the leather settees in the foyer, her duty to escort Cathy Jordan and her husband to the reception. David Tyrell had claimed the task of collecting Curtis Woolfe, who had flown in earlier in the day from Switzerland, which was where he now lived. The third major guest, the octogenarian British crime novelist, Dorothy Birdwell, was being driven directly to the reception by her assistant.

Mollie, Resnick thought, was looking decidedly smart, rising to greet him in a loose-fitting pearl trouser suit which might have been silk. Something held him back from making the compliment out loud, a sense that, to Mollie, that kind of remark would be less than acceptable.

'Nice tie,' Mollie said, with a little nod. 'Interesting design. Paul Smith?'

'Spaghetti vongole.'

To his surprise, Mollie laughed and Resnick grinned back. 'What happened,' he asked, 'when you showed her the letter?'

'Oh, for a minute or two, I thought she was going to throw a wobbly, but then she just laughed and told me for all it was worth, I might as well tear it up. That was when I told her about you.'

Before Resnick could reply, the lift doors opened and Cathy Jordan appeared in an ankle-length, off-white dress from beneath the hem of which poked the toes of her boots.

Mollie moved quickly to meet her.

'Is there time,' Cathy Jordan asked, after Resnick had been introduced, 'for the inspector and me to have a chat?'

'Sure,' Mollie said. 'I think so.'

'Great!' Cathy said, appropriating Resnick's arm. 'Why don't we go to the bar?'

Perched on a stool, Cathy Jordan asked Resnick to recommend a single malt and, although it wasn't really his drink, after a quick glance along the bar he came up with Highland Park.

'Two large ones,' Cathy said. And to Resnick, 'Ice?'

He shook his head.

'One as it comes,' she said to the barman, 'one with lots of ice. That's L-O-T-S.' Turning towards Resnick, she made a face. 'What is it with this country? Is ice still rationed?'

He smiled. 'We're a moderate people. Maybe we don't like too much of anything.'

'That include crime?'

58

'Not necessarily.'

'Violent crime?'

'Well, we don't have guns on the streets...' He corrected himself. 'At least, not as many as you.'

'But you're getting there.'

'Maybe.' He said it with regret. He knew it wasn't only the more publicised areas of the country – Brixton, Moss Side – where weapons were increasingly easy to obtain, increasingly likely to be used. There were estates there in the city where firearms were heard being discharged far more frequently than gunshot wounds were ever reported. He didn't imagine their aim was always less than true.

Cathy clinked her glass against his. 'Cheers.'

'Cheers,' Resnick said. And then, 'Miss Jordan, about this latest letter...'

'Cathy,' she said. 'For God's sake, call me Cathy. And as for the letter, it's a crock, just like all the rest. Some scuzzbag shut off in a sweaty room, only way he knows of getting off, you know what I mean?'

Resnick throught that he might. 'Then you've no worries about security?' he said, after tasting a little of the malt.

Cathy rattled the ice cubes around a little inside her glass. 'I'm in a strange country, right. It wouldn't hurt to have someone watching my back.'

'All right. Mollie's given me a copy of your schedule. Maybe we could go over it and see which events you're most concerned about?'

'Sure,' said Cathy, but then became aware of Mollie Hansen hovering with intent and drained her glass in a double swallow. 'Gotta go. Look, couldn't we meet tomorrow? Go through things like you said?'

Resnick got to his feet. 'Of course.'

'Good. We Americans are big on breakfast meetings, you know.'

'Here?'

'Half eight, how's that sound?'

'Fine.'

'Good.' And Mollie steered Cathy Jordan away towards their waiting car, while Resnick sat back on the stool and nursed his way down the rest of his Highland Park.

# Thirteen

Art Tatum and Ben Webster: they did it for him every time. Resnick lowered the stylus with care and watched as it slid into the groove; listened, standing there, as Tatum played his practised, ornate way through the first chorus of the tune, tightening the rhythm at the beginning of the middle eight, before stepping aside with a simple little single-note figure, falling away beneath the glorious saxophone smear of Webster's arrival. Resnick turned up the volume and wandered through into the kitchen: coffee was pumping softly inside the silver pot on the stove. He set a match to the gas on the grill, sliced dark rye bread and put it to toast. Cream cheese, not too much pickled cucumber, smoked salmon. While none of the other cats were looking, he sneaked Bud a small piece of the salmon. Some days he liked to drink his coffee, rich and dark, from one of a pair of white china mugs, and this was one of those.

Settled in his favourite chair in the living room, coffee and sandwich close at hand, album turned over and turned back down, Resnick lifted Cathy Jordan's book from the small table beneath the lamp and began to read:

> *If anyone had told me, Annie Jones, you'll end up spending your seventh wedding anniversary alone in the front seat of a rented Chevrolet, outside of Jake's at the Lake in Tahoe City, I'd have told them to go jump right in it. The lake, that is. But then if that same anyone had told me, the day I appeared,*

fresh out of law school, ready to start work at the offices of Reigler and Reigler, bright and full of promise in my newly acquired dove-grey two-piece with a charcoal stripe, skirt a businesslike three inches below the knee, that I would swap what was clearly destined to be a famous legal career for that of a lowly private eye, I would gleefully have signed committal forms, assigning them to the nearest asylum, and tossed away the key.

'You know, Annie,' my mother had said, the first time I plucked up courage to explain, 'you can't really be a private eye, they only have them in the movies. And books. And besides, they're always men.'

My mom, God bless her, always seemed to have a vested interest in remaining firmly behind the times.

'Sure, Mom,' I said, 'you're right.' And inched back the business card I had proudly given her, stuffing it back down into my wallet. There'd be another time.

And so there had. My first major cheque safely paid into the bank and cleared, two other clients waiting in the wings, I had invited my long-suffering mother out for cocktails and dinner at her favourite Kansas City restaurant.

I didn't mention that, did I? About my mother being from Kansas City. Well, that's an important part of it; it explains a great deal.

But back to cocktails. Emboldened by the second Manhattan, I had showed my mother my bank balance and launched into the spiel. Adventure, independence, the chance to be my *own boss, run my own life – 'Mom, I'm a big girl now. This is what I want to do. You see, it'll work out fine.'*

*Which so far, pretty much, had been true. During my time practising law I had made a lot of useful contacts, in that profession as well as the police. I was in pretty thick with a few good working journalists, too – the kind that still spend more time on the street than in the office staring at their computer screen.*

*And Mom, I like to think, surprised herself with a smile of pride when some new-found friend asked over coffee, 'Marjorie, just what is it that your daughter does out there in California?' And my mom, smiling, saying, 'Oh, she's just a private eye.'*

*There were things about my life, though, that I didn't tell her. A little knowledge may, in some circumstances, be a dangerous thing, but in my mother's case it's positively beneficial. I didn't tell, for instance, about the six weeks I spent in hospital after being stupid enough to get trapped up an alley with three guys who made Mike Tyson look like Mickey Mouse. Nor the occasion I stepped in front of a light and two .38 slugs tore past me so close I swear I could feel the wind of their slipstream. And the bodies. I didn't tell her about the bodies. The one I had found tied upside down, offering freebies to half a hundred flies; the little girl I had discovered buried in a ditch. I hadn't told her about any of these things on account there was no need to upset her without cause – which was why I had never told her about Diane.*

*My mom, you see, is strictly old school. The*

reason she can come to terms with what I do for a job is because, when it comes right down to it, the job I do is not that important. At best it's a stage, a phase, it's what I do to fill in time before I finally settle down and get on with what the Good Lord set me on this earth for, get married, of course, and have children.

Somewhere, she has a picture of me, taken at a cousin's wedding when I was but thirteen. The same age as that poor child who ended her days in a shallow grave. There I am, on the left of the photo, wearing my pretty pink bridesmaid's dress and smiling through the jungle gym of my new braces as I cling on to the bride's bouquet which I have just caught.

When Miller and I were divorced, she took it pretty well. 'Everyone,' she said, 'is allowed one false start.' Since when, despite the fact that in child-rearing terms, the years are no longer exactly on my side, she has continued, optimistically, to wait.

As, I suppose, had I. Oh, you know, a dinner date here, a concert ticket there, but pretty much I'd laid low, let my work carry the load, kept my powder dry while making sure my underwear was always clean just in case.

Diane had been a columnist for the Chronicle when I met her, women's issues mostly, date rape, who has the key to the executive wash room, the right to choose, you know the kind of thing. Her byline and a photograph (not flattering) and five bucks a word. Someone had persuaded her, with all the women PIs appearing on the book-racks, she should do a piece on the real thing.

Diane rang me and after a couple of false

starts we finally got to meet in a bar out by the ocean in Santa Cruz. We hadn't shaken hands before my stomach was bungee jumping and ... well, you're pretty sophisticated or you wouldn't have stuck with it this far, so you can guess the rest. That was almost a year ago – almost, hell! – it was eleven months, five days and around seven hours, and still, first thing I do once I've made sure my charge is seated safely at her table, is phone Diane's number just to hear her voice on the answer machine.

If that kind of thing happens in Kansas City – and I'm sure it does, both in Kansas City, Kansas and Kansas City, MO – then I'm sure my mother doesn't know about it. For now, for at least as long as Diane and I go on maintaining separate apartments, I intend to see it stays that way.

Right now I check my watch against the clock on the dash and they both tell me it's fifteen minutes shy of ten o'clock. The coffee the woman at the reservations desk organised for me is long reduced to a residue of cold grounds and, even in the expanse of my extravagant rental, my legs are beginning to cramp up and feel in need of a stretch.

At the desk the woman remembers me and says again, if I'd care to take a seat at the bar ... But I assure her I'm fine and while she sends a waiter nimbly down the carpeted stairs in search of a fresh cup of coffee, I move close enough to the stained wood balustrade to see the young woman whose safety I am charged with protecting. She's sitting at a table, center room, pretty blonde head inclined towards the pretty young man who is *her dinner date, a poet from Seattle and a pretty serious one. A first collection already published by Breitenbush Books of Portland (he happened to have a copy with him and was kind enough to show me) and another from Carnegie Mellon on the way. They seemed to have reached the dessert stage, so we could be on the road by ten thirty.*

*'They make a lovely couple, don't they?' The receptionist has come to stand next to me and I nod in agreement. 'Yes, they do.'*

*'Do you work for Mr Reigler?' she asks.*

*'Sort of,' I say.*

*By then the waiter has returned with my coffee so I thank them both and carry it outside, back into the parking lot. The air is warm enough for me to be only wearing a light sweater and even though we're close to the lake, it isn't too buggy. I stroll for a while between the cars, remembering the morning Reigler asked me to his office. It was only the second or third time I'd seen him since resigning from his law firm; the first time since his stroke. It had left him with some paralysis down the right side, not so bad that he couldn't stand, with help, and, although it was necessary to concentrate, he could speak and make himself understood. Once out of hospital and through his period of convalescence, he had insisted on coming to the office every day. Much of the time, I guessed, he just sat there and they ran things past him, playing up to the formality that all decisions were his.*

*What Reigler had wanted to talk to me about was a series of threatening calls, someone, anonymous, who felt their life had been ruined by some case or other Reigler's firm had handled.*

*'Now it ain't worth doing anything to you, you sorry bastard,' the last one had said, 'but you best watch out for your family, 'cause they can get hurt and there isn't a damn thing you can do to stop it.'*

*Aside from notifying the police, one thing Reigler did was to hire me. His daughter April was, I suspected, the one true love of his life. She was a beauty, of a fragile kind; she was bright, dutiful enough, but stubborn. She was prepared to humor her father by agreeing I could drive her places, keep an eye out, but made it clear this wasn't going to be like the secret service and the President. 'Besides,' she reminded her father, a little, I thought, unkindly, 'what could they do when Kennedy was shot? Reagan?'*

*Reluctantly, April agreed that I could go along on her trip to Tahoe, as long as I didn't get too close. This evening she has made it clear that any ideas I might have of sitting alongside herself and her poet while they share beautiful thoughts and a lobster and mango salad are not going to pan out. And in all honesty the only danger I suspect she might be a prey to in the midst of that crowded and fashionable restaurant rests in the depths of the poet's brown eyes.*

*Another turn of the parking lot and I'm back at the Chevy and there they are, April and her own Byron or Keats, stepping through the restaurant door. I set my empty cup down on the roof of the car and head towards them.*

*Seeing me, April's face breaks into a genuine smile and I am touched. She is a lovely girl.*

*'How was dinner?' I ask.*

*'Wonderful!' she enthuses. 'Wasn't it, Perry?' And she turns to where he has stopped, a pace behind as if suddenly uncertain of the etiquette of dating young women who have personal bodyguards. Which is when the shot rings out and April screams as she is catapulted into my arms and I know what is clinging to my face and hair, most of it, is blood, and at that precise moment I don't know if it is April's blood or mine and, in all honesty, right then and there, I don't care.*

Aside from one of the cats purring somewhere out of sight, it was quiet. The record had long finished. Half the sandwich lay uneaten on its plate. Resnick sat where he was for several minutes more before closing the book, placing it on the arm of the chair, getting up and leaving the room.

# Fourteen

'I read your book. *Dead Weight*.'

'You did? What did you think?'

'Well, maybe I didn't read all of it. Not yet. I'm sure I will.'

Cathy Jordan was looking at Resnick with amusement, her head tilted a little to one side, waiting for the truth. They were having breakfast at her hotel, sharing the decanted orange juice – produce of several countries – the pineapple chunks and the already solidifying scrambled eggs with a scattering of executives and Japanese tourists. The majority of visitors to the festival were saving their pennies elsewhere.

'The first few chapters,' Resnick said. 'One last night, the others earlier this morning.'

'I didn't think earlier than this existed.'

Resnick shrugged. 'The older I get . . .'

'I know, the less sleep you need. With Frank it's the opposite. I swear that man'd sleep twenty hours of any twenty-four if you'd just let him.'

'And Frank is . . .'

'My husband. But stop evading the issue – what did you think of the book?'

'I liked it.'

'You did.'

'Yes. You sound surprised.'

She smiled with her eyes. 'No, but I figured you might be.'

Resnick cut his sausage, skewered a section with his

fork and dabbed it in the mustard at the side of his plate. He knew she wasn't about to let him off the hook.

'It's direct, isn't it?' he said after a little chewing. 'Like you – like you talking.'

Cathy was pointing at him with her knife. 'Not a good mistake to make. Annie isn't me. A long way from it.'

'All right, then. Somebody who sounds like you.'

'Who'll talk with her mouth full over the breakfast table and threaten her guest with sharp implements?'

'Exactly.'

She laughed: okay.

'I suppose,' Resnick said a few moments later, 'I was expecting something more – I don't know – wordy. More description, is that what I mean?'

'Probably. Three quarters of a page detailing the stained glass window over the door, a couple more pages describing what our suspects are wearing, from the make of their brogues to the pattern on their pocket handkerchiefs, that kind of thing?'

'I suppose so.'

'Potential clues.'

'Yes.'

'Well, if that's the kind of writer you want . . .' Cathy was pointing her knife towards an elderly woman, slightly stooped, grey hair pulled back into a bun, waiting while a younger man in a navy blue blazer pulled out her chair. 'Dorothy Birdwell,' Cathy said, 'spinster of this parish.'

'She's a writer?' Resnick asked.

Cathy arched an eyebrow. 'Rumour has it.'

The waitress, a student on a six-month visit from Lisbon to learn English, offered them more coffee; Cathy Jordan spread a hand over the top of her cup, while Resnick nodded and smiled thanks.

'Toast,' Cathy said to the waitress, 'we could use more toast.' And then, to Resnick, 'One literary novel when she was at Cambridge or Oxford or wherever it was. Love between the wars; unrequited, of course. After that, nothing for a decade. More. Up to her scrawny armpits in academia. Then, out of nowhere, comes *A Case of Violets* and everyone's frothing at the mouth about the new Allingham, the new Marsh, the new Dame Agatha. Right from then till practically – what? – ten years ago, everything she wrote was guaranteed, gilt-edged bestseller.'

Resnick watched as the man in the blazer and light grey trousers carefully eased Dorothy Birdwell's chair into the table, bending low to enquire if she were all right before taking his own seat.

'Who's that?' Resnick asked.

Cathy lowered her voice, but not by very much. 'Marius Gooding. Her nephew. Or so she says. Of course, we like to think he's something more.' Cathy laughed, quietly malicious. 'Can't you see them, every night after she's taken her teeth out, getting at it like monkeys, swinging off the chandeliers?'

Resnick could not. Marius seemed fastidious, slightly effete, his moustache daintily trimmed. Resnick watched as he leaned forward to tip a quarter-inch of milk into Dorothy Birdwell's cup, before pouring her tea. Marius was possibly forty, Resnick thought, though he contrived to look younger – the kind of man you expected to find hovering around the edges of Royal Ascot, the Henley Regatta, though since Resnick had never been to either, that was a mixture of prejudice and conjecture.

'Dorothy Birdwell,' he said. 'What did puncture her career ten years ago?'

Cathy Jordan laughed. 'We did. Women. Marcia Muller, Paretsky, Grafton, Patsy Cornwell. Linda Barnes. Julie Smith. A whole bunch of others. Took old Dottie's space on the book-racks and wouldn't give it back.'

'Just because you're women?'

'Some say. Pretty much.'

'Dorothy Birdwell's a woman.'

'Another rumour. Nothing proven.'

Resnick smiled but continued. 'These authors you mentioned, they're all American? Is that the reason?'

'Maybe it used to be. Part of it, anyway. But not any more. Liza Cody, Val McDermid, Sarah Dunant – you've got people of your own, doing pretty good.'

'So what is the reason?' Resnick asked. 'Why the big change?'

Cathy pressed butter onto her toast and shattered it into a dozen brittle pieces. 'Okay. Fact: most crime readers are women. Fact: we give them protagonists they can identify with. Heroines. Never mind old biddies purling two and two together or chief inspectors with aristocratic leanings and patched tweed jackets, this is the age of the female PI. Smart, sassy, full of spunk, as likely to lay you out as get laid. On her terms. And enjoy it.'

'So she's out of date? Birdwell?'

'She was always out of date; that was the attraction. The thing is, now she's out of fashion. Which doesn't mean she doesn't still have her readers, just less of them and they're getting older all the time.' Cathy leaned closer. 'Rumour has it, her agent's on the hunt for a new publisher; after twenty years with one house. Something's hurting.'

Resnick set down his coffee and glanced round again at Dorothy Birdwell. 'You don't think, if she's got reasons to be jealous . . . ?'

'Dorothy? Behind those letters? I'd like to think she had it in her. But, no, not a chance. Malicious looks at thirty paces, that's her mark.' Cathy reached out and lifted up Resnick's tie, the end of which had been mopping up what remained of the mustard.

Resnick nodded and sat back, drawing the copy of Cathy's schedule from his pocket. 'This afternoon, you're signing books at Waterstone's; early this evening, introducing a film at Broadway . . .'

'*Black Widow*, d'you know it? No? Great little movie. Sexy. Debra Winger doing mouth to mouth with Theresa Russell, then busting her for murder.'

'After that?'

'There was something about a bunch of us going out to dinner. This director they've dug up. They're screening one of his films after mine. You should come. Some place called Sundays? David promised the food was pretty good.'

'Sonny's,' Resnick said. 'And, yes, it is.'

'Then you'll be along?'

'Maybe. I can't promise.'

'The policeman's lot . . .'

'Something like that.'

'Suit yourself.'

'How about earlier?' Resnick asked. 'The signing. Would you feel happier if I had someone there? Just keeping an eye?'

Cathy smiled. 'The author who got stabbed with a poisoned dagger behind the mystery shelves? Sounds too much like something out of a Dorothy Birdwell to me.'

'Okay. As long as you're sure.' Resnick checked his watch, then pushed back his chair and reached for his wallet.

'Don't bother,' Cathy said. 'It's covered.'

'No, I don't think I can . . .'

She covered his hand with hers. 'You're my guest. It's charged to the room. Which gets charged to the festival. Relax. It's not a crime. Not a bribe. Honest. Besides, young Mollie would be thrilled at the idea of buying you breakfast.'

'I doubt it.'

Cathy's half-snort, half-laugh was loud enough to turn heads.

'What?' Resnick said.

'You may be good at your job – I hope to hell you are – but you sure know shit about women!'

Flushing, Resnick tried for a smile.

'I'm sorry,' Cathy said, taking his hand again and giving it a squeeze. 'I didn't mean to be insulting.'

'That's okay.'

'Or just another brash American.'

'You're not.'

She held his gaze before replying. She liked the way the skin crinkled around his eyes when he smiled. 'Good. I'll look forward to seeing you tonight.'

'If I can,' Resnick said. 'I'll try.'

He was conscious of Marius Gooding watching him all the way to the dining room door – only one reason he didn't stop and look back at Cathy before passing through. He would check the roster, have a word with Skelton, see if they couldn't send somebody down to the bookshop in their lunch hour just the same. As for later, the invitation to the restaurant, he didn't know, though the last time he'd been to Sonny's, he remembered, on the occasion of his friend Marian Witczak's fortieth birthday, he'd had the rack of lamb and it had been very tasty, very sweet.

# Fifteen

'Listen,' Divine was saying into the telephone. Not saying, shouting. 'No, listen. Listen. Listen up a minute. Bloody listen!'

Most of the CID room did exactly that; stopped whatever they were doing to stare at Mark Divine, standing beside his desk, brown hair pushed back from his forehead, blue shirt, dark trousers, tie twisted round, anger reddening his cheeks in ragged circles, telephone tight in his hand.

'For once in your life, just listen.'

Whoever was at the other end of the line chose to ignore the advice. Connection broken, Divine stared at the receiver in frustration before slamming it back down. 'Stupid tossing woman!'

'Nice,' Lynn Kellogg remarked. 'No wonder you're so successful at pulling. All that suave sophistication.'

Divine mouthed an everyday obscenity and kicked his chair back against the wall, stuffed both hands deep into his pockets and slouched out.

'Must be,' Lynn said, enjoying a little tit-for-tat retribution, 'his time of the month.'

'Time you weren't here, isn't it?' Millington said from the far end of the room. 'One of your snouts, give you a lead on those break-ins, didn't he?'

Lynn lifted notebook and ball-point from her desk and found space for them inside her shoulder bag. She was almost at the door when Resnick walked in, breathing a little heavily after hurrying up the hill from Cathy

Jordan's hotel, patches of mustard yellowing nicely on his tie.

'Off far?'

Lynn shook her head. 'Ilkeston Road.'

'How long d'you reckon?'

'An hour. Hour and a half.'

'Think you could get yourself into the city centre, middle of the day? Waterstone's, corner of Bottle Lane . . .'

'And Bridlesmith Gate. Yes, I know it. Why?'

'This American author who's over. Jordan, Cathy Jordan.'

'*Sleeping Fools Lie.*'

'Sorry?'

'One of her books. I read it last year.'

Resnick was quietly impressed. Aside from anything else, where did she get the time? 'There've been a few threatening letters. Offering her harm. Doesn't seem to take them too seriously herself and I'm not sure how far we should, but it might be no bad idea, to have someone around. She's doing some kind of book signing, one o'clock. Don't want to stick a uniform in there, scare people off.'

'Okay, fine. Be interesting to meet her, I should think.'

'Pop back in on your way down, I'll fill you in.'

Lynn nodded and was on her way.

Resnick beckoned Millington closer. 'Young Divine stormed past me and up the stairs as if you'd given him a good earful. Blotted his copybook again, has he?'

Millington shook his head. 'Mark? No, nothing I've said. Just off up the canteen, most like, have a good sulk.'

'What about?'

Millington's best malicious smile slid out from under his moustache like a ferret on the loose. 'Course of true love, never did run smooth.'

*

Kevin Naylor took two mugs of tea over from the counter, two sugars in Divine's, one in his own. 'Here. Drink that.' Divine continued glowering at a sausage cob, which sat encircled on his plate by a moat of brown sauce. Two tables away, three uniformed constables and a civilian clerk were arguing the merits of the present Nottinghamshire side. 'Give this lot a white ball with a bell in it, and they'd not top three figures against a blind school.'

'What's up?' Naylor asked. 'Lesley?'

Lesley Bruton was a staff nurse at Queen's Medical Centre. Divine had met her during the course of an enquiry and been immediately attracted. Nothing in itself unusual in that. Divine in the vicinity of an attractive woman was like a water diviner in overdrive. What had been unusual was that, despite her early indifference, he had stuck with it.

Months it had taken him to wear Lesley Bruton's patience down to the point where she would even talk about going out with him. Divine, week after seemingly thankless week, just chancing to be driving past the entrance to the hospital as she was coming off shift, more often than not still wearing her staff nurse's uniform beneath her outdoor coat. When finally he caught her at a weak moment and she conceded a quick drink, he had surprised her by making her laugh; surprised her more by not making a play for her when he dropped her at the house she shared with two housemen and three other nurses. Though she could see in his eyes it was what he was set on.

Since then she had put him through a series of arbitrary tests, from keeping him waiting one hour and forty-nine minutes due to an emergency admission, to holding a handful of her damp Kleenex as she sobbed her way through the sentimental bits of *Mrs Doubtfire*. Last night it had been an ordeal by association: Lesley had organised a leaving do for one of the other nurses on the ward and made it clear to Divine she wanted him along. It had all been fine until he'd lost count of his lagers and graphically propositioned one of Lesley's friends.

'Jesus!' Naylor said, hearing the story. 'Don't believe in asking for trouble, do you?'

'All I said was, one into two, how many times d'you reckon it'd go.'

'Pillock!'

Divine dipped his head and savaged the sausage cob. 'Wasn't as though I was trying to have it away behind her back.'

'Might've been better if you were.'

'Yes, happen you're right.' And then, eyes brightening: 'Got to admit, though, can't beat a threesome to get your hormones in an uproar. Remember those sisters whose caravan caught fire out at Strelley . . .'

But Naylor had other things on his mind, more compelling than his colleague's compulsive sexual shenanigans. Now that the baby was up and toddling, walking really, baby no longer, Debbie was only making noises about trying for another. As if eighteen months of post-natal depression had never happened. Perhaps blowing what little they'd saved on a trip to Florida would be worth it after all, shift her mind on to a different tack.

'I hope we're doing enough, Charlie, that's my concern. I'd not be happy coming out of this with egg all over our faces.'

Skelton held the milk carton up questioningly and Resnick merely shook his head; as it was, calling the superintendent's coffee black was asking to be summonsed by the Race Relations Board. 'If anything should happen to her, you know what I mean.'

Resnick set cup and saucer on the floor beside his chair. 'Watching brief, that's what I thought. Public appearances

78

and the like. There's a dinner tonight, just informal, I thought I might go along.'

Skelton looked at Resnick with interest before fidgeting with the papers on his desk. 'No follow-up on that stabbing in Alfreton Road?'

Resnick shook his head. 'We've done a check of the hotels. Nothing. Bloke's likely off home, thanking his lucky stars, shooting a line to his wife about where the scar came from.'

The photograph of Skelton's wife, Resnick noticed, had still not found its way back on to his desk.

'Nothing else I should know about?' the superintendent asked. 'Advisory meeting's tomorrow.'

'Maybe just get some advice,' Resnick said. 'Like how are we supposed to increase the percentage of successful investigations when there's a ban on overtime.'

'Remember the old story, Charlie,' Skelton said, 'the one about the rabbit and the hat . . .'

# Sixteen

Lynn had no trouble recognising Cathy Jordan. Red hair
tied back with green ribbon, blue denim shirt, pale cord
three-quarter skirt, tan boots, she stood, relaxed, alongside
a table on which copies of her books had been piled high.
A glass of red wine in her hand, she was chatting amiably
to a pleasant-faced man in a dark suit whom Lynn took to
be the Waterstone's manager. There were quite a few
people already hovering in the general area of the table,
glancing almost surreptitiously in the author's direction,
waiting for the official business to begin.

Lynn stood by this month's best-sellers, making sure
she had the layout of the shop clear in her mind: the main
doors onto Bridlesmith Gate were at her back, a second
entrance, from the foot of Bottle Lane, was in the corner
of the travel section, several steps up to her left; around
the corner at the far end, she remembered, were children's
books and – what? gardening? – something like that, yes,
gardening. Lynn moved through the steadily growing
crowd and introduced herself.

Cathy Jordan took half a step back to look at her – Lynn
with her newly short hair almost flat on her head, navy
cotton jacket and dark skirt, black low-heeled shoes.

'Resnick, you work with him?'

'Inspector Resnick, yes, that's right.'

'Sent you along to hold my hand.'

'Not exactly.'

A line was beginning to form now, curving its way back
between the other tables; those at the front coughing a

little nervously, wondering how it was Lynn had some-how got in before them.

'You're not armed or anything?'

Lynn shook her head. 'Should I be?'

'God, I hope not.' Cathy Jordan smiled. 'Just, if someone's standing behind my back with a gun, I like to know.'

'Don't worry,' Lynn said. 'I probably won't be at your back at all.'

'Prefer to merge into the crowd, huh?'

'Something like that.'

'Good.' Still smiling. 'Good.' And, turning back towards the manager: 'Shall we get to it?'

Derek Neighbour had made sure of getting there in plenty of time. Parking, he knew to his cost, was always a problem after mid-morning, so he had left his home in Newark shortly after eight, called in briefly at the antique shop he ran with his partner, Philip, and arrived in plenty of time to find a space on the third floor of the Fletcher Gate multi-storey. From there it was only a short walk down the steps on to King John's Chambers and Water-stone's was just to the right – which was as well, considering the weight of what he was carrying.

Derek hadn't discovered Cathy Jordan until *Shallow Grave*, which, of course, was her fourth, the fourth Annie Q. Jones, and, even then, he had almost never read it at all. For at least six weeks it had lain on the nice Victorian wash-stand below the bedroom window, six weeks when Philip would say to him, 'Have you read that book yet?' and he would reply, 'Well, no, not exactly. But I'm getting around to it.'

What Derek normally liked was what the Americans, who had to invent a category for everything, called 'Cosies'. Old-fashioned would have been another way of putting it, but then, what was wrong with old-fashioned?

Craftsmanship, attention to detail, control. Dorothy Birdwell, now, she had long been one of Derek's favourites.

But Philip could be persuasive. 'Cathy Jordan, I do think you'd like her. She's good. The genuine article.'

Since some of Philip's bedtime reading was, well, dubious to say the least, Derek had remained noncommittal. Till, one day, or to be precise, two, he had been laid up in bed with flu. The Patricia Moyes he was rereading for the third time had come to its same, careful ending; Dorothy Birdwell had pottered around in the East Anglian fog to disappointingly little purpose, and there were just so many times you could reread the letters page of the *Telegraph*.

So, propped up on his pillows and with some Beechams and hot lemon close to hand, he had started *Shallow Grave*:

> *The first time I saw Anita Mulholland she was a happy twelve-year-old with braces on her teeth and a smile that would have knocked out the angels; next time I saw her was a year later, to the day, and she was dead.*

The voice, Annie's voice, had gripped him from that first sentence and hadn't let him go. The story, oh, the story was fine, perfectly fine, though in truth, there was little about it that was particularly original. But there were moments when Derek's skin had tightened about him, moments when the cold of shared fear slid along the backs of his already feverish legs and arms. And there was the disgust and shock of what had happened to that young girl. But without the voice, the sure, buttonholing quality of the voice, none of the rest would have been enough.

He finished *Shallow Grave* and, when he had recovered, set out to acquire the others. Philip had copies of the book that preceded it, *Sleeping Fools Lie*, and the one which came after it, *Dead Weight*. But now Derek had been well and truly bitten, he wanted to read all five Annie Q. Jones mysteries from the beginning. The second, *Uneasy Prey*, he finally found in an *Any two for 50p* box on the market, dog-eared and marmalade-stained, but, as far as he could see, intact. *Angels at Rest*, the first of the series, proved more difficult. It had been brought out in paperback in Britain by a firm that had rapidly gone into liquidation, and had been published in hardback in a small edition intended primarily for libraries. Derek had finally tracked down a copy through the *Books Wanted* section of Philip's *Guardian*.

Derek, of course, was more than a mere reader: he was a collector with a collector's mentality. Completism was his unquestioned faith. Inside the heavy cardboard box he was carrying were British editions of all five Annie Q. Jones mysteries, five American paperbacks, American first-edition hardbacks – the 'true' firsts – of everything except *Angels at Rest*, and, just for fun, a few assorted foreign-language versions he had picked up here and there – German, French, Danish, South Korean, Taiwanese.

A complete English-language set, except that it wasn't, to Derek's eternal chagrin, quite complete. Rumour had it that a mystery bookstore outside Phoenix had a first edition of *Angels at Rest* for sale at six hundred and fifty dollars, US, but it had proved sadly untrue.

Derek was still searching.

He turned his back towards the glass door into Waterstone's and eased it open, the box held tight in front of him on aching arms. The queue at the signing table was long, but that didn't matter in the least. If Derek only reached Cathy Jordan at the end of her session, so much the better, there would be more time to chat.

Lynn refused the glass of wine which the manager offered her and opted for mineral water instead, sipping it now from a vantage point by the side wall, close to the books on poetry and theatre.

She admired the way Cathy Jordan dealt with her fans; a smile for each one, not forced but seeming genuine, to each she offered a palatable slice of conversation; copies of her books she signed in black ink with a flourish, using a fat Mont Blanc pen she carried especially for the purpose:

> For Emily
> from Annie Q.
> & me!
> *Cathy Jordan*

The C was round and deep enough to contain, almost, the rest of her first name; the J swooped towards the bottom of the title page before sweeping through its final curve.

'Well,' Cathy Jordan said, 'it's good to meet you, too.' Her voice, American, slightly nasal, sounded overlarge within the confines of the store.

Lynn had decided she would buy a copy of *Dead Weight* for herself, but wouldn't bother, probably, to get it signed. The line was dwindling to an end: a youngish man wearing a black *Anthrax* T-shirt and with two gold rings in his right ear, one immediately above the other, was having his book signed now, and behind him two women waited together, deep in conversation. The taller of the two was wearing a brightly coloured ethnic dress, a green rucksack slung casually over one shoulder; her companion, several years younger, wore a black shirt over blue jeans, one hand resting on the leather shoulder bag slung from her shoulder. Behind them another man, older, with gingery hair and glasses, stood with an open cardboard box of books at his feet; and finally, a fortyish woman with a Warehouse carrier bag in one hand and a small child, already beginning to grizzle, clinging to the other.

84

Lynn glanced at her watch; she thought, I can be back at the station by half past two.

The man in the T-shirt moved away and the taller of the women swung the rucksack from her shoulder. The boy at the back of the queue had started to cry and his mother gave his arm a tug, causing him to cry louder. A couple of fourteen-year-olds, arms loose around each other's limber bodies, passed carelessly in front of where Lynn was standing.

'We've read all of your books,' the woman in black was saying. 'They really made an impression.'

'And since it's your first visit,' her friend said excitedly, 'we've brought something for you.'

'Well, that's real nice,' Cathy Jordan said, giving it her best smile.

The woman raised the rucksack high and swung it towards the table: what was inside was a plastic container and what was inside that was blood. A lot of blood. It poured over Cathy Jordan's face and hair and down her front, splashing across what was left of the piles of books.

'We thought,' one of the women was shouting, 'you'd like to know what it was like.'

Lynn pushed the two youths aside and in four paces she was at Cathy Jordan's side; Cathy standing, arms outstretched, blue of her shirt adrift in blood.

'Are you all right?'

'What the hell do you think?'

On his knees, Derek Neighbour was lifting books from their box as deftly and carefully as he could; those that had been lying on top were thickly spotted and stained.

Lynn part-swerved round him, part-vaulted over him; the mother with the Warehouse bag dragged her screaming child towards her and Lynn cannoned into the shelves avoiding him. Ahead of her she could see the two women pushing their way through the doors on to the street.

'Make way!' she called. 'Make way, police!'

Nobody moved.

Lynn ran between them, failing to notice the table opposite the cash desk until she struck it hard, somewhere between hip and thigh, her cry lost in the crash of books against the floor.

'Stop!'

They were running full-pelt down the middle of St Peter's Gate, ignoring the traffic, both pavements clogged with lunchtime shoppers, grazing on their take-away burgers or baked potatoes.

'Police!'

Halfway down, they separated: the one in black continuing on, actually gaining speed, the woman in the dress dodging her way into the arcade of fashionable shops that led towards the square.

Lynn ducked into the narrow alley higher up and emerged on to Cheapside before the woman was in sight; for a moment, Lynn thought she might have doubled back, but no, there she was, pushing between a knot of people outside Saxone's window.

'Right!' Lynn yelled, catching hold of the collar of the woman's dress. 'That's it!'

The dress ripped and, stumbling, the woman, all but bare-chested, fell across the kerb by the pedestrian crossing. A green double-decker bus pulled up not so far short of where she was sprawling.

Lynn seized one of the woman's arms and yanked her back on to the pavement; leaning over her, a crowd gathering quickly round, she drew out her warrant card and held it high in the air. 'I'm a police officer and I'm placing you under arrest. You do not have to say anything unless you wish to do so, but anything you do say may be given in evidence.'

Someone at the back of the crowd began a slow handclap and several more jeered; the majority started to drift away. On the ground, without bothering to pull the

**material of her dress around her, the woman began to laugh.**

# Seventeen

'Well, I suppose,' Marius said, pausing by the bathroom door, 'you could say that some kind of natural justice has been done.'

The door was open just a crack and he could smell the sweet, urine-like smell of baby powder, the kind with which Dorothy liked to dust herself after her bath. At first, Marius had found it almost repellent, but now he savoured it along with almost everything else – the small and delicate ways in which she kept her body sweet to the touch.

'Marius, dear. Hand me my dressing gown, would you?'

Quilted, pink, it slid around her shoulders like satin over old silk.

'Tea's ready,' Marius said. 'And I found some more of those nice little cakes. The butterfly ones with the cream.'

Stepping out into the main room of their small suite, Dorothy Birdwell smiled her thin-mouthed smile. 'Marius, you spoil me. You really do.'

'Not really,' he replied, smiling back. Not nearly enough, he thought.

'Now, dear,' said Dorothy, settling carefully into a high-arched chair. 'I want you to tell me all about what happened in the bookshop. And I don't want you to miss out a single thing.'

'Will you please state your name?' Lynn asked. 'For the record.'

'Vivienne Plant.'

'And your address?'

'Flat seven, Ancaster Court, Bairnbridge Road, Mapperley.'

Like all of the interview rooms at the police station, this was small and airless and hung over with the unmistakable pall of stale cigarette smoke. Vivienne Plant, with her bright dress and upright posture, the after-image of a sneer on her well-tended middle-class face, looked impressively out of place.

'What is your present occupation?' Lynn asked.

'I'm a lecturer in Women's Studies.'

'Here in the city?'

'In Derby.'

'And are you married or single?'

'Neither.'

'I'm sorry?'

'I have lived with the same partner for seven years; we have a three-year-old child. We are not married. Is that clear enough?'

As a manifesto, Lynn thought. 'Ms Plant, you do admit the assault on Cathy Jordan . . .'

'Demonstration. I was making a demonstration.'

'In relation to Ms Jordan?'

'In relation to her work.'

'You disapprove of her books, then? You don't like them?'

'Which question do you want me to answer?'

No wonder she didn't want a solicitor, Lynn thought, she thinks she is one. 'Aren't they the same thing?' she asked wearily.

'Disapproving and not liking?'

'Yes.'

'I like eating Terry's Chocolate Oranges, sometimes two at a time; I also like popping into McDonald's last

89

thing at night for apple pie. I don't really approve of either.'

Someone walked past along the corridor outside, heavy feet set down slowly and with purpose. Lynn tried not to look at her watch or the clock on the adjacent wall. 'Can you tell me,' she asked, 'why you disapprove of Cathy Jordan's books so strongly?'

'Which version do you want? The fifty-minute lecture or the single-paragraph outline?'

Lynn was reminded of those times she had been lectured by her head teacher at school. 'The outline will be fine.'

'Right. What I object to about her books is that they rely on an almost exclusive portrayal of women as victims, usually victims of violent and degrading assault. Their degradation and pain are in direct proportion to Jordan's profit. She's got rich on women's suffering. She should know better.'

'And your intention was to teach her that lesson?'

'I thought it was appropriate.'

'Covering her with paint?'

'Yes, don't you?'

'Then you do admit to throwing paint over Ms Jordan?'

'I thought of it more as pouring, but yes, all right. I do.'

'You assaulted her.'

'Surely that's for the court to decide?'

'You want this to go to court?'

'Of course.'

Oh, God, Lynn thought, spare me from people who know what's right for me better than I do myself. The whole Greenpeace, civil liberties, feminist bunch of them. 'This action, was it carried out on behalf of some group or organisation?'

'Not officially, no. It was an individual act.'

'Aside from your accomplice.'

Vivienne Plant's shoulders braced back even further. 'There was no such person.'

'Ms Plant, I was there in the shop. I saw you standing in line with another woman, talking. A woman wearing a black shirt and jeans. You came into the shop together. Approached Ms Jordan together. After the incident, you ran out together. You were not acting on your own.'

'Well, that's going to have to be your word against mine.'

Lynn shook her head. She could have thought of places she would rather be than shut up with Ms Self-righteous, plenty of them. 'All right,' she said, 'we'll come back to this again.'

'Look,' Vivienne said, leaning forward, holding Lynn with her eyes, 'the responsibility for what happened is mine. Okay? But what I did, I did for all women, not just me.'

'All women?' Lynn said.

'Of course.'

'I don't think so.'

'No?'

Lynn pushed back her chair and got to her feet. 'You didn't do it for me.'

Vivienne pitched back her head and laughed. 'Well, you really do need the fifty-minute version, don't you?'

Lynn reached sideways, towards the Off button on the tape machine. 'This interview stopped at thirteen minutes past three.'

Once Naylor had settled him down, assured him that in all probability he would be able to drive back to Newark ahead of the evening rush hour and allowed him to make a call to his partner, Derek Neighbour had proved a good witness. He had seen Vivienne Plant's actions clearly and described them with accuracy. Yes, she and the other woman, the one in the black shirt, had chattered away all the time they were waiting in the queue and although he hadn't heard a great deal of what they had actually been saying, the impression they gave was not of two people who have only just that moment met. Absolutely not.

'So it was your impression that the two women were friends? That they knew one another quite well?'

'Very well, more like.'

'And their names? Did you hear either of them address the other by names?'

'No. Come to think of it, no. Not that I can recall. I don't think they did.'

'All right, Mr Neighbour. Thanks a lot. We've got your address and if we need you again we'll be in touch.'

Naylor got to his feet. Derek Neighbour continued to look up at him, uncertain.

'Was there something else?' Naylor asked. 'Something you wanted to add?'

'It's just, well, you know, the damage . . .'

'To Miss Jordan? Apart from the shock, I don't think it was too serious. Her clothes, of course, and . . .'

'No. To me. My books.'

'Well, I don't know. Perhaps Waterstone's, in the circumstances . . .'

'You don't understand. There's a first edition of *Uneasy Prey*, absolutely ruined. I don't even know if I'll be able to find another one, and if I do, the cost is going to be close to three hundred pounds. More.'

Three hundred, Naylor was thinking, for one book. Only a crime book, at that. Debbie's mum got through four or five a week from the library, large-print editions in the main. Debbie reckoned she could get one finished between *Neighbours* and *Countdown*. Why would anyone pay three hundred quid for something you could get through in a few hours and never want to look at again? It didn't make a scrap of sense.

*

'The stuff with the paint she's ready to admit to. Eager. Not that she could do anything else.' Lynn was at her desk in the CID room, talking to Graham Millington. Vivienne Plant she had left to stew a little in the interview room. 'The woman who was with her, though, she won't give us a thing. Denies knowing her altogether.'

'No chance she's telling the truth?'

Lynn looked up at him. 'None.'

'Charlie,' Skelton said, 'we're not going to let this woman wrap us round her little finger, commit time and money, all so's she can garner free publicity for whatever cockamamie idea she's spouting. Women's Studies, that's her, isn't it? Jesus, Charlie! Women's Studies, Black Studies, Lesbian and Gay Studies, what in God's name happened to good old History and Geography, that's what I'd like to know?'

Resnick couldn't oblige. Though he had recently been taken to task for carelessly using the masculine pronoun by a very intelligent and thoughtful young woman, who, it had turned out later, believed Norwich to be located in the middle of Hampshire.

'What about the American?' Skelton said. 'Is she keen to press charges?'

'We don't know yet . . .'

'Then it's about time we bloody did!'

Right, Resnick thought, getting to his feet, and it's about time you went back to running before you have some self-induced heart attack. Whatever was going on behind closed doors in Skelton's executive home, it wasn't happy families.

Lynn was waiting outside Resnick's office. 'Graham and I had another go at her. Still won't budge. Didn't know the other woman from Adam. I mean Eve.'

'She's lying?'

'Not just that. She knows we know she is, but at the moment there's not a lot we can do to prove it. Loving that, isn't she? Clever cow!'

'Not your favourite person, then?' Resnick smiled.

'Women like that,' Lynn scowled, 'whatever their intentions, just end up making women like me feel inferior.'

'Well, looks like you can have the pleasure of kicking her free. Last thing the old man wants to do is contribute to her publicity campaign.'

'What about Cathy Jordan? Suppose she wants . . .'

'To lay charges? I doubt it. Wouldn't exactly help her, would it? But if she does . . .' Resnick shrugged. 'I don't suppose Ms Plant's about to do a runner, do you? Suddenly turn into a shrinking violet?'

Lynn looked back at Resnick, concerned; unless she was very much mistaken, he had made a joke.

# Eighteen

'Catherine, dear. How awful for you. How perfectly awful.'

How Cathy Jordan hated being called Catherine; especially by Dorothy Birdwell, wattled hands flustering all around her, smelling her old maid's smell of face powder and malice.

'Yes, well, you know, Dottie, it really wasn't so bad.'

'Perhaps you should consider following my example, dear, and have a nice young man to look after you.'

Marius Gooding was standing a short way off, blazer buttons glistening. For the first time, Cathy noticed his manicured hands, long fingers flexing slightly at his sides. Catching Cathy's gaze he made a quick dipping gesture with his head, somewhere between a nod and a bow, a token smile of sympathy passing across his face. Without her understanding exactly why, something deep inside Cathy shuddered.

'I don't need a nice young man, Dottie,' she said, 'I have a husband.'

'So you have, dear, sometimes I forget.'

'What in hell's name happened to you?' – Frank's first words when Cathy had appeared back at the hotel in borrowed clothes, face oddly aglow, hair clotted red. 'Something go wrong at the beauty shop?'

'Screw,' she'd said, pushing past him on her way to the bathroom, 'you!'

'Nice idea, Cath, if you could remember how. Wait for

95

you to screw me, might as well hand my dick to Lorena Bobbitt for surgery.'

The only answer was the sound of water bouncing back from the shower. Frank poured himself a drink and took it across to the window, looking out. There was a plane rising slow between the small, off-white clouds and for a moment, wherever it was heading, he wished he were on it. Then he laughed. The thing that had most fascinated him about the whole Bobbitt affair, the way the guy had made a living later in a Californian nightclub, women handing over good bucks to dance with him in the hope of scooping ten grand by giving him a boner.

For Frank, whose childhood had been spent in cast-offs and hand-me-downs and who had stolen his first quarter at age five, it was eloquent testimony to what made his country great. The ordinary American's ability to make entrepreneurial capital in the face of any adversity.

Tyrell had insisted on living as close to the centre of the city as his and his wife's combined salaries would allow. After all, he had reasoned, the one thing we don't want to add to my already antisocial hours is a lot of unnecessary travelling time, right? And Susan Tyrell had nodded agreement and said nothing about the fact that buying a house where her husband was suggesting would give her a forty-five-minute drive each way to the comprehensive where she taught.

Besides, she had liked the house: substantial, large without being sprawling, one of those late-Victorian family homes near the Arboretum which she and David had redecorated and were steadily filling with books and videos instead of children.

Another of those decisions that Tyrell had talked her into with his usual mixture of enthusiasm and dodgy rationalisation. She had, Susan knew, allowed it to happen too often, agreed to far too much for too long and in favour of what? A quiet life, contentment? When most of their friends were already into their second divorce or separation, what was she trying to prove? That she was a survivor? That, despite all the odds, she and David still loved one another, that they had found a way of making it work?

The first time she had spoken to him, really spoken, had been after a seminar at the University of Warwick, where they were both doing Media Studies. The only one of the group not majoring in Film, Susan had sat there for eight weeks, listening, contributing very little. Finally, she had plucked up her courage and launched into a mild attack on the film they had been watching, a fifties musical called *It's Always Fair Weather*. Pretty enough, she had said, but pretty vacant. Fun, but why all the fuss? David had told her in no uncertain terms and after twenty minutes she had bowed her head and agreed with him and a pattern had been set.

On the way out of the seminar, he had invited her for coffee; in the coffee bar he had invited her to a movie. The movie turned out to be two, an Elvis Presley double bill, and David had made them sit on the front row. *King Creole* was okay, he pronounced, but the really interesting one was *Change of Habit*, Presley's last feature, 1969. And Susan had kept her thoughts to her popcorn, watching Dr Elvis falling sanctimoniously in love with a speech therapist she had only later identified as Mary Tyler Moore.

'Didn't you think it was great,' Tyrell had enthused later, 'the way our sense of Presley as star bifurcates the diegesis of the narrative?'

'Um,' Susan had said. 'Yes. Absolutely.'

She looked up now from the pile of books she was marking, hearing the front door open and Tyrell's voice calling her name from the hall. 'Susan, you there?'

She would, he thought, be in the long kitchen which

97

doubled as dining room, marking another thirty-three pastiches of *EastEnders*, ever ready to pop another frozen pizza into the microwave.

'My God! You won't believe what happened. In the middle of the day, broad daylight. Must have been like that scene in *Carrie*, the one with the pig's blood, you know.'

Susan was on her feet, filling the kettle. 'I heard about it on the car radio.'

'National?'

'No, Radio Nottingham.'

'Oh,' Tyrell sounded disappointed, ferreting in the cupboard for what was left of the packet of custard creams. 'I thought at least we might've got some good publicity out of it.'

'I wonder if she felt the same? The woman – what's her name?'

'Come on, Susan. Cathy Jordan, how many more times? You'll meet her tonight at Sonny's.'

'I'm not sure if I'm going.'

'What? Don't be ridiculous, of course you're going.'

'I don't know, I think I'm getting a headache. I've got all this work to do.'

Tyrell swore as the last biscuit crumbled between his fingers and fell to the floor. 'Susan, it's all booked. Arranged. Besides, you want to meet everybody, don't you?'

'Do I?'

'Of course you do. You'll have a great time once you're there, you always do.'

Susan reached for the tea bags. 'Earl Grey or ordinary?'

'Ordinary.'

What Susan could remember was sitting at one end of the table, drinking glass after glass of Perrier while the conversation spun around her.

Tyrell smiled. He had found a cache of plain chocolate

digestives. 'I don't want to go without you, you know that. Still, if you've really got your mind made up . . .'

When she looked at him, what Susan saw was relief in his eyes; he would be so much happier not having to bother about her. 'Yes,' she said, pouring boiling water into the pot, 'you go on your own.'

Tyrell shrugged and sat down at the pine table, reaching for the *Guardian*. First chance he'd had to look at the paper that day.

# Nineteen

*Angel Eyes*. The first film in the Festival's Curtis Woolfe season and, to Tyrell's mind, the best. Made in 'forty-five for Republic, and photographed by John Alton, it featured Albert Dekker as a middle-aged businessman lured to destruction by slinky, wide-eyed Martha MacVicar who, a year later, her name changed to Martha Vickers, would come to brief fame as Lauren Bacall's thumb-sucking, promiscuous sister in the film of Raymond Chandler's *The Big Sleep*. Woolfe, who collaborated on the script with an uncredited Steve Fisher, persuaded 'Wild Bill' Elliott, a Western star under contract to the studio, to shed his buckskins and play the honest cop who investigates Dekker's murder and almost falls for MacVicar's wiles himself.

Despite the film being almost unknown, Mollie had garnered enough publicity around Curtis Woolfe's re-emergence to ensure a three-quarter-full house. Woolfe had limited his spirits intake to a half-bottle of vodka and rather less of gin. The plan was for Tyrell to introduce him briefly to the audience before the screening and invite anyone who wished to remain behind for a question-and-answer session at the end.

As the house lights dimmed and the stage spot flicked on, Tyrell dabbed sweaty palms against the sides of his black suit and with a whispered, 'Let's go to work,' set out down the sloping aisle towards the microphone.

At about the same time that Tyrell was introducing Curtis

Woolfe, Peter Farleigh was stepping out of the shower and sipping the Dewar's and ginger ale he had poured for himself earlier. A little something from the mini-bar to set him up for the evening. And why not? Whatever he was about to treat himself to, Farleigh thought that he deserved it. He had had a good day. Now it was a few drinks in the bar, a meal and then he'd see. But one thing was certain, even if he ended the night back in his hotel room watching a Channel Four documentary about Tibet, it was preferable to driving the relatively short distance home; better than enduring Sarah's pained indifference and cold back.

Even before his seven-thirty alarm call that morning, he had been wide awake, eager to go. *Telegraph* and *Mail* delivered to his room, he had browsed the front pages between buffing his shoes and shaving, the sports and financial sections he had read over breakfast – the full English as usual when he was travelling, but careful to use sunflower spread instead of butter, pour skimmed milk into his coffee, half a spoonful of sugar, no more. Time to telephone his wife before leaving, remind her the Volvo had to be taken in for service; maybe she could check the wardrobe, see if any of his suits needed dropping off at the cleaner's while he was in town.

His hire car was a new Granada, almost pristine, one of the perks of the job. His first meeting, at Epperstone Nurseries, had been over by lunchtime. Oh, there'd been one or two potentially dodgy questions about increased resistance to the new systematic fungicide he was pushing, but that was what he was paid to deal with. A few fancy charts prepared by the research department, a joke about not going back to the bad old days of mercury pollution, and they had been falling over themselves to sign on the dotted line.

Farleigh had joined them for a swift half in their local before driving to a little place he favoured just this side of

Loughborough; very nice smoked mackerel with goose-berry sauce. By twenty past two, he had been steering the Granada into the car park at the University School of Agriculture, Sutton Bonington.

Whenever people asked his line of work, more often than not he would temper sales executive with a wink and a self-deprecating smile: fifteen years in fertilisers, best make sure you're sitting downwind.

He had been back in the city by six and by seven had written up his sales reports, called his secretary on her home number and checked his appointments for tomorrow, thought about phoning his wife – got halfway through dialling the number – before deciding against it. One of the things he couldn't stand, men who behaved as if they were on some kind of leash.

Peter Farleigh sucked in his stomach beneath the hotel towel, made a fist to circle steam from the mirror and leaned forward to examine his face; he could leave shaving till morning. A splash of aftershave would do.

Dry, he put on clean socks, underpants and shirt, the same suit and tie. In the lounge bar, he ordered a G & T, evinced enough of an interest in the forthcoming test series to have the waistcoated barman smiling, tipped in the rest of his tonic and carried his glass over to a table near the smoked-glass window. Blurs of light passed along the street outside, trailing orange smoke.

When Farleigh turned his head, she was sitting across from him, relaxed into one of the easy chairs near the piano, leaning back. Black dress, dark hair curling away from the nape of her neck. Thirty? Thirty-three? He watched as she bent forward to pick up her bag, the way the button-through dress eased itself a little higher above her knees when she sat back. Oblivious to anyone around her, the woman tapped a cigarette from the pack, clicked her lighter, no response, gave it a shake and tried again,

102

finally dropped the lighter back inside her bag and began rummaging for a match.

'Here,' Farleigh said, walking towards her. 'Allow me.'

'Thanks.' Perfume, red nails matching the dark of her lipstick; smoke that moved soft across her face.

'Staying here at the hotel?'

Shaking her head, she smiled. 'No. I'm meeting a friend.'

Back at his seat, Farleigh thumbed through the menu, vacillating between the steak and the salmon. A light-toned Afro-Caribbean sat down at the piano and almost immediately began with 'Over the Rainbow', sleeves of his lightweight cream jacket pushed high above his wrists. For some moments, Farleigh was nagged by the thought that he had missed his daughter's birthday; once they were off at university, it was so difficult to keep tabs. At the edge of his vision, the woman shifted her position casually, leaning forward to the ashtray and back, crossing and recrossing her legs.

If she looks at me when I get up, Farleigh thought, I'll speak to her again. Instead, her head was turned towards the pianist, who had eased the microphone over the keyboard and was lightly crooning, 'Me and Mrs Jones'. For God's sake, Farleigh told himself, stop being so bloody pathetic!

In the dining room, he decided fish twice in one day wasn't a good idea and ordered the steak. One bite and he knew that hadn't been a good idea either.

'Everything satisfactory, sir?'

'Fine, thank you.'

As compensation, he sent back his glass of house red and ordered a bottle of good Bordeaux. Before now he'd paid the earth for stuff that tasted more like the copper sulphate fungicide known to the trade – his trade – as Bordeaux Mixture, but this was the real thing.

By the time he had risen to his feet, one bottle later, his

head was slightly muzzy and it had taken him a while to realise that the dark-haired woman from the bar was now sitting at a corner table of the restaurant, evidently still alone.

That's all right, Farleigh lectured himself, keep on walking; couple of phone calls, early night. Just as long as she doesn't look up. But it hadn't even taken that.

The woman was surprised when Farleigh stopped beside her table. 'At least you made the right choice,' he said, nodding towards her plate.

'I'm sorry?'

'The salmon. I had the steak. Like the proverbial, I'm afraid.'

'The proverbial what?' There was just a hint of lipstick, dark against the white of her teeth.

'Old boots.'

Farleigh smiled and she smiled back with her eyes; she was older, he decided, than he had first thought, but not by too much. Still the right side of forty.

'It was never an issue,' she was saying. 'The steak. I'm vegetarian.'

'Ah.'

'All that stuff they pump into the poor animals, mad cow disease and everything.' She smiled, more fully this time. 'Perhaps you think that's foolish?'

'Not at all.' Things I could tell you, he was thinking, put you off your food for a lifetime. 'What happened?' he asked, indicating the empty chair.

Vaguely, she waved a hand. 'Oh, you know . . .'

'It's difficult to imagine.'

'What's that?'

'Anyone standing you up.'

He had hoped for some response, a laugh, an explanation. Instead, she looked down at her plate and pushed at a piece of pink flesh with the edge of her fork. Farleigh knew he had blown it. 'Well, enjoy the rest of your meal.'

She waited until he had almost turned away. 'Why don't you sit down? Join me for a drink.'

# Twenty

Curtis Woolfe's film had been well received. Of course, there were always those who wanted nothing more than the latest glossy mishmash of unarmed combat and special effects, and who found anything pre-seventies slow and dull and boring. 'Nothing happens,' they would say, mooching down to the bar for their designer lager. Nothing happens. Well, nobody's head came off, nobody's blood spurted a perfect technicolour parabola across the screen, nobody humped naked in the shower or the kitchen sink; there was no Chuck, or Steven, or Cynthia, no Jean Claude, Arnie, or Sly; not even (the heavens forfend) Bruce Willis. But the moment when Albert Dekker steps into the darkness of his hotel room, twists the key in the lock behind him, slides the bolt and turns back into the room to see Martha MacVicar's feral face illuminated through the slanting blinds by the light across the street, still had most of the audience catching its breath. The smile that died in her eyes as her teeth bit down into her lower lip.

In the auditorium, Curtis Woolfe had been pleased with the audience's reaction and had answered questions with self-deprecating charm. What had it been like working with Mitchum? 'Delightful, especially when he was stoned.' Who was the most beautiful *femme fatale*? 'Gail Russell – ask John Wayne.' What was his favourite *film noir*? 'Aside from my own, *Out of the Past*.' Why hadn't he made a film in over twenty years? 'Nobody asked me.'

Here in Sonny's restaurant, he was even more relaxed. Gesticulating over the food in his assumed Gallic manner, almost anxious to talk about the other films in the season, Woolfe was lavish in his praise for Tyrell and the festival.

Resnick had arrived early, drunk a Beck's alone at the large reserved table and been about to leave when, through the curved corner window, he had seen Mollie Hansen leading the group along Carlton Street, past the George Hotel. There were a dozen of them in all, Dorothy Birdwell the last to arrive, leaning on Marius Gooding's arm. Cathy Jordan, her hair trimmed back and partly covered by a black velvet beret, had taken a seat alongside Resnick; her husband, facing them, sat beside Mollie.

'So how was the film?' Resnick asked, starting on his second beer.

Cathy Jordan speared a piece of bread, spread it lavishly with butter and took a generous bite. 'I had an aunt once, lived all her life in this town near Jackson, Wyoming. So small it didn't even rate a pimple on the map. You could turn up there any time, day or night, unannounced, nothing in her store cupboard to speak of, yet inside half an hour you'd find yourself sitting down to the tastiest snack you could ever have imagined.' She brushed a crumb from the side of her mouth and tried the wine. 'Well, Curtis's film was like that. Considering what he had to work with, it was a small miracle.' She lifted the menu towards the light. 'How d'you think this rack of lamb would be? I'm good and tired of steak and chicken.'

Across the city in his hotel, Peter Farleigh and the dark-haired woman were back in the bar. Michelle – she had told him that was her name, Michelle – had developed a taste for blue cocktails afloat with tinned fruit and Farleigh had kept pace with her, drinking brandy now and talking in a voice that was just this side of loud. On and on about crop yields, fertilisers, EEC farming subsidies.

When Michelle's eyes began to glaze over he changed the topic to his family, his three kids – the one at university, the one who was already an accountant, the one who had gone off with a bunch of travellers and sent them marigold teas and pictures from the I-ching. The pianist had trawled his way from *Cats* to *Carousel* and eventually given way to piped music: bland arrangements of the Beatles for saxophone, six strings and a drum machine.

From behind the bar, a voice called last orders. Farleigh looked hard at Michelle and she looked away; he let his hand drift down towards her leg and with a look she stopped it well short of her knee.

'I hope, Peter, you're not going to make a move on me.'

'I'm sorry, no, look, I . . .' He could feel his face reddening and that only made it redden more. What was he doing sitting there, blushing like a schoolboy whose mother had chosen the wrong moment to come into the room?

'What was going to be the next step, Peter?' She was leaning towards him, almost touching her shoulder to his arm. 'Asking me up to your room?'

'Look . . .'

'Well . . . ?'

'Michelle, I . . .' Suddenly he became aware of his own sweat, sweet and rancid; the muscles of his stomach tightened and refused to let go.

'Was that it?' her voice rising. 'Because if it was, Peter, well, I have to say you'd have been disappointed.'

Farleigh was certain everyone else in the bar could hear. 'All right, look, it's been a nice evening, let's just forget it.'

'Forget it?'

'Yes.' He pushed an almost empty packet of cigarettes down into his pocket, brushed the heel of his hand across the eyebrow of his right eye. 'I think that's best, don't you?'

'Best?'

'Yes.' Standing now, while she leaned back into the comfort of the chair and surveyed him with amused eyes.

'Peter?'

'Mmm?'

'You know I'm teasing you, don't you?'

He could still smell himself, hear his own breath.

'I am teasing you.'

'Yes, well, like I say . . .' All the while, backing away.

'I would – if you asked me – I mean, I would like to . . . go with you, you know, to your room.'

Farleigh looked clumsily round. A man with a shock of almost pure white hair was staring back at him from a stool at the corner of the bar. As Farleigh continued to look, the man smiled, more a simper than a smile, and Farleigh quickly looked away.

'Unless,' Michelle said, 'you've changed your mind.'

He sat back down. There was a mole, a small one he hadn't noticed before, just to the right of her cheek, and her eyes, what would you call that shade of brown?

She inclined her head towards him. 'Have you changed your mind?'

The answer, not instant. 'No.'

'Good. Let's not waste any more time, then, down here.' She was on her feet now, holding out her hand.

Peter took it, but as soon as he was standing she pulled it away.

'After you.'

As they were waiting for the lift, she slipped her arm through his. Another couple stood waiting, a little behind them, younger, the woman fidgeting with the cuff-links on the man's right sleeve. They had been out to some formal occasion and were wearing evening dress. The woman was pretty in an obvious kind of way and somehow reminded Farleigh of his daughter, not the one at university, the other one. The one who sent him tea and blessings and whom he rarely saw. She was wearing a silver dress cut low and once they were in the lift, despite Michelle's proximity, he found it difficult not to stare at the tops of her breasts.

'A hundred and fifty,' Michelle said.

At first, Farleigh wasn't even sure she was talking to him.

'A hundred and fifty.'

'What about it?'

'That's what it'll cost.'

'What?'

'Me. For the rest of the night. A hundred and fifty pounds.'

Farleigh was still staring at the young woman, unable to look at Michelle. The young man, embarrassed, was staring at the buttons beside the lift door.

'Well?' Michelle said. 'Don't you think I'm worth it?'

Close to Farleigh, the young woman suddenly threw back her head and laughed. The lift stopped at the sixth floor and the couple scrambled out. After a moment, the doors sighed shut and the lift continued its ascent.

'I thought you knew,' Michelle said. Farleigh shook his head and she smiled. 'Knew that I was working.'

'No, how could I?'

The lift stopped again and they got out into the empty corridor.

'What did you think was going on then?'

'I don't know. I suppose I just thought, you know . . .'

'That I'd let you pick me up? That I fancied you?'

'Yes.'

'Marvellous, isn't it?' Michelle said. 'The way we deceive ourselves.'

Threading through the sounds of the restaurant, the voice of a woman singing 'Someone to Watch Over Me.' Resnick thought it might be Carmen McCrea, but he couldn't be sure. Whoever had decided, ten years or so ago, that jazz was a good accompaniment to fashionable eating, he felt he owed them a vote of thanks.

Beside him, Cathy Jordan was tucking into an unhealthy portion of sticky toffee pudding, while Resnick, with unusual restraint, confined himself to his second large espresso.

'See that?' With her spoon, she made a dismissive flicking gesture across the table. 'Lothario in action.'

Oblivious, Frank Carlucci was engaging Mollie Hansen in intense conversation; if he got any closer he would be eating his creme caramel out of her lap.

'Doesn't bother you?' Resnick asked.

Cathy glanced across at them and then away. 'Not any more.' The look in her eyes suggested she might almost mean it. 'Besides, that young woman can handle herself.'

Resnick drew breath slowly and nodded. About that, he thought she was right. Along the table, Dorothy Birdwell, back upright, head tilted forward, sat quite asleep.

'That was all it took,' Frank Carlucci was saying to Mollie, 'a little investment here, little advertising there. One minute I'm the guy who won silver snatching the big one at the Games, face all over the sports pages for weeks. The Olympics, right? A big deal.'

Mollie yawned.

'A while after that,' Frank said, 'things got kinda slow. That's till I met Cathy there. Married her. Wake up and what am I? Mr Cathy Jordan, that's what.'

Oh, God, thought Mollie, here we go. Another everyday story of emasculation. Tennessee Williams without the style.

'I could only take that for so long,' Frank was saying. 'I knew I had to do something for myself. Something big. So I look around, talk a little here, a little there, a favour to be called in, you know what I mean? Now here I am, heading up the fastest-growing catering franchise on the West

Coast. Shops everywhere, those little carts, signs – Carlucci's cappuccino, the coffee with muscle. Truckers pull over and drink my stuff without there's guys looking at 'em strange for drinking something with a fancy name, bunch of froth on top. You understand what I'm saying?'

'I understand,' Mollie said quietly, 'if you don't take your fucking hand off my leg, I'm going to stick this fork right through it.'

There was a scar on one of her breasts, curving beneath it, a thin ridged line, small and white. Peter Farleigh lay on his back and Michelle knelt above him, straddling his thighs. She was still wearing skimpy bikini pants. They had fooled around for a while earlier, Michelle finding some baby oil in her bag, and now a small pool of it floated in one of the folds of his stomach, glistening a little in the light from the window, the only light in the room.

'Are you ready?' she said.

She could see he was ready.

'All right,' she said, 'just a minute.' And leaned sideways, reaching down again to where her bag lay beside the bed.

Bloody condoms, Farleigh thought, shifting his position to accommodate her move. Still, better safe than sorry.

But then he saw what was in her hand, the look in her eyes, and he knew that wasn't true.

# Twenty-one

Resnick had just walked into the CID room when the call came in, Millington picking up and listening only long enough to beckon him over, pass the phone across.

'Right,' Resnick said, a minute later. 'We've got a body. Graham, you come with me. Mark . . .'

'Boss?'

'I shall need you and Kevin knocking on a few doors.'

Divine didn't need telling twice.

'How about Lynn?' Millington asked. They were in the corridor, heading for the stairs. 'Seeing the shrink, isn't she? Could always get her to cancel. Reschedule.'

'For the sake of fifty minutes? No, I don't think so.'

Millington pushed open the rear door to the car park. 'How long till all this psychobabble business is over and done with, that's what I'd like to know?'

'Graham,' Resnick said, with a slow shake of the head, 'I doubt it ever is.'

To say the body was in the bath was not quite accurate. The left arm and leg and most of the trunk were hanging inside, the right leg outside, trailing at an awkward angle to the floor. The right arm stretched along the bath's rim, the head resting, open-mouthed, against the crook of the elbow. From the position alone, it was unclear whether the dead man had been trying to climb into the bath or crawl out.

A patchy trail of blood contoured its way across the carpet, leading from the bed into the bathroom; blood had dried in tapering lines down the plastic-coated side of the bath beneath the body and more had collected around the plughole like a pressed rose.

'Dragged there, d'you reckon?' Millington asked.

Resnick's mouth tightened. 'Possible. Dragged himself, could be.'

'Why the bath, then? Not the door?'

'Might not have known. Just getting away. Disorientated. Then again, maybe it was deliberate. Wanted to wash it off.'

There was a uniformed officer outside the door, another further along the corridor, shepherding curious staff and guests on their way. From the hotel register, it had been established that the occupant of the room was a Peter Farleigh, with an address Resnick recognised as one of those villages in the Wolds, north of Loughborough.

The clean towels which the maid had been carrying were in a heap near the door where she had dropped them; the maid herself was lying down in one of the vacant rooms, according to the manager, in a right old state.

'We don't know, of course,' Millington said, 'if this is Farleigh or not. Not for a fact.'

Resnick nodded, stepping back into the main room. Both he and Millington were wearing plastic coats over their street clothes, white cotton gloves on their hands.

A wallet lay on the table beside the bed, nudged up against the base of the lamp. Cautiously, Resnick fingered it open. Whatever money it might have held was gone. Surprisingly, though, the credit cards seemed to be in place. Behind a kidney donor card was a membership card for a squash club in Melton Mowbray which bore a small, coloured photograph above an address and the name, Peter John Farleigh. The man poised over the bath looked different, in the way that dead people do, but Resnick had no doubt that he was one and the same as the person pictured in the photo.

Resnick stood where he was, focusing on the bed, the ruck of clothes, darkly stained; under the almost silent hum of the air conditioning, the scent of sweat and blood were unmistakable. He tried to imagine what had happened in that room, tried to magic words, expressions out from the walls. If that address were still correct, then Farleigh lived no more than an hour's drive away, so why opt for the hotel in preference to going home?

Sex, Resnick thought.

A lover.

A liaison, bought and paid for, bought and sold.

Sometimes this was what it cost.

The door opened from the corridor and Parkinson, the pathologist, came in: tall, bony, thinning hair, neat in a mossy tweed suit. Automatically, he fingered an extra-strong mint from the roll in his side pocket and slid his glasses from their case. 'Now then, Charlie, what have we got here?'

Lynn thought, this room always smells of flowers. Roses, though there were none that she could see. She sat in the same chair, wooden arms and a curved back, comfortable, but not so comfortable that you would drift off to sleep. Not even through these long silences. Petra Carey, Dr Petra Carey, sitting near to the window, seemingly relaxed. There was a desk, but the doctor ignored it, except sometimes at the beginning of the session when Lynn arrived, she would be there, finishing writing up her notes, glancing, perhaps, at Lynn's file. 'Lynn, it's good to see you. How are we today?' Petra Carey, today in a short jacket and loose, long skirt, white blouse with a slight frill, wedding ring wide on her hand. Scrubbed face and careful hair, attentive eyes. 'What would you like to talk about today?' Lynn supposed she might be five years older than herself. Quiet, she could hear the ticking of the clock.

*

There were seven wounds in all: four to the chest, one between the ribs to the left-hand side, two low in the stomach, approximately two inches above the line of pubic hair. All but one of the chest wounds were scarcely more than superficial; the deepest seeming the one which had passed between the ribs, close, Resnick guessed, to where the heart had been still beating.

After the scene-of-the-crime team had finished shooting off several rolls of film and videoing Farleigh's body *in situ*, it had been removed from the bath and laid on thick, opaque plastic sheeting.

'What time are we looking at?' Resnick asked.

Parkinson wiped the thermometer with care and returned it to its case. 'Ten hours, give or take.'

'Midnight, then?'

'Round about.'

Resnick grunted. At midnight, he had been leaving Sonny's restaurant, exchanging handshakes and goodbyes with David Tyrell, hoping that the heated words being exchanged between youths outside the pub opposite would not escalate into blows, causing him to intervene.

'Any chance you'll get to my panel tomorrow?' Cathy Jordan had asked.

Resnick had replied non-committally, uncertain; now it was clear that he would not.

He had picked up a cab across the street from Ritzy's and, home, had poured himself a half-inch of bison grass vodka and read a little more of Cathy Jordan's book. So far, the most likely culprits behind April's murder seemed to be a former ex-criminal client of her father, a rejected would-be lover, or – just out of the woodwork – April's half-brother by one of her father's previous liaisons. Resnick's money was on the brother. In the book, it was easier; in the book it didn't matter if he were wrong.

'Nothing else for me here now,' Parkinson said. 'You'll be at the post?'

Resnick nodded.

In a room along the corridor, Kevin Naylor was patiently questioning Marie-Elisabeth Fournier, having to remind her almost every other sentence to speak in English, not French. Earlier, he had tried a few remembered phrases from his schooldays and she had looked at him blankly, as if he were speaking another language. Then finally she told him everything she knew.

Divine had found two of the guests with rooms on the same floor, still lingering over their breakfast in the dining room, but they claimed neither to have seen nor to have heard anything. Names and addresses of the other guests he obtained from the hotel register.

Computer records showed that Farleigh had stayed at the hotel on three occasions in the past eighteen months, the first time for a single night, the others – of which this was the last – for two. Always a single room, always on his own.

'Visitors?' Millington asked. 'You know the kind I mean.'

'We try not to encourage it, but . . .' The manager shrugged. 'People do what they do.'

'And Farleigh, you don't know if . . .'

'I've no idea.'

'No gossip amongst the staff? No . . .'

'You'll have to ask them yourself.'

'We will.'

The first of the night staff to respond to urgent requests that they make themselves available for questioning, was one of the waiters from the restaurant. Yes, he recognised the man's photo and, no, he had eaten alone, but after he had finished his meal he had sat down again with somebody else. The description the waiter gave was backed up by the barman when he arrived some forty minutes later. Late thirties, early forties, dark hair, black

117

dress. On the game? Could be, nowadays it was increasingly difficult to tell.

Had either of them seen the woman there in the hotel before?

No, they didn't think they had.

If they were to be shown some photographs?

Oh, surely, they'd be happy to oblige. Tickled pink. Couldn't let the likes of her be running around free, now, could they? Was it true, as they'd heard, she'd stabbed him fifteen times or was it just the twelve?

'Sure you're up for this?' Resnick asked.

Lynn was looking through the car window at alternations of hedgerow, sunlight catching silver along arable fields. 'I'll be fine,' she said.

At the outskirts of the village, Resnick slowed behind a dozen sheep, a lad no older than fourteen herding them slowly through a farm gate. When Resnick glanced across at Lynn, the skin around her eyes was drawn. He knew he shouldn't have asked her to come with him; knew also that in situations such as this, she was irreplaceable.

The house was well back from the road, a small Fiat parked in the drive.

'Mrs Farleigh,' Resnick said to the middle-aged woman who came to the door. 'I'm Detective Inspector Resnick and this is Detective Constable Kellogg. I wonder if we might come inside?'

# Twenty-two

Sarah Farleigh had gone through all the normal reactions to her husband's death: disbelief, shock, anger, finally tears. Lynn had moved to hold her and the older woman had shrugged her off, stumbling from the kitchen in which they had been talking, through the French windows of the living room into the garden, which was where Resnick found her, squatting in the middle of half an acre of lawn, face in her hands.

For several minutes he hunched there beside her, while a blackbird noisily disputed their presence from the branch of a nearby apple tree. When the worst of the crying, the kind that scrapes against the chest, tears the back of the throat, had stopped, to be replaced by intermittent, stuttering sobs, Resnick reached for her hand, the one in which a sodden Kleenex was tightly balled, and she clutched at his fingers as if they were all that could prevent her from falling. Clung to them until they hurt.

'Do you know,' she said a little later, letting go of Resnick's hand, accepting the handkerchief that he offered her, wiping her face and blowing her nose. 'Do you know, he would never lift a finger in this garden? Not as much as mow the lawn. These trees, the flower beds, all of the shrubbery down along the south wall, that was all me. My work. I even used – of course, he used to get it at a discount, he would do that – I even used the fertiliser the company made, you know, the one where he worked. Whose goods he sold. It could have been anything, you see. Kitchenware, clothing, anything, just as long as it was something he could sell. It didn't matter that . . . it didn't matter that . . . it was used to make things grow.'

Resnick was ready; he shifted his weight and caught her as she half-turned, her body, stiff and thickening into middle age, falling across him, his arms supporting her, her brown hair harsh and soft against his neck.

Over the top of her head, he could see Lynn standing in the doorway, watching; after a while she turned back into the house.

The telephone rang and then was still.

Sarah Farleigh straightened and, shakily, got to her feet. 'I'm sorry. Thank you. I shall be all right.'

Resnick smiled a wan smile. 'I shouldn't be surprised if Lynn hasn't made some tea.'

She looked at him. 'No. I expect she has. It's what women are good at. It's what we do.'

Resnick walked with her, back to the house.

The scene-of-crime team had lifted seventeen good prints from the hotel bedroom, the bathroom had yielded eight more. Likelihood was that most of the prints would have come from Farleigh, others either from the hotel staff or previous occupants of the room. So much for cleaning. All these people would have to be contacted, checked and eliminated. If everything worked out the way it did in the textbooks, if luck and logic were on their side, any prints unaccounted for would belong to Farleigh's attacker. If that person had a record, well, while not exactly home free, the police would have a suspect, clear in their sights.

Everyone involved in the inquiry knew things were rarely that simple.

'Any sign of those photographs? From the hotel?' Resnick was barely into the office, loosening his tie, undoing the top button of his shirt.

'Promised half-hour back,' Millington said, looking up from the computer printout splayed across his desk.

'Give them a chase.'

'Right. Mark . . .'

'Boss?'

'Ten-by-eights from this morning, find out where they are. And while you're about it, check out the arrangements for viewing the scene of crime video.'

'On it now.'

'Good lad.'

Resnick was reading the printout upside down. 'From the hotel,' Millington explained. 'Three lists. Guests registered for the past two nights, previous occupants of Farleigh's room, going back two months, and all staff on duty in the past forty-eight hours.'

'Any headway?'

'Kevin's got a couple in now, running through photos with them. Maybe they'll pick out the woman, maybe not. If not, best haul our tame artist in, get a composite.'

'How about the hotel?'

'We've got three lads out of uniform, questioning the staff as they clock in.'

Resnick picked up the list and let it fall. 'We'll need more bodies.'

'Too right. I can hear 'em bleating about overtime already.'

Resnick sighed. 'I'll have a word with the old man. He can lean on the ACC. Budgets should be their problem, not ours. Meantime, we should get the names on this list checked with Intelligence at Central. Never know your luck.'

Millington nodded. 'Next thing up.'

In his office, Resnick wondered if it weren't time to call down to the front desk, see if someone wasn't nipping across to the deli.

\*

They were getting tired, Naylor could see that; losing concentration. Time and again he was having to stop them, not leading, not wanting false information, but slowing them down, bringing them back. Not wanting their eyes to gloss over another page of photographs without discriminating, letting individual features sink in. Known prostitutes, working the city centre, with a possible preference for hotels.

'Jesus,' the waiter said. 'How much longer are we going to be?'

'Not too long now.'

'Yes, but how long?'

'Till we're done.'

'Don't worry,' the barman said, winking. 'I know him. This is how he spends his breaks; feet up in the bogs back of the kitchen, looking at pictures of women. Only difference, these've got more clothes on.'

'Up yours!' the waiter said, cheerily feigning offence.

'No, ta. Not today. It's Friday and I'm a good Catholic, remember?'

'Here,' Naylor said, turning the page. 'Take your time and have a careful look at these.'

Resnick had the scene-of-crime photographs spread across his desk; the gorgonzola and radicchio sandwich he was eating lay on a paper bag in his lap. What held his attention most, aside from the unfocusing depth of the dead man's eyes, was the haphazard pattern of stab wounds in the chest, the single blow – the first to be struck, or delivered later, after the fury of the first assault? – that had penetrated the ribs and found the heart. Resnick imagined Farleigh struggling from the bed, endeavouring to escape, only to fall across the mattress-end before the blade was driven home again. Was that how it had been? And then the slow crawl towards the bath . . . ?

Resnick looked again at the pictures of Farleigh's face,

the spread of his overweight body. What had he done or said, Resnick wondered, to provoke such an outburst?

He brought the remaining half-sandwich to his mouth with both hands and chewed thoughtfully. Catching a stray drip of mayonnaise on the back of his hand, he looked around for something to wipe it on, finally resorting to licking it away; the last thing he wanted to do was get splotches all over the photographs.

'There!' the waiter said.

'Where?'

'There.'

The face he was pointing to, finger wavering stubbily above it, was of a woman who was probably in her forties, with dark hair that hung, puppy-dog-like, around her ears and over equally dark eyes. There was no humour in those eyes. For all the world, she looked as if she had been willing the police photographer to shrivel up and – yes – die.

Marlene Kinoulton.

'You're mad.' The barman said, shaking his head. 'That's never her.'

'I say it is.'

'She's too old, way too old.'

'You didn't see her as well as I did. You were never as close.'

'She was at the bar.'

'How many times? Twice? Once? You think how many times I was over to the table, bending over to serve her . . .'

'Gawping down her front.'

'Never mind that. You know what I'm saying. I had a better sight of her than you. And for my money, that's her.'

The barman swivelled away in his chair, gestured towards Naylor. 'The hair. It's wrong.'

'What d'you mean wrong?' the waiter asked.

'It didn't look like that at all.'

'So what? Aren't women changing their hair all the time?'

'But this – look – it's thicker, bushy. Can you not imagine feeling that? What it'd feel like? Coarse, am I not right? Where that one last night in the bar, her hair was fine, well looked after, finer than this. No, no way, this is never her.'

For several moments there was silence, both men sneaking glances at Naylor and Naylor not wanting to influence either of them unduly.

The barman finally jumped to his feet. 'Well, I don't care what you say. I reckon that's her and I'm sticking to it. And now, if there's anything you want me to sign or whatever I'll sign it, because then, I don't mind telling you, I've had quite enough and, if it's all right with you, I'm out of here, so I am, now.'

Kevin Naylor was looking at the photograph. Marlene Kinoulton. The name meant nothing to him. He would pass it on down the line and, as long as she was still working the city, they would bring her in. He knew that both men were looking at him, waiting for him to say something positive, send them on their way. His back was aching from bending over the albums for so long and he knew he could do with a pint, but it was at least an hour before he would get one, possibly longer. Always, jarring at the edge of his mind, the conversation he had had with Debbie over breakfast, over children, another baby.

'Thanks,' he said. 'Thanks for all your time. You've been very helpful.'

# Twenty-three

Frank Carlucci had picked up the first edition of the local paper on his way back from the municipal pool. Thirty minutes of steady lengths, interrupted only by the arrival of the first batch of schoolkids of the day. Juice and coffee hadn't been as difficult to find as the last time he was in the country, ten years before, but even so, his request for a caffe latte had been treated with disbelief and the cappuccino he ordered instead was weak and boasted no more than a quarter-inch of froth. Let me into this market, Frank thought, and I could clean up.

Cathy was in the shower when he got back, between the groans and the splashes singing one of those old Brill Building songs by Carole King, Neil Sedaka, one of those. Later that day was when *Shots on the Page*, the literary segment of the festival, began, and she would be at her busiest, fans simpering round her for autographs, coming off with the same stupid questions – 'Who are your favourite mystery writers, Ms Jordan?', 'Where do you get all your ideas?', 'Just how much of you is there in Annie Q. Jones? Is she really you?' One major difference between them, Frank knew for sure, no way his wife was a dyke.

The water stopped and a few moments later Cathy came through from the shower, a towel about her hair.

'Jesus H. Christ!' Carlucci whistled in wonder. 'You still got a great body, you know that?'

'Frank,' Cathy smiled, her voice slipping into the

125

mock-innocent tone with which she often teased him, 'you didn't drown. You're back.'

For once, Frank refused the bait. 'Maybe it's 'cause you never had kids, I don't know, but you're in as great shape now as when you was twenty-one.'

'Bullshitter! You didn't know me when I was twenty-one.'

Carlucci laughed. 'More's the pity.' He cupped one of her buttocks with his hand and she slapped him away.

'Hey, you don't want to get felt up, shouldn't walk around that way.'

'What's that, Frank, rape defence A? Your honour, she was asking for it.'

'What you talking, rape? Husband pats his wife's ass, that's not even sexual harassment. Not even today.'

Cathy pulled on a pair of white underpants and began sorting through her tights. 'I know, Frank, you're right. It's just, well, sometimes I have difficulty remembering — that you're my husband, I mean.'

'Listen,' said Frank, serious now. 'I ever force myself upon you?'

Cathy straightened away from the bed. 'No, Frank, I can't say you have. Not recently anyway. Not since that time in Atlanta I broke your nose.'

'You didn't break my nose. A few seconds maybe, it was out of joint. Hey, you even helped pop it back, remember?'

'And got snot and blood all up my arm for my trouble.'

She had her back to him, snapping on a brassière, and he waited until she turned, wondering if she were really mad, remembering. She didn't look mad. Standing there, white bra with some cleavage and a little lace, blue jeans, even with her snarled-up hair, she looked great.

He told her so.

'Look,' he said. 'I'm serious. You don't think we could . . .' Eyes straying towards the bed.

'Come on, Frank. I just got out the shower. And I've got this radio interview in less than half an hour. Mollie's coming by to pick me up.'

Right, thought Frank, always something. He tossed her the paper and Cathy caught most of it, the second section sliding from the bed down to the floor. 'Maybe you should take a look at this before you go. Hung on to your front page spot, but only just. I'll see you later,' he said and left the room.

The piece describing the affray in the bookshop was boxed towards the bottom of the page, two columns. Beneath the headline, **STAR US CRIME WRITER ATTACKED**, Cathy Jordan's face smiled out from one of her standard issue publicity shots. *'Presumed feminist protest . . .'* it read. And: *'Although clearly shaken by the unprovoked assault, the visiting best-selling American author insisted she would not be curtailing her very full programme during the city's top film and fiction festival. This evening, Miss Jordan is appearing on a* Shots on the Page *panel discussing the future of crime fiction.'*

Terrific, Cathy thought, every weirdo and closet voyeur coming out of the woodwork, eager to see what I'm going to get doused in this time.

But she didn't think about that for long; her eyes kept being pulled back to the top of the page:

## Police Probe Hotel Slaying

### DEAD MAN FOUND NAKED IN BATH

*Police launched a major inquiry today after the body of 53-year-old Wymeswold man, Peter Farleigh, was found in his hotel room earlier this morning. Farleigh, a married man with three grown-up children, who worked as a*

*sales executive for Myerson Chemical
and Fertiliser, had been stabbed a number of times in the chest and abdomen.
His body was discovered when Marie-
Elisabeth Fournier, a maid employed by
the hotel, entered Mr Farleigh's room.
She found Mr Farleigh's naked body
lying in the heavily blood-stained bath.*

*Miss Fournier, who is nineteen, and
studying English here in the city, works
at the hotel on a part-time basis. She is
understood to have been sedated and
treated for shock.*

*An incident room has been set up at
Canning Circus police station and the
inquiry is being headed by Det Insp
Charlie Resnick.*

*A police spokesman said they were
not sure if there was any link between
Mr Farleigh's murder and a recent
incident in which an unidentified man,
apparently naked, was found with stab
wounds in the Alfreton Road area of the
city. This man, whose injuries were
treated at Queen's Medical Centre, has
since disappeared without trace.*

*Forensic experts are continuing to
examine the room in which Mr Farleigh
was found for clues and a post-mortem
examination will be carried out by
Home Office pathologist Prof Arthur
Parkinson.*

*Det Insp Resnick declined to give any
further details of the death until the
post-mortem has been carried out, or to*

*detail any lines of inquiry being fol-
lowed.*

*Speaking from her five-bedroomed
detached home in the village of Wymeswold, a grief-stricken Sarah Farleigh
said, 'Peter was a model husband and a
perfect father to our children. We are all
heartbroken at the news of what has
happened.'*

Well, Cathy Jordan thought, that puts the occasional pot
of paint into perspective, doesn't it? She slid a green silk
shirt from its hanger in the wardrobe and held it against
herself in front of the mirror. Radio, for God's sake, she
was about to do radio. What did it matter what she looked
like? Now that he had his very own murder inquiry, she
doubted that good old Charlie Resnick would have much
time left over to think about her.

Mollie Hansen was waiting for her in the lobby, one of
Cathy's books and a folder of publicity material under one
arm.

'The car's waiting. It isn't far.'

'Fine. And, look, I hope you made it clear. I'll talk
about anything but that stupidity with the paint.'

'Of course,' Mollie said, holding open the door. 'I've
spoken to the producer twice.'

Cathy Jordan sat in front of the goose-neck microphone, a
plastic cup of water near her right hand. Across the broad
desk, the morning presenter picked his way through
several cassettes before finding the trail for that evening's
live broadcast from Mansfield Civic Centre and slotting it
into place. A recording of 'Up, Up and Away' by the Fifth
Dimension was coming to an end. He had already checked
Cathy's voice for level.

'More music later. But now I've been joined here in the

studio by the American crime writer Cathy Jordan, one of the people most responsible for the amazing increase in the popularity of women in this field. Good morning, Cathy.'

'Hi.'

'Tell me, Cathy, while it's true that your books have proved almost as popular here as back home in the States, this hasn't been without some opposition. I believe, for instance, there was an incident yesterday involving some paint . . .'

# Twenty-four

The questions didn't finish there.

Even without the additional publicity, the hotel's principal convention room would have been full for Cathy Jordan's evening panel, but, as things had developed, it was close to overflowing. Delegates who had been unable to get seats were standing at both back and sides, or leaning against ledges and walls; several more were sitting cross-legged between the front row and the platform. Cathy, herself, was sitting to the left of Maxim Jakubowski, the chairman; the young Scottish writer, Ian Rankin, sat, toying with his water glass, alongside her. On the chairman's right, Dorothy Birdwell and the tall figure of South Londoner and ex-Who roadie, Mark Timlin, sat in unlikely alliance.

'Excuse me, I have a question . . .' The voice was articulate, middle-class, used to making itself heard. 'I have a question for Ms Jordan . . .' From the chair, Jakubowski leaned forward and acknowledged the speaker from the floor.

The woman was standing now, a few seats in from the central aisle near the back of the room – rimless glasses, greying hair pulled back, a perfectly unexceptional print dress. Alongside Jakubowski, Cathy Jordan had poured water into her glass; everything had been going smoothly up to now, as predictable as discussions on the future of crime fiction tended to be.

'I should like to ask Ms Jordan if she shares my

concerns about the way women are increasingly being represented in crime fiction?'

Cathy sipped her water and counted to ten. Ian Rankin coughed and winked. 'Here we go,' he whispered.

Cathy set down her glass. 'Well,' she said, 'doesn't that depend on what those concerns are?'

'Those of most women.'

'*Most* women?'

'Yes.'

There was an uneasy stirring amongst sections of the audience; some, having heard of the bookshop incident, had come anticipating conflict and so far had been disappointed, others were inwardly flinching, steeling themselves against embarrassment.

Cathy took her time, waiting until the hum of expectation had faded into an expectant silence. 'Now I don't know, of course, how you're calibrating "most". I mean, is that most women in this country? This city? Or are you claiming to speak for most women in this room?' She paused and looked slowly around and heard a few disclaimers from amongst the crowd. 'Maybe, you mean most of your own little circle of friends?'

There was a sprinkling of laughter, mostly self-conscious, during which the questioner stepped out into the aisle. For the first time, Cathy caught Marius Gooding's eye. He was sitting four rows back, staring not at Dorothy Birdwell, but at her, staring hard.

'No,' the questioner was replying, her voice louder now, more openly aggressive. 'I mean any women. All women.'

Again there were mumbles of dissent, but not many, not enough to deflect shouts of acclamation which seemed to come strategically from around the room. Cathy glanced towards the chairman, who undemonstratively shook his head, happy to let things proceed.

'I'm speaking for any woman who has any sense of her

own strength or dignity, her own independence or sexuality . . .'

'Oh, come on!' Cathy Jordan said. 'Spare us the speeches.'

'. . . and who could not fail to be appalled and threatened by the excessively violent way . . .'

'Always did like a bit of violence myself,' Timlin said, as much to himself as anyone else.

Dorothy Birdwell, much like the Dormouse in *Alice*, seemed to be sleeping.

'. . . the violent ways in which you and others like you, serve up women as a series of passive victims at the hands of men.'

'Hang on a minute now,' Cathy protested, as Ian Rankin leaned towards her with a few words of encouragement.

Amongst the growing hubbub, a handful of people were heading for the exits and a number of women – half a dozen now, several others prepared to join them – were on their feet and pointing towards the platform.

'I intend to make my point . . .'

'You made your point.' Cathy said, louder now, close to losing her temper. 'The same old tired point I've heard half a hundred times before. Women as victims. Poor damned women! What is the matter with you? Don't you live in the real world?'

Some of those standing had begun a slow handclap, drowning Cathy's words. The expression on the questioner's face was a satisfied sneer. Marius had still not taken his eyes from Cathy's face.

'Pick up a paper,' Cathy said into the din, so close to the microphone that it distorted her voice. 'Any paper, switch on the news, what do you see? Women *are* victims. You think I invented that? You think I made it happen?'

'Yes!' they chorused back. 'Yes!'

Cathy Jordan sat back with the gasp of mock surprise and shook her head.

'Every time you attack a woman in your books . . .' another voice from another part of the room. 'Every time you rape, or kill, or maim . . .'

'*I* rape?'

'Yes, you. You! You! You!'

Beside Cathy, Ian Rankin was shaking his head in a mixture of bewilderment and anger, and at the far end of the table, Mark Timlin was smiling happily. Dorothy Birdwell had awoken and, like the Dormouse in *Alice*, was looking around in dazed surprise. The chairman tapped a warning on the end of his microphone, but to no avail.

'Every time you do those things, one woman to another . . .'

Cathy Jordan was on her feet, pointing. 'I do not *do* those things.'

'Yes, you do!' It was the original questioner, closer to the stage now and pointing. 'And as long as you go on perpetrating this myth of female weakness, it will go on happening.'

'That's a crock of shit!'

'Is it? Is it, Ms Jordan? Well, I hope next time you open your paper and read about some poor fifteen-year-old, or some old woman of eighty being raped and beaten, you should think about that a little more carefully.'

'Jesus!' said Cathy, slamming back down into her chair. 'I don't believe this is happening.'

'All right,' Jakubowski said, raising both hands in an appeal for calm. 'Thank you very much, thank you very much indeed. I'm sure we all appreciate your point, but now I feel we should move on. Yes, thank you, there's someone over there . . .'

Cathy continued to sit there, taking no further part in the discussion, staring at the blank sheet of paper in front of her as her anger began slowly to subside.

# Twenty-five

The photographs of Peter Farleigh had been enlarged and pinned, head height, to the wall. Slightly below them, to left and to right, the other, earlier, non-fatal victims: Paul Pynchon, from Hinckley, stabbed in the red-light district near the Waterloo Road; Marco Fabrioni, beaten and tied up on the Forest; Gerry McKimber, the sales rep stabbed in his hotel room; a quick drawing from memory of the still-anonymous man who had disappeared from hospital after being found, stabbed and naked, on the Alfreton Road. The one they were now, thanks to the rare flash of inspiration from Divine, calling Polo after his sock.

Maps, dates, approximate times.

Details of wounds, weapons used.

Data.

Three colour ten by eights of Marlene Kinoulton, left profile, right profile, full face: the woman identified by the waiter in the hotel where Farleigh had been killed.

There were twenty officers in the room, most with mugs or styrofoam cups of tea, Players' Silk Cut between their fingers, Benson King Size; expectation adhering to the walls like yellow smoke.

Skelton, straight-backed, stood near the main door, watching. His responsibility, not his show. Resnick rose purposefully to his feet.

'Pynchon, Fabrioni, McKimber, Polo, Farleigh: five stabbings, one fatal. Five male victims, all of them – and this is not entirely confirmed, but I think we can assume it

135

for now – engaged in some kind of sexual activity involving prostitution.'

Resnick paused, making sure of everyone's attention.

'Now if we look at where the attacks took place, they break down into two basic groups: outside, in the red-light area, and inside, in one hotel or other. From that first group, two attacks – those on Pynchon and on the Italian – were carried out by more than one person, male as well as female, and the injuries received were more general. Personally, I think we can disregard these as having any direct connection with Peter Farleigh's murder. Our friend, Polo, I'm not so sure about.

'We think he was running from his attacker, that's the only reasonable assumption, and that would place the attack in the same general area as those on Pynchon and Fabrioni. But what have we got? A single wound, no more. Nothing to suggest the kind of group attack that took place in the earlier cases. So, let's presume, one assailant. All the other evidence suggests a woman, some kind of assignation that went wrong. Likely, but only conjecture. The wound is interesting, though; a single blow with a sharp implement, most likely a knife, in an area that closely corresponds to where most of the stab wounds in Farleigh's body were found. So, although Polo's stabbing is the incident about which we know least, and therefore it might be convenient to push it to the back of our minds, I don't want that to happen. Not yet. It may connect.'

He paused, glanced over towards Skelton, who avoided his eyes and fidgeted instead with the knot of his tie. What did that mean, Resnick wondered? That I'm going on too long and he's bored? Or does he think I've got it wrong? Barking up the wrong tree? Maybe his tie was simply too tight.

'Now,' Resnick said, moving towards the photographs, heads turning to watch as he pointed with the first two fingers of his right hand. 'These pair, McKimber and Farleigh, this is where our main focus has to be. Look at the similarities. Both men attacked in hotel rooms, attacked with knives, stabbed more than once. In both instances, the most likely scenario, the assailant was a woman. A woman who was there for the purposes of prostitution, though it's only in McKimber's case we know that for a fact.'

Lynn Kellogg's arm was raised. 'Surely, sir, we don't even know that? The woman he claims stabbed him, she's never been identified.'

'That's right.'

'So, he could be lying. I mean, we've only his word.'

'Right, he stabbed himself,' Divine called out, sarcastically.

'No,' Lynn snapped back. 'But it could have been a man, right. A boy. Men are prostitutes too, you know.'

'Okay,' Resnick raised his hand for silence. 'We're going to be talking to McKimber again. I'm seeing him myself. I'll bear what you've said in mind. You're right, it wants double-checking. No harm.'

He moved across to the pictures of Marlene Kinoulton. 'This is the woman identified by the waiter in the hotel restaurant as the one Farleigh was talking to earlier on the evening he was killed. They'd been eating at separate tables till Farleigh went over and joined her. Afterwards they went out, the waiter thinks, into the hotel bar, and although the barman confirms that Farleigh was there with a woman, sat there with her until past eleven, he wasn't able to confirm the identification. His general description of the woman Farleigh was with is close enough though, for us to take this woman, Kinoulton, very seriously.

'She is a known prostitute, here in the city, we've established that. Also works in Sheffield, Leicester and Derby.'

'Anywhere she can get a Cheap Day Return,' somebody said.

Resnick waited for the laughter, what there was of it, to fade. 'On five previous occasions, she's been issued a warning for soliciting in the big hotels. She wants finding and fast. Mark, Kevin, you're already liaising with the Vice Squad, she's your target, down to you. As I've said, I'm talking to McKimber. The rest of you, we have to keep checking other guests at the hotel, the rest of the staff, so on. We really need another ID to back up the one on Kinoulton. Or some positive forensics. We're also going to do a little digging into Farleigh's work, appointments kept on this trip, general background. Why he chose to stay in a hotel in the city when an hour's drive at most would have seen him home.' He looked around. 'All right. Questions? Sergeant Millington's got your assignments. Let's be diligent. Not miss anything. Let's get this wrapped up as fast as we can.'

'You think I'm wrong?' Resnick asked. He and Skelton, out in the corridor, officers spilling past them, voices raised from the stairs, banging of doors, the same old chanting of telephones.

'No, why?'

Resnick shrugged.

'If I thought you were going down the wrong road, as your superior officer, I'd say so. Only . . .'

Resnick looked at him expectantly. A shout, distant, from the area of the cells, was followed by a metallic slamming sound, then silence.

Skelton stood back, nodding, still fiddling with his tie. 'Not wanting to chuck a spanner in the works, Charlie, not at this stage. But like you said, tunnel vision, it's a dangerous thing.'

'Yes,' Resnick said. 'Thanks. Thanks, I'll keep it in mind.'

*

Breakfast had been a rushed affair, needing to be in at the station early, make certain everything was up and ready for the briefing. Now, Resnick stood in line behind a pair of purple-shirted tax accountants, waiting for the assistant at the deli to make him a couple of sandwiches for the drive down into the neighbouring county, something tasty on dark rye and caraway, an espresso for now and another for the journey. The tape machine in his car had been on the blink for weeks, all he'd been able to listen to was GEM-AM, recycling the glorious moments of some-body's youth, though rarely, it seemed to Resnick, his own. But now it was fixed and he could play the new – to him – Joshua Redman to his heart's content: 'Moose the Mooche', 'Turnaround', 'Make Sure You're Sure'.

Clicking the seat-belt into place, Resnick turned the key in the ignition and switched on the stereo, tenor sax loping in at mid-tempo as he eased out into the mid-morning traffic.

# Twenty-six

The pub was flat against the main road, a thin line of pavement all that separated its windows from the heavy lorries shuddering down towards the A5, the M69, the M6. Inside four men, worn down by middle-age, sat at four separate tables, nursing pint glasses through until lunchtime. All four looking up when Resnick entered, but none looked up for long. The landlord, restocking shelves behind the bar, paused to glance at Resnick's warrant card, listened to his question and pointed towards the stairs. 'First floor, back.' If the radio had been switched on and if it had been playing David Whitfield or Perry Como, Resnick would not have been surprised.

There were three boards, bare along the landing, and each one of them creaked.

'Gerry McKimber?'

A tall man, spindly with a nose like a wedge that had been driven hard, and not quite straight, into the centre of his face, McKimber stared at Resnick's identification, then stepped back, shaking his head. 'Christ! It's not taken her so bloody long!'

'Her?'

'I told her I'd pay, Jesus, she's knows I'll pay just as soon as I can. She knows I've lost my fucking job, for Christ's sake, what does she expect?'

'Mr McKimber?'

'I've told you . . .'

'Mr McKimber . . .'

'What?'

140

'You're talking about maintenance, child support?'

'No, I'm talking about winning the fucking pools!'

'That's not why I'm here.'

'Not? Not the pools, then?' He laughed, more a bark than a laugh. 'Not here to tell me that? Half a million quid? Am I going to let it change my life?'

Resnick shook his head.

'Well, thank Christ for that. 'Cause I forgot to post the sodding coupon.'

'Mr McKimber, can I come inside?'

There were two beds pushed back against the far wall, narrow divans low to the floor, only one of them recently used. On the other, McKimber had piled, not neatly, some of his possessions, cardboard boxes, motoring magazines, clothes. A wardrobe, a table, what might euphemistically have been called an easy chair. The single window, with a view over beer crates and barrels and an outside urinal, was open a crack.

McKimber stubbed out the cigarette that had been smouldering in the ashtray and lit another. He held the packet towards Resnick, who shook his head.

'If it's not that cow, then what is it?' But then he saw Resnick's face and thought he knew. 'You've caught her, that cunt as stabbed me? You've got her, right?'

'Afraid not.'

'Then what the fuck . . . ?'

'There's been another incident . . .'

'Like that? Like what happened to me?'

'Similar. Enough to make us think there might be a connection. I need to talk to you again.'

McKimber walked towards the window and looked down, pushing fingers back through his unkempt hair. 'You know, at first she never believed me, the wife, I don't know why. It was a fight, she said, you were in a fight. Some pub or other. Same as before. Why bother making up an excuse? Why bother lying?'

McKimber turned back into the room, cigarette cupped in his hand. 'As if what I'd said, you know, what really happened, the hotel and that, as if somehow she'd never have minded so much.'

He went over to the bed, sat down. 'I used to get into these scrapes. Once in a while. You know what it's like, on the road. Travelling. Well, you can imagine. Chatting up people all day, trying to. Half the time getting doors closed in your face. Abuse. You wouldn't believe the abuse. Come evening, had a bit of a meal, too far to go home, too tired, what do you do? Well, me, like a lot of men, I like a drink. Trouble is, when I drink I suppose I get careless 'bout what I say. Don't care who hears me, either. Gets me into trouble, I admit it. The firm, they'd warned me, Gerry, this has got to stop. So many last warnings, I never believed them and then they gave me the push for something else altogether, but that's another story.'

He drew on the cigarette, releasing the smoke, slow, down his nose. 'The wife, see, she'd been on at me, an' all. Forever on at me. Just once more, Gerry McKimber, you come home looking like you've been in a brawl and you're out of my house. My house!' McKimber repeated his barking laugh. 'Not now. Not when she's crying out for me to pay something towards the sodding bills. Oh, no. Now it's our house again. Our house!'

He looked across towards Resnick, who waited, listening, prepared to listen, saying nothing.

'This business with the woman, the one as cut me, the wife, she thought I'd made it up. Of course, I never told her, what I never told her, that I was, like, paying for it, you know. Christ, I wasn't about to tell her that now, was I? Paying for it. Give her that satisfaction. No, what I said was, what I told her, this woman and I, we get talking in the bar, one thing rolls into another, I've had a few too many to know properly what I'm doing, next thing she's with me, up in the room. Would she believe that? Not for weeks would she fucking believe that, blue in the sodding face from telling her. Well, it was the truth, more or less the truth, I didn't want her mingeing on at me for something I'd never done. Jesus! When I finally get it through her thick head I'm not lying, what does the stupid cow do? Fucking slings me out!

'All my stuff, clothes, everything, out the window, out the door. Out the house. Receipts, samples, God knows what, all over the front garden, next door's, up and down half the bloody street. Some of it I never even bloody found. "You believe me now, don't you?" I said. "You're filth," she says. "You're scum. You're never setting foot in this house again." The kids upstairs, hanging out of the upstairs, taking it all in.'

He ground the nub end of his cigarette into the threadbare carpet with his heel. 'What was it you wanted to know?'


Sharon Garnett had been on court for the best part of an hour and a half; two games down in the fourth set and any rhythm in her service had gone. A couple of double faults, an attempted lob off her backhand which had landed closer to the next court than the one on which they were playing, and it had been over.

'Thanks, Sharon. Good game.'

'Sure,' Sharon grinned. 'I was crap.'

Her opponent laughed. He was a nice enough bloke, sergeant in Surveillance, wife and two-point-four kids, semi-detached south of the city at Ruddington. 'Time for a drink after?'

'After?'

'Shower, change, whatever?'

'Thanks, no. Maybe some other time. I'm going to shower at home.'

She was almost at her car before Divine spotted her, Divine and Naylor, leaning up against their own vehicle, taking in what there was of the sun. The rhododendron bushes thick along the perimeter of University Park behind them.

'Will you look at that?' Divine said. 'Legs that go all the way up to her arse!'

'Right,' Naylor said. 'New design. Don't know if it'll catch on.'

'Clever bugger!'

Naylor gave a shout and Sharon turned and saw them, no more than a couple of big kids, standing there in shirtsleeves, grinning. She wished she had stopped for a shower now, changed; aware of her sports shirt sticking to her, the sour-sweet smell of her own sweat.

'Called in at the station, said you might be here,' Divine said.

'Day off.'

'Win?' Naylor asked.

'Not exactly.'

'This bloke copped it in the hotel,' Divine said. 'You heard about it?'

She nodded.

'Witness made an ID . . .' Naylor said, taking over. 'Waiter, works in the hotel restaurant.'

'She's a tom,' Divine said, interrupting.

'Local?'

'So it seems.'

'Name?'

'Kinoulton. Marlene.'

Sharon wished they weren't having this conversation out there, cars driving in and out of the tennis centre behind them. Sweat growing cold.

'Know her?' Divine asked.

'I've not been here long enough to know all the girls.'

'But this one, this Marlene?'

'I might.'

They waited.

144

'You know the girl I contacted you about? Doris. The one said she might have something interesting to tell me, about the night that man was knifed near the Alfreton Road? Well, turns out, as far as Marlene Kinoulton's got a best friend, she's it.'

Divine grinned across at Naylor and Naylor winked back: at long last they might be getting somewhere.

Resnick had taken McKimber back through the evening in low gear, beginning to end. 'Never occurred to me at first that she was on the game. Never cottoned on. I thought, I suppose, nothing special, even so, not going to let themselves get turned into a knocking shop. But then I thought, yes, well, why not? Where all the money is, isn't it, after all? Blokes with time on their hands, money to spend.'

'So, as far as you were concerned, at the beginning, it was what? Just a casual chat?'

'Well, no, not exactly. Way she was coming on to me, right off like, knew it was more than that. But, well, like I say, I suppose I thought I'd clicked, you know. Pulled.'

'And when did she make it clear that wasn't exactly the case?'

'When we got to the room.'

'Once you were inside?'

'No. I was just, like, about to use the key. One of them bits of plastic, not really a key at all. She leaned past me, hand against the door. "You know this isn't your birthday, don't you?" That's what she said.' He looked over towards Resnick. 'She was there, then, wasn't she? What was I supposed to do?'

'What kind of a woman would you have said she was?' Resnick asked. 'Based on that first part of the evening.'

'Woman? She was a tart, wasn't she?'

'Yes, but before you knew that. I mean, was she pleasant, well-spoken? How did she come across?'

McKimber shrugged. 'Just sort of normal, you know.'

'Intelligent? Bright?'

'Bright enough to know she had my balls in her pocket.'

'But, aside from what you've already said, were you surprised to find out she was apparently a prostitute?'

'Surprised?' McKimber shook his head. 'One way or another, they all are. I mean, that's the way it works. If you can get someone to pay for it, why give it away?'

Resnick showed him six sets of photographs, six different women, all similar, all with dark hair.

'Look,' McKimber said, 'you're wasting your time. I've already been through this.'

'Humour me,' Resnick said. 'Let's try again. Just these few.'

McKimber lit another cigarette. A good minute before he answered, Resnick could see that he'd stopped really looking. 'I'm sorry,' McKimber said. 'It isn't any good.'

'You're quite sure.'

'Yes, I said. The only one . . .'

'Go on.'

'The only one it just might possibly be . . .'

'Yes?'

McKimber transferred the cigarette to his mouth and jabbed a finger – 'That one. That's the only one, if you told me I had to pick out one of these, had to, that's the only one comes close. Only one that's near.' And he picked out, not Marlene Kinoulton, but the woman in the set of photographs immediately above her, gazing into the camera with a slight squint.

Divine and Naylor had driven Sharon Garnett back to her flat and waited while she had cleaned up and changed into tan leggings, a purple T-shirt, black cotton jacket. Together, Naylor driving, they trawled the red-light district looking for Marlene Kinoulton and her friend

Doris Duke. Nowhere to be seen. None of the girls out working claimed to have seen them for several days. A week. Sheffield, try Sheffield. Leeds.

'Sorry,' Sharon said eventually. 'We're wasting our time. We'd be better trying again later tonight. Late.'

'Fair enough,' Divine said and Naylor pulled in towards the kerb.

'I might have a problem,' Naylor said. 'With later. I'm supposed to be off round Debbie's mum's. She's got this relation over from Canada. Nephew or something. Having a bit of a celebration.'

'Sounds,' Divine said with a smirk, 'like the kind of thing you wouldn't miss for the world.'

'Yes, well. I'll see what I can do.'

Sharon opened the car door. 'Half ten in the Arboretum then, okay?'

'Get there first,' Divine grinned, 'and mine's a pint of Kimberley.'

'You wish! I'm the one doing you a favour, remember? And mine's a Bacardi and Coke. Large. Ten thirty, right?'

Divine watched as Sharon walked away. 'Second thoughts, why don't you go hobnobbing with the in-laws after all. Leave this to me.'

'Thought you were being faithful this month?' Naylor said. 'One-woman man.'

'Yeah, so I am,' Divine grinned, grabbing his crotch. 'It's just this that doesn't understand.'

# Twenty-seven

'Honey, you sure you're up for this?'

Cathy Jordan hesitated in what she was doing, adjusting her silver Zuni earrings in front of the mirror; her favourites, the ones she had bought in Santa Fe. 'God, Frank, I wish you wouldn't do that.'

'What? Show a little concern?'

'Call me honey that way. Makes me feel like something out of Norman Rockwell.'

'Not *The Shining*?' He came up behind her with arm raised, as if holding a knife, leering his manic Jack Nicholson leer. 'Honey, I'm home!'

'Jesus, Frank.'

'What?'

'All that's been going on, that's not so funny.'

Dipping his head towards her shoulder, an oddly tender gesture, he slid both arms around her. 'That guy, huh? The one in the paper. Poor bastard!'

She was looking at his reflection in the dressing table mirror, both their reflections: familiar and strange.

'Frank?'

'Umm?'

'Did you read any of the new book?'

'Your new book?'

'Uh-huh.'

'I didn't think you'd even shipped it off to the publishers yet.'

'No, but . . .'

'You're still working on it, right?'

'Fiddling, that's all. The manuscript.'

'You remember one time you caught me reading these pages you'd left lying around? I thought you were going to go crazy.'

Cathy Jordan smiled into the mirror. 'That was a while back. I was more cranky then. Nervous, I guess.'

'What you mean is, back then, you cared what I thought.'

'That's not what I mean at all.' Looking at him, defiance and concern in his eyes, the stance of his body, strength of his arms. So easy to have turned inside those arms.

'Anyway,' Frank said. 'I didn't look at it, not a peek. How come you ask?'

'Oh . . .' Her voice drifted off and she looked away; how strange desire was, months in which she had felt – God! – nothing, at best a mixture of comfort and irritation, and now this. 'It doesn't matter,' she said, and moved her mouth over his.

They kissed until it was difficult to breathe.

'Jeeze,' Frank said, as she released him. 'What's got into you?'

Cathy let her smile spread wide and when she laughed it was down and dirty. 'Recently, not a whole lot.'

He reached for her and she reached for him.

'Well,' Cathy said, eyebrow arched. 'Have you been working out?'

They were midway between the dressing table and the bed when the phone rang.

'Leave it,' Frank said.

'All right.' But she could see the time, winking at her, green-eyed, from the clock radio beside the bed.

'Cathy, come on.'

She reached out a hand and the ringing stopped. 'Hello,' she said, listening a moment before dropping the receiver back down. 'It's Mollie. She's in the foyer, waiting. We have to be there in thirty minutes.'

Frank rolled clumsily round and leaned forward, elbows on his knees, fingers pressed against his temples.

'Don't, sweetheart,' Cathy said, giving his arm a squeeze. Her voice tenderly mocking. 'Don't have a headache.'

'What do you suggest?' he said. 'A shower? Maybe there's time to jerk off? I know, I could jerk off in the shower.'

Already she was on her feet, reaching her coat from the hanger. 'You could come with me to the store, that's what you could do. Protect me from any more militant paint-throwers. Radical *femmes*. With this murder on their hands, I doubt the police will have officers to spare.'

Frank looked across at her from the bed, still undecided how grouchy he was going to be.

'Don't be mad,' Cathy said. 'Do this for me. Once it's over, we've got the rest of the afternoon to ourselves. We can come back here, what do you say?'

But Frank knew, they both knew, whatever he replied, the moment was gone.

Cathy hadn't known what to expect, but the city centre on a Saturday lunchtime wasn't it. The way people pushed, wall to wall, along the pedestrianised street leading towards the Victoria Centre, all Cathy could think of was one of those paintings by – who was it? – Brueghel. A medieval vision of Hell.

The bookshop, where she and Dorothy Birdwell were to do a joint signing, was on the ground floor of the shopping precinct. Signing with Dorothy, needless to say, had not been Cathy's own choice, but it was at the shop's request and, as her publisher had been quick to point out, the shop was capable of shifting a lot of product. Cathy presumed she meant books.

Mollie steered Cathy and Dorothy between groups of teenagers wearing high-tops, reversed baseball caps and T-shirts, Frank and Marius, unspeaking, following close behind. Between River Island and HMV they passed several mothers, dragging squawking children in their wake, fathers striding several paces ahead, the fuss and commotion no concern of theirs. Cathy saw one woman spin a small boy, no more than three, out of the path of a pushchair and give him a slap, hard, across the backs of his bare legs. 'There! Now stop scraighting, you mardy little sod, or I'll slap you again.' For a moment, Cathy caught her eye: blonde hair tight like copper wire, cigarette, eyes hard as coal. Pregnant again. No way was she more than twenty, twenty-one. A moment, then she was gone.

'Here we are,' Mollie said cheerfully. 'And look, there's a queue already.'

Cathy's face beamed back at her in full-colour from a poster in the window. Inside the shop, it was reproduced many times: smaller posters on the walls, dumpbins at the ends of aisles, a whole shelf of paperbacks and hardcovers, book back to front, displaying the same image. How did she look to all these people, Cathy wondered? Sunny, smug, self-satisfied. American. But, in truth, most of the people pushing round her seemed quite oblivious, not to care.

In contrast, the publicity for Dorothy Birdwell, who stood talking now to Marius, was noticeably less prominent, her books less visible.

'Cathy Jordan?' She shook hands with a surprisingly young woman in a light grey suit with a faint stripe. 'It's a pleasure to welcome you. We've got you set up over there.' Cathy shook her hand and she turned aside to Dorothy. 'Miss Birdwell, how are you? If you'll excuse me, I'll be with you in just a moment.'

Leaving Dorothy and Marius stranded, she led Cathy

past the line of fans towards a table piled high with yet more copies of her books; those waiting to speak to Dorothy Birdwell were far fewer and mostly older.

'Is that her?' one woman said of Cathy as she passed.

'That's never her.'

'Bet you it is.'

'Some of those photos don't do her any favours, do they?'

'Not much. Lop a good ten years off her age, that's all.'

'Get away!'

The manager saw Cathy installed and moved swiftly across to deal with Dorothy Birdwell and an increasingly irate Marius, who was quick to complain about what he saw as second-rate treatment.

Responding to Cathy's request, Frank had positioned himself midway along the queue, feigning an interest in a shelf of books dealing with railways. If he went and stood right behind her, he'd only succeed in looking like a semi-pro bodyguard, with his brains firmly in his biceps.

'Hello, Miss Jordan. It's really nice to meet you. My husband and I've read all of your books, haven't we, Trevor? I wonder if you could just sign this for me? Yes, that's it. Janice and Trevor. That's lovely. Oh, yes, and the date. Ta ever so much. Bye-bye.'

The first railway in Britain, Frank read, was a simple set of wooden beams laid on the ground in Nottinghamshire in the reign of Elizabeth I, to transport coal from the coalfield.

Mollie drifted off towards the contemporary fiction shelf and thumbed through the latest Michèle Roberts.

'You're not going to stop writing them, Miss Jordan? I mean, you won't pack it in will you? You'll not get bored with Annie? You can't, not while there's so many of us, all waiting for the next.'

Confused between the LMS, the GWR, the Southern and the LNER, Frank set the book back. Mollie moved on to find something that would do for her mother's birthday. Fay Weldon or Joanna Trollope, perhaps. Something that would take away the taste of the Jeanette Winterson she had given her the year before.

Cathy Jordan's hand was beginning to ache and she still hadn't got to the additional copies she was sure the manageress would want her to sign for stock. But at least the end of the line was at hand, and not a single troublemaker in sight.

The queue to Dorothy Birdwell's table had long since dried up and she was still sitting there, straight-backed and hopeful, Marius gently massaging away a little stiffness in her shoulders, whispering in her ear.

'What name would you like me to put?' Cathy asked for the umpteenth time. And, 'How do you spell that?'

With only a few people still to go, Frank had seemingly got bored with watching over her and was chatting to Mollie instead, the pair of them up at the front of the shop, near the cash desk. Cathy dipped her head to sign another book and the next time she looked up, there was Marius, immediately in front of her.

Cathy jumped, surprised at his being there, disturbed by the intensity of his stare. 'Marius, you don't want me to sign a book for you, I suppose? For Dorothy?'

She forced herself to smile, but Marius was not smiling back. Instead, unnervingly, he slowly leaned towards her, the table edge gripped with both hands. His stare was fixed on Cathy and would not let her look away. 'What I want,' he said, his voice intense and low, 'is for you to understand what's happened here today. All these people, foolish, small-minded people flocking around you, I want you to understand what that is about. It's not you. Not talent. Not originality, not skill. That woman over there has more of those qualities in her little finger than you'll ever have in the whole of your life. No, what this . . . this charade is all about is publicity, media, money. That and the sordid muck you wallow in every day of your writing life. Sensationalism of the kind that real writers would never for one moment soil their hands with. Or their minds.'

He held her gaze a moment longer, straightened, and turned away, leaving Cathy shaken and pale.

'What the hell did he want?' Frank asked, moments later, glancing over to where Marius was now helping Dorothy Birdwell from her chair.

Cathy shook her head. 'Nothing,' she said. 'Nothing important.' But the coldness that had spread along her arms and the backs of her legs was still there and although Marius now had his back to her, she could still clearly see her image, reversed, reflected in his eyes.

# Twenty-eight

Back in the Book Dealers' Room at the festival hotel, business was in full swing. Derek Neighbour had spent some time moving from stand to stand and had finally come upon Ed Leimbacher, from *MisterE Books* in Seattle, who had assured him that he could he could lay his hands on a first edition of *Uneasy Prey* in mint condition. Something of a snip at four hundred and sixty pounds. Plus commission. And handling. And packing. And insurance. 'And a bargain at that,' Leimbacher had smiled reassuringly.

Neighbour wondered why he wasn't reassured.

There was no getting round the fact, though, that the damage to the copy of Cathy Jordan's book he had taken with him to Waterstone's was even worse than he had feared; as many as fifty pages were stuck together irretrievably with paint, many of the others spotted and splotched. And the dust-jacket . . .

'Look,' Neighbour had finally said, fingering his cheque-book nervously inside his jacket pocket, 'I'll have to think about it a little longer. I'm sorry.'

'You could be,' Ed Leimbacher said. 'Pass it up and by the time you've done another circuit of the room, it could be gone.'

'I know, it's just . . .'

But the book dealer had turned aside and was no longer smiling – not until the next potential customer came along moments later. Books may be books, but business, well, that was business.

155

Dorothy Birdwell was leaning back in the armchair of their hotel suite, a damp cloth lightly across her eyes. Marius had helped her to remove her shoes and stockings and now was slowly massaging her feet, first one and then the other, each held close against his chest as he worked his fingers around the ball and carefully across the instep, knowing exactly when and where to apply pressure, when his touch should be little more than a breath.

'Marius, my dear . . .'

'Mmm?'

'When you went across to speak to the American, you didn't say anything too, well, distressing, I trust?'

'Oh, no. No.' Sliding one of his fingers along the delicate curl of her toes. 'Of course not. Nothing like that.'

'I know. I know. Some people, some men, if they were annoyed, they could be a little crude. But not you. I don't think you could ever be crude in the slightest.'

Mouth curved into a smile, Marius bent forward and lightly kissed the underside of her foot.

'How'd it go at the signing?' Tyrell asked. It was mid-afternoon and he was snatching the chance for a quick sandwich and a pot of tea at the convention hotel.

'Okay,' Mollie said. 'At least as far as Cathy was concerned. It was Dorothy Birdwell I felt sorry for. I doubt if she had more than half a dozen people standing in line. Still, I'm arranging transport for her and Marius to go out to Newstead Abbey. Apparently she's got this big thing about Byron.'

Tyrell's eyes brightened. 'Did you know Curtis was going to make a film about Byron? Ages ago. Late fifties biopic. Script, locations, everything. Apparently, some of his original drawings are around somewhere. Sounds like a really interesting project. James Mason as the man himself – can't you just see it? Mad, bad and dangerous to know. Patricia Medina. Vincent Price as Shelley. Aside from that Steve Reeves thing he did in Italy, it would have been the only costume piece he made.'

'How is Curtis?'

Tyrell inclined his head in the direction of the bar. 'Keeping himself topped up.' He lifted up the pot and gave it a gentle shake, offering it towards Mollie, who shook her head.

'What amazes me,' Mollie said, 'he seems able to drink all the time and never get drunk.'

'He explained it to me the other night,' Tyrell said. 'Claims he attained a state of perfect equilibrium in 1965 and he's been balancing there ever since.'

'What crap!' Mollie said. 'All Curtis has done, like a lot of other pissheads, is attain a state of being perfectly unemployable.'

Tyrell was on the verge of arguing back, but thought better of it; no sense in taking on Mollie when he didn't have to. Easing his slim body back into the comfortable chair, he opted for enjoying his tea instead.

As soon as the signing was over, Cathy Jordan had decided what she wanted most was to walk. She didn't know where and perhaps it didn't matter. She just wanted to walk.

'Want me along?' Frank asked.

Cathy gave a suit-yourself shrug and began to push her way through the crowds entering the Victoria Centre. Crossing the road in dangerous defiance of a black and white cab and a green double-decker bus, she hurried past the Disney shop on the corner and plunged into the Saturday afternoon throng.

Frank knew his alternatives: let her go her own way and head off back to the hotel and watch TV; or do what he actually did, tag along several yards behind and wait for her to slow down, for whatever was irking her, gradually to become less troublesome.

With no clear idea where she was heading, Cathy found herself on a recently re-cobbled road that led towards the castle; dropping down below the sandstone rock, she turned past the Trip to Jerusalem, local bikers and Japanese tourists sharing an uneasy space outside the proclaimed oldest pub in England. Beyond Castle Boulevard, Cathy crossed the bridge above the canal and walked down towards the lock.

Pigeons roosted in the broken windows of abandoned warehouse buildings. Brickwork blackened and cracked. Iron gates bloomed rust. Idling past, a freshly painted longboat leaked colours onto the oily surface of the water. Mallards, unconcerned, rocked and resettled in its wake.

'I'm sorry,' Cathy said, pausing.

'No problem.'

Ruefully, Cathy smiled. 'Why do we say that? No problem, all the time. Waiters in restaurants, cab drivers, clerks. You. Especially when it isn't true.'

'Hey, I didn't mean anything.'

'Exactly.'

'You mean there is a problem? That's what you think?'

'Don't you?'

They were walking slowly now; heels of Cathy's boots clipping the uneven concrete of the canal path.

'It's not that guy, Marius, is it?'

'Marius? What about him?'

'I don't know. Just the way he came up to you at the end, there. I thought maybe he had you spooked.'

'Jesus! It'd take more than a creep like Marius to spook me.'

They walked on. Between the buildings on the far side of the canal, traffic shunted eastwards in a slow line.

'Is it the letters?' Frank asked.

Cathy sighed. 'I've hardly thought about the damned letters.'

'Then it's somebody else.'

Cathy laughed, short and humourless. 'You mean, a man?'

'Unless you've changed a lot more than I thought.'

She shook her head. 'You know you amaze me, Frank. There you are, shaking your dick at anything in sight, telling me it doesn't mean a goddamn thing, where if it's me . . .'

'There is somebody then.'

She stopped, folded her arms across her chest. 'Frank, you have my word, I have not been screwing the home help.'

'Maybe not. But that might have been better than banging that plastic surgeon.'

Cathy didn't respond. She set off walking again, watching as a pair of ducks, grey-green, floated past along the canal. 'Water under the bridge, Frank. Old water under an old bridge. And, besides, he was interested in offering a little liposuction, that was mostly all.'

'I can imagine.'

'God, I hope not, baby.'

'What?'

'The two of us hacking at it in that hotel room, the size of a domestic freezer. Me struggling with my thermals and Mr Plastic with the kind of all-over body hair that puts King Kong in the shade.' She shuddered. 'Not a pretty sight.'

Frank strode on ahead, putting some distance between himself and his wife's revelations. He didn't know how much she was joking, if at all. After twenty or thirty yards, Cathy caught up with him, touching the fingers of her left hand to his neck, the ridge of muscle just above the collar. 'I'm sorry, I'm a bitch. You don't deserve that.'

'I do,' Frank said.

'Okay,' Cathy agreed, laughing. 'You do.'

Thirty minutes later and they were sitting at one of the

wooden tables outside the Baltimore Exchange, staring off towards the water with a couple of beers. Away to the east, where the canal disappeared between low, suburban houses on its way to join the River Trent, the sky was suddenly thick with clouds and the near horizon had misted over with slanting rain and violet light.

'How many years,' Cathy asked, 'have we been together?'

'Seven,' Frank said, not looking at her direct. 'Eight.'

'I wonder,' Cathy said, 'if that isn't long enough?'

# Twenty-nine

Resnick's friend, Ben Riley, had never been much of a ladies' man. Back in the late sixties, early seventies, when they had been young constables there in the city, there had been girls, certainly – nurses from the old city centre hospital, since rationalised out of existence, workers from the hosiery factories strung out along the roads north-east of the city, long since pulled down for DIY stores and supermarkets, Toys R Us. But the drinking, hobnobbing with the lads, to Ben they had always been more important. Until Sarah.

Sarah Prentiss had been a librarian who worked at the central library when it was on Shakespeare Street, close behind the Central Divisional police station. It was a place Resnick himself had liked to wander through, sit in sometimes, reading through the jazz reviews in back issues of the *Gramophone*. A solid building, thick stone walls, monumental, long corridors and high ceilings, shelves of books that seemed to stretch on forever, a pervasive silence – to Resnick, it was the essence of what a good library was about. Some years back, it had become part of the new university and the main library had moved even closer to the city centre. Now you had to push your way through a conglomeration of sales goods, advertising, magazines, videos and CDs before coming face to face with a good old-fashioned book. As far as marketing went, Resnick was sure it was successful, he was certain the library boasted a greater number of clients than before; he just wasn't one of them.

Neither was Ben Riley, who, to Resnick's continuing regret, had relocated to America some ten years ago. He doubted whether Sarah Prentiss visited the library much either, now that she was Sarah something else, and living in Northamptonshire with a husband, kids, and a couple of cars. He had learned this from Ben, with whom she had, for some years, exchanged the obligatory Christmas cards.

Why was Resnick thinking of all this?

Betty Carter was singing 'Body and Soul' on the car stereo as he drove, mingling the words and tune with those of a second, similar song, so that the final, climactic chorus seemed forever delayed, but that wasn't it. Not exactly. More confusing still, the words of yet another song were worrying away at some part of Resnick's mind.

'Send in the Clowns.'

He had heard Betty Carter live just once. A rare trip to London, a weekend in early spring, and she had been at Ronnie Scott's. A striking black woman, not beautiful, not young; warm and confident, good-humoured, talking to the audience between numbers with that slight show-business *bonhomie* that set Resnick's teeth painfully on edge. But when she sang . . . He remembered 'But Beautiful', 'What's New?', the way she would move around the stage with the microphone, her body bending to the shapes of the words with a combination of feeling and control that was unsurpassable.

Scott himself, nose like a hawk and gimlet-eyed, his sixty-odd years showing only where the skin hung thinly at his neck, had been leading his quartet through the support slots on the same evening. Tenor saxophone, piano, bass and drums. After several rousing numbers, Scott had played a two-chorus version of Sondheim's 'Send in the Clowns', almost straight, bass and drums dropping out, the tone of his saxophone ravishing and hard, one of the best ballad performances Resnick had

162

ever heard, silencing the club and striking him straight to the heart.

Ben Riley's heart.

Resnick had never known his friend fall for any woman the way he had fallen for Sarah. 'Don't know what she sees in me, Charlie, but thank Christ that she does!' And soon after, 'Not going to believe this, Charlie, but I think we're going to do it. You know, yes, tie the knot.' During the preparations for the wedding, little by little, Resnick had sensed Sarah withdrawing; the way she would react sometimes when he saw them together, snatches of conversation that were reported back. He tried to say something about it once and it was the first and only time Ben had come close to hitting him. Three weeks before the ceremony, Sarah had told Ben there was somebody else.

When Ben had scraped himself back off the ground days later, he sent her flowers and a telegram – *I guess they sent in the clowns* – a line from the song, which was popular at the time. With Sarah, certainly. She had bought Ben a record of it, Judy Collins.

He didn't know her response, whether she laughed or cried. He wouldn't talk to Resnick about her for months, years, wouldn't hear her name; then, one day, Ben said she had phoned him, from nowhere, out of the blue. Almost, he had failed to recognise the voice and the name; of course, it was no longer the same. Feeling low, lonely the way only marriage can make you feel, she had got to thinking about him. What he was doing. Where he was. They met once on a country road and she held his hand but turned aside from his kiss; there were things she wasn't telling him about the marriage, she made that clear, a tiny hook that bit deep. Then came the Christmas cards: *With love from Sarah and family*. The last few were returned to sender: Ben Riley had gone to the States.

Why was Resnick thinking of all this now?

*

163

She was out in the garden and hadn't heard the bell. Resnick let himself in through the side gate and walked along the gravel path. Honeysuckle climbed the wall. She was bending over one of the flower-beds, using a tool Resnick recognised but couldn't have named, to lever out weeds. As she straightened, she put her hand, no more than a moment, against the small of her back.

'I didn't think you'd recognised me, Charlie,' Sarah Farleigh said.

'I hadn't.'

She smiled at the ground. 'When did you realise?'

'Today. Oh, no more than an hour ago.'

She paused in pulling off her rubber gloves to look at him, asking the question with her eyes.

'I don't know,' he said. 'I mean, exactly. It came to me suddenly, I don't know why.'

'Why don't we go inside?' Sarah said. 'It's getting cold.' This time the smile was fuller, more real, and for the first time he saw her as she had been, the woman with whom Ben Riley had fallen in love.


The interior of the house was not ostentatious, but neat. Comfortable furniture, wallpaper Resnick would have guessed came from Laura Ashley, not an Aga but something similar dominating the broad, flagstoned kitchen where they now stood.

'Do you really want tea?'

'Coffee?'

'All right,' she set the kettle to boil, balanced coffee filters over two green Apilco porcelain cups, and reached the sherry bottle down from between glass jars of puy lentils and flageolet beans. Resnick shook his head and she poured a good measure for herself, tilted the glass and poured again.

'You'll think I'm becoming an alcoholic,' she smiled.

'No.'

Her hair was thick the way it had always been, streaked now with grey. The skin around her eyes was red from too much crying, but the eyes themselves were green, the green of slate that has stood fresh in the rain, and bright. Her wrists were thin, but strong, and her calves and ankles fleshed out and solid. She had aged more heavily, more hastily than Resnick had ever imagined she would.

'Will you come to Peter's funeral, Charlie?'

He took a first sip of his coffee, surprised.

'Isn't that what they always do, Morse and the others? I've watched them on television, standing in the background at their victims' funerals, looking for suspects among the guests.'

'I don't think that would be appropriate,' Resnick said. 'Not in this case.' He looked into her eyes. 'But, yes, if that's what you want. Yes, I'll be pleased to come.'

'Thank you,' she said. And then, 'Peter has family, of course, had, but I can't say we ever really got on.'

'You have children, though.' He had seen their photographs in the hallway and on the mantelpiece in the living room when they had walked past.

'Yes, three.'

'All grown up?'

'All grown.'

Sarah took her sherry to the window; it was darkening steadily outside and somewhere was getting rain. 'Do you ever hear from him at all?'

'Ben?'

'Yes.'

'Not for a while. He's in America, you . . .'

'Yes, I know. Montana, isn't it? Nebraska? One of those western states.'

'Maine, he moved to Maine.'

'Married?'

'There's someone, yes.'

'Children?'

'Yes, there's a child. A boy. I . . .'

'Charlie, I don't want to know.' There were tears in her eyes, but she was damned if she was going to cry. There had been crying enough lately and with good reason. What was the point of crying over impossibilities? Spilt milk gone sour.

'Sarah, what happened to your husband, I couldn't be more sorry.'

'Thank you. I know.' She smiled again, a generous, smile, almost a laugh. 'You always were a sympathetic man.' Turning, she rinsed the sherry glass beneath the tap. 'Maybe I should have married you.'

'I don't think so.'

She did laugh then. 'No, neither do I. Why don't we sit for a while in the other room? Have you got time, before you need to be getting back?'

Resnick got to his feet. 'A little, yes.'

They sat in armchairs on either side of an open fireplace which had a centrepiece of dried flowers in the grate. The curtains, full and dark and with a recurring motif of leaves, were closed. There was one photograph of Peter, arm around one of his daughters, laughing into the camera. The others were of the children, none of Sarah herself. On the polished coffee table lay copies of *Good Housekeeping* and *Vanity Fair*, several paperback books.

'Did you marry, Charlie?'

'Uh-hum.'

'Elaine, is that what she was called?'

Resnick nodded. 'Yes.' Christ, he didn't want to talk about this.

'What happened, Charlie?'

'We divorced.'

'For better or worse.'

'Something like that.'

'Which was it for you?' Sarah asked.

'Oh, worse. I suppose it was worse.'

'And now? Have you come to terms with it now?'

'I think so.'

'And you're still in touch?'

'Not really, no.'

'A shame. But, then, I suppose it's better that way.'

He didn't answer immediately. 'It is for me.'

Sarah drank more of the gin and tonic that had replaced the sherry. 'You think I treated him badly, don't you? Your friend, Ben. What I did, the way I behaved, you think it was pretty inexcusable.'

Resnick shook his head. 'No. I don't think that. I think, at the time, I was sorry he was so hurt. But, you know, my job, it's hard to sit in judgement about what people do.'

'You surprise me. Seeing what you see, I should have thought you did that all the time. Pass judgement.'

'I know. Only that doesn't seem to be the way it works. What happens, most of the time anyway, whatever it is someone's done, somehow you come to understand. No way you could talk to them, else.' Resnick looked across at her. 'At some point in our lives, we're all capable of anything. I suppose that's what you learn most.'

Sarah sipped her drink. 'You don't know any more yet,' she said, 'about what happened to Peter? I mean, why or . . .'

'Not really, although . . .' He stopped, uncertain, and she leaned forward a little, waiting for him to carry on. 'There's a chance, just a chance, mind, we might have a lead, something to go on.'

Sarah set down her glass. 'It's funny, isn't it? These days, you think, oh, people fooling around. Prostitution. Casual sex. Aids, that's what leaps to mind, isn't it? Aids, that's the danger. Not . . . not this.'

'I think,' Resnick said, 'if you're going to be okay, I ought to be moving.'

'Yes, of course, fine. You don't have to worry about me. I'm not about to do anything stupid.'

'I didn't imagine you would.'

She walked with him to the door. 'The funeral . . .'

'You'll let me know.'

'Of course.'

He was almost at the car, when she called him back. 'That girl, the one who was here with you the other day.'

'DC Kellogg. Lynn.'

'She's in love with you, you know.'

# Thirty

'Thought you weren't coming,' Divine said, as Naylor materialised through the crowd. He had nabbed a seat to the side of the pub, close against the windows that looked out over the trees and sloping shadows of the park. Quiet half-hour with Sharon Garnett, who knew what might develop? But not now. 'Here,' he said, trying not to sound too grudging. 'You can just about squeeze in here.'

Naylor set down his own pint and the refill he had bought for Divine, and sat next to a youth in a cotton shirt with sleeves rolled back, who grudgingly made space for him.

'Sort out all the under-age drinkers amongst this lot,' Naylor said. 'Have the place to ourselves.'

'Aye, well. Better things to do, eh?'

'Happen.'

'How was Canada's feller-made-good?'

'Prick of the first water.'

Divine laughed. 'Maybe should've brought him along. There's women here, not seen a good shagging since Forest last won bloody Cup.'

Naylor nodded absent-mindedly and drank.

'Hey up, though. Here we go. There's one I'd not mind putting it to myself.'

Dressed in a black roll-neck, leather jacket and blue-black jeans, Sharon Garnett was making her way past the raised platform of the stage, where a tubby retread of Elton John was fiddling with the wiring of the electric piano and preparing to excite the crowd with a despairing version of 'Crocodile Rock'.

'What are you having?' Divine said, out of his seat and reaching for his wallet.

'A headache. I've heard this bloke before. What say we drink up and leave?'

A few minutes later they were walking along Arboretum Street and heading for Balmoral Road, a narrow cut-through that would take them to the Goose Fair site and the Forest Recreation Ground.

'This tart we're looking for,' Divine said, 'how well d'you know her?'

'Doris? Like I say, I've not been here long enough to know the girls well, but, yes, I've had words with her once or twice.'

'And?'

'She's all right. Straightforward enough. Honest.'

'Honest?'

'Yes. She doesn't make any bones about what she does. Doesn't make a fuss if she's nicked.'

'Back on the street the next night, probably carrying a dose of Aids.'

Sharon stopped walking. They were on the corner of Forest Road East, the cemetery that took up one corner of the recreation ground, off to their right. Immediately before them, open space dropped to near darkness and, beyond that, the lights of the terraced houses of Forest Fields. 'You don't know that,' Sharon said. 'And if she had, who gave it to her, answer me that?'

'A needle?' Kevin Naylor said.

'I don't reckon Doris does drugs,' said Sharon.

Divine laughed, the sound carrying on the wind. 'Makes her the only scrubber round here who doesn't.'

Doris Duke was short as Sharon was tall. They finally tracked her down some forty minutes later, climbing out

of a Mazda saloon in four-inch heels that still left her well
below average in height. She was wearing a pink T-shirt
that stopped between belly button and ribs, a waist-length
nylon jacket, midnight blue, and a skirt which, when she
backed out of the car, left little to the imagination. A small
handbag hung from one shoulder by a gold chain.

'Doris.'

She almost smiled when she saw it was Sharon; a smile
that fast turned sour when she saw the two men in her
wake.

'Doris, we'd like to talk.'

'Oh, we would, would we?'

Divine wanted to slap the sneer from her face for a start.

'Yes, about your friend.'

'Which friend's that, then?'

'Marlene.'

'No.'

'Marlene Kinoulton. Don't let on you don't know who I
mean.'

'I know who you mean, all right. Just she in't no friend
of mine.'

'Since when?'

'Since she legged it with fifty quid she owed me.'

'And when was that, Doris?'

'Couple of days back.'

'And the fifty pounds?'

'Lent it her, didn't I? Slag never give it me back.'

'Why did she want the money?' Divine asked.

'I don't know, do I? Never asked.'

'Come on, expect us to believe you handed it over, just
like that?'

'I don't give a toss whether you believe it or not. So
happens it's the truth. One of your mates says they're
short, you don't go through some sodding inquisition,
right? If you've got it, you hand it over.'

Divine wasn't so sure.

'Even if it's fifty pounds?' Naylor asked.

Doris Duke laughed. 'Fifty? What's fifty quid? I can thumb down the next punter comes along here, earn that in twenty minutes.'

'Then why,' said Sharon, 'are you so steamed up about it?'

'Christ, you don't understand anything, do you? It's the principle of the sodding thing.'

They went to sit in Sharon's car to talk, Doris insisting that they drive well clear of the Forest first. 'Certain people see me sitting with you lot, they'd be less than well pleased.' Doris had grown up in the same part of east London that Sharon had lived in before striking out for the provinces, and because of that, and the fact that Sharon was clearly different – the Vice Squad wasn't exactly overflowing with blacks – Doris felt that, underneath it all, Sharon was all right.

But now it wasn't Sharon asking the questions.

'And you last saw Marlene when?' Divine said.

'I told you, Tuesday.'

'The day you lent her the money?'

'Yes.'

'Lunchtime. In the Queen.'

'Jesus, yes.'

'All right, Doris,' Naylor said, 'we only want to be sure we've got it right.'

'Oh, yes, I know,' sarcasm edging her voice.

'Don't want to put words into your mouth.'

Or anything else, Divine thought. Under the car's interior light, Doris's make-up was thick enough to chip and there was the clear residue of a bruise, dark above her left eye.

'And she didn't say anything about her plans? Taking off somewhere for a few days? We know she used to work in Sheffield and Derby. That wasn't why she wanted the money? For the fare?'

'Look,' Doris said, her voice taking on the pained expression people reserve for children, the old or the very deaf, 'I don't know where she is. Don't even know where she's been. We were mates, yes, but we never lived out of one another's pockets. Sometimes she'll be off somewhere, weeks at a time; I don't see her around and then I do. This business, you don't ask too many questions. And the fifty . . .' She pulled open the ashtray beside the dashboard and stubbed out her cigarette. '. . . Most likely she owed someone. Either that or she just fancied going into town, buying herself a new dress.'

'Why would she do that?' Sharon asked.

'Why would you? Cheer herself up, of course.'

'Or make herself look smart.'

Doris gave it a moment's thought. 'Maybe.'

'So as to work the hotels.'

'Maybe.' Doris started rummaging for a cigarette in her bag and Sharon offered her one instead. 'Thanks,' angling her head towards the window as she lit it and exhaled.

'If you knew,' Sharon said, wishing that the two detectives weren't there, doing her best to exclude them with her voice. 'If you knew that was what Marlene was going to do, try the Victoria, say. The Royal. Maybe the Crest. If Marlene had told you that was what she had in mind and then you read about what happened to that man in his hotel room, well, I wouldn't blame you for keeping quiet.'

Doris looked at her, blinking through the veil of cigarette smoke. 'Yes, but I don't know that, do I? If she did that, I don't know nothing about it.'

Sharon gave a brief sigh and sat back. 'You're sure you don't know Marlene's new address?'

'Sure.'

'Okay,' Sharon said, swivelling round and snapping her

seat-belt into place. 'Why don't we take Doris back to work?'

They watched her walk away to join the knots of girls on the edge of the Forest. 'Wouldn't know the truth,' Divine said, 'if it jumped up and bit her in the arse.'

Naylor shook his head. 'I don't think she knows anything,' he said.

'I'm not so sure about that. I think she does,' Sharon said. 'And if I don't push too hard I think she might tell me, but I'd have to be on my own.'

'Aside from us, then,' Naylor asked, 'why wouldn't she open up now?'

'Partly, it's against her instincts. And I think she's frightened.'

'What of?'

'I don't know. And maybe it's not for herself, maybe it's on account of her friend.'

A car slowed as it neared them, the window rolled down on the driver's side. 'Get home to the wife,' Divine called. 'Before you get nicked.' The window went back up as the driver accelerated away.

'Why don't we call it a night?' Sharon said. 'I'll try Doris again tomorrow, all right? And we'll keep in touch.'

You run on, Divine wanted to say to Naylor, just run on ahead and let me give it a try. A drink some time, Sharon, how about that? Something to eat. Clubbing, maybe? Black Orchid's not too bad. But something in Sharon's eyes, the way she held herself, standing there and watching as they walked away, made him realise, no, it wasn't such a good idea after all.

# Thirty-one

*Slowing off the freeway, I can hear the sirens and already I'm thinking, hey, it's okay, how many times do you hear that in this city, night and day? Doesn't have to have anything to do with this case, anything to do with me.*

*But the closer I get to Fairlawn Avenue, the louder the wailing gets, not just the police, either. As I slow for the light, an ambulance shoots past me, causing traffic travelling on the cross street to swerve and brake. By the time I arrive at the house, my stomach is cramping fit to beat the band and I know what I will find.*

*Fifty yards away from the gathering furore and the flashing lights, I swing my car into someone's front yard and start to run. Paramedics are scuttling into the house with all their gear and a uniformed cop is standing guard on the sidewalk, while, behind him, two of his colleagues are threading out the famous yellow tape:* **Crime Scene, Do Not Cross.** *I show the cop my ID and can tell he isn't about to be impressed, when Lieutenant Daines appears on the square of trimmed lawn at the front of the house, badge clipped to the lapel of the black tux he must have been wearing when the call came through. His black tie is unfastened and hangs loose from the collar of* *his dress shirt and he has that look that homicide detectives get once in a while, no matter how long they've been in the job. The look that says, no matter how bad you thought it could get, it just got worse. Looking up, he sees me and waves me through.*

Resnick turned down the corner to mark his place and set Cathy Jordan's book aside. A little more than two thirds of the way through and the body count was rising. Whoever had killed April Reigler at the end of chapter one, seemed to be working his or her way through April's college friends. Resnick thought it was an elaborate blind, a series of otherwise unnecessary crimes whose only purpose was to confuse the investigation and lead the police – and the redoubtable Annie Q. Jones – off along the wrong track. For his money, the answer lay closer to home. In his experience, that was usually the case. But he wasn't betting on it.

In the kitchen, he switched the radio on and swiftly off again. What was it about the BBC that the first few hours of Sunday morning were devoted so resolutely to pretending nothing had changed since 1950? From 'Morning has Broken' through to the Appeal for This Week's Good Cause, it was as though God were still benevolently in His heaven and all, in thought, word and deed, were right with the world. Even 'On Your Farm', which was allowed to interrupt the predominantly religious programmes, regularly featured one of its journalists sitting down to a trencherman's breakfast of sausage, bacon and eggs with commonsensical good-hearted country folk of the kind Resnick had long thought existed only in the minds and brochures of the English Tourist Board.

The clock above the dresser showed it was still shy of seven. He had been up since half past five, unable to sleep; had made two pots of coffee and now he was about to make a third. This time he would have toast and some of that marmalade he had bought at the Women's Institute market in the YWCA opposite Central police station. Wonderfully sweet and runny, the kind that always slid off the knife blade and on to your hand before you could hope to spread it on bread. Annie Q. Jones, he knew, would have already done her work-out to Cher's fitness video and would be standing with her coloured pens in front of the giant whiteboard on which she noted all the significant incidents in her current case; arrowing connections, circling clues. All Resnick could do, standing there waiting for the water to heat through, was allow the bits and pieces of the investigation to trundle round inside the washing machine of his brain. Turning the toast, he smiled, remembering how it had begun, the loneliness of the middle-aged runner with only one sock. One of the mysteries of the age, which neither he nor Annie Q. Jones would ever solve – why was it that whenever you took six pairs of socks to the laundry, nine times out of ten, you only got five and a half pairs back? Lynn? In love with him? What on earth had Sarah Farleigh been talking about?

Millington and his wife had this Sunday morning routine: as soon as the alarm sounded, Millington would push back his side of the duvet (John Lewis Partnership goose down, acquired only after his wife's careful perusal of comfort ratings and tog numbers in *Which?* magazine) and hurry downstairs, returning some fifteen minutes later with a tray, laden with tea (Waitrose organically grown Assam), slices of fresh granary bread (for which Madeleine had stood in line at Birds the Bakers the previous day), butter (now that the latest dietary reports had suggested a low level of dairy products was actually good for you, they were allowed butter) and Wilkin and Sons' 'Tiptree' morello cherry conserve. Not jam, conserve. And, for Madeleine, the *Mail on Sunday*.

Millington placed the tray in the centre of the bed, and prepared to climb back in, knowing full well no matter how circumspectly he did this, his wife would tell him to be more circumspect still.

'Careful, Graham,' she said. And, with Millington joining her in harmony, 'You'll spill the tea.'

Madeleine detached the sports pages from the paper and passed them across; that done, the drill was this: Graham would butter the bread, which he had already cut into two; Madeleine herself would add the jam. Graham would pour milk into the cups and she would pour the tea, now brewed to a good colour and strength. The only occasions he stirred in a little sugar was at the station, when he could be good and sure Madeleine wasn't looking.

'Ooh look, Graham, that writer, there's something about her in the paper.'

'Mmm? Where?'

The photographer had posed Cathy Jordan alongside the statue of Robin Hood beside the Castle wall, Cathy's hand reaching up to touch the bow. The headline: **MAKING CRIME PAY**.

'You know, Graham, I was thinking of going.'

'Where's that, love?'

'She's being interviewed this afternoon, by that woman from the box. The one I like, with the glasses, you know. From *The Late Show*. Oh, what is her name?'

'Don't ask me.'

'It was on the tip of my tongue just now.'

'Thought that were jam.'

'Oh, Graham, be serious.'

'So I am. Get your head over here and I'll lick it off.'

'Graham, don't! You'll upset the tray.'

'Not if we park it on the floor.'

'But I've not finished my tea.'

178

'Stewed by now. Any road, I can always nip back down later, mash some more.'

'Graham!'

'What now?'

'I shall have to go to the bathroom first.'

'Whatever for?'

'I shall just have to, that's all.'

'All right, then. If you must. But for heaven's sake, don't take all day about it.'

And Madeleine hurried into her dressing gown, leaving Millington to read about Notts' first innings against Middlesex, nibble another piece of bread and jam and hope the mood didn't desert him before she returned.

'Come on, Mum,' Lynn Kellogg was saying down the phone, 'that's just the way Auntie Jane is. You've been telling me that for years.'

And while her mother launched into another familiar family diatribe, Lynn, half-listening, sipped her Nescafé and struggled with seven down, four across in yesterday's crossword. At least, she thought, as long as her mother could find the energy to get worked up about her sister's failure, for the third year running, to send a birthday card, it meant there was nothing more urgent to worry about. Meaning Lynn's dad.

Not so long after Christmas, her father had had an operation to remove a small, cancerous growth from the bowel. 'We'll be keeping an eye on him, naturally,' the consultant had said, 'but so far, fingers crossed, it looks as though we might have nipped it in the bud.' And her father, slow to recuperate, shaken by everything that had happened – the strangeness of the hospital, the discomfort of endoscopy, the myth that no one who was ever admitted to an oncology ward lived more than a twelve-month after, the persistent threat of the knife – *was* getting better. When last Lynn had driven over to Norfolk to visit,

179

he had been back out again, pottering between hen houses, cigarette hanging from his lips.

'Away with you, girl,' he had said, Lynn lecturing him for the umpteenth time about the dangers of cancer. 'There's not a thing wrong with these lungs of mine and you know it. Doctor told me so. So, less you see me pulling down these overalls and smoking out my backside, bugger all for you to get aerated about, is there?'

Lynn hoped he was right. She thought, hearing a bit of the old fire back in his voice, that probably he was.

'Yes, Mum,' she said now. And, 'No, Mum. That's okay. He's doing fine, just fine.'

*A psychological process in which painful truths are forced out of an individual's consciousness* – six letters. With her mother prattling on like that, Lynn couldn't, for the life of her, think what it was.

'Frank?'

Cathy Jordan rolled off her stomach and reached towards the clock radio, angling it in her direction. Jesus! She hadn't intended to sleep so late.

'Frank? You in the bathroom or what?'

No reply. Most likely he was off swimming, maybe found a gym downtown to press a few weights. Cathy eased herself up on to one elbow and dialled room service, ordered fresh orange juice and coffee, croissants and jam. If she was going to pig out most of the morning, she might as well enjoy it. Give some thought to what she was going to say that afternoon, not that it would be any different from what she'd said half a hundred times before.

The one thing Marius didn't like, the thing he could barely stand, the way she would introduce him as her nephew all the time. As if somehow she were ashamed of him, felt a need to explain. Secretary, that would have been something; personal assistant. She hardly referred to him by either of those titles any more, though, naturally, they explained what most people imagined his function was. And it was true. Dorothy's correspondence, he saw to that; appointments, meetings with publisher or agent, requests for interviews by the media, any and every little thing. Most people looked at him, accompanying her everywhere, helping her off and on with her coat, pulling out her chair, and they assumed one thing. About him. Poor Marius, camp as a clockwork sixpence, gay through and through. Well, if only they knew.

He had the oil ready now, a mixture of sweet almond and camellia, scented with dewberry, her favourite. It was just a matter of warming his hands. He knew she was waiting for him, towel spread over the sheet, face down, patient. Undemanding. Most of the world, Marius thought, didn't realise how beautiful old people could be. Their skin. Lightly freckled, the delicacy of fine lines patterned like honeycomb: he thought Dorothy had lovely skin.

# Thirty-two

When Resnick's wife had entered into an affair, she had been driven to it; driven by what had disappeared from their own lives, by passion. It had also been a sign: clear, not negotiable. This is over for us; I want out. Of course, it had not been clean, nor without pain. It rarely is. But clear, yes, that's what it had been.

Whether passion had driven Jack Skelton beyond the bounds of propriety with the self-possessed DI Helen Siddons during her brief sojourn in the city, Resnick had no way of knowing. He had only seen the looks, the late-night conversations conducted in corners, the lingering glances. What the superintendent would have seen in her, attractiveness and intelligence, both well honed, was easier to judge; aside from the fact that Skelton was her senior officer, what might Siddons have seen in him? She was not, Resnick thought, the kind of person to commit to any action unless it contained an advantage. And if passion was what had been at stake there, would passion for Jolly Jack have been enough? Enough for her to risk losing her footing on the fast track towards the top? Not too many points for engaging with a superior in an extra-marital affair; not unless that superior was of the rank of assistant chief constable at the very least.

God, Charlie, Resnick thought, as he approached the Skelton house, you're getting cynical in your old age. It must be Sundays, that's what it is. All that bell-ringing and sanctimonious ill will. All those cars queuing to get into DIY centres.

He was pleased finally to have arrived, to have parked behind the Volvo in Skelton's drive, climbed out and automatically locked the door, walked towards the house in his response to the superintendent's early summons.

'Had breakfast, Charlie?'

Resnick nodded, yes.

'You'll have some coffee, though?'

'Thanks.'

Skelton's daughter, Kate, was sitting with her feet drawn up under her, in one of the easy chairs in the L-shaped living room. Walkman in place, the usual tinny whispers escaping, she sat reading an A-level textbook, occasionally scribbling a biroed note in the margin. His wife, Alice, with an expression for which the word sour could have been invented, had barely stopped to greet Resnick as he entered; hurrying on past him and up the stairs to the first floor, from whence the whining suck and bump of the vacuum cleaner could now be heard.

All the little nudges, Resnick thought, that make a home, that make a marriage.

He and Skelton sat on stools in the kitchen, alongside what Resnick guessed the brochures called a breakfast bar; the smell of grilled bacon was tantalising on the air and a scrambled egg pan had been left in the sink to soak. Resnick tried to remember the last time he had seen the superintendent unshaven.

'Sure you won't have anything?'

'No, thanks. I'm fine.' Resnick accepted the coffee and drank some without tasting.

'You've seen the Sundays?' Skelton asked.

Resnick shook his head. 'Always try hard not to.'

'What with this bloody crime festival being here, and now the murder, they're having a field day. Already got us down as the most violent city in the country. Load of bollocks! Give a roomful of monkeys a set of statistics and a computer and they'll prove bloody anything. Anyway, goes without saying, the chief constable's been breathing down my neck for a result. Invited Alice and myself out to his place this afternoon, high tea.'

Resnick smiled; the thought of Alice Skelton having to put on her best frock *and* be polite to people she probably despised, was something he'd rather imagine than actually see.

'Laugh all you want, Charlie, while they're carving into the Yorkshire ham on the lawn, I'm going to be carpeted inside, good and proper. Unless you've got something you've yet to tell me.'

Resnick wished he had. 'Marlene Kinoulton, she's still our best shot. About the only shot we've got.'

'And she's disappeared.'

Resnick shrugged. 'May not mean a great deal. Sounds as if she's never in one place for long. You know how it is with these girls, some of them, all over the shop.'

'If I could say we had confirmation of her identity, that would be something, but so far not a bloody thing.'

Resnick drank some more coffee. 'It's amazing to me, though I suppose by now it shouldn't be, just how unobservant most people are. Close on sixty potential witnesses we've questioned so far. Vast majority of them, couldn't even place Farleigh as being there at all, despite the fact he must have spent a total of over two hours that evening, downstairs in the hotel, either in the restaurant or the bar. Of those that did remember him, half of them have no recollection of his having been with a woman, and those that do . . . well, it's a lottery if she was fair or dark, caucasian or Chinese.'

Skelton reached up towards one of the fitted cupboards, lifted out a bottle of cooking brandy, tipped a shot into what was left of his coffee and pushed the bottle in Resnick's direction, where it stayed, untouched. Little early in the day for his boss to be hitting the hard stuff, Resnick thought. He said nothing.

Skelton said, 'At least that business with the letters, threats to that woman, Jordan, that seems to have died down.'

Muffled but on cue, Resnick's bleeper began to sound.

Cathy Jordan had fallen back to sleep. One of those shimmering dreams that refused to touch ground. Railway carriages, aeroplanes, other people's bathrooms. Silk. Steel. Slivers of skin. She woke with the undersheet wound tight between her legs and her hair plastered to her scalp with sweat. 'Frank?' Frank was still not back. Breakfast? The breakfast didn't seem to have arrived. If room service had knocked, they had got no answer and gone away. Cathy prised herself from the bed and made it, less than steadily, to the shower.

Testing the temperature of the water with her hand, she stepped beneath the shower, letting the water stream over her neck and shoulders and as, eyes closed, she lifted her face towards it, she felt braced, revived.

Ten minutes later, Cathy briskly towelled herself down. Through the curtains, she saw it was another fine day. Not exactly sunny, but fine. Better than she had anticipated. Maybe she'd laze around a little longer, take a look at the Sunday papers. Wasn't that interview she'd done being printed today?

She glanced around. Frank could have taken the newspaper with him when he went out, but that seemed unlikely. Probably, they were still outside in the corridor.

Wrapping a towel around her, Cathy pulled back the door and looked out. There they were, and a full breakfast trolley, too. A glass cafetière with silver trim, juice, several pots of honey and jam, a bread basket covered with a starched white cloth. Oh, well, the coffee would be cold, but nothing was wrong with orange juice and a couple of cold croissants. Cathy wheeled the trolley back inside and snapped the door closed with her hip. Letting the towel fall to the floor at her feet, she flicked back the cloth from the basket and screamed.

Where she had expected croissants, a baby nestled snugly, its limbs, where they showed through its baby clothes, skinned and streaked with blood.

# Thirty-three

The flesh was rabbit, not the supermarket kind, but bought fresh and skinned, none too expertly at that. The blood, it seemed, had been squeezed from a pound or so of liver, the richness of the smell suggesting pig as the most likely source. Baby clothes, otherwise new, had been purchased at Mothercare. The face, cherubic and brittle, had been detached from a child's doll, the old-fashioned kind.

It was not until later, when the trolley was being carefully checked and searched, that the note was found, a single sheet inside a small envelope which had been slipped between two napkins, folded beneath an empty glass.

'You don't want to see it,' Resnick said.

'Yes, I do.'

'There's no point, not now. Why don't you wait?'

'Till when?' Cathy Jordan had laughed. 'Till I'm feeling better?'

When Resnick had first arrived, she had been standing by the window, dressed in denim shirt and jeans, an absence of colour in her face. Someone from the hotel had brought her black coffee and brandy and she had drunk the latter, allowed the coffee to get bitter and cold. The trolley and its contents were where she had left them, towards the centre of the room.

Frank Carlucci had arrived back from the pool a little after Resnick, unaware that anything was wrong. Immediately, Cathy had rounded on him, shouting, where in God's name had he been, why the fuck was he never there

187

when she needed him? Once, hard, she had pounded her fist against the meat of his shoulder and Frank had lowered his head, eyes closed, bracing himself for her to strike him again. 'Can't someone, for Christ's sake, get me some fresh coffee up here?' she had said, turning away, letting her hands fall by her sides.

Since then she had been quiet, almost controlled, patient while Resnick made calls, issued orders, people came and silently went. Conversations were held in hushed tones beyond the door.

Handling the edges carefully with gloves, Resnick held the note towards Cathy Jordan's face. It had been typed on an ill-fitting ribbon, black shadowing into red:

> *How do you like this? The only misbegotten child you're likely to have.*

Cathy read it slowly, again and again, tears filling her eyes until she could no longer see. Blindly, she moved towards the bathroom, banging her shin against the low table laden with magazines. When Frank went to help her, she pushed him angrily away.

The two men looked at one another, Resnick replacing the note inside its envelope.

'What kind of a sick bastard does something like this?' Frank asked.

'I don't know,' Resnick said. All the while thinking, this weekend the city is full of them, writers, film-makers, people for whom thinking up things like this is meat and drink.

'Frank,' Cathy said, coming back, tiredness replacing the shock in her eyes, 'would you be a sweetheart, see what's happened to that coffee?'

'Sure.'

As Frank picked up the phone, Mollie Hansen appeared in the doorway and Resnick motioned for her to stay where she was, walking over and leading her into the corridor outside.

'I only just heard,' Mollie said. Her face, usually unblemished and even, was beginning to show signs of strain. 'I'm not sure I know everything that happened.'

Concisely, Resnick told her all she needed to know.

'How's she taking it?' Mollie asked.

'She's angry, upset, pretty much what you'd expect.'

'And those threatening letters she had – do you think this is the same person?'

'It's possible. As yet there's no way of knowing. At first sight, the note doesn't seem to have been written on the same machine. But that might not mean a thing.'

'And you don't imagine . . .'

'What?'

'Well, that business with the paint. This couldn't be another stunt to get publicity for their cause?'

'Vivienne Plant and her friends? I don't know. I'd have thought she'd have had a photographer on hand, at least. But we'll talk to her, all the same.'

'Good.' They were standing near the lift doors, opposite a lithograph of trees and a beach, shaded pink. 'Can I talk to her? Cathy?' Mollie asked.

'From my point of view, no reason why you shouldn't. But you might leave it a while longer. Give her some time to settle down.'

Mollie sighed, looked at her watch. 'I suppose so. It's just she's got this interview this evening with Sarah Dunant. If she isn't going to be able to go ahead with it, I ought to let Sarah know.'

'Why don't you give her half an hour?' Resnick said. 'I can let her know you're around. If she says she wants to talk to you now, I'll let you know.'

'Fine,' Mollie smiled tiredly. 'Thanks.'

Behind her, the lift shushed to a halt and Lynn Kellogg

stepped out, Kevin Naylor immediately behind her. 'Thought you could use a little help,' Lynn said.

Resnick nodded his thanks and set them both to work.

Susan Tyrell stood in the centre of the kitchen, door open to the garden, whisking meringue and wondering how long it had been since she and David had made love. Probably it had been Christmas, that squeaky bed in her parents' spare room, several bottles of cheap champagne and some good port enough to stir a little life into David's libido. Even then, he had called out the name of some movie star at the point of climax. His and not hers. Hers had been an altogether quieter, more private affair, later.

Since then it had been a cuddle last thing at night, those long moments before falling into sleep, David's last waking act to turn away from her arms.

'Why do you stay with him?' her friend, Beatrice, had asked.

Susan had sat there like a contestant on *Mastermind*, stumped for the right answer.

'This damned festival,' Tyrell said, coming into the kitchen, cellphone in his hand, 'is getting more like a Quentin Tarantino screenplay every day.'

Terrific, Susan thought, blood and gore and bad seventies pop songs, continuing to stir the meringue as he relayed the events at the hotel.

'You are coming to the show this afternoon?' Tyrell asked.

'Oh, yes, I expect so.'

'You should. Aside from one screening at the Electric in 1982, *Dark Corridor* hasn't been shown in this country since the fifties. And Curtis himself hasn't set eyes on a print of *Cry Murder* since he was still in the States.'

'Really?' Susan said with barely feigned interest. The meringue was just stiff enough now to cover the pie. She could have got into an argument about rarity not always equalling quality – if the damn films were any good, *why* hadn't some enterprising programmer shown them? – but she lacked the energy. Umpteen eleven- to eighteen-year-olds, nine till four, Monday to Friday, she knew well enough to reserve her strength for what really mattered.

Back at the hotel, Lynn Kellogg and Kevin Naylor were questioning as many of the staff and guests as they could find. Resnick had phoned Skelton and arranged to meet him back at the station to make his report; he had promised to talk with Cathy again later. Frank sat in the chair before a silent television, watching a ball game that, for all its apparent similarities to baseball, he just didn't understand.

Cathy Jordan lay on the bed, fully dressed, staring up at the ceiling with blank, blue eyes.

# Thirty-four

'I guess when I married Frank, that was more or less my last chance. Kids, I mean. Oh, we talked about it, back and forth, you know. Frank he would have been keen, keener than me, if you want to know the truth, but, well, the time never did seem right. This book to be finished, that book; another damn tour. In the end, I suppose the idea just ran out of steam.'

Cathy Jordan had wanted to get away, clear her head, and Resnick had brought her to Wollaton Park, green slopes and a golf course, ornamental gardens round an old ancestral pile and down below where deer were grazing, the lake they were walking around.

'You have kids?' Cathy asked.

Resnick shook his head.

'But you're married, right?'

'I was. Not any more.'

'I'm sorry.' She laughed. 'I say that, sorry, automatically, you know, without thinking. Truth is, half the friends I've got are divorced and most of the others wish they were, so . . .'

They emerged between brightly coloured rhododendron bushes at the far end of the lake, a middle-aged couple walking amongst other couples who were exercising their dogs, simply enjoying the sunshine. Here and there, men sat transfixed beside fishing rods, immovable as stone.

'Mostly, now, I never think about it. Kids, I mean. Then something happens like today – well, never *like* today,

192

not, thank God, exactly like that – and somehow it starts up again . . .' Her voice trailed away and it was a good few moments before either of them spoke. A pair of Canada geese skidded noisily on to the water, scattering blue. 'I guess it gets easier, right? I mean, the point finally has to come, you accept it: I am not going to be a parent.'

Resnick shrugged. 'Maybe,' he said, not believing it was so. Even now it would lurch at him, unsuspected, out from the darkest corner of the house or through the glare of a midsummer street – the urge to have a child of his own.

'Well, I tell you,' Cathy was saying, 'I'm from a big family and whenever we get together, nephews and nieces every which way, I get home after one of those things and I'm glad of the rest.' She laughed. 'I've got three sisters, five cousins, seems they pop another one out whenever they stop to take a breath.'

Resnick smiled and together they walked on past the lake's edge and up the slow incline towards the Hall. By the time they had turned through the gateway past the stables and the small agricultural museum, it was time to drive the short distance back to the city.

'You going to be okay?' Resnick asked. They were standing beside the car in the hotel forecourt, motor idling. 'Mollie seemed concerned about this interview you have to do.'

Cathy gestured dismissively with her hand. 'I'll be fine. And listen, thanks for this afternoon. Most people wouldn't have taken the time. I'm only sorry I wasn't better company.'

'That isn't true.'

She threw back her head and laughed. 'Along with everything else, I'm fucking premenstrual!'

Resnick watched her walk towards the doors. 'Take

care,' he said, then climbed back in the car and drove to the station.

Millington's wife was spending the afternoon rehearsing *The Merry Widow* and he had come in to the office in an open-neck shirt and his third-best sports jacket, the one with the leather-patched sleeves, and was threading his way, painstakingly, back through the statements that pertained to Peter Farleigh's murder. Something whose importance they had failed to grasp, a connection they had missed – if it were there, so far it had eluded him.

'Call for you from the wife,' Millington said, seeing Resnick walk in.

Resnick's stomach went cold; without reason, his first thought was of Elaine.

'Ex-wife, that is,' Millington went on. 'Widow. Farleigh's.'

'Sarah,' Resnick said.

'Yes, that's it. Wants to know, once the inquest is over, will we be prepared to release the body?'

Resnick's breathing was back to normal. 'I'll talk to her, thanks.' He looked down at the material on the sergeant's desk. 'Anything?'

Millington shook his head. 'About as enlightening as shovelling shit.'

Resnick nodded and moved away.

'Boss.' He turned again at the sound of Divine's voice; Mark coming into the room with a slice of part-eaten ham and pineapple pizza folding around his hand. Lunch, Resnick thought, I knew there was something. 'Had a bell from Garnett. Says she's going to have another go at Kinoulton's mate later, reckons as how she knows more'n she's letting on.'

'You think she's right?'

'Could be. Let's face it – some bugger's got to know something.'

'Okay,' Resnick said. 'Keep on top of it.'

Sharon Garnett, Divine thought, I shouldn't mind. Tilting back his head as he lifted the pointed end of pizza to his mouth, he wandered over towards his desk.

In the corner near the kettle, Resnick found the remnants of a packet of chocolate digestives and dunked them in lukewarm tea. He was considering phoning Sarah Farleigh, still wondering exactly what he might say, when Kevin Naylor and Lynn Kellogg got back from Cathy Jordan's hotel.

Naylor had talked to the room service staff on duty, the young woman who had prepared Cathy Jordan's breakfast tray, the man who had taken it up to her room, knocked, received no reply and left it on the trolley outside the door. He had talked to the maid who had been changing bed linen and towels on that floor. Everyone had followed procedure; no one had noticed anything amiss. Unless one of the staff were lying, and Naylor didn't think this was the case, the most likely scenario was that the macabre 'baby' had been exchanged for the proper contents of the basket while the trolley was outside the room. Which raised the question – since, presumably, the thing had required planning, and since whoever was responsible could hardly have been sure the breakfast trolley would be so conveniently standing there – what other means had been envisaged for its delivery?

After helping Naylor a while at the hotel, Lynn had gone off in search of Vivienne Plant, who, after a few obligatory warnings about harassment, had been only too happy to give the names and addresses of three witnesses who could testify that she had been engaged in a fortnightly badminton game that morning, after which she and her friends had progressed to Russell's bar for a good, unhealthy fry-up brunch.

'Okay,' Resnick said, having listened to their reports.

'Without getting into a lot of lengthy forensics and committing more hours than we can afford, that may be as far as we can go. For now, anyway.'

'That's okay, then,' Naylor said, walking with Lynn across the CID room. 'We can get back to doing something important.'

Lynn stopped in her tracks. 'What?'

'Well, you know. Not as if there was any real harm done,' Naylor said.

'No harm?'

'You know what I mean. It's not as if anything actually happened.'

'Something happened all right,' Lynn said.

'Yes,' Naylor agreed, digging an even deeper hole for himself, 'but not serious.'

'Suppose it had been Debbie, though, Kevin, how would you feel, then? How would she feel, d'you think?'

'She'd be upset, course she would . . .'

'Upset?'

'Yes, but she'd get over it.'

'Which means it's not worth our bothering with?'

'Not as much as some other things, no.'

'If she'd been hit, though? Physically attacked, raped even?'

'Then, of course, that'd be different.'

Lynn laughed, more a snort than a laugh. 'Fact you can't see wounds and bruises, Kevin, doesn't mean a person hasn't been damaged. Hurt. Doesn't have to mean it's less serious.'

# Thirty-five

Doris Duke didn't look as if she were working. Instead of high heels, she was wearing a pair of scuffed trainers and there was a hole at the back of her black tights big enough to slip a hand through. Aside from what still stuck, haphazardly, to her face from the previous night, she wore no make-up. Her hair had been pulled back from her head and hung raggedly down, secured by a couple of pins and a rubber band. There was a cigarette in her hand.

Sharon eased the car over to intercept her and Doris's head instinctively turned; she wasn't out looking for business, but she wasn't going to shunt it away.

As soon as she recognised Sharon, she knew it was business of a different kind. 'What d'you want now?' she asked, trying to summon up a belligerence that wasn't really there.

Sharon set the handbrake, slipped the car into neutral. 'Talk.'

'Oh, yeah? What about now?'

'This and that?'

'Pay for my time, will you?'

Sharon smiled. 'You've been watching too many of those TV movies, Doris. That's the only place girls like you get paid to talk to the likes of me.'

Doris stood uneasily, shifting her weight from one foot to the other, cigarette cupped in her hand. 'From what I've seen, your sort are either looking to bang you up and slap the hell out of you, or they're sniffing round for freebies.'

She gave Sharon a look that was meant to be provocative. 'Which is it with you?'

'Neither. I told you. I just want to talk.'

'And I said, what about?'

'Marlene.'

Doris dropped her cigarette to the pavement, quickly ground it out and began to walk away.

'Doris . . .'

'No,' she called over her shoulder. 'I already told you everything I know.'

Sharon released the handbrake and let the car coast after her. 'All right,' she said through the window, 'we'll talk about something else.'

'Yeah? Like what? Swap recipes and tips on chipping away old nail polish?'

'If you like, yes. Why not?'

'You know sodding well why not!'

Sharon let the car roll on down the hill, Doris, head down, crossing the road behind her. By the time Sharon had stopped the car and got out, they were level.

'Come on, Doris. A deal.'

'Yeah? What's that?'

'I'll buy you a meal and we'll talk and if you don't want to say anything more about Marlene, that's fine.'

'I thought I didn't get paid for my time?'

Sharon was standing next to her now, taller, having to stoop down; Sharon wearing a leather jacket, unzipped, over her souvenir T-shirt from a Prince concert, blue jeans and a pair of ankle-high Kickers, green with a grease mark on one heel. 'This isn't buying your time, it's buying you lunch.'

'Lunch?'

'Tea, dinner, whatever. Come on, when did you last eat?'

'That's where I was going now.'

'So fine. Where to?'

Doris grinned, just a little, not giving it too much. 'McDonald's. Got these vouchers I've been saving from the *Post*. Two McChicken sandwiches for a couple of quid.'

'Okay,' Sharon said. 'Why don't we go in the car? That way, we could go to the one by the canal, what do you say?'

Sharon told Doris to keep her McChicken vouchers for another occasion and splashed out on two Big Macs, fries, apple pies, cola. They had stopped at the paper shop on Lenton Boulevard so that Doris could buy another twenty Bensons, king size. There was a seat by the window, and although they couldn't actually see the canal from there, they could work out where it was, across the other side of Sainsbury's car park, to the right of Homebase.

Doris picked out most of the middle of her Big Mac, toying with the bun but never really eating it. The fries she dunked in a generous puddle of red sauce. Sharon ate slowly, saying little, trying to make the younger woman feel at ease.

Doris told her about a childhood bounded by Hackney Marshes and Homerton Hospital; Dalston, Clapton, Hackney, Leyton. A familiar enough story, familiar to Sharon certainly, not so very different from her own; the same story many of the working girls had to tell. When it was told at all. And Doris, not a product of what sociologists and politicians called a broken home; no one-parent family hers. Her father, on the dole, had always been there. Always. Through the unbroken veil of cigarette smoke, beneath the slow-fading bruise, Sharon looked for the child in Doris's eighteen-year-old face but it had long been driven out.

*she says:*
*if only I could be*

199

*three again, struggling with my shoe laces;*
*start all over, go back to the beginning*

*shake my mother*

*abuse my father*

'You reckon her for it, don't you?' Doris said suddenly, pushing away the carapace of her apple pie. 'That bloke got himself knifed. You reckon her for that.'

'Do you know where she was, Doris? That evening? Where she was working? Was it the hotels?'

'I already told you, I hadn't seen her since the Tuesday.'

'Tuesday afternoon.'

'Right.'

'When you lent her the money. The fifty pounds you never got back.'

Doris mouthed an oath. Sharon reached for her cola and drank a little more. Doris lit another cigarette. Two lads walking past outside shouted something they could neither of them make out and one of the lads went into a swagger, cupping non-existent breasts. His mate laughed so much he nearly got clipped by a passing car.

'She wanted it for drugs, didn't she?' Sharon said.

Doris nodded. 'Crack.'

'How bad is she?'

It seemed a long time before Doris answered. 'Look, you know as well as what I do, there's girls out there, they don't keep high, they go crazy and once it gets like that, there's nothing they won't do to score. These dealers, they play 'em along, let 'em get in debt, serious now, hundreds I'm talking, easy. Once it's like that, they can do what they like with them. Sex shows, dyke stuff, animals. This one bloke, charged his mates a tenner each to wank off over this girl while his alsatian licked her out.' Doris shuddered and made a face. 'Marlene, though, she wasn't like that. She was bright, dead clever. Older, too. Been around, but it didn't show. That's how come she could work the hotels. Me, now, I walk in and they've got me walking right out again, regular revolving door. Not Marlene. That's why I was surprised when she started doing crack. Oh, we'd have the odd spliff once in a while, who doesn't? But crack.' Doris shook her head. 'First, it was just weekends, fifteen, twenty quid a rock. You know, when we was busy. Never ends up like that, though, does it? Marlene, she could see what was happening to her. Kept trying to kick. Even went to that place, you know, down by the Square. What's it called? Crack Awareness, something like that. Got worse anyway. Got so she hated what she was doing, couldn't stand being touched. Being with some bloke, any bloke, but, of course, that's what she had to do. Keep earning, more and more, trying to stay ahead.'

In another part of the restaurant, twenty or so eight- and nine-year-olds were having a party, flicking Chicken McNuggets across the tables, wearing cardboard cut-out hats.

'How much,' Sharon asked, 'had she got to hate it?'

'She used to say, next man who touches me, I'm going to kill him.'

'And you thought she was serious? You thought she meant it?'

'No, don't be bloody stupid, course I didn't! We say that all the time.'

'Then what?' Sharon said.

Doris took a long drag on her cigarette. 'Week or so back, the night that other bloke was done, you know, stabbed. It was in the paper, found him starkers in the road.'

Sharon waited, Doris taking her time.

'I ran into Marlene,' Doris said, 'she was leaning on this wall off Forest Road, looked like she'd just been throwing up. There was blood all down her front. Up her hand and arm.'

To an almighty roar from the children, one of the McDonalds staff jumped up on to the middle of their table dressed as Mr McChicken, and started flapping his wings.

Sharon bided her time.

'Who did she cop from, Doris?'

Doris blinked at her across the smoke from her cigarette. 'Richie. I don't know . . . I don't know where, but yes, Richie that's the only one I ever heard her mention. That's who she said.'

# Thirty-six

Dorothy Birdwell's fingers fumbled with her water glass, almost sending it tumbling, and for once Marius was not poised to intervene and set everything to rights. Marius, in fact, was nowhere to be seen. It gave her a pinched feeling in the back of the throat, making it difficult to breathe. And as for talking . . .

Dorothy steadied herself and, with almost exaggerated care, brought the glass to her lips. The forty or so people who had gathered to hear her thoughts on Christianity and the crime novel, with special attention to the work of Dorothy L. Sayers, watched and waited patiently. After all, she could sense them thinking, at her age you can't expect too much.

Well, expectations were strange things. She reached out towards the small table at her side and lifted her copy of *Such a Strange Lady* into her lap.

'As we can be only too aware,' she began, 'living as we do in these particular times, it is difficult not to see the art of biography and the wish of the individual for privacy as being incompatible. Think then only of a young woman, an only child, born at Christchurch Cathedral Choir School, a Christian scholar whose second book of poems was titled *Catholic Tales and Christian Songs*, and yet who nevertheless became pregnant out of wedlock and secretly gave birth to an illegimate son. How irreconcilable the gulf between the life that is apparent and expected and the life that is actually lived.'

She paused and caught her breath. If only she had not

been forced to have words with Marius earlier that afternoon – some of them, she would have had to agree, significantly less than Christian. If only Marius had not stalked off in such high dudgeon, no word of where he was going or when he might return.

Dorothy looked out at her audience and continued. 'In her religious play *The Devil to Pay*, Dorothy Sayers explicitly deals with Faustian themes, the extent to we are all of us prepared to go, the amount we will pay for happiness on this earth even though it might mean we risk damnation in the next . . .'

'How about a couple of drinks, honey?' Cathy Jordan said in a mock-seductive, mid-Western voice. 'One way or another, I reckon we've earned them.' She was leaning against the frame of the bathroom door, a towel wrapped around the middle of her body. A tumbler of tap water, with the aid of which she had just swallowed aspirin, was held lightly in her right hand, wrist resting on the swell of her hip.

'Go to hell, Cathy, why don't you?' Frank said, flipping over the pages of the magazine he was reading – a copy of *Première* he'd picked up at the airport, everything you ever wanted to know about Demi Moore except what does she ever see in that asshole actor.

'What does she ever see in that asshole actor?' Frank asked.

'Which particular one did you have in mind?'

'Demi Moore. You know. The one with Demi Moore.'

'Oh, him.'

'Yes, him.'

'He was great in *Pulp Fiction*.'

'Didn't catch it.'

'Just terrific.'

'I still don't see . . .'

She lifted the magazine from his hand and then dropped

it back down. 'They're a partnership, that's what it is. That's why it works.' Playful, she nudged him with her bare toes. 'She works. He works. Simple. A partnership.' She threw him a face and headed back towards the bathroom door. 'We should try it some time.'

'What?'

'Nothing.'

'What the fuck was that about?'

He was on his feet now, close behind her, and Cathy turned to face him. 'Work it out for yourself.'

'Every cent you earned this last year, I earned as much.'

Cathy shrugged. 'I had a bad year.'

'Bitch!'

'Sure, Frank. Love you too.'

For an instant, she flinched and closed her eyes, thinking he was going to strike her, but what he did was jerk the towel from around her, so that she stood before him, naked.

Her breasts were heavier than when he had first seen her, the skin across her belly less taut, but there was nothing to deflect from the fact that she was still a beautiful woman; more beautiful as she stood there now, unclothed, than in her boots, bright shirts and jeans. Most women Frank knew, the reverse would be true.

'Well?' Cathy gave him a look that said, what now? and he didn't know. She held out the glass towards him and automatically he reached to take it. Swiftly, she stepped back inside the bathroom and shut the door, flicking the bolt across.

Mollie Hansen was sitting in the Broadway Cinema CaféBar, nibbling at a portion of cabbage stuffed with peppers and drinking Red Raw ginger beer. Slides of scenes from various forties *films noirs* were being projected on to the far wall, and she was idly checking them off as she ate: *Mildred Pierce, Gilda, The Lady from Shanghai.*

'Hi, Mollie.' Susan Tyrell was standing at her shoulder, an empty glass in one hand, a bottle of Cabernet-Shiraz in the other. 'Okay if I join you?'

'Sure.'

Susan pulled out a chair and sat down.

'In for a long wait?' Mollie said with a grin, indicating the bottle.

Susan's eyes rolled upwards. 'David's just getting going on Hollywood *femmes fatales*. Stepping out of the shadows in tight black dresses with guns in their hands.' She filled the glass to within a quarter-inch of the rim and brought it to her mouth without spilling a drop. 'Once he gets started on that little fantasy, I might as well be invisible.'

Mollie forked up some more stuffed cabbage. Larger than life on the wall, Joan Crawford, in poor lighting and a fur coat, stood over the dead body of Zachary Scott.

'You see what I mean?' Susan asked, 'Who ever paid any attention to her when she was just plain old married Mildred, wearing an apron morning till night and baking pies?'

Mollie waited for the laugh, but it didn't come. 'That's a movie,' she said. 'Not real life.'

Susan drained her glass and began pouring another. 'Try telling that to David.'

Mollie looked at her seriously. 'Then maybe it's time to get out of the kitchen?' she said.

Susan looked away. 'Yes, well, I'm afraid that time is long past.' And then she did laugh, but it was loud and forced. 'Listen to me, carrying on. Complaining about David to you of all people.'

Mollie leaned closer and covered Susan's hand with her own. 'If you feel this bad, you've got to sit him down and talk to him. Make him listen.'

206

'Really. And when did you last succeed in doing that?'

Marius Gooding had let himself back into the hotel suite he had been sharing with Dorothy Birdwell and locked the door. Pulling the blinds, he stripped down to his undershorts and vest. 'Bitch!' he said, as he pulled out drawer after drawer of her neatly folded clothes and spilled them across the floor. 'Bitch!' as he jerked her satin and taffeta dress from its padded hanger and tore it neck to hem. *Bitch!* he scrawled across the photograph in the back of her new book. *Bitch!* in black felt-tip on the centre of the sheet. *Bitch!* on the wall above the bed. *Bitch!* along one arm, the inside of his legs, across his face, and all around his head. *Bitch! Bitch! Bitch! Bitch!* Marius curled up on the floor, knees to his chest, head in his arms, and cried.

# Thirty-seven

Frank didn't recognise the woman sitting up at the bar; no reason that he should. It was early yet, early for serious drinking, and the place, long and narrow with stairs leading to a high balcony at the rear, was quiet. Music – which he recognised as Joe Sample, Frank having been a major fan of the Crusaders since seventy-two, 'Street Life' one of his favourite records of all time, the one he always instructed DJs to play when he and Cathy hosted parties of their own – was pumping quietly from large speakers suspended from the ceiling. The barman, fresh-faced and possibly as young as he seemed, set aside the newspaper he was reading and asked Frank what he wanted. The answer was a whisky sour, large, a little salt on the glass; iced water on the side. And something to pick on. He hadn't eaten since lunch and reasoned this was the start of what might prove a long night.

'Nachos,' the barman suggested. 'Chicken wings? Potato skins? Onion rings?'

'Forget the nachos and the onion rings. Let me have the chicken and the potato skins, okay?'

'Sir.' The barman passed Frank's order through to the kitchen and began to slice the lemon, fresh, for his whisky sour.

Frank toyed with the drink when it came, checking the temptation to swallow it right down; ever since the talk with Cathy down by the canal, he'd felt like he was walking on the proverbial eggshells. He laughed and the woman four seats along turned her head; never understood what that meant before, eggshells, what it was like. Now he thought if it was going to crack and let him tumble through, why not take a hammer to it, smash it first himself? Do unto others instead of being done to.

He finished his drink and called along the bar for another. The woman, sipping what Frank thought was some kind of rum cocktail, rum collins, cuba libra, one of those, glanced at him again. Not giving it too much. Still light outside, in the bar it was cool and dark. There were rings on the fingers of both the woman's hands, Frank noticed; dark hair which fell past her face due to the way she was sitting, partly shielding her from his gaze. Thirty-five, Frank thought, forty. Waiting for a friend. Nothing to get worked up about.

'Your whisky sour, sir.'

'Sure,' Frank said. 'Thanks.'

When Cathy arrived outside the main convention room for her interview, she had managed to patch up most of the damage, though the skin around her eyes was darker than usual and her face was pinched as if she were suffering from too little sleep. Which was partly the truth.

'You okay?' Mollie asked, concerned, stepping forward to greet her.

Cathy nodded: fine.

And from anything other than close up, she did look good: a cream linen suit with wide lapels, a green satin shirt and, poking out from beneath slightly flared trousers, the ubiquitous boots.

'Cathy, I think you know Sarah Dunant.'

'Sure. We met at the Edgars last year.'

The two women smiled and brushed cheeks and set off towards the platform, Mollie leading the way.

'So which part of the States are you from?' the woman was saying.

And, 'How long are you over for?'

And, 'Oh, interesting.'

Frank all the while hearing Cathy's voice – *I wonder if that isn't long enough?* Eight years. Close to. Saying it, it didn't seem so long. But living it. He shook his head. Some days he could scarcely remember when there had been anything else.

'Sorry,' Frank leaned sideways towards the woman's stool. 'I didn't catch what you said.'

'I said, do you want another drink here or are you ready to move on somewhere else?'

The music had shifted again, back from some guitar band that reminded Frank of the Byrds, back to the Crusaders, the album they made – eighty-one, eighty-two? – with Joe Cocker.

'I'm okay here,' Frank said. 'Unless you're getting restless?'

She shook her head and slid her empty glass towards his; all this time they'd been talking and he still hadn't got a good look at her face.

'Two more,' Frank called along to the barman. 'Same as before.'

The convention room was comfortably full, without being overcrowded. Mollie had been able to spot a few of the more vocal feminists, identified them from previous events she had helped to organise. *Representations of Women in the Media. Melodrama and the Family.* She had talked to quite a few of them at length, respected what they had to say. Liked them.

After a brief introduction in which Sarah Dunant had placed Cathy Jordan's work within the context of post-seventies crime fiction, she led her through a series of questions about her career, its false starts and now its successes. Dunant then summarised the prevailing politically correct readings of crime fiction and asked Cathy for her opinions. There were questions from the floor, searching rather than hostile, and then the interview was over: polite, professional, non-contentious.

Cathy had opted to close the session with a reading and she chose the opening chapter from *Dead Weight*. Instantly, the caustic, slightly self-deprecating voice of Annie Q. Jones buttonholed the audience and when she finished it was to warm applause.

Mollie came on to the platform to thank both women formally and bring the proceedings to a confident close. Now she could take them to the hotel bar, buy them a drink, make her excuses, take herself home and rest, thankful that the evening had passed without incident.

Still in the bar, Frank was explaining the difference between a latte and a mocha, though he wasn't sure if his companion were still listening and if she were, whether she had understood. Where previously there had been several feet of space behind them, now they were constantly being banged against and jostled by one or other of the young people who stood in groups around them, smoking and drinking and laughing. The volume of the stereo had increased four-fold and whatever was being played now seemed to consist of a thumping bass and very little else.

'You want to try somewhere else?' Frank asked, mouth close against her hair.

'I thought you weren't interested?'

'I'm interested.' He wondered how long her hand had been on his knee.

'Then let's go back to your place.'

'How d'you mean?'

'You've got a room, haven't you? You're staying at a hotel?'

Frank shook his head. Now that he could see her, he

liked what he saw. Liked her breath, slightly sweet, upon his face. 'We can't go there.'

'I thought you were here on your own. Have you got a wife or something?'

'That doesn't matter. We just can't go back to my room, that's all.' He let his hand cover hers, where it was still resting, high on his thigh. 'What's wrong with your place?'

'We'll go to another hotel,' she said, and smiled. 'As long as your credit card's good for it.'

'Hey, don't worry about the money. But d'you think we'll get into somewhere this late? Town strikes me as pretty busy.'

'Don't worry about that,' she said, getting carefully down from her stool. 'Just trust me.'

# Thirty-eight

The first time Resnick had seen Sharon Garnett, the sun had been showing weakly through winter clouds and the earth beneath their feet had been coarse with frost. All around them, the high stink of pig food and pig shit. Other officers, silent, as they lifted a stretcher across the ruts, the body of a young woman sealed beneath thick plastic that was spotted here and there with mud.

Now, as she pushed her way through the bar towards him, Resnick realised that she was both taller than he had remembered and likely older too. The only black face in the Sir John Borlace Warren.

'Your local?'

Resnick grinned. 'Not exactly.'

After Sharon had rung him with the information about Marlene Kinoulton's probable drug supplier, he had put through a call to Norman Mann at Central Station and the choice of meeting place had been the Drugs Squad officer's shout.

'Pint?' Sharon asked.

'Guinness, thanks. Half.'

By the time she had been served, Norman Mann had joined them, lager in hand, dark hair thick on his head and curling up over the collar of what had clearly been bought from a job lot of black leather jackets.

Resnick shook his hand and did the introductions.

'This Richie,' Mann said, once they had elbowed their way into a corner, 'had our eye on him for quite a while. There's a blues he does his drinking some nights. No sense looking for him there too early, but by the time we've supped a couple of these, we could wander down. See what's what.'

'You think he'll talk?' Sharon asked. 'Give us anything we need to know?'

Norman Mann winked broadly. 'Always a chance. Smoked enough weed, we'll be lucky to shut the bastard up.'

The room was small and, in the way of most hotel rooms, anonymously airless. Frank had tried to kiss the woman as she leant back against the door, clicking the lock, but she had swerved her head aside. Then, as he had reached towards the light switch, she had caught hold of his arm and ducked beneath it, twisting him round till he was hard against her. She had kissed him then, her mouth slippery over his, teeth blocking out his tongue.

'At least now you're going to tell me your name?' he said.

'Why? Isn't it better like this?'

'In the dark?'

'Yes.'

But it was not quite that, the curtains only partly pulled across and light enough from the city shining through; he touched her face and she shuddered, almost before the touch, as if anticipating something else. His skin against hers was surprisingly soft. At first, she squirrelled the tip of her tongue into his palm and then drew her teeth down and around one of his fingers, nipping it a little at the knuckles before drawing her lips back along it so slowly that he moaned. With a laugh, she bit down into the fleshy round beneath his thumb.

'Hey!'

'Hmm?'

Frank fumbled her open at the front and bent his head into her neck, squeezing her breasts. Whatever moment he

214

might have pulled back at had long passed. She touched him and, arching back his head, he closed his eyes.

'Frank?'

'Yeah?'

'Let's go to bed.'

Soon she was kneeling over him, kissing him, deft pecks like a bird's, delicate and sharp. His trousers had been pushed and kicked down to his ankles, shirt thrown sideways to the floor; his boxer shorts were tight across his thighs.

'Like me, Frank?'

'Sure I like you.'

'I mean me. Really me.'

'Sure.'

'You're lying, Frank.'

'I'm not.'

'Lying.'

'Look, I swear to God . . .'

'Anyone, Frank. I could be any woman in the whole wide fucking world. Any woman, Frank. Any cunt in a storm.'

He made to roll aside and she leaned her weight against his arms, surprisingly strong. 'What's the matter, Frank? Don't want me any more? Huh? Don't fancy me?'

Head sideways below the pillow, he didn't answer.

'Don't you like it when a cunt talks back, Frank? That the problem?'

'There's no problem,' he mumbled, only just audible above the hum of the air conditioning.

'What?' Her face lowered close to him, laughter in her voice, teasing.

'I said there's no fucking problem.'

'Temper,' she scolded. 'Temper.' And rocking back on his hips, she reached a hand behind and between his legs and he could sense rather than see her smile. 'You're right, Frank. No problem at all.'

She moved again, her buttocks lower on his thighs, the front of her pale-coloured briefs against his balls. Spreading his hands, straightening his arms, he raised his face towards hers and she kissed him, he kissed her, her fingers tugging at his hair.

'Wait,' she said, minutes later. 'Wait.'

'What for?' His breathing was harsh.

'What do you think?' Swivelling off him. 'I have to go to the bathroom, of course.'

He watched her dart away, pale, no longer slender, saw the shimmer of electric light before the bathroom door closed it out. With a slow sigh, he lay back down, rested an arm across his face and once more closed his eyes.

A blues club in Radford or Hyson Green didn't mean laid-back, Mississippi Delta bottleneck, the kind that might grace TV advertisements for beer or jeans; it didn't even mean second- or third-generation bump and grind, juke blues, South Side Chicago, T-Bone Walker or Otis Rush. It meant after-hours drinking, Red Stripe and rum, the sweet scent of marijuana drifting in lazy spirals down the stairs.

They were illegal, of course, and the police knew where they were and who ran them, and those that ran them knew the police knew and, unless something exceptional happened to upset the racial apple cart, that was how it stayed.

This particular club was off the Radford Road, more or less across from where the Hyson Green flats used to be, until they had been bulldozed down and the land leased to house another supermarket. Perish the thought the Council would build more homes. The fact that the club was above the premises of what had been some kind of outreach office of the Probation Service, only added a little extra piquancy.

Norman Mann paused at the foot of the stairs and drew

in a deep, long breath. 'What d'you reckon, Charlie? Worth inhaling, eh?'

Smelled a sight better than a lot of things illegal, Resnick thought, and likely did a lot less harm, but that was as far as he was prepared to go.

The treads on the stairs were cracked in places and bare. As they climbed higher the bass from recorded reggae made the walls vibrate. Norman Mann motioned for Resnick and Sharon to stay at the end of the landing, went to the door and knocked. There followed a long and fairly tortuous conversation Resnick couldn't hear.

'We'll wait down there,' Mann said, when the head he'd been talking to withdrew and the door was sharply closed.

In what had once been the Probation office, a forty-watt bulb hung from a length of fraying flex. Miraculously, it still worked. What it cast light on were an old desk, empty boxes, balls of dust, a stack of forms waiting forever to be filled in and signed – those that hadn't been shredded by the mice for their nests. A hungry cat would have thought it had died and gone to heaven. Next time Dizzy nips my trouserleg because he thinks I've put him on short rations, Resnick thought, I'll bring him down here and lock him in.

Richie made them wait. When he finally appeared in the doorway, he was wearing a skinny-ribbed V-neck jumper in bright colours and tight trousers which, even in that dim light, shone when he moved. He was slightly built and about as pale as a black man can be without becoming Michael Jackson. He stood lounging against the door frame with a can of lager in his hand.

'Who's these?' he said, indicating Resnick and Sharon with a nod of the head.

Norman Mann made the introductions.

'Marlene Kinoulton,' Resnick said. 'We'd like to find her.'

217

'Slag! I'd like to find she first.' The syntax was right, but at root the accent was no more Caribbean than if he'd gone down the pit at sixteen – which conceivably he might have done, except that by then they were already closing them down.

'She owe you?' Norman Mann asked.

'She owe everybody.'

'That why she's keeping her head down? Maybe skipped town?'

'She not even got the sense to do that. I saw her fat white ass only this afternoon.'

'You sure?' Resnick asked.

'I not blind.'

'Then you would have had a word with her,' Norman Mann said. 'Her owing you, and all.'

'She getting into this car, in't she?'

'Which car?'

'I don't know. Big white car. She's working, in't she? Doing business. Drive off before I can say a thing.'

'No way you could have been mistaken? You're positive it was her?'

'Yeah.'

'Where?'

'Round near her place.'

'You got an address for her then?' Resnick said.

'What's it worth?'

Both men stared at him and Richie stared back for long enough to show no way were they going to intimidate him. Then he gave his can a little chug.

'How about peace of mind?' Norman Mann said. 'Good will.'

'What you want she for?' Richie asked. He was looking at Resnick.

'Something serious,' Resnick said. 'Nothing that would affect you, I can promise you that.'

'Promise?' Richie drained the can and tossed it into the nearest corner. 'What's that?'

Over their heads, someone had turned up the volume and the ceiling had started to shake.

'That gives way,' Norman Mann said, glancing up, 'going to be a lot of people hurt bad. Crying shame.'

'Forest Fields,' Richie said. 'She have a room, Harcourt Road.'

'Number?'

'Top end, corner house.'

'Which side?'

Richie grinned. 'Depend which way you looking, don't it?' And then, addressing Sharon directly for the first time, ' 'stead of hangin' out with these guys, get your black ass down here some night, show it a good time.'

# Thirty-nine

Frank Carlucci couldn't be certain how long he had lain there before he realised the woman wasn't coming back. However much sexual anticipation he was experiencing, the effect of innumerable whisky sours had meant that the meeting between his head and a pair of the hotel's comfortable pillows had so far resulted in one thing only. The woman was, he seemed to remember thinking, taking one hell of a long time in the bathroom, but aside from that, he didn't recall very much at all. A sound that, he now realised, might have been that of the room door opening or closing, and that was all.

Sitting up – first quickly, and then, as his head informed him speed was ill-advised, cautiously – he looked at his watch. Too dark too see. Reaching across, he snapped on the bedside lamp. Blinking, then squinting, he tried again. A quarter past one. He had scarcely been asleep any time at all.

Easing himself off the bed, he checked the bathroom, the door to which was wide open and, of course, it was empty. Only then, with sinking desperation, did he scrabble on the floor for his jacket and fumble his wallet out into the light. He knew what remained of his English cash and all his credit cards would be gone, but, contradicting him, they were there, the money, as far as he could tell, intact.

Back in the bathroom, he splashed cold water in his face and then wondered why he was bothering. Cathy was bound to be asleep in their own room by now, another hotel across the city, and what was to be gained from waking her, he didn't know. Better to face her the next day with a fresh face and a good story.

Frank hung the *Do Not Disturb* sign outside the door, climbed back into bed and inside five minutes he was snoring, first lightly, then loudly.

They had been parked across the street some ten minutes, Norman Mann smoking two Bensons while he and Resnick listened to one of Sharon's anecdotes about policing deepest Lincolnshire. 'Go into some of those places,' Sharon said, 'and I'd know how my relatives felt, getting off the boat at Tilbury in the 1950s.' Or mine, Resnick, thought, in 1938. Except, of course, that they'd been white.

'Well, what d'you think, Charlie? Shall we give it a pull?'

Resnick pushed open the car door and stepped out on to uneven paving stones. Apart from a stereo playing too loud a half-dozen doors down, the street was quiet. The end terrace to the right, facing north, had stone cladding on the front and side walls, window frames and ledges which had been newly painted, yellow, and a small sign attached to the front door to show that the householders were members of the local Neighbourhood Watch. The house opposite had a derelict washing machine upside down outside in the scrubby front garden, one of its upper windows covered in heavy-duty plastic where the glass had been broken and not replaced, and at least a dozen milk bottles beside the front door, each containing a varying amount of mould and algae.

'So, Charlie – no call to be much of a detective here, eh?'

'Give me a minute,' Sharon said at the space where the front gate should have been. 'I'll get round the back.'

Once she had disappeared from sight, the two men

slowly walked towards the door. When Resnick rang the bell it failed to work; he knocked and no one answered, but from the sound of the television they knew somebody was at home. Norman Mann leaned past him, turned the handle and pushed and the door swung grudgingly inwards.

'Thanks very much,' he said with a wink, 'we'd love to come in.'

They followed the sound of amplified voices into the front room.

Three youths, status unemployed, were watching a video of *Naked Gun 2½* amongst a plethora of beer cans and empty pizza boxes and the faint scent of dope.

'What the fuck?'

Resnick showed them his identification, while Norman Mann walked past them towards the television set and switched it off.

'Hey! You can't . . .'

'You live here?' Mann asked.

'Yeah.'

'All of you?'

'Yeah.'

'Who else?' Resnick asked.

One of the youths, his head partly shaven, a trio of silver rings close in one ear, got awkwardly to his feet. 'Look, you gonna tell us what's going on? What the fuck this is all about?'

'Easy,' Mann said. 'We ask questions, you answer them. So, now – who else is there, living in the house?'

The youth looked round at his mates before responding. 'There's Terry, right, up on the first floor at the front . . .'

'He's not here now,' put in one of the others. 'Off home to see his old man.'

'Who else?' Resnick said.

Two of them exchanged quick glances; the one with the

shaven head stared at a stain in the carpet, one amongst many. 'You won't let on?' he finally said.

'To who?' Norman Mann asked. 'And about what?'

'The landlord. See, the bloke as was up there moved out and he left it to us to let out the room.' A few more shifty looks wove back and forth. 'On his behalf, like.'

'And you forgot?'

'No, well, we got someone in, all right . . .'

Norman Mann laughed. 'Just a bit slow in letting the landlord in on it?'

'Something like that.'

'Well, I know how it is, lads,' Mann said. 'Busy life like yours. Going down the video shop, cadging fags, jerking off, signing on. Understandable, really, you've never quite found the time.' One of the youths sniggered; the others did not.

'This unofficial tenant,' Resnick said. 'Got a name?'

'Marlene.'

'Kinoulton?'

'Yeah, that's right. Yes.'

There were footsteps outside and then Sharon walked into the room. 'Back door was open. Didn't reckon anyone was about to do a runner.'

'Here,' said the shaven youth. 'How many more of you are there?'

'Hundreds,' Norman Mann grinned. 'Thousands. We're taking over the fucking earth!'

The room Marlene Kinoulton had rented was on the first floor at the back. No lights showed under the door and when Resnick knocked there was no response. A hasp had been fitted across the door and a padlock secured.

'Have that off in two ticks,' Norman Mann said, flicking it up with his forefinger.

'And have anything we find ruled inadmissible by the

'court,' Resnick said. 'Let's wait for the morning, get a warrant.'

'Suit yourself.' Norman Mann looked quite disappointed. He was more of a knock-'em-down-and-reckon-the-consequences-afterwards man himself.

'I'll babysit the place the rest of the night,' Sharon offered, once they were back downstairs. 'If she's around, she might come back.'

'Good,' Resnick said. 'Thanks. I'll send Divine round to relieve you first thing. Meantime, I'll chase up a warrant. See what she's got in there, worth keeping a lock on.'

In the front room, Norman Mann took a swallow at the can of lager he'd popped open and set it back down with a grimace. 'What you're scrounging off the DSS, ought to be able to afford better than that.' Reaching round, he switched the TV set back on. 'Thanks, lads. Thanks for inviting us into your home.'

# Forty

Cathy Jordan woke early, with the creamy taste of another late-night supper still rich in her mouth. She lay without moving, aware of Frank's absence, accepting it without surprise. They had tried, in the time they had been together, handling her enforced absences, these trips to the conventions and booksellers of the world, in a number of ways. At root, however, there were two alternatives: he went with her or he stayed home. Cathy liked to claim she left the choice to him.

If Frank waved her off at the airport with a hug and a kiss and a see-you-in-six-weeks, within days he would be calling her erratically around the clock, unable to settle; and she would return to smiles and flowers and rumours of drunken nights and drunken days and always there would be messages from women Cathy had never previously heard of, backing up on the answering machine.

Or he travelled with her, bemoaning the cappuccinos and gymnasia of the free world; frequently bored, listless, quick to take offence and give it. And there were mornings like this, Cathy waking to one side of the bed, the other unslept in and unsullied, and later, around lunchtime, Frank would reappear, without explanation, his expression daring her to ask. Which at first she had, and, of course, he had lied; or she had made assumptions, right or wrong, and he had responded with counter-accusation and attack. It was after one of these, she had finally said, 'Frank, I don't give a flying fuck what you do or who you do it to, but if I ever contract as much as the

225

tiniest vaginal wart as a result of your fooling around, I will never – and I mean, never – speak to you again.'

Sniping aside, not a great many words had been exchanged on the subject since.

Cathy sat up and surprised herself by not wincing when her feet made contact with the hotel carpet. It had been past midnight when Curtis Woolfe had insisted on buying several bottles of champagne and then doctoring everyone's glass with four-star brandy. For the umpteenth time he proposed a toast to David Tyrell and thanked him for, as he put it, restoring his life's work to the light of a new day. It didn't seem as if Curtis was going to be a recluse any longer. Amongst the other rumours which abounded was one that he had been asked to film Elmore Leonard's non-crime novel *Touch*, with Johnny Depp as Juvenal, the beautiful healer, bleeding from five stigmata on prime-time television and Winona Ryder as the record promoter who falls in love with him.

Cathy, who to date had fielded approaches, official and unofficial, from Kim Basinger, Sharon Stone, Amanda Donohoe, Melanie Griffith, Phoebe Cates, Jamie Lee Curtis, Michelle Pfeiffer, Bridget Fonda and Jennifer Jason Leigh to play Annie Q. Jones, had leaned across and warned Curtis not to hold his breath. In most cases, it was far better to bank the option fee and pray no one ever got around to making the movie.

She was about to get into the shower when the phone rang and she lost her footing to the sudden thought that it was someone calling with the news that something had happened to Frank. Something bad. The skin along her arms pricked cold as she lifted the receiver. Frank, out on the town in a town where men where getting stabbed and worse.

It wasn't Frank, or anything about him; it was Dorothy Birdwell, asking if Cathy would consider joining her for breakfast.

Cathy drew breath. 'Sure, Dorothy. Why not?' And she returned to the shower, relieved, surprised, wondering if there was a certain British etiquette to these occasions she was supposed to observe.

Skelton and his wife were making brittle conversation over the toast and marmalade. Frank Carlucci had not been the only person to stay out all night unannounced. At a little after seven, Kate had phoned from Newark and said she was sorry, but she'd got stuck, missed the last train, missed the bus, there'd been some confusion and she'd missed her lift; it had been all right, though, she'd been able to stay with friends. She hoped they hadn't been too worried. Why, Skelton had asked, his temper conspicuously under wraps, had she not called to tell them this earlier, before the worrying had begun? Kate's explanation had been too complicated and devious to believe or follow.

'What on earth was she doing in Newark in the first place?' Alice had demanded, tightening the belt to her dressing gown.

Skelton had shaken his head; aside from a vague idea that they sold antiques, he had never been certain what people did in Newark anyway.

'What time did she say she would be back?' Alice asked.

'She didn't.'

He had been pouring another cup of rather tired tea, when the doorbell sounded.

'There she is now,' said Alice. 'And she's forgotten her key.'

But it was Resnick, braving another episode of happy families in order to persuade Skelton to apply for a search warrant for the end terrace in Harcourt Road.

'The whole house?' Skelton asked, when he had listened to Resnick's explanations.

'Might as well. While we're about it.'

While Cathy Jordan's breakfast was heavy on the grains and fruit, heavy on the coffee, Dorothy Birdwell's order, carefully enunciated, was for one poached egg – 'And that's poached, mind, properly poached, not steamed' – on dry wholemeal toast and a pot of Assam tea.

'Cathy,' Dorothy Birdwell said, once her egg had been delivered (a poor, shrivelled thing, in Cathy's opinion) to the table. 'I may call you Cathy, may I?'

'Sure, Dottie. That's fine.' She could tell Dorothy didn't like *that*, but the older woman took it in her stride.

'You know, dear, I am not the greatest fan of the kind of thing that you write.'

'Dorothy, I know.'

'In fact, I would go so far as to say, in a way I find it quite pernicious. I mean, this may be old-fashioned of me, I'm sure that it is, but I do think there are certain standards we have a moral obligation to maintain.'

'Standards?' Great, Cathy thought, she's invited me down to receive a lecture, a *grande-dame* rap across the knuckles.

'Yes, dear. A certain morality.'

Cathy speared a prune. 'Let me get this straight. Are we talking sex here?'

'My dear, you mustn't think me a prude. Sex is fine, in its place, I'm sure we would both agree to that.' (We would? Cathy thought, surprised.) 'But its most intimate details, well, I don't think we need to have those spelled out for us, you see. Not in all their personal intricacies, at least. And the violence we most certainly inflict upon one another, if I wish to learn of that, I can always read the newspaper – though, of course, I prefer not to – I do not wish to find myself confronting it inside an otherwise charming work of entertainment. You do see my point, dear?'

In polite company, Cathy wondered, what did you do with a prune stone? Spit it out into your hand, or push it under your tongue and risk being accused of speaking with your mouth full. Either way, it didn't matter. Dorothy's question had been rhetorical.

'But I do want to say that I think the way those ghastly women have been ganging up on you is perfectly dreadful. And in no way could I ever bring myself to support their actions.' She fluttered her hands above the remains of her poached egg. 'That silly business with the paint.'

Cathy nodded. 'To say nothing of the rabbit.'

Dorothy inclined her head forward. 'Yes, dear. It was about that I most particularly wanted to talk.'

'You did?' The antennae in Cathy's brain were beginning to stand up and point, but she couldn't yet tell in which direction. She set down her spoon and fork and waited.

'Marius,' Dorothy said earnestly, 'has always been such a sweet boy, so single-minded in his attentions. I really couldn't begin to tell you all the things he has done for me.' For a moment, Dorothy paused and dabbed at her mouth with a napkin. 'But, I now realise, there are times when he has allowed his – I suppose the only word I can use is devotion – his devotion for me to, well, blind his judgement.' She sipped her tea, grimaced in a ladylike way and added just a touch more milk. 'I am sorry, dear.'

Cathy didn't say anything: she couldn't immediately think of anything – aside from the scatological and the profane – to say. She stared across the table at the older writer instead and, in return, Dorothy Birdwell smiled one of her perfunctory smiles and tipped some more hot water from the metal jug into the teapot.

'Are you telling me,' Cathy finally got out, whispering because she was afraid anything else would be a shout, 'that it was Marius pulled that gross stunt with the rabbit dolled up as a fucking baby?'

It was no good, the whispering hadn't worked; she was shouting now, not quite at the top of her voice, but loud enough to have half the dining room turning round and an assistant manager heading towards them at a fast trot.

'Yes,' Dorothy said, head bowed, 'and I'm afraid that is not all.'

'Not all? Not all? Jesus, what's the little creep done now?'

'My dear, I can only assure you, you have my deepest sympathy and apologies.'

'Sympathy? Apologies?' Cathy was on her feet now, stepping back. 'With all due respect, Dorothy, your apologies, my ass!'

'Really, dear, I don't think this kind of a scene . . .'

'No? Well, I don't give a fuck what you think. What I do give a fuck for is where in sweet hell is your little lapdog, Marius?'

'I dismissed him, of course. I'm afraid there was quite a little scene. He was very upset. Very. But in the circumstances, there was no way in which I could change my mind.' Again, she paused. 'I am sorry, dear, believe me.'

'Where,' Cathy said, 'is Marius now?'

'I can only imagine he's gone to the station . . .'

'Train station? He's heading for where? London? Where?'

'Is everything all right?' the assistant manager asked. 'Is there anything I can do?'

'Keep out of my face,' Cathy snapped.

'Manchester,' Dorothy Birdwell said. 'He has a friend, I think, in Manchester.'

'Thanks,' Cathy said, 'for the breakfast. Thanks,' over her shoulder, as she hurried off towards the nearest phone, 'for everything.'

Resnick had just got back to his office, warrant signed and

delivered into his hand, when Millington beckoned him towards the phone he was holding.

'Cathy Jordan, for you. Likely wants to know if you've finished her book.'

'Hello,' Resnick said, and then listened. After not too many moments, he asked Cathy to stop, take several deep breaths and start again. Slowly. 'Right,' he said when she had finished. 'Right. Yes.' And, 'Right.' He passed the receiver back into Millington's hand. 'Graham,' Resnick said, 'get on to the station. Manchester train, I think it's the one comes across from Norwich. Have it stopped.' He swivelled round to see who was available in the office. 'Lynn, pick up this bloke at the railway station, I'll arrange back-up. Marius Gooding. Late thirties, five seven or eight, shortish hair, dark. Smart in an old-fashioned kind of way. Maybe a blue blazer. Keep it low key, just ask him in for questioning, that's all.'

'What if he refuses?'

'Arrest him.'

'What charge?'

'Threatening behaviour, that'll do. Okay?'

'Right.'

Millington was still talking to the stationmaster; any immediate developments he could handle here. Divine and Naylor had already gone out to relieve Sharon at the house where Marlene Kinoulton had her room. As he left to follow them, Resnick patted his inside pocket, making sure the search warrant was in place.

# Forty-one

They found: one three-quarter-length coat, navy blue; one leather jacket, hip-length, black, badly scuffed along one sleeve; five skirts, three short, one calf-length, one long; two sweaters; one white, ruffle-front shirt; one black-beaded fishnet top with fringing; eight other assorted tops, including two T-shirts and a blue silk blouse with what looked like blood on one sleeve; one black velvet suit; two pairs of jeans, Levi red tab and Gap denim; three pairs of ski pants, one badly torn, possibly cut; five pairs of ribbed woollen tights; seven pairs of regular tights, one red, one blue, mostly laddered or holed; three pairs of stockings, all black, two with seams; two pairs of cotton socks, off-white; eleven pairs of briefs, two of them crotchless; one black suspender belt; three brassières; one bustier; one nurse's uniform, badly stained; one school gymslip, bottle green.

Two pairs of ankle boots, a brown and a bright red; one pair of black leather lace-up boots, knee-length; two pairs of trainers, Reebok and Adidas; seven pairs of shoes.

Condoms: Durex Featherlite and Elite and Mates liquorice ribbed.

K-Y lubricating jelly, three tubes.

Vaseline.

Body Shop body massage oil.

Cotton buds. Smoker's toothpaste. Safeway frequency wash shampoo. A diaphragm. A pregnancy testing kit, unused. Soap. Boots face cream. Nail polish, seven different shades. Nail polish remover. One Philips electric razor, lady's model. One set of make-up brushes. Navy eyeliner. Green mascara. Dejoria hand and body lotion. Aloe hair gel. Max Factor Brush-On Satin Blush. Princess Marcella Borghese Pink Marabu Blusher, hot pink. Three kohl pencils. Three bottles of aspirin. One packet of Nurofen. Lipsticks, seven ranging from Coral Reef to Vermilion. Panty liners. One box of tampons, extra absorbency, five remaining. Perfume. One plastic bottle of Tesco antiseptic mouthwash, peppermint flavour, family size.

Paperback books: *Dark Angel* by Sally Beauman; *The Silence of the Lambs* by Thomas Harris; *Rosemary Conley's Hip and Thigh Diet*; *Rosemary's Baby* by Ira Levin; *Tess of the D'Urbervilles* by Thomas Hardy.

Assorted copies of *Elle, Vanity Fair, She, Cosmopolitan, Fiesta* and *Men Only*.

One video tape of *Sex Kittens Go Hawaii.*

Kleenex.

An Aiwa radio-cassette player, with a copy of the Eurythmics' *Greatest Hits* inside. Assorted cassettes by Phil Collins, Chris Rea, Chris deBurgh and Tina Turner.

One medium-size suitcase, a tan handbag, two imitation leather shoulder bags. Inside one of the bags, a purse containing forty-seven pence in change, several used tissues, a torn half-ticket for the Showcase cinema and a strip of four coloured head-and-shoulder photographs of an unsmiling Marlene Kinoulton.

In a drawer, one Coke can, a hole punched through approximately one inch from the end, around which there were signs of burning. Two boxes of matches. A container of aluminium foil.

In a buckled metal dustbin in the back yard, and partly covered by grey-black ashes, several fragments of dark material – synthetic mixed with cotton – singed, but not burnt.

In the kitchen on the ground floor, somehow stuffed

down behind the piece of narrow, laminated board that separated the washing machine from the swing-top rubbish bin, one dark blue, Ralph Lauren, wool and cotton mix sock with a red polo player logo.

# Forty-two

On its way to Liverpool, via Manchester, the twin-carriage train stopped at Langley Mill, Alfreton and Mansfield Parkway, Bolsover, Sheffield, Edale and Stockport. At that moment, it had stopped within sight of the station, small knots of would-be passengers staring along the track towards it, checking their watches, the overhead clock, the monitor screens on which the slightly flickering green lettering announced no delay and clearly lied.

Lynn almost approached the wrong man, before she spotted Marius, standing close to the window of the buffet, glancing distractedly at the copy of the *Telegraph* folded in his hand. He was wearing a blue blazer, grey trousers with a deep crease, black brogue shoes that shone. There was a smart, double-strapped, leather suitcase at his side.

'Marius?' Lynn said softly, so softly that he only just heard.

'Hmm? I'm sorry?' He looked at a youngish woman, with brown hair cut, he thought, rather savagely short. A round face that seemed, somehow, to have sunk, like early-punctured fruit.

'Is your name Marius?'

'Marius Gooding. Yes, why? Have we met? You'll have to forgive me, I don't remember.'

What she was taking from her pocket was her warrant card. 'I'm a police officer. Detective Constable Kellogg. I...'

He was still smiling his well-mannered, tentative smile

when he struck out, the arm that held the newspaper jerking towards her face. For an instant, Lynn was lost in tall pages of newsprint, crisp and self-righteous editorials, as Marius followed up his blow with a push and took to his heels. Twenty yards along the platform, heading for the stairs, he collided with an elderly couple, loaded down with walking boots, binoculars and rucksacks, off for a day in the Peaks. Spinning around, close to losing his footing, Marius started off again in the opposite direction, aiming for the far side of the buffet, the steps that would take him up to the bridge and the open car park, the streets beyond.

Lynn positioned herself well, feet firmly set; she made a grab for his upper arm, ducking beneath his open hand as he made to fend her off. Her fingers grasped the sleeve of his coat and held fast. Marius's impetus rocked Lynn back, but not totally off-balance. Buttons sprang free as threads snapped.

Most of the people waiting on the platform had ceased worrying about their train. Fingers pointed; cries of 'There!' 'There!' and 'Look!' A black porter, white-haired, too small for his blue-black uniform, hovered anxiously, wanting to do something but unsure what.

Lynn ducked again under a flailing arm and tightened her grip on Marius's opposite wrist, forcing it high towards the middle of his back.

Marius gasped with sudden pain.

'Go on, duck,' someone called admiringly. 'You show 'im right and proper.'

Releasing one of her hands, but not the pressure, Lynn caught hold of Marius's hair, just long enough at the back to give her leverage. Marius cried out as first one knee, then the other struck the concrete platform.

'Nesh bugger!' a voice came dismissively. 'Be scraightin' next, you see if he ain't.'

And, in truth, there were tears in the corners of Marius's eyes.

'Marius Gooding,' Lynn said, a little short of breath, 'I'm arresting you on suspicion of threatening behaviour . . .'

'That's ridiculous! When did I ever threaten . . .?'

'For assaulting a police officer and resisting arrest.'

The socks matched: a perfect fit. The youth with the earrings and the shaved head had remembered finding the second sock, the one that Naylor had triumphantly discovered in the kitchen, but not exactly where. Somewhere on the stairs, he thought? Out in the yard? Anyway, he had assumed it belonged to one of the other lads (knowing it not to be his, his came from a stall in the market or at Christmas and birthdays from Marks and Spencer, via his parents) and had stuffed it in the washing machine along with an accumulated load. How it had ended up wedged where Naylor had found it, he had no idea, except, socks, well, almost as if they had a mind of their own.

The Coke can still contained minute traces of what Resnick was certain would prove to be crack cocaine.

And the blood on the silk blouse? If blood indeed were what it was? Forensic tests would be carried out with as much haste as urgent calls from Resnick himself and Jack Skelton could engender. If the blood proved to match that of the late Peter Farleigh, they were as good as there, home free. If not . . .

'So, Charlie,' Skelton said, turning away from the window behind his desk, clear blue sky beyond the edge of the building outside. 'Are we there, do you think, or what?'

'Nudging close. Got to be. Business with the sock, could be coincidence, but that's asking a lot. Circumstantial, though, at best.'

'This, er, friend of hers – Doris Duke. She'd give

evidence about seeing the blood on Kinoulton's clothing, as well as her deteriorating mental state?'

Resnick shifted his weight in the chair. Close and yet still far. 'Maybe, though what credence the jury'd give to her, I don't know. Something concrete, that's what we need. Positively linking Kinoulton with the attacks, any one of them. That's what we still don't have. If Farleigh's hotel room had given up a clearer print that'd be a start, but no. Smudge and fudge. I can lean on McKimber again, but he's got his own reasons for not wanting to get dragged in too far. Desperate to get back with his wife and kids, poor bugger.'

Skelton coughed, a sudden, sharp attack and Resnick waited while it subsided.

'Course, if we could lay our hands on Kinoulton herself, ask her some questions direct, it might be a different picture.'

Skelton nodded neat agreement and flicked out the sides of his suit jacket before sitting back down. 'Not to fret, Charlie; something'll turn up.'


Once his panic and anger had subsided, Marius Gooding had apologised so abjectly, his tongue must have tasted of the interview room floor. Over and over. You have to believe, I've never done such a thing in my life. Never struck anybody at all, never mind a member of the opposite sex, a woman. No, Lynn, had observed, but you have done other things.

'What? What other things?'

One by one, she showed him the Polaroids that had been taken inside Dorothy Birdwell's hotel suite. *Bitch! Bitch! Bitch!*

Without further hesitation, Marius had demanded a phone call and a solicitor. The call was to Dorothy Birdwell, who listened patiently to his pleading and then hung up without answering.

The solicitor who arrived was actually a solicitor's clerk, Heather Jardine; a forty-three-year-old Scot, divorced with two teenage children, who had abandoned a stuttering career as a playwright and enrolled in evening classes in law. She knew Lynn Kellogg fairly well – they had been through this and similar procedures before – and the two women treated one another with more than grudging respect.

Jardine made sure her client was aware of his rights, had been fairly treated and asked if he might not have a cup of tea.

Lynn waited for Kevin Naylor to join her and set the tape rolling, identifying those present in the room and the time.

'All right, Marius, why don't we talk about the incident with the rabbit first off?'

After a less than ten minutes of prevarication, Marius asked if he could speak to Heather Jardine alone. This allowed, he admitted the incident with the breakfast trolley, said that he had got it ready the previous day and had intended to leave it outside Cathy Jordan's door; seeing the trolley there, waiting to be taken into the room, he had elaborated his plans accordingly.

'And what was the point?' Lynn asked. 'I mean, why go through all of this rigamorole?'

Marius didn't reply immediately. Instead, he swivelled his head and asked Heather Jardine if he had to answer, and she said, no, he did not. Another few moments and he answered anyway. 'It was a symbol,' he said. 'Of what I think of her work.'

'A symbol?' Lynn repeated carefully.

'Yes.'

'Perhaps you'd best explain.'

'Oh, if you'd read any, you'd know.'

'In fact, I have,' Lynn said. 'A little.'

'Then you'll know the awful things she does; little

239

children tortured, abused, defiled.' His face was a mask of disgust.

'Do you have children, Mr Gooding? Yourself?' Lynn asked.

'I don't see what on earth . . .'

'I was interested, that's all.'

'Well, no, then. No, I don't.'

'But it's something you feel strongly about?'

'Yes. Yes, of course. I mean, it's only natural. At least, that's what you would think. And the fact that she's a woman. That it's a woman, perpetrating these things . . .'

'Not exactly, Mr Gooding.'

'What do you mean?'

'I mean, Ms Jordan isn't actually *doing* any of these things. She isn't *doing* anything. Other than writing books. Isn't that so?'

'Yes, but . . .'

'Let me be clear here,' Naylor said, leaning forward for the first time. 'The business with the rabbit, that was to teach Miss Jordan a lesson, frighten her into stopping writing, what?'

'Huh, she's never going to stop, is she? Not with a formula like that. Raking it in. God knows what she must have earned, the last few years. Though, of course, she hasn't got the respect. Not from the critics, nor the affection of her readers. True affection, like Dorothy.'

'That was what you had for Ms Birdwell? Yourself, I mean. Affection and respect?'

'Of course, yes. Why I . . .'

'Then why this?' Lynn's finger hovered over the first of the photographs. 'Or this? Or this?'

Marius closed his eyes. 'I was upset. I . . .'

'You seem to get upset a lot,' Lynn observed quietly.

'I thought . . . I know it was stupid and foolish and very, very wrong . . . but I thought she didn't . . . Dorothy didn't . . . after everything that had happened between us, all the

240

time we had spent together . . .' His body was racked by a sudden sob. 'I thought she didn't love me any more. And I am deeply, deeply ashamed.'

The faint whir of the tape machinery aside, the clipped clicking of the clock, the only sounds were the contortions of Marius's ragged breathing as he struggled to recover himself, regain some element of control. Heather Jardine looked at the notepad on her lap and wished she could light up a cigarette; Kevin Naylor simply looked embarrassed. It was Lynn whose eyes never wavered. If ever anyone was in need of therapy, she was thinking, it's this poor, pathetic bastard and not me.

'These feelings you had about Cathy Jordan,' Lynn asked, 'about her work. Would you say that Ms Birdwell shared those?'

'Most strongly, yes.'

'But she didn't approve of the methods you used to express what you felt?'

'*Grand guignol* was the term she used. Over-theatrical. Too close for Dorothy's liking to the kind of thing you can imagine Jordan doing herself. Though, of course, that was the point.'

'She was happier with the letters, then, was she?' Lynn asked, making a leap of faith.

Marius's face was a picture.

Reaching down for the folder that was leaning against one leg of the table, Lynn extracted copies of the threatening letters Cathy Jordan had received and set them carefully down along the length of the table.

'The letters,' Lynn said. 'Have a good look. Remind yourself.'

Marius wobbled a little in his seat.

'I think,' Heather Jardine said, rising to her feet, 'my client is in need of a break.'

'This interview,' Lynn said, face angled towards the

tape recorder, 'suspended at seventeen minutes past twelve.'

At four minutes to two, Alison and Shane Charlton rang the buzzer at the Enquiries desk below and asked if they could speak to somebody about the Peter Farleigh murder.

# Forty-three

'We had a message,' Alison Charlton said, 'you wanted us to get in touch. We've been away, you see. The weekend.' She smiled at her husband, who smiled, a touch self-consciously, back. 'We came in as soon as we heard.' The wedding rings, Resnick noticed, were shiny and new on their hands.

'The man who died,' Shane Charlton said, 'Alison's mother had saved his picture from the paper. She knew we'd been staying there that night. The same hotel.'

'It was Shane's firm's do,' Alison explained.

'I recognised him, we recognised him right off,' Shane said. 'Didn't we, Ali?'

'Oh, yes.' Her face, bright already, brightened still further. 'We were right facing him, him and her. Going up in the lift. Must have been – I was saying to Shane, wasn't I, Shane? – after that that it happened.'

'What time was this?' Resnick asked. 'Can you remember?'

'It would have been round eleven thirty,' Shane said.

'Nearer quarter past,' Alison said.

'You said, him and her,' Resnick reminded her.

'The woman . . .'

'The woman he was with . . .'

'Nice looking, she was. Well, quite . . .'

'Considering.'

'Like you say, considering. And I think she'd been drinking, don't you, Shane?'

'Didn't act drunk, though, did she? Not exactly.'

'No, it was what she said.'

Shane nodded, remembering.

'Come right out with it, didn't she? We might as well not've been there, might we? For all she cared. Well, I'd never've had the guts to have said it. Not the way she did. One hundred and fifty pounds, she said, just like she was talking about, oh, you know, the weather. A hundred and fifty pounds, to spend the night. I said to Shane after, when we was in our room, would he, like, if he was off on business and on his own, without us being married, of course, would he ever spend that amount of money. And you said you might, d'you remember, but only if she looked like me. I thought that was really sweet.'

She giggled and Shane, embarrassed, fidgeted in his seat.

'Could you describe her?' Resnick asked. 'The woman.'

They looked at one another before Alison answered. 'She was, well, she wasn't young.'

'She was never old,' Shane said.

'Thirty-five, should you say, Shane?'

Shane shrugged. 'Something like that.'

'And she was dressed, you know, not tarty. Smart, I suppose you'd say. She had this black, button-through dress. Satiny, sort of. Sleeveless. A blouse underneath.'

'Colour?'

'Blue. It was, wasn't it, Shane? Quite a dark shade of blue.'

'I don't know. I don't think I ever noticed.'

'I'm sure it was. Midnight blue, I think that's what you'd call it. Midnight blue.'

'How about her hair?' Resnick asked. 'What do you remember about that?'

'Well, it was dark. Definitely dark. And she wore it up like this . . .' Alison demonstrated as best she could with her own hair, even though it was too short to give the proper effect. '. . . pinned, at the back.'

'She had one of those things,' Shane said.

'What things?'

'I don't know, those things you put in your hair.'

'A ribbon? She didn't have a ribbon.'

'No, not that. One of those plastic thingummies . . .'

'A comb?' suggested Alison.

'She wasn't just standing there with a comb in her hair, don't be daft.'

'That's what they're called, though. Combs.'

'Don't you remember?' Shane said.

Alison shook her head.

'It was on the right-hand side,' Shane said.

'Well, that was over towards you. Where you were standing.'

'That's right.'

'What colour was it?' Resnick asked, hanging on to his patience. 'This comb.'

'White. Off-white.' And, as though plucking the name from the air, smile on his face as if his answer had just won a prize. 'Ivory.'

Alison smiled for him.

'I'd like you to look at some photographs,' Resnick said. 'Down at Central Station. The Intelligence Bureau. I'll get someone to drive you down.'

'Oh, great,' Alison exclaimed. 'We'd like that, wouldn't we, Shane?'

The officer set out the photograph of Marlene Kinoulton along with eleven others of similar colouring and general age and appearance. Neither Alison nor Shane picked her out immediately, but when they did, there was little or no uncertainty.

'It was the hair that threw me, wasn't it you, Shane?'

Alison said. 'She didn't have it down when we saw her. Like I told the other policeman . . .'

'Inspector Resnick,' Shane said.

'Inspector Resnick, yes. Like I told him, her hair was up then. Made her look quite a bit different. Bit older, of course, but smarter. I'd wear it like that all the time, if I were her.'

Heather Jardine and Lynn Kellogg were standing out at the rear of the station building, the ground around them dark and slick from the quick summer shower. Heather Jardine was having her second cigarette in succession, all the more necessary having given up smoking from New Year's Eve until a week ago last Friday. Now, it was as if she couldn't get the nicotine back into her bloodstream fast enough.

'So how's it been?' she asked and they both knew what she was referring to, Lynn standing there with a polystyrene cup of lukewarm coffee in her hand, not wanting to talk about the kidnapping and its aftermath, not at all, but understanding the other woman's need to ask, the concern.

'Not so bad,' Lynn said. 'You know . . .' Letting it hang.

'I don't suppose,' Heather said, 'it's the kind of thing you ever really forget.'

Lynn swallowed a mouthful more coffee; though the sun had come back out, the recent rain had left a nip in the air and she caught herself wishing she had worn a cardigan, some kind of a sweater.

'He's not come up for trial yet, either, has he?'

Lynn shook her head.

Heather drew smoke in heavily and held it in her mouth before exhaling. 'These letters, they're pretty nasty, I know. Threatening, it's true. But even if you could prove in court he actually did send them, there's never any real sense he was intending to carry any of those threats out.'

Lynn let her continue.

'I suppose if you took some of it literally, there might be a charge of threat to kill, but well . . . I don't think the CPS would be over the moon about that, do you? Without that, unless the woman wants to press charges herself, take out a civil action, where are you?'

Lynn smiled wearily. 'Public Order Act, section five.'

'Ah, you'd not bother. Most your boss is likely to press for, bung him up before the magistrate and have him bound over.'

Lynn had a mouthful more coffee and tipped the remainder out on to the wet ground. 'And what about all the rest?'

'Resisting arrest?'

'Assault.'

Heather stubbed out the butt of her cigarette on the sole of her shoe. 'First offence, no record, previous good behaviour. I'd be surprised if it got anywhere near court, and if it did, any barrister worth half his fee would argue a hole through the prosecution a mile wide.'

'Maybe.'

'If I'm wrong,' Heather laughed, 'I'll buy you a bottle of twenty-year Macallan.'

Not really a drinker, Lynn took this to be an impressive offer. 'Shall we go back in? At least, we can make him wriggle and squirm a bit longer.' She shuddered, not from the cold. 'It's not just his public-school accent or that pathetic little moustache, don't know what it is, but there's something about him, makes my skin crawl.'

Involuntarily, Heather had begun scratching her thigh. 'Mine, too.'

Skelton was standing behind his desk, about as close to being at ease as he ever seemed to get. 'Pulled in all the extra bodies I can, Charlie. Go through the city tonight like a fine-tooth comb. If she's still here, we'll find her.'

'If not?' Resnick asked.

'Then we'll release her picture in the morning.'

# Forty-four

*'. . . Police today took the unusual step of releasing a photograph of a woman they wish to interview in connection with a number of attacks on men, including the murder of Peter Farleigh, whose body was found with fatal stab wounds . . .'*

Susan Tyrell reached over and pushed one of several preset buttons, switching the radio to Classic-FM. 'Did you see the picture, David?'

'Mm? Sorry, which picture?' He was standing by the microwave, concentrating on the controls; one second too many and the croissants would be reduced to slime. Close by stood the matt black espresso machine he had talked Susan into buying him the Christmas before last and which he had never learned to use.

'In the paper,' Susan said. 'The woman they think's been stabbing all those men.'

'On the game, isn't she?'

'So it says.'

The microwave pinged and David slid the warm croissants on to plates. It was warm enough again for them to sit out in the garden, make use of the deckchairs Susan had picked up on sale at Homebase. He picked up the paper from where Susan had left it and carried it back to his chair. Centre columns, page three. 'Marlene Kinoulton, doesn't have much of a ring to it, does it? Not exactly stunning, either. Can't quite imagine who'd want to shell out for her.'

'Really?' Susan said, pouring the coffee. 'I should have thought she was just your type.'

David laughed. 'What on earth's that supposed to mean?'

'Oh, you know, one of those raddled creatures you fantasise about, short on morals and long on hearts of gold. I can remember you dragging me off to see *Cutter's Way* . . .'

'Jeff Bridges.'

'. . . just for the scene where Lisa Eichhorn looks so pained and awful after he's walked out on her. What did you say? You'd never seen a woman looking so bereft . . .'

'Or beautiful.'

'Right.' Susan broke into the croissant with her fingers. 'And then she gets killed.'

David raised an eyebrow and passed her the jam. 'Goes with the territory.'

'Prostitutes and whores, you mean? Victims.'

'I suppose.'

Susan looked at him hard. 'I wonder why they're always the ones you fancy so much?'

A butterfly landed for an instant on David's sleeve, then fluttered off towards the cotoneaster. 'I liked Julie Andrews once.'

'You were seven. And you're avoiding the issue.'

'Is it an issue?'

Susan brushed crumbs from the front of her blouse. 'It might be.'

David wriggled his lean body against the striped canvas. Just when he was having a nice, relaxing morning for a change. 'Then I suppose it's to do with – oh, you know what it's to do with – fallen angels, forbidden fruit.'

'Like her?' Susan said, nodding in the direction of Marlene Kinoulton's picture in the newspaper. 'But you don't fancy her.'

'That's different.'

'Why? Because she's not pretty, screen-star pretty?'

'For God's sake, Susan, because she's real. And because what goes with her is real.'

'Such as?'

'How long a list do you want? Herpes, gonorrhoea, Aids.'

'Oh,' Susan said, 'for a moment I thought you were talking about commitment.'

'Commitment? To a whore?'

'Yes. Why not? That's what it is, after all. You start off fancying her, you decide to pay for her, you end up sticking a condom on your cock and sticking it inside her. I'd say that called for quite a lot of commitment, wouldn't you?'

David had jerked to his feet, spilling coffee down one leg of his trousers and across the seat of the deckchair. 'Christ, Susan, what's this all about?' He couldn't remember her so animated, so angry.

Susan put down her cup and plate, folded her hands across her lap. 'The night before last, I went out and picked up a man.'

David stared at her, mouth slightly open. Just stared. As if hearing it for the first time, he heard the harsh, bright call of the magpie on the overhanging branch of their neighbour's pear tree.

'I picked him up in a bar and we went to a hotel.'

David turned towards the bottom of the garden, walked five paces, turned back around. 'Look, Susan, I'm sorry, I can't deal with this now. I have to go.'

All she could do was shake her head from side to side and laugh.

Hurrying past her into the house, David froze at the entrance to the hall. Where was his briefcase? Where were his keys? What was going on with his life?

'David,' Susan touched his arm and he flinched.

'David, look at me.' And she leaned back against the front door the way she thought Claire Trevor might have done, Barbara Stanwyck or Jane Greer. 'I didn't tell you so that you could deal with it. It's done. Over. I just wanted you to know.'

As he tried to push past her, reaching for the handle to the door, she added, close to his ear, 'I thought you might look at me differently, that's all.'

He hesitated for a second before tugging at the door and Susan stepped to one side, letting him go.

She was still standing in the hallway when she heard the car start, tyres spinning a little as it sped away. She hadn't told him exactly how drunk she had needed to be, the way excitement and revulsion had tasted in her mouth; nor about the way her face had looked in the bathroom mirror before she had decided to cut and run.

Susan looked at her watch: nine seventeen. They would have realised at school by now she wasn't coming in. She was surprised they hadn't phoned. In the living room, she poured herself a generous glass of gin, lit a cigarette: isn't that the kind of thing Lisa Eichhorn would do? Claire Trevor. Barbara Stanwyck. Jane Greer. All those women who rarely made it in one piece, through to the final reel?

# Forty-five

Resnick sat at the coffee stall, taking his time through his second espresso of the morning. A sudden shower had surprised him as he was walking his way down from the Woodborough Road and he had ducked into the market by the rear entrance.

Marlene Kinoulton's photograph was prominently displayed on the front page of the local paper. All of the previous night's searching had brought them nothing but sore feet and abuse. Urgent messages had gone out to Leicester, Sheffield, Derby, the other cities where it was known she had worked. It was too early to gauge the extent and accuracy of public response, though early signs were far from promising; what had come through via the information room so far had been patchy and poor. Nowadays, it seemed, unless you went on television, *Crimewatch UK* or one of those, chances of lighting a fire under the public were poor. And he supposed, in time, if Kinoulton weren't traced, that was what would happen. Actors and a film crew and a researcher asking to interview him so that they could get it just right. *'Later tonight, on* Crimewatch UK, *the intriguing story of the missing prostitute and the hotel-room murder . . .'*

A woman with a child of under two clinging to her skirt, climbed on to the vacant stool next to him, lifted the child into her lap and stuck a dummy in its mouth. Directly across from where he was sitting, a man he had put away for two stretches for burglary, joked with one of the Asian stallholders over a cup of tea. He did not acknowledge Resnick, nor Resnick him. When the festival was over and all the visitors and writers and film-makers had returned to wherever they had come from, this was what it would come back to. People who lived here; who did what and to whom?

'Another espresso, inspector?'

'Thanks. Better not.' Lifting the small cup to his mouth, he swallowed down what was left. Dark and bitter, why was it so good?

Cathy Jordan and Frank Carlucci had tiptoed around each other, exchanging no more words than were necessary. Neither of them wished to begin a conversation that could reopen old wounds and, in all probability, inflict new ones. Mollie Hansen had phoned earlier to enquire whether Cathy were happy to be interviewed on *Kaleido-scope* that evening, she had to ring John Goudie back and let him know.

Now Mollie was there at the hotel, making sure that the travel arrangements to London were clear; after the radio programme, there was a book signing in the Charing Cross Road at Murder One, at which point the publicist working for Cathy's UK publisher would take over and Mollie was in the clear. That is, she could get on with attending to the rest of the festival.

She was leaning against the counter at reception, just through speaking to Cathy on the internal phone, when Resnick came in.

'Not more trouble?' she asked, intercepting him with a guarded smile.

'No.' He realised he was staring at her and looked away.

Mollie laughed. 'My God! You don't like it, do you?'

'What?'

'And now you're embarrassed to have noticed.' She

had had a small stone fitted in the right side of her nostril, bright blue.

'Not at all,' Resnick blushed.

'You don't approve, body adornment?'

He shook his head. 'I don't suppose I've ever thought about it. I was surprised, that's all.'

Mollie smiled. 'Do you like it, though? Be honest. I'd like to know what you think.'

'I think you looked fine before.'

It was Mollie's turn, almost, to flush. 'You're here to see Cathy?'

He nodded. 'Just quickly. I shan't be long.'

'If I hang on,' Mollie said, 'I don't suppose I could scrounge a lift?'

'If I had the car with me you could.'

'Never mind. Some other time maybe?'

'Maybe.'

'Well,' backing away, 'see you around, I guess. Come to a movie, why don't you?'

'I'll try.'

Mollie raised a hand, fingers spread, and turned towards the doors. By the time she had walked from sight, Resnick was standing by the lifts, watching the numbers descend.

When Resnick got out of the lift on Cathy Jordan's floor, Frank Carlucci was waiting to get in. The two men exchanged cursory nods before Frank, hands in pockets and ample shoulders hunched, stepped inside and the doors closed behind him.

Cathy opened the door on Resnick's first knock and was surprised to see him standing there and not Frank.

'Sorry. Figured you for the penitent husband, back to crave forgiveness.'

'Does he have something to be forgiven for?'

Cathy's mouth turned upwards into a smile. 'Don't we

255

all? And wouldn't life be a deadly bore if we did not?' She moved aside to let Resnick enter. 'But in Frank's case, this particular case, I have no idea.' She shrugged. 'Going on his track record, I'm prepared to give him the benefit of the doubt.'

'Innocent as charged.'

Cathy grinned. 'Guilty.'

'Marius likewise.'

'He owned up?'

Resnick nodded.

'The letters as well?'

'Yes.'

Cathy's fist punched the air. 'The bastard! The snivelling lousy bastard!'

'He got a friend in the States to send the letters for him; everything that happened over here was down to him. He swears he never had any intention of carrying any of it through. Just wanted to frighten you, shake you up; make you think about what you were doing.'

'Frighten me?'

'Yes.'

'The little shit!'

'As far as it's possible to tell, my guess is he's telling the truth. It's difficult to see him as actually dangerous, more of a nuisance.'

'If I didn't know better, I'd think you were building up to telling me you're about to let him go.'

Resnick stood there looking at her.

'Jesus! You are! You're going to give him a friendly pat on the head and a warning. Be a good slimebag and don't do it again.' She turned, shaking her head. 'I can't believe it. I can't fucking believe it!'

'Dorothy Birdwell insists she won't press charges. Also, she's paid to have the room set back to rights and the hotel's keen to avoid any adverse publicity.'

Cathy's face was white with anger. 'Which just leaves

me, right? And who the fuck am I, that you should give a good god-damn?'

Resnick took a pace towards her, then a pace back. 'Cathy,' he said.

'What?'

'Whatever you decide to do, it's unlikely, given all the circumstances, that the CPS will recommend prosecution.'

'Shit!' Cathy crossed the room to the whisky bottle, poured a stiff shot and carried it back with her to the settee. 'So what will happen to him? Exactly.'

'Most likely, he'll be bound over not to repeat this or any other behaviour.'

'And then he'll walk?'

Resnick nodded. 'Yes.'

Cathy took one sip at her Scotch and then another. 'Where is he now? You've still got him in custody?'

'Yes, why?'

All energy, Cathy jumped to her feet. 'Fine. I want to see him.'

'I don't know . . .'

'Come on, just see him, right? One final time. Tell him goodbye.'

Resnick looked a long way short of convinced.

'Inspector . . . Charlie . . . Surely it's the least you can do? After all, I'm not exactly about to stick a knife in him, pull out a gun.'

'I still don't know . . .'

'Please.'

'All right. But just five minutes. No more. And I shall have to be there all the time.'

Cathy smiled at him with sweetness dropped in acid. 'But of course.'

The police cells were full so Naylor had stuck Marius Gooding in one of the interview rooms and turned the key.

'Half an hour,' he had said. 'Forty-five minutes. Tops.'

Marius had been there for not far short of three hours. Silent, a uniformed officer had brought him a cup of tea and a copy of a three-day-old *Daily Mail*, which Marius had read through several times, cover to cover.

When Resnick entered, he was quickly on his feet, a protest forming on his lips; then, when he saw who was with him, he remained silent.

'Hello, Marius,' Cathy Jordan said, not halting until she was an arm's length away. 'Been treating you okay, have they?'

Marius looked at her, eyes refusing to focus; Resnick had remained near the door and was picking at something that seemed to have lodged on the cuff of his shirt.

'I just wanted to see what you looked like, remember you, in case there was any chance I might have the misfortune of running into you again. And to thank you. No, really, I mean it. Thank you for showing me how low a piece of phlegm like you can go. Exciting, though, was it, Marius? Give you a little hard-on? Thinking up all that stuff in those letters you sent me. Writing about it. What had happened to those women. Those kids.' A fleck of spittle had landed on Cathy's chin and with the back of a hand she wiped it away. 'Must have known those books of mine pretty well, Marius, to quote them so well. So accurately.'

Marius didn't want to look at her, but he wasn't able to look away.

'Might make a point of asking your therapist about that, your fascination with all those nasty incidents you profess to hate. That is, after you talk to him about your mother, your relationship with her.'

He flinched as if he had been struck and clenched both hands fast by his sides.

'Got to be something there, right? Explain this thing you've got for old women.'

'Cathy,' Resnick said, moving forward. 'I think that's enough.'

'No,' shaking her head. 'No, it's not nearly enough.'

Lightly, he placed a hand on her shoulder. 'It'll have to do.'

She tilted her head towards him and smiled. 'Okay. Okay, Marius. No hard feelings, maybe. Well, not too many. And I do hope, whoever the shrink is you go to see, he can help you sort yourself out.'

She looked at him and the first vestiges of a grateful smile appeared at the edges of Marius's eyes. 'Here,' Cathy said softly. 'Have this to remember me by.' And, with a fast swing of the arm, she hit him hard across the face and he rocked backwards, the ring on her finger opening a cut deep below his eye.

Resnick grabbed her but she was already stepping away. 'Well,' she said, 'let's see if your DPP or whatever it is, reckons it's worth prosecuting me for that.'

Releasing her, Resnick pulled a handkerchief from his pocket and gave it to Marius to hold against his face. Then he opened the door and called along the corridor for someone to administer first aid.

Cathy paused in the doorway. 'Then there's a tooth for a tooth, Marius. You remember that one, don't you?'

They stood on the steps outside the police station, watching the traffic playing ducks and drakes with the traffic lights around Canning Circus.

'I tricked you,' Cathy saaid. 'For that, I'm sorry.'

'You had that in your mind all the time?'

'Pretty much.'

'I should have known.'

Quickly, she glanced at him. 'Maybe you did.'

Resnick didn't reply.

A pair of uniformed officers exited behind them and walked around the corner to the official car park.

Cathy offered Resnick her hand and he took it in a firm grip. 'That book of mine,' Cathy said, 'if you ever finish it, you could always drop me a line, let me know what you think.'

'Of course.'

They both knew, whatever his intentions, he most probably would not. Cathy gave him her card regardless and he slipped it down into the top pocket of his coat.

'See you then.'

'Yes, see you.'

For some minutes he stood and watched her go, a tall woman with cropped red hair, wearing a red silk shirt, blue jeans and heeled boots, walking away.

# Forty-six

At a little short of nine the next morning, Sarah Farleigh was sitting in Resnick's office, black leather handbag resting in her lap. She was wearing a black suit that looked new, hemline stretched across her knees.

'Asked to see you, sir,' Naylor explained outside. 'In the circumstances, I thought you'd not mind.'

'Okay, Kevin. That's fine.'

There was a moment to look at her, through the glass, before she turned. One of her hands moving distractedly from her side to the brooch on the lapel of her coat, from the corner of her mouth to a stray twist of hair.

'Sarah.' As he entered she rose and came towards him and, although he held out his hand, she moved inside it and gave him a brief hug. Where her face had rested on his sleeve, it had left a smudge of make-up and, stepping back, she brushed it away.

'Is there any news?'

'News?'

'The woman – have you caught her?'

'Not yet.' Resnick went round behind his desk and sat down.

'I don't suppose you've any idea why she did it?'

'Not really. Not till we talk to her.'

'And if you don't?'

'We will.'

'You sound sure.'

'Murders,' Resnick said, 'one area where our clear-up rate is good.'

261

'I thought that was usually the – what do you call it? – family ones?'

'Domestics. Yes, I suppose it is. More often than not.'

Sarah had resumed her seat and retrieved her bag from the floor. Now she opened it and took out a photograph, square and a little creased, bent at the edges. 'I don't know what I was doing, looking through stuff of Peter's, I suppose, and I found this.' She leaned forward and placed it on the desk, for Resnick to swivel round.

It showed Sarah and Ben Riley in a rowing boat, Sarah leaning back, her face, sharper-featured than now, smiling out from beneath the brim of a large, white sun-hat. Ben had the oars in his hands, a cigarette dangling from one side of his mouth. He looked – the phrase leapt immediately to Resnick's mind, somewhat archaic, but appropriate – as pleased as Punch.

'You know where that was taken, don't you?'

Resnick looked again. There was a small, curved bridge in the background, flowering shrubs. 'It's up by the university, isn't it? The lake?'

'That's right. And you know who's behind the camera.'

'No, I don't think so.'

'It's you.'

He looked at it once more, trying to cast back. 'I'm sorry, I'm afraid I don't remember.' He made to give the photograph back to her, but she held up her hand and shook her head. 'Keep it.'

'Well, I . . .'

'I thought you might like it. You never know, you might see Ben some time. Or write . . .'

'Okay. Thanks.' Resnick glanced at it again before sliding it into the drawer to the right of his desk.

'If you don't find her, this woman, I mean, suppose it takes a long time – it could now, couldn't it? – what happens about the body?'

'As I told you when I phoned, it remains the property of the coroner.'

'But not forever. What if you never find her?'

'Sarah, I don't think that'll be the case. Believe me.'

'So I can't bury him?'

'Not yet. I'm sorry.'

For several moments, she closed her eyes; body held taut. 'A memorial service, then. That's what I'll do. There'll have to be something.'

Resnick was on his feet. 'As long as you think you're up to it, that sounds a good idea.'

'Thanks.' This time, she was the one offering her hand and he took it. 'You will come?' she said.

'Of course.'

Sarah smiled her thanks.

'I'll see you out.'

'Nice car,' Resnick said, as Sarah unlocked the Volvo. He said it as much to make conversation as anything else; since leaving his office, she had fallen quiet. Not that that surprised him; he was glad to see her coping as well as she seemed to be.

'It was Peter's. I've got an old Fiat, just for nipping about, locally. Longer distances, I use this if I can. It's a lot more reliable.'

'Well, take care, Sarah. Drive safely. And you will let me know about the memorial service?'

Millington met him on the stairs. 'Call from Sheffield, possible sighting of the Kinoulton woman; sounds promising. Local CID're running it down.'

'Good.'

'Oh, and the report's in on that blouse found at the house. It was blood. And it is the same group as Farleigh's.'

'Let's hope Sheffield turn up trumps, then. Put this one away before it gets too long in the tooth.'

# Forty-seven

Sheffield, not for the first time, was a wash-out. As were Birmingham, Bradford, the Chapeltown district of Leeds. There was a twice-confirmed rumour that Marlene Kinoulton had been working the streets of Butetown, down near the Cardiff docks. A Vice Squad officer had warned her off, only recognising her from the circulated description when it was too late; a bevy of the local girls had backed her into a corner and given her a tongue-lashing, warned her to piss off out of their territory or they'd get one of the pimps to see to her face and legs.

Millington and Divine drove down to Cardiff; Mark Divine pleased at the chance to make a rugby player's pilgrimage to Cardiff Arms Park. It was about the only part of the trip that worked out well. The co-operation which the local force had promised was dissipated in a miasma of broken promises and missed appointments. They did persuade one of the runners working for a high-flown dealer to talk to them over a late-night biriani and chips. Marlene Kinoulton he swore he'd seen just two nights before, sold her the last two rocks he'd had.

Millington and Divine stayed another couple of days and, as far as they were able, turned the underbelly of the city upside down. Afterwards, only one thing seemed certain: Marlene Kinoulton had been there and now she had gone.

Resnick allowed Marian Witczak to talk him into accompanying her to a midsummer dance at the Polish Club and, after several generous glasses of bison grass vodka, remembered how to polka. A card from Cathy Jordan, a street scene in Dublin, reminded him that he had still to finish *Dead Weight* and, between other things, he got not quite to the end, but almost.

Debbie Naylor waylaid Kevin one night with a bottle of wine and something racy she'd bought from an advertisement in the back of the Sunday paper and now she woke in the mornings with carry-cots and Babygros dancing before her eyes.

Kate Skelton, who not so long before had driven her parents close to despair, shoplifting to pay for her drug problem, astonished them by getting three good A levels and applying to university.

Sharon Garnett applied to be transferred from the Vice Squad into CID and her application was turned down.

Lynn Kellogg came into Resnick's office one morning at the end of July and told him she was seriously thinking about moving back to East Anglia and had been sounding out an old friend about a vacancy in a Norwich force.

'Can we talk about this?' Resnick said. He felt as if something solid was being pulled out from beneath his feet. He felt something he didn't understand.

'Of course,' Lynn said, and waited.

'I meant, I suppose I meant, not here.'

'You're busy.' His desk was the usual clutter of reports and forms, empty sandwich bags.

'Yes. No. It's not that. I suppose . . . well, to be honest, you've taken me by surprise.'

'Yes, well, it's nothing definite yet, although . . .' She stopped, reminded of the look that had come into her father's eyes, the first time she had told him she was applying to join the police. 'How about a drink then?' she said. 'If you want to talk it through.'

'It's a long time since you were at the coffee stall,'

Resnick said. 'They've just about given up asking where you've got to.'

Lynn smiled; just a little, not too much; just with the eyes. 'All right.'

Amongst the other things on Resnick's desk, unopened, the invitation to the service at Wymeswold Church dedicated to the memory of Peter Farleigh.

He thought she'd changed her mind. Several of the stallholders had taken in the goods that hung around the outside of their sections and pulled down the metal sides. Resnick had read the cricket report in the local paper twice.

'Sorry,' Lynn said, a little out of breath, her cheeks flushed with colour for the first time in weeks. 'Something cropped up.'

'Important?'

'No, just fiddly.'

'Here,' the assistant said, setting down a cappuccino, 'for you the first one free.'

'Thanks,' Lynn said, 'but best not.' She pushed a pound coin across the counter and grinned. 'Probably consitutes a bribe.'

Now they were there, there was no rush to talk. Resnick sipped his espresso as Lynn tasted the chocolatey froth from a cheap metal spoon. With a thump and clatter, another stall was locked away for the night.

'Your dad,' Resnick finally said. 'Is that the problem?'

'How d'you mean?'

'The reason you're thinking of moving back.'

'Oh, partly, yes. In a way.'

'I thought he was better. Doing okay. Stable, at least.'

'He is. But cancer, you know, so hard not to think, whatever the doctors say, it's not going to come back. Somewhere else.'

'There's no sign, though?'

267

'No, not yet. No. Touch wood.' She glanced around. The couple who ran the corner vegetable stall were laughing together, lighting up, just for a moment holding hands. 'It's my mum, more.'

'She's not ill?'

Lynn shook her head. 'Just works herself up into such a state.'

Resnick finished his coffee; wondered if there were time for one more. 'That's the reason, then? To be near your mother, close?'

Lynn drank some of her cappuccino. 'Not really, no.'

Something had begun pressing against the inside of Resnick's left temple, urgent, hard.

Lynn tried to choose her words with care. 'Ever since what happened. When I was ... taken prisoner. I can't stop, haven't been able to stop myself, well, thinking ...'

'That's only natural ...'

'I know. Yes, I know. And Petra says ... That's my doctor. Petra Carey. She says I have to take time, open myself to it; she says there's a lot I have to talk myself through.'

'Like what?'

'Like you.'

Resnick's left eye blinked. If the assistant turned around, he would order another espresso, but, of course, the man continued stubbornly washing down the counter at the other side.

Lynn was speaking again, her voice measured, trying to talk the way she would to Petra Carey if Petra Carey were there. 'Tied up there at night, in the caravan, never knowing when he might come in. Knowing what had happened to that other girl, knowing what he'd done, what he might do. I was scared, of course I was scared. Terrified. Though I knew the last thing I could afford to do was show it. To him. And underneath it all, somehow -- I'm not sure, I was dreaming a lot of the time, I think I must have been; trying not to let myself fall asleep, but not being able to stop myself – but somehow there was always this idea that it would be all right, that someone – no, you – that you would come and – God, it sounds pathetic now, doesn't it, hearing myself say this – but that you would come and save me.' For a moment, Lynn pressed her face into her hands and closed her eyes. 'Except,' she went on, 'it wasn't always you. It wasn't as straightforward as that. Sometimes, I would think it was you but then when I saw your face, it was my dad. You were ... my dad.' She shook her head, low towards her hands, which were folded over one another now, beside her cup. 'It isn't even that simple. There are things, other things, I can't, I don't want to say.'

Resnick put one hand over hers, ready to retract it if she pulled away.

'I haven't been able to talk to you,' Lynn said, not looking at him, looking away. 'Not really talk, not since it happened.'

'I know.'

'I just haven't felt comfortable, being with you.'

'No.'

'And it's difficult. So bloody difficult!' With surprise, the assistant looked round at her raised voice. 'And I hate it.'

'Yes,' Resnick said, taking away his hand. And then, 'So this is why you want to go; this rather than your mother, anything at home.'

'Oh, they want me back there, of course. My dad doesn't say so, but my mum, she'd love it. But if it wasn't for this other business, no, I don't think I'd go.'

'And you don't think we could work it out. Somehow, between us, I mean. Maybe, now you've started talking about it?'

'That's what Petra says.'

'That you, we, should talk it over?'

Lynn nodded, still not looking at him. 'Yes.' And when Resnick was silent, she asked him what he was thinking.

'I was wondering why you hadn't felt able to come to me before?'

'You're hurt, aren't you?'

'By that? Yes, I suppose I am.'

'She said you would be. But, I don't know, I just couldn't.'

'You were afraid of what I'd say?'

'No. What I would.'

Resnick's intention, that evening, had been to go along to the refurbished Old Vic and listen to the new Stan Tracey Duo. But by the time he'd fed the cats, fiddled around with a smoked ham and stilton sandwich, he didn't seem to feel like going out. Sitting on the back step with a bottle of Czech Budweiser, he found out how Annie Q. Jones was getting on, embroiled in plot and counter-plot in the last fifty pages of *Dead Weight*. Poor Annie, sapped on the head from behind, going down a narrow side street in pitch darkness – at least she had her lover to provide a little comfort in the small hours.

His neighbours, also enjoying the light, pleasantly warm evening, had thrown open their windows and were treating him to muffled television laughter and the smell of chicken frying. Resnick finished his beer, took the book back inside, page at the start of the final chapter folded down, and set off to walk down into the city.

He arrived at the pub in time for the last two numbers. Stan Tracey, hunched over the keyboard, angularly manoeuvring his way through 'Sophisticated Lady', taking the tune into seemingly impossible blind alleys and then escaping through a mixture of finesse and sheer power. Finally, Tracey and an absurdly young-looking Gerard Presencer on trumpet had elided their way along a

John Coltrane blues, the audacity of Presencer's imagination more than matched by his technique.

Just once, in the middle of the trumpeter's solo, eyes closed, Resnick had seen a perfect vision of Lynn, her face, round and open and close to his. And then it had gone. While the applause was still trickling away, he lifted his empty glass and set it down by the end of the bar, nodded towards the landlord, and made his way towards the door.

Back home again, Bud nestled in beside his feet, Resnick finished the book:

> *I know that Reigler has suffered another stroke, but still I'm not prepared for what I find. One side of his body seems totally paralysed, the same side of his face sunken and lined, one dark eye staring out. His speech is slurred, but I get the jist. As confessions go this one's pretty simple and to the point. He nods when he's finished and I switch off the tape that's been resting on one arm of his wheelchair.*
>
> *Seems he's got one more request.*
>
> *I don't know why I should raise a finger for him and then I find out what it is.*
>
> *The gun is in the drawer and I'm careful only to handle it with the gloves I conveniently have in the pocket of my coat. There's a wind got up from the ocean and the temperature has plummeted. There's one shell in the chamber and just a moment of doubt when I think it might be intended for me, but one more look at his wrecked body and I know that's not the case.*
>
> *The trigger mechanism seems light, though even so, I'm not convinced, the state that he's in, he's going to be able to find enough*

*pressure, but I figure that's his problem, not
mine.*

*I hear the gunshot as I'm climbing into my
car, and I guess it's worked out all right. I
don't go back. There'll be a call box on my
way home and I can pull over and perform my
anonymous civic duty. I risk the last ten miles
way above the limit. I know Diane's going to
have something ready, maybe even something
we can eat in bed, and I don't want to keep her
waiting.*

*Well, no longer than she finds enjoyable.*

So that was how it ended, he thought, clear-cut and happy,
no loose ends. With a wry smile, Resnick closed the book
and reached across to switch off the light.

# Forty-eight

The church was small and most of the pews were filled
with the Farleigh family and neighbours, Peter Farleigh's
colleagues from work and a few representatives of
organisations he had regularly supplied. After several
hymns, carefully chosen but randomly sung, the vicar
spoke with a pious briskness of Peter's devotion as
husband and father, his dedication and selflessness as a
breadwinner, the admiration and respect with which he
was held within the community. The managing director of
Farleigh's firm, who turned out to be Japanese, talked
briefly and in perfect, Oxford-accented English of his late-
lamented model employee. Then the youngest Farleigh
daughter, wearing a long, loose-skirted floral dress, sang
'Where Have All the Flowers Gone', accompanying
herself on the guitar.

People cried.

Resnick stood in line to grasp Sarah's hand and kiss her
on the cheek, express his condolences to her children,
strung out awkwardly beside her. 'You will come back to
the house afterwards?' He looked into her red-rimmed
eyes and agreed.

There were scarcely more than a dozen there when
Resnick arrived: immediate family, and the vicar,
exchanging pieties with Peter's mother, who had the good
fortune to be profoundly deaf.

Resnick ate several skimpy sandwiches, making them
more palatable by taking separate triangles of tongue and
cheese and pressing them together. He chatted in a

desultory manner with Peter and Sarah's son, who replied in monotones and couldn't wait to get away.

'I don't know what she's looking so sad about,' the older daughter spat out towards Resnick, glancing over to where her mother was standing. 'It wasn't as if she loved him anyway.'

Overhearing this, her younger sister burst into tears.

Once he noticed people beginning to slip away, Resnick retreated to the kitchen and rolled up his sleeves, stacking and washing up the glasses, cups and plates. The son borrowed his mother's Fiat to drive his grandparents to the station and the two sisters, reconciled, went for a walk.

'Thanks for staying, Charlie,' Sarah said, when she had seen the last visitor off. 'And for doing all of that.'

'It's nothing. Glad to be of help.'

'Well, it's sweet of you. And now I need a drink. You?'

'No, thanks.'

'Driving?'

'That's right.'

Sarah smiled, the first he had seen all day. 'You were always that way, Charlie. I remember. Careful to the point of being almost boring. Ben, now, he didn't care. Not that much. I've driven back with him when he probably wasn't safe at all.'

'Sarah,' Resnick said, more sharply than he had perhaps intended.

'What?'

'Stop it. For heaven's sake.' He wiped suds and water from his hands with the tea towel and dropped it on the counter beside the sink.

'Charlie. I'm sorry, I don't understand. I was only . . .'

'I know what you were doing. Bringing up Ben again and again, pretending we were forever doing things together, one big happy trio.'

'Elaine, too . . .'

'Sarah, aside from that time at the lake I doubt if we

274

spent more than a couple of dozen hours together, all told.'

'Charlie, I don't know, is that true? It certainly isn't the way I remember it. I . . . Oh, Charlie, I just keep thinking about him, that's all. All day today, when I should have been thinking about Peter . . .'

'You had your chance to marry him and you turned him down.'

'And I made a mistake.'

'I'm sorry.'

'God, Charlie, I was wrong. You're not the way you used to be. You've changed. You've become hard, mean.'

'Maybe that's the way I have to be.'

She drank some of her sherry, barely tasting it, then set the glass back down. 'To do this?'

'Yes.'

She walked into the living room and he followed her through; the French windows into the garden had been left open and there was a breeze. A cat, ginger and black, that Resnick had not noticed before, was curled up on one of the armchairs.

'Yours?'

She shook her head. 'Next door's.'

For an instant the words caught at the back of Resnick's throat. 'You used his car, didn't you?' he said.

Sarah looked back at him. 'Yes,' she said. She seemed smaller already, as if she had shrunken a little inside her smartly tailored suit. Her green eyes had ceased to glow.

'There was a list on the computer, vehicles that had checked into the hotel garage. When I saw the number had been traced through to Peter as owner, I assumed he had been using it himself.' Resnick looked across at her, but whatever she had focused on was way down the garden, beyond the shrubbery. 'It took a while for all our routine checks on the car hire returns to go through the computer, but when they did, there was a Ford Granada under Peter's name.'

'Two and two then, was it, Charlie?' She had turned to face him now, moved towards him; the shine was back in her eyes but it was of quite a different nature than before.

'Most of the prints we lifted from the hotel room were too smudged to be of any use; there was one inside the rim of the bath, only partial, but enough to get a match off the invitation you sent me . . .'

'You bastard!'

'Not enough in itself.'

'Too bad. Too bloody bad!' She turned her back to him, leaned her head and arm against the mantelpiece and started to cry. Resnick left her to it. After a while, she pulled a small handkerchief from her sleeve and dabbed at her eyes.

'He phoned me that morning, telling me to take the car to the garage; as if I needed reminding, like a complete child. And would I run around the house after him, picking up his dry cleaning and take that in as well?' She blew her nose. 'He said he'd ring me that evening, but, of course, he didn't. He rarely did, when he was away, and I knew why. I knew what he would be doing, some cheap little tart or other, some whore. And, of course, I was right. I was right.'

She started to cry again, really cry this time, and Resnick went over to her and placed his hands, lightly, on her upper arms.

'I was outside, in the corridor, when she left. I can even describe her for you, if you want. Except that her hair was up, she was pretty much like her photograph. In the paper. When I went in, Peter was on the floor, just past the end of the bed. He was crawling towards the bathroom, crawling on his hands and belly and leaving these trails, like a snail, except they were red, all along the floor. I felt sick. I couldn't stop watching him. It was horrible, disgusting.

He got himself up on to the side of the bath and then stopped, Collapsed. Unconscious. The knife, the one she'd stabbed him with, it was still on the bed; I could see the handle sticking out from the sheet. Maybe she'd looked for it and not found it, I don't know. Anyway, I took it and went into the bathroom. Peter still hadn't moved. I thought I could still hear his breathing, but I couldn't be sure. I remember his buttocks were all flabby and loose, almost white except for these purple spots. And the awful flab of his belly, pushed out on both sides by the bath.' Resnick felt, rather than saw, her shake against his hands. 'I only stabbed him once, in the side. I couldn't believe how easily the blade went in.'

Resnick had heard the car pull up a while since, back along the road. He wondered how long they had been out in the garden, how much they had overheard? He called out and Millington and Lynn Kellogg stepped inside.

'Sarah Farleigh,' he said, 'I am arresting you for the murder of Peter Farleigh . . .' He was glad she was looking away again, not directly up at him; glad to have got the business done before the children returned.

# Curtis Woolfe

## FILMOGRAPHY

*Death by Night*
RKO, 1994
Photography: Nicholas Musuraca
Screenplay: Albert Maltz and Warren Duff
Jean Brooks, Lawrence Tierney, Paul Lukas

*Angel Eyes*
Republic, 1945
Photography: John Alton
Screenplay: Curtis Woolfe and Steve Fisher
Bill Elliott, Albert Dekker, Martha MacVicar

*Dark Corridor*
RKO, 1946
Photography: Robert De Grasse
Screenplay: Lawrence Kimble and Daniel Mainwaring
(uncredited)
Gail Russell, Albert Dekker, Kent Smith

*Cry Murder*
Republic, 1947
Photography: John Alton
Screenplay: Curtis Woolfe and Doris Miller
Dane Clark, Coleen Gray, Luther Adler

*Dead Ringer*
Monogram, 1948
Photography: Mack Stengler
Screenplay: Steve Fisher
Steve Brodie, Jennifer Holt, Myron Healey

*High Tension*
Allied Artists, 1952
Photography: Joseph F. Biroc
Screenplay: Curtis Woolfe and Warren Douglas
Dan Duryea, Dorothy Malone, Charles McGraw

*Lone Justice*
Allied Artists, 1953
Photography: Ernest Miller
Screenplay: Steve Fisher
Bill Elliott, Coleen Gray, Myron Healey

*The Last Gun*
Allied Artists, 1954
Photography: Ernest Miller
Screenplay: Daniel Mainwaring (as Geoffrey Homes)
Bill Elliott, Peggie Castle, Dorothy Malone

*Days of the Gunfighter (I Giorni des Pistoleros)*
BRC Produzione Film/Estela Films, 1965
Photography: Francisco Marin
Screenplay: Jesus Navarro
Rod Cameron, Hally Hammond (Lorella de Luca), Henry
Silva

*Second Unit Director* (uncredited)

*A Long Ride From Hell (Vivo per la tua Morte)*
Cinerama Releasing Corporation, 1968
Director: Alex Burks (Camillo Bazzoni)
Screenplay: Steve Reeves, Camillo Bazzoni
Steve Reeves, Wayde Preston, Silvana Venturelli

# Cathy Jordan

## BIBLIOGRAPHY

*Annie Q. Jones Mysteries*

*Angels at Rest* (1989)
*Uneasy Prey* (1990)
*Sleeping Fools Lie* (1991)
*Shallow Grave* (1993)
*Dead Weight* (1995)
*Living Proof* (scheduled for publication, 1996)


Other Fiction

*Family Affairs* (1982)
*Rimrock* (1984)
*From Shore to Shore* (1987)

## OTHER BESTSELLING TITLES
## BY JOHN HARVEY

ALL ARROW BOOKS ARE AVAILABLE THROUGH MAIL ORDER OR FROM YOUR LOCAL BOOKSHOP.

PAYMENT MAY BE MADE USING ACCESS, VISA, MASTERCARD, DINERS CLUB, SWITCH AND AMEX, OR CHEQUE, EUROCHEQUE AND POSTAL ORDER (STERLING ONLY).

EXPIRY DATE ...................................... SWITCH ISSUE NO.

SIGNATURE ..........................................................................................

PLEASE ALLOW £2.50 FOR POST AND PACKING for the first book and £1.00 per book thereafter.

ORDER TOTAL: £................................. (INCLUDING P&P)

ALL ORDERS TO:

ARROW BOOKS, BOOKS BY POST, TBS LIMITED, THE BOOK SERVICE, COLCHESTER ROAD, FRATING GREEN, COLCHESTER, ESSEX, CO7 7 DW, UK.

TELEPHONE: (01206) 256 000
FAX: (01206) 256 914

NAME ...................................................................................................
ADDRESS...............................................................................................
..............................................................................................................

Please allow 28 days for delivery. Please tick box if you do not wish to receive any additional information. ☐

Prices and availability subject to change without notice.